Also by
Stanley Elkin
Boswell
Criers and Kibitzers, Kibitzers and Criers
A Bad Man
The Dick Gibson Show
Searches and Seizures
The Franchiser
The Living End
Stanley Elkin's Greatest Hits
George Mills
The Magic Kingdom
Early Elkin
The Six-Year-Old Man
The Rabbi of Lud
The Coffee Room

the

MACGUFFIN

Stanley Elkin

LINDEN PRESS
SIMON & SCHUSTER

New York London Toronto
Sydney Tokyo
Singapore

Linden Press
Simon & Schuster Building
Rockefeller Center
1230 Avenue of the Americas
New York, New York 10020

Linden Press/S&S and colophon are registered trademarks
of Simon & Schuster Inc.

DESIGNED BY BARBARA M. BACHMAN
Manufactured in the United States of America

1 3 5 7 9 10 8 6 4 2

Library of Congress Cataloging-in-Publication Data
Elkin, Stanley, date
The MacGuffin / Stanley Elkin.
p.   cm.
I. Title.
PS3555.L47M25   1991
813'.54—dc20   90-13233
CIP

ISBN 0-671-67324-6

An excerpt from this novel originally
appeared in *Playboy* magazine.

I' d like to express my gratitude to the Rockefeller Foundation for putting Joan and me up in Ballagio on Lake Como over in Italy in the villa they run there for the villaless, where I not only wrote part of and got a pretty good handle on the rest of *The MacGuffin*, but also managed to spend the five happiest weeks of my life.

to Joan

Though he was probably about the right age for it—fifty-eight—Druff didn't suppose—not even when he was most fitfully struggling to bring forth a name like something caught in his throat, or spit out the word momentarily stuck on the tip of his tongue—that what he was experiencing was aphasia, or Alzheimer's, or the beginnings of senility, or anything importantly neurological at all. Though he wouldn't have been surprised if *some*thing dark was going on in the old gray matter—— a kind of lava tube forming, say, or, oh, stuff creeping in the fossil record, putty leaking into his creases and crevices, his narrows, folds and fissures, some sluggish, white stupidity forming and hardening there like an impression formed in a mold. He hadn't become absent-minded. Indeed, if he was asked to do anything, anything at all—call up to his son when he had finished his shower, pass on telephone messages, tell Rose Helen that the jeweler had called, the clasp on her necklace was ready, she could pick it up when she wanted—not only did he deliver the messages intact, he couldn't rest until they *were* delivered; the light, ordinary tasks being what they'd always been, annoying chores, petty charges of being, small anxieties, like, oh, de-tours on unfamiliar roads whose extent was not known to him, or the go-here, go-there arrangements of red tape. Which was ironic, wasn't it, his being City Commissioner of Streets and all.

It wasn't fugue state, although he'd noticed of late (of late? of late? when did you first notice it?) that information seemed to go in one ear and out the other. He'd become impatient with information unless it was organized as opinion, a column in a newspaper was an example, or a memo someone in his department had signed off on (signed off *on?*), and then he might recall only the opinion but couldn't for the life of him give the reasons for it. It wasn't even that Druff was particularly forgetful, and his character, though it occasionally failed to concentrate, *never* forgot.

Rather—there was no way he could measure this—it was as if he had somehow mysteriously lost, well, *force.* It seemed to him that people made allowances for him, that he lived under some new and infuriating dispensation, on some plane of condescension, like the handicapped, or at least the elderly, in a sort of wit-reamed oblivion. The same people, his oldest acquaintances some of them, who in the past had always been at least a little afraid of him, or at least a little wary—not, mind, obsequious, *never* obsequious; for they'd known that, caught in their kindness, they had more to fear from him than ever they did from mere opposition, or even open confrontation—fell all over themselves to dredge up anecdotes about him, ancient tales of his old heroic sangfroid. (If they only *knew* how froid! Druff thought over the chirps and squeaks and other freezing noises in his head, helpless to provide anything for their conversation, to add or detract, chilly behind his smile.)

Though it was Druff's opinion they were still afraid of him, not of his power, but of their own. (Why, they'd traded places!) As if, when it came to Druff, they chose forbearance and restraint. No, that was dumb. They chose nothing. It was still a women-and-children-first world, and they weren't afraid of their power at all, merely mindful of it. City Commissioner of Streets or no City Commissioner of Streets, Druff, in his *real* avatar, the one they automatically rose to give up their seats to or hold open doors for or help with his packages, was their little old lady. (So what, incidentally, was all that shit about that they had to fear from him if he caught them in their kindness? A lump on stumps could have caught them in their measly, inchworm charities.) What was a poor City Commissioner of Streets to do? Well, if he was *really* getting stupid, hold on tight, disclose nothing, do whatever he could to muffle the dark screech of the slow stalactites—stalagmites?—dripping in his skull. Trump their tolerance with tolerance, and other-cheek the very breath from their bodies. As, knowing his limitations, but calling it delegation of responsibility, some entirely honorable division of labor, he was on terms with, though dared not second-guess, the civil engineers who worked for him, educated hard-hat types who did the scientific heavy lifting in his department. Hey, he was only little old Bob Druff, City Commissioner of Streets. Not His Highness, not Your Lordship, or

Senator, or the Right Honorable anyone at all. He wasn't even Professor Druff, less real clout to his title than the president of a humane society. Only the buck stopped there.

And, God help him, the bucks. For his dubious kid kenneled in graduate school, for the built-ins in his back yard—the barbecue, the pool—for the tall, unlovely weathered gray wooden fence around that yard, for the additions to his home—the deceptive bungalow in the modest neighborhood, as riddled with gear (high-tech furnishings in the snazzy basement and remodeled rooms) as an embassy, for the top-of-the-line Chrysler in his garage, for his cashmeres, silk suits and cambrics—— all the difficult cloth of their—Rose Helen's and his—compromised wardrobe.

Honest? He was honest. He supposed he was honest. Though the graft poured in. They threw it at him, the graft. He didn't even have to solicit. (As councilman, as council president, and later as under-mayor, he'd taken even less advantage.) So he was honest. In those days, the golden age of his brains, he knew where they were, but had never sought to find, the buried bodies. (He was a politico. It was a kind of received wisdom, the gossip you took in with your mother's milk. You didn't seek out information. You didn't buy it. Aldermen didn't have spies. You just knew. As far as he was concerned, there were no marks against his innocence.)

Anyway, it was his force he'd have liked to recover, or was at least nostalgic for, his edge and intelligence.

"Though maybe," he informed Dick, the plainclothes chauffeur whisking him on this beautiful spring day on a leisurely cruise through the park, searching out potholes, "that famous 'golden age of my brains' I do so like to discuss, was only the absence of overload, in the days before my computer chips, say. Incidentally, I see by the morning paper on my lap here that scientists working on three continents have succeeded in photographing atoms blown up ten million times—count 'em, Dick, ten million—in some new superconductor material. Researchers came up with this compound. They mix these powders and bake them up in ovens. Copper and oxygen. A couple others. Barium. One your commissioner never heard of. Yttrium? Copper, oxygen, yttrium and barium powder. Oxygen cookies. The copper, yttrium and barium assortment. They think what lets them carry so much current with such little energy loss—sounds like crowd control; we know about *that* in the department of streets, don't we Dick?—are 'flaws, imperfections in the alignment of the atoms.' "

"I was reading that paper myself, Commissioner."

"Were you, Dick?"

"Well, the obits anyway. Macklin died."

"Macklin, Macklin . . . Marvin Macklin? He died, Marvin Macklin?" (God knew how he'd come up with that first name; he had not a clue who the guy was.) Dick took the limo deep into the bottom of a pothole. "After a long illness."

"Oho. We know what *that* means."

"Cancer."

"Well, that's the thing, Dick. There could be incredible spin-offs."

"Spin-offs from cancer?"

" 'Waste-free electronics,' it says. 'Powerful new magnets.' Old Macklin comes back, in eight or nine years they sprinkle his tumors with iron, suck them right up in the Hoover."

"Really?"

"We ain't seen nothing yet."

"Speaking personally, Commissioner, I think I have."

"You've seen squat jackshit, Dick," the City Commissioner of Streets said. "What there was whizzed by you just like it did me and about everyone else. Oh, you mean corruption, you mean what goes on. I see what you mean. You're talking about downtown. You're talking about significant bricks through important windows. You're talking about bending some colored guy's head. Watered cement you could go fishing in, swimming, maybe skate on in winter. You're discussing the hear-no-see-no-speak-no evils— bribery and blackmail raised to the levels of professions. That's what *you're* on about. Forgive me, Dick, but you're missing the point, I think. You ain't, you really ain't. Seen nothing yet, I mean. We're living on the cusp here. Like guys standing up in canoes in heavy seas. My goodness, the boneyard of history is shtupped with folks like us, knifed on the cutting edge, caught short between technologies.

"What are they going to do, *retrain* us? You hear they're going to retrain you, you run for the hills."

"As a matter of fact," the chauffeur said, "there *was* some talk."

1 4

"Yes? What? No, let me guess. They offered to put you into a program where they teach you evasive procedures, bodyguard driving, executive protection. The swerve and dodge skills, all the eat-my-dust, change-directions, push-them-off-the-road ones."

"Yeah, that's right," Dick said. "You heard about that."

"No. I swear," Druff said gloomily. "I love it when I guess."

Because where there's smoke there's fire, Druff thought, and now maybe they were going to take his drivers—he had two, Dick was one, Doug the other—away from him. (Besides himself, only the mayor, police and fire commissioners had limos.) And he'd been a show-the-flag sort of commissioner. There were times, plenty of them, when he'd sent a riderless limousine out into the neighborhoods. Or, cloning his power, ventriloquizing it—he and his drivers were more or less the same size—ubiquitized himself, had one of them drive while the other rode statesmanlike in the back, a fleeting, shadowy sit-back stand-in for the commish, his deputized decoy presence, like some false Hitler's. (Being City Commissioner of Streets was not without its perks and splendors.) Though most of the time, of course, it was really only him, genuine Druff, back there. Well, quite frankly, he rather enjoyed being snatched through the city, siren screaming, Mars light flaming on the roof of the big car, to any emergency which required his attention, or at least his presence—he filled the nooks and crannies of his sinecure like a suit he'd been measured for by tailors—in the streets he commissioned. And delighted in municipal occasion, the reviewing-stand condition. Give him a hot day, a parade, and let him strut his stuff (comfortably in place) on a folding chair, or even along the hardest, backless bench. Despite the fact that his was an appointed position, he had an image of a bleachered , shirtsleeved America. Registered voters were his countrymen, pols his tribe. But had some vague aversion, this niggling atavism in the blood, a soft xenophobia—hey, he knew people who wouldn't give someone from a different precinct the time of day!—toward the whole participatory democracy thing, the League of Women Voters, proclaimed Independents, reformers, kids better off taking the fresh air outdoors but who volunteered to stuff envelopes instead, man phone banks—— airheads with all their muddled notions of good government, the various tony freedoms and constitutional amendments. (*He* believed in good government. Druff did. Anyone would be a fool not to, but good government was services. It was meat inspectors, guys who checked the restaurants, the building codes. It was the department of sanitation, the fire department, a strong police. It was knowing what to do with the infrastructure, making the trains run on time without harming the Gypsies.)

His ease he meant, taking his ease in the heat. His ease he meant, that he wished he could have over again, like a second chance, his ease he'd have liked to recover, the way some people wanted their youth back. His force and edge and intelligence.

"I stand by the system. I stand by the system up to my ears."

"Sir?"

He hadn't realized he had actually spoken.

"Because, Dick," he said, putting one past his driver, making the fellow think he hadn't been paying attention (and maybe he hadn't; maybe he was figuring the pros and cons, mulling over the offer to become a Counter-Chauffeur in the Counter-Chauffeur Division, weighing his age against his chances), "if the mayor hadn't appointed me to this job, God knows I couldn't have made it through another campaign."

"You, Commissioner? Sure you would. You had a lock on those people. Those people were your people."

"No," Druff said, "you can't think that way. I don't know, how does anyone declare for the statehouse even? And the federal fellows, how do the federal fellows do it?"

"It's their calling. Why I drive a limo instead of set up for a taxi."

"I guess," Druff said. And then, leaning forward to close down some of the distance between them, "Just between us, Richard. Answer a question?"

"Sir?"

"No no. Between us. Two guys. I'm not City Commissioner of Streets, you're not my driver."

"Yeah?"

"What's the morning line on me?"

"On you, Commish?"

"On Bobbo Druff, yes."

"Well, to tell you the absolute honest-to-God truth, that you could have been a contender."

"Ah," satisfied Bobbo.

"And but so how come?"

"That I'm not? The absolute honest-to-God?"

"Tit for tat."

"It was all that Inderal I was putting into my system," he told him, naming the old blood-pressure medication, the drug of choice for any-one—politicians, actors, TV and radio people—who had to speak in public.

"A stand-up guy like you?"

"I missed my hard-ons, yes."

"You, Commissioner? Stage fright?"

"Jack and Bobby had to have been iron men. Gary Hart."

"You're telling me Lee Harvey Oswald and Sirhan Sirhan weren't disaffected, just two jealous husbands?"

Sure, he thought, my ease. That bright, cold composure.

"But I was *at* that debate. You never even broke a sweat," said the driver.

"That's right." Druff remembered. "You *were* there."

"Jesus," Dick said, "the time the guy said 'my opponent,' and you interrupted him and spelled out your name? And then when he said 'my opponent' a second time and you spelled 'opponent'? My, that was lovely. He didn't stand a chance. And him screaming 'Speak to the issues, speak to the issues.' And you said, 'The issues? Right, *I'll* speak to the issues.' "

" 'Clear the snow,' " Druff said, recalling.

"Clear the snow, yeah."

" 'Test for safe chlorine levels in the municipal pools.' "

"Yeah," said his driver, giggling, "the chlorine levels."

" 'Enforce the bus schedules. Rip out all unnecessary stop signs, but plant them like trees wherever there's been an accident. More time for your nickel on the parking meters.' "

"Oh, God yes. 'More time for your nickel.' Beautiful lovely. Your famous 'Fourteen Points.' Continental Divide politics, watershed rheto-ric. *That* caught the old hack off balance, *that* tumbled him."

"Now now," Druff, like a pop, remonstrated gently, "language. We don't say 'old hack.' A little generosity, Dick, please. We say 'old trouper.' They also serve."

But didn't it just, the commissioner thought fondly, cheered by the memory of his inspired old promises. (With an Inderal assist, the soft toxins of his chemical ease, the solid confidence under his evaporated flopsweats like the stout barbecue, cunning pool and beautiful patio furniture on the beautiful patio behind his homely gray fence.) Flabbergasting *his* opponent with a sudden, off-the-cuff agenda, the sweet reasonables of ordinary life; astonishing the reporters there, the wide-eyed ladies and gentlemen of the press patting down their pockets for a spiral notebook or a pen that worked while he, on a roll, continued: "If the able-bodied won't mow their lawns, the city gets someone on welfare to mow them and presents a bill." Enforcing the weekend curfew for teenagers at the fast food hangouts. All moving violations to be paid by mail. No more futzing with City Hall's byzantine arrangements. Free jump starts on cold winter mornings if the temperature hadn't risen into double digits by 9 A.M. ("It's all traffic," he'd told them, "government is all traffic and threats to tow your car.") "In the fall," he'd said, and quoted himself directly now, in the car, "in the fall, until the first snow, we come by for regularly scheduled leaf pickups. And haul off your oversize objects too, your ancient washing machine, your moldy box spring and mattress. And, if I'm elected, no one—*no one*—will ever again be required to put anything on the windshield or rear window of his car, safety inspection or tax or city sticker, that has on it any adhesive stronger than the glue on the back of an ordinary envelope." ("No more senseless scraping!" he'd vowed.)

"I liked the one where you promised to pull the cops out of the inner city and put them back into the good neighborhoods," his chauffeur reminisced.

"Yeah," said the quite suddenly downed City Commissioner of Streets (who *could* have been a contender), "that was a good one."

"Yes," Dick the chauffeur said, "the Fourteen Points. Let's see now, the snow, the chlorine and stop signs and bus schedules. The parking meters, settling fines. Mowing the lawn, curfews. Jump starting the cars is nine. Leaf pickups, no senseless scraping, cops in the low-crime areas, coming by for the furniture in the alleys. I make that thirteen. Did I mention the parking meters? I think so. That's thirteen. I leave something out?"

"Deuces and one-eyed Jacks are wild," the stupid old man said sadly.

"God," said his driver, "you could have been landslide material."

"Through every Middlesex village and town."

"What's that, a Middlesex village and town?"

"Don't rightly know."

So they traveled over the potholes in the park, cruising the wintertime, salt-bruised paving, Druff, withdrawn and brooding in the deep, plush recesses of the outlandish automobile. (Because if you traveled in chauffeured limousines they really oughtn't to have city seals blazoned on their sides, his department's blacktop, bulldozer heraldics.)

But Dick wouldn't let it go, relishing, almost licking, his memory like some kid in a school yard, say, recollecting the best parts in a movie, recounting the combinations, all the "he saids" and "you saids" of their (to hear Dick tell it) mythological confrontation. "Remember, Commissioner? 'Hell no,' you told him, 'I'm not mudslinging. It ain't even gossip. Gossip would be if I named you your lovers.' Then you listed the facts and figures for him, all the old trouper's inadequacies and ineptitudes, so that 'incompetent' was the least of it, the part the reporters crossed out when they wrote up the story. Hot damn!"

"Now now," said City Commissioner of Streets Druff, "it was hardly the Lincoln-Douglas debates."

"Hardly the Lincoln-Douglas, he says." And then respectfully, seriously, even gravely, "As close as *this* town gets, Commissioner."

And Druff, who at his time of life—it was at *least* past late middle age in his head and even later than that in the cut of his cloth, his chest caving behind his shirts, emptying out, and his torso sinking, lowering into trousers rising like a tide and lapping about him like waves—was actually old enough to think "at my time of life" and so may have been—admittedly—subject to a sort of soft paranoia, all the compounding interest on disappointment, the wear and tear of ambition—hard by, as he was, the thin headwaters of the elderly—and was the first to admit the outrageousness of his surmise and discount the chinks in his argument, discounted his vulnerabilities anyway and suddenly knew the man, his driver, the chauffeur Dick, was some kind of spy.

Well well well.

And even appreciated the fact that he ought to have felt flattered. How many men his age had spies on their case? Even when he'd been on the campaign posters and big outdoor advertising there hadn't been spies. It was a tribute at his time of life. So why, given his blues and vapors, didn't Dick's probable double agency perk him right up? Or at the very least offer some red alert of consciousness or push him to action? Why, if after all these years he was finally a target, didn't he behave like one and get moving?

Ask him outright, Druff thought. Just put it to him. Say, Why, Dick?

And would have if, just then, a mounted policeman hadn't called "Top of the morning there"—they were stopped at a stop sign—to them through the open window of the limousine. Druff turned sideways to wave and return the greeting. (Cops, he thought, in all their supposititious ethnics and green, adoptive blarneys; in their drawled, beefy flagpatch, redneck sheriff's ways; in their designer shades and presumptive cool.)

"And the same back to you, Offi—" the politician offered when the horse, or what was more likely, the man himself—startled—did this aborted, electric bolt, a maneuver like a double take.

"Oh," the cop said recovering, smiling, "it's *you* back there, Commissioner. Who's that up front? Doug-go?"

"Stosh-o wants to know if it's Doug-go, Dick-o," the policeman's City Commissioner of Streets told the driver, frowning.

"How you doing?" Dick said.

"Filling the quotas," the centaur joked, "no complaints. Ain't ten A.M. yet, maybe fifteen tourists took my picture. And yourselves?"

"On the trail of fresh potholes."

"Well," the cop said, "you've a grand morning for it."

"Just how many people know you and Doug drive each other around?" the commissioner asked when they were again under way. (Under way indeed, thought Druff in the big, nautical-seeming car.)

"You know," Dick said, "that's a question that says something about people's human condition. Lisher? Lisher," he repeated. "The rough-rider, the steed cop. Well, I'll tell you something, Commissioner Druff. We get our share. More than our share. It ain't only cavalry guys up on their coursers see that kind of action. You know how many people during the course of a day regard us as a photo opportunity? If I had a dollar."

"Really," Druff said.

"Oh," Dick said, "six bits, four even. You don't always see this.

Often you'll be indoors on important street business when they come up. They'll want to know if it's the mayor's, the governor's. They don't know, it could be their senator's. Your average citizen is easily impressed but don't understand his city's seals from Shinola."

Bold, thought Druff. My spy is a bold spy. Indoors on street business.

Though of course Druff knew—or at least used to—all about photo opportunities—— posing with constituents and cronies like Dan Dailey tricked out in a straw boater in a musical. How many rec rooms, he wondered, were still decorated with such pictures, the flash distorting their faces, darkening or overexposing them like flesh in a photograph taken in a nightclub?

The commissioner dipped a hand into a pocket in the jacket of his suit and withdrew a pouch of chewing tobacco from which he removed, staring steadily into Dick's eyes in the driver's rearview mirror, a few dried coca leaves which he put into his mouth, holding them carefully against his gums like some pleasure poultice and allowing the bolus of leaves to fill with syrups from his gums and face before he began to grind it in his jaws. (A cousin in Peru sent him the stuff in two-pound cans of mountain-grown coffee once or twice a year.)

"How can you stand to chew that shit?" Under his crowns Druff had the decayed and withered posts of an Indian, brown, twiglike teeth. "No," Dick said, "really, how can you? These days they blow Tops even in the majors."

"That's because they're superstitious," the commissioner said. "They cut it with the gum and chew each other's pictures on the baseball cards."

(At fifty-eight, he liked to get high. He loved the euphoria, of course, the sidebars of music and landscape, everywhere beauty arranged, composed as a photograph; loved the concentration, his lasered focus, the sense drugs gave him of recovered obsession, the small motor movements of the will, his resumed patience with the world, with everything, even the pure plain humanness of his mistakes, his kid's, his city's, the tolerance and good intentions dope revealed to him. Though this, doing numbers on the job, was a new wrinkle.)

"What gets me," Dick said, "I never see you spit."

Druff spit on the floor of the limo. "Play ball," he said.

"You're the commissioner," said the spy.

2 1

And, energy up, told his driver they'd discovered enough potholes for one day, that one day they'd be remembered as the Lewis and Clark of potholes and that they should proceed to City Hall.

Less than fifteen minutes later they were there.

The City Hall in Druff's city had been built in 1871. It was a tall, narrow structure of dressed limestone, four stories high and only eight windows across, a classical descending hodgepodge of balustrades, cornices, dentils, friezes, keystones and quoins. There were engaged columns between the arched, Italianate windows. There were crests and garlands, a portico with a pediment like a diving platform on which stood a statue of the founder of the department store City Hall had originally been. (Some air of the mercantile about it still, of emporium and records filed years, or of some great commodity exchange, furs, even diamonds, or cotton, or tobacco factorage, something if not actually anachronistic about the place then at least geographically off, as if Druff's city were three or four hundred miles south of where it really was.)

Druff's rooms on the fourth floor reminded him of theatrical agents' or producers' offices in old thirties films. (When he thought of them he saw them in black and white.) A gate, activated by a buzzer, opened in the low wooden railing that separated the public from the private suites and offices, a toy obstacle, some playpen of the governmental, civil, decorous, beyond which young hopefuls (in those old movies) cooled their heels while waiting not for the appointments which even they knew they would not be given, but for fabulous breaks in the routine, three minutes of extemporaneous, gift democracy to show their stuff when the door to the sanctum opened and Ziegfeld appeared. Which now, since San Francisco, since Harvey Milk and Mayor Moscone, didn't happen so much. An armed security guard posted outside the little low fence mitigated the old honorable ambience of the place. Up in smoke, gone with the hopefuls themselves. Unless something was on the chest and burning the heels of the security guard too.

Though there were computers in Druff's building now of course, modems, fax machines. Some people in data processing had desktop-published a pamphlet on sidewalk repair and replacement for his department, another on gutters and pavements, others on street signs, on markers and street graphics, on leaf collection and snow removal, on

how to obtain permits for street fairs and block parties, on detours and
barricades. And put out brochures on lighting and traffic signals, on
street cleaning and lawn maintenance. (Not "lawn." What was it called,
that little strip of grass easement between the pavement and the curb
the home owner was responsible for? The City Commissioner of Streets
had forgotten.) Both the pamphlet on gutters and pavements and the one
on markers and street graphics had won first prize in a national competition, and the lawn maintenance—*verge* it was called—brochure was a
classic, better than Beverly Hills', better than West Palm Beach's, *those*
garden spots. Druff, who hadn't even known there *was* such a competition, had been sent by the mayor to the awards banquet in St. Louis.
(He was a good old City Commissioner of Streets, and when he was
called up to the dais to collect the citation in his category—public
service publications in cities of between one and two million people—he
made a speech without benefit of Inderal—"I'm totally unprepared for
this," he'd told them, "because whoever thought for a minute we'd
win?"—and became, with that "we," an instant favorite with the crowd.
He was a good old City Commissioner of Streets. And, afterward, took
a drink with a few of the boys, some whom he knew from the days when
he was political, but most of them new to him, a kind of under-profes-
sional—not docs or the lawyerly or of an insider-anything, killer-M.B.A.
imagination, accepting burnout ten or so years down the road like some
teenager the cancer she takes in with her suntan—municipally manage-
rial, infrastructure type—— hospital administrators, parks commissioners, fellows from water, from tunnels and bridges, low-income housing.
Talking with one in particular, not a bad sort if you accepted up front
that he was a bore, who'd asked him questions about his town and then
confessed he'd never been there himself. "What, not even to change
planes?" "No," the guy said, "never." And really wanted to know the
sort of shop his city was, what the museums were like, if the zoo was
any good, how come it didn't have a baseball team. "It's a great place
to raise children," Druff told him truthfully, then added, "not great
children." "Is it?" "Probably because our housing stock is so good."
Offering "housing stock," because, Druff being Druff, he had to, since
honor had it that tie went to the bore and Druff, thinking of the children
he'd not too greatly raised, owed him.)

Then, back in town, an altered man, or at least an altered City

Commissioner of Streets, thrown back on his old affection for the electorate, for shirtsleeve America and the July Fourth condition, his meat inspector–cum–fireman notions and mail-must-go-through priorities. His own shirtsleeves rolled and actively inventing campaigns, promoting civic pride, this patriot of the local, this hustling jingo of the here. ("What's *this* all about?" Loft, the director of the airport, had asked. "A little slogan I thought up," Druff said. "What? A slogan? 'Change planes in our town and we'll show you a time'?" "Sure," Druff told him, "if they had even a two- or three-hour layover, we could pick them up in buses and show them around. No city in America has thought of this yet." "There's such a thing as turf, Druff. You're the street man here. You of all people ought to know that." So took his case over Loft's head. "Look," he'd argued to a chilly City Council, "what's the worst that could happen? That the bus has an accident and everyone in it is killed or maimed. Don't worry, it won't happen, we'll use only the most seasoned drivers. It *won't* happen, but even, God forbid, if it does, most of these people are covered by the credit cards they use to purchase their airplane tickets, by their travel agencies, by the bus company itself. I asked counsel to look into this and he assures me we're in the clear." Going at his job in those mercantile rooms of yore as if City Hall were still a department store. He was a good old City Commissioner of Streets and only wanted to be a better one. Why not? Streets were roads, roads were what the Romans built, and he, Druff, was road man here, Imperial Commissioner of the Way to the Empire! So give me a little credit please, he'd thought. I understand about empire, why wouldn't I know about turf?)

And, honored by his honors (all the more splendid for his not having known about the national competition or such categories in the first place, or even all that much about the project itself, and all the more moving for his having merely signed off on it—signed off *on?*—their having come to him not so much a sign that he'd cashed in on other people's efforts as much as a tribute to the smooth functioning of his department), by his Academy Awards in Gutters and Pavements, in Markers and Street Graphics, and his Lifetime Achievement Award in Mowing the Lawn, continued for a time to press his campaigns.

His shame campaign.

The oversized, non-removable Day-Glo stickers he'd have had the city slap on the windows of trucks and vans, of commercial vehicles double-parked in the street, tying up traffic, the sample copy for which he'd written himself. ("This vehicle is double-parked in violation of city traffic ordinances and has been appropriately ticketed. Citizens who feel they have been personally inconvenienced, either by being unable to move out of their parking spaces, or by being denied access to parking spaces which might otherwise have been available to them, or by being unduly held up in traffic, are, in light of the selfish disregard shown them by the other driver's lack of consideration for his neighbors, encouraged to take down the name of the company, its phone number or address when available and vehicle license plate number, and report all such incidents to the appropriate authorities.") If he'd been a mathematician or scientist such a solution to so longstanding a municipal problem might have been termed elegant—he didn't mean his copy, his copy was merely a detail, an example, an instance, a first draft; he put no great stock in his copy; his copy could always be improved—so he was disappointed, though not surprised, when the city fathers to whom he'd shown mock-ups, complete, right down to Druff's improvable text on the Day-Glo sticker and its permanent bond shaded in on the verso, had thrown up objections that were, well, political. ("Yes," said the mayor—Dick's "guy" and "old hack" of the morning's reminiscences—"that would do the job all right, but those vans and trucks that block up the traffic are doing deliveries, dropping stuff off, picking stuff up. This is commercial traffic you're talking about, acceptable lifeblood traffic. We have to deal with it. You're mixing babies and bathwater, what do you call it, apples and oranges. Good government is knowing who should get the tax abatements." A shot, Druff thought, a shot and a hit. "Yes," he said, "I see what you mean, Mr. Mayor. I'm old and stupid, too caught up by ancient history and old times. Maybe what appealed about my idea was that it was so purely an adaptation of the eleventh of my Fourteen Points, 'no senseless scraping,' brought up to date." The mayor brushed away Druff's dismissal of himself. "Now now," he said, "it's a *good* idea. It is. Maybe its time hasn't come but it's a *good* idea," adding, too cruelly for any absolutely first-rate pol, thought Druff, "and whenever my City Commissioner of Streets feels he has another one up his sleeve, I want my City Commissioner of Streets to feel free to stop the presses and let me know." Saying "my

City Commissioner of Streets" as in ancient history and old times he'd said "my opponent," for, yes, this was he, his old opponent from the Lincoln-Douglas. And might have assured Hizzoner right then and there that Druff would no longer trouble him with any more bright ideas from that sleeve of his. Which he didn't because you never ever made a campaign promise you didn't absolutely have to.) But abandoning the last of his promotional schemes right then and right there, returned to the easy status quo of Awards Banquet ante.

For the rest of the morning Druff accepted phone calls and answered letters, working routinely within the soft parameters of the job description. Twice he had fifteen-minute meetings, one with the department's chief engineer, who'd been assigned to draw up plans for an enclosed walkway above Kersh Boulevard where three or four months earlier a young woman, a foreign exchange student from Lebanon, on her way back from campus to her dormitory after an evening lecture, had crossed not at the corner but at one of those push-button traffic signals in the middle of the block, and been killed by a hit-and-run driver. The engineer had shown him blueprints ("What's this," the City Commissioner of Streets said, "sheet music?" Then asked the engineer to rough the bridge in for him in terms—no cross sections, no esoterics—Druff could understand. "This won't fall down, will it?" he'd asked. "No? You don't think so? Well, what can we rely on if not our informed guesses? Go ahead, put a crew together.") and now reported back to him that it was his, the chief engineer's, understanding that the city was unwilling to proceed with construction until the university agreed to pay the costs on whatever was built on university property. The second meeting—Druff had forgotten that it had been scheduled for today—was with a lawyer, some bagman type from the university. He'd come with its sealed, lunatic bid. "Obviously the school regrets this tragedy, but isn't this all a little like locking the barn door after the dish has run away with the spoon?" the fellow said. "The city should never have put up a pedestrian-activated traffic signal in that spot in the first place. It fair screamed 'attractive nuisance' to any beered-up kid who chanced by." However, in the interest of putting all this behind them, he'd told Druff, the university was willing to help out, but preferred that the university's builders be engaged on, well, the university's buildings, that this was essentially a city project and that city contractors ought to be used on it, and it needn't bother that the walkway be built in conformity with campus style, that a strictly neutral municipal architecture would serve, it was a matter of indifference to the university if the city failed to match its distinctive and rather expensive limestone. Druff, who smelled kickback the minute the guy opened his mouth, thanked him for coming and told him he'd convey the university's position and get back to him with a decision.

If I live long enough this is how I'll spend the rest of my life, thought fifty-eight-year-old Druff on the downhill side of destiny, folding his stale, foul, used-up juices into a clean handkerchief and placing three or four fresh leaves from his pouch of chewing tobacco into his mouth. It was not a disagreeable prospect. A sedentary, lackluster office life held no terrors for him. The worst that could happen was that he'd be bored. If it was too late for anything to happen to him, why that was all right, too. Enough had happened to him already. He suffered from two or three major illnesses—— heart disease (three years earlier, he'd had bypass surgery, after having a heart attack years back); spontaneous pneumothoraxes (four times a lung had collapsed on him; it was, they liked telling him, a young man's disease; runners burst blebs while they were still in their teens); and peripheral circulatory blockage in his legs (wounds, below his knees, took forever to heal; a stubbed toe could turn into gangrene just like that). Also he couldn't always, or even very often, get it up. What was more troubling was that he didn't very often even want to.

Which might, thought Druff, explain, I betcha, the power fantasies, all that If-I-Were-King subjunctivication of his life.

Only it wasn't Bobbo the Roman Numeral I in those fantasies, but Bobbo, Prez of the Free World As We Know It. An American first, pictures don't lie. That was no crown on his head, it was a straw boater; no throne under his ass, a folding chair. RD to the constituents, those who'd put him into office and those who'd voted against him. RD in the black banners of the national press. RD'S STUBBED TOE TO COME OFF! RD DRAWS DEEP BREATH SMELLING FLOWER, COL-LAPSES LUNG! RD REPORTS HARD-ON, MAY RUN FOR SEC-OND TERM!

And it wasn't always, or even all that often, in terms of headlines that RD appeared to himself. No no. He knew, was on talking terms with, his priorities. Heady, daring stuff. Missions to bring the hostages out. And had worked out position papers not only on the emergencies but on the back burners too, credits to Canada for dropping acid rain on their forests and wildlife, how to accommodate revolutions in place, what to do about an ailing dollar, how to deal with the burdens of secrecy in a dangerous world—— Why, go public! All *sorts* of innovative shit.

For one thing, he would allow no one to run for office—this was complicated and controversial and would almost certainly require a constitutional amendment—who was not fluent in Japanese or some other language du jour.

Am I ridiculous? Well, I don't mean to be.

Dick, Druff thought suddenly, his spy and sometime chauffeur, had probably soft-soaped the security guy in the outer office, sent him to lunch, and was probably his guardbody now.

And *laws?* The laws in his country would be the best on the books. Free speech, free press, the right to worship where one pleased, everything state-of-the-art in those departments. Holland couldn't hold a candle. But that was only the beginning. Because, face it, how often, how often *really,* did the average man have this stuff jeopardized? And how many times in the course of a normal, decently led life did your garden variety citizen have to worry about a Miranda decision and the safeguards against self-incrimination and all the rest of the illegal-search-and seizure-provisos and stipulations? Because didn't it finally come down to what he told his constituents, the good folks who'd put him in the White House in the first place, that government mostly *was* traffic and threats to tow? It has *nothing* to do with you, my fellow Americans. (Except for the fact that I'm its ruler and have to give its dinner parties, it has scarcely bugger squat jack all to do with *me!*) And that's why I've convened this Constitutional Convention, my ladies and gentlemen, to see if after two hundred and some years since its founding we can't put together some laws that might actually *mean* something to the man in the street. We will, and right in front of the gaze of an interested world, now turn our attention to those areas of governance which have been too long neglected. For this purpose I will, and in the not-too-distant, be naming a blue-ribbon committee to consider subjects such as Used Car Law, Points and Closing Law, Improper Credit Card

Charges Law, Bank Statement Error and Utilities Bills Law, and the Rules of Guarantee, Warranty, and 7/70,000. In addition, a special Presidential Oversight Commission will be addressing everything ever written into a lease pertaining to the payment of the last month's rent in advance—— Rent Deposit Law. Because, well, to tell you the truth, my people, you don't all that many of you look like Virginia gent farmers and country-fed, all-purpose, Jeffersonian aristoi to me, or even, when it comes right down, artisans and mechanics either. Good night and God bless.

Druff enjoyed these reveries, the long stretch of his incorporeal cock-and-bull pipe-dream life. It wasn't even wishful thinking. Not the press-conferenced, carefully worded announcement of his candidacy, or his campaign speeches, or the debates, or his acceptance speech, or even his address to the nation when he took the oath of office at his inaugural. None of it was. Indeed, it was only a sort of mental doodling, what you catch yourself doing with a pencil while the other guy is speaking. There was nothing ta-pocketa-pocketa about it. The only voice, the only sound he heard, was his own.

(And didn't it really come down, always, to one tired man's extinguished or diminishing capacities? Because, like he said, enough had already happened to him. If the truth were known, if nominated he would not run, if elected he would not serve.)

Now, about that dead Lebanese girl.

He didn't actually mean kickback, not kickback as in payoff. He supposed (on closer examination) he meant something fishy, things rotten in Denmark. It mightn't be bucks changing hands here (though money, Druff knew, along with that attenuated man's diminishing capacities and Druff's old rule of traffic and threats to tow, was what it almost always came down to) but the buck, some paper trail of deniability. What was all that malarkey about municipal stone and neutral architectural styles? Or the bag guy's conditions, his objection to using any but city contractors, the dig about that traffic signal being an attractive nuisance? Druff was an old-timer, that rotten fish-stink he smelled was probably only just ass. No matter how you covered it, or what you covered it with, a little something always came through.

"By God, Mrs. Norman," he told his receptionist/secretary over the intercom, "the thing I can't take about this job is the machinations. I mean, I'm a politician, a political appointee anyway, you think I'd be used to it. I sure as hell ought to be, but all this cat-and-mouse gives me the headache. Look up"—he read a business card—"Hamilton Edgar, for me, will you, kid? See can you find out when his appointment was scheduled?"

"Hamilton Edgar?"

"The lawyer the university sent out. When did he go on our dance card?"

He heard male laughter.

"That you out there, Double-O-Seven?"

"It's Dick, Commissioner."

"Carry on, then."

"He phoned this morning, sir."

"Ah," Druff said.

"Is that important, Commissioner?"

"Don't rightly know, Dick, can't rightly say. I'll tell you this much—— hold on a min. Who else is out there besides you and Mrs. Norman? Any armed folks?"

"No sir, Commissioner, just me and Mrs. Norman."

"Do you want me to come in, Commissioner Druff?"

"What's that, Mrs. Norman? No no," the commissioner said, "it's getting on toward quiet time."

Now, thought Druff, about that dead Lebanese girl. About that dead Lebanese girl *really*.

He knew her. Well, *knew* her. He'd met her. She'd been out to the house a couple of times. Mikey had brought her over. (His son Michael. Thirty years old his last birthday, it was Michael himself who insisted people still call him Mikey. I told you, Druff thought, enough has already happened to me.) And introduced him to Su'ad al-Najaf. ("Call her Suzy, Daddy.") This would have been months before the accident. A woman in one of those massive, all-in veil/shawl/head-to-toe arrangements—what were they, *chadors?*—all wrapped up like the Nun of the World. She reminded him of that spokesterrorist on TV in the days of the Carter administration—the Georgian was right, RD thought; he'd have handled it about the same way himself—when Iran held the fifty-two American hostages, the one always out by the embassy gates where the demonstrators shouted their slogans. "Mary" her name was, always set off in quotes as though the networks were protecting the innocent. This one was a sloganeer, too. She had her own Fourteen Points. More, probably.

And had taken them (though Druff was certain from the way his son beamed up at her during her presentation that he'd heard it before, that he listened to her recitation as if she were his protégée and he'd had a hand in helping her prepare it, grinning, moving his lips) through the history of the Sunni-Shiite discord, telling them about Mohammed's son-in-law Ali, Ali's kid, Hussein, the Imam's martyrdom by the troops at Karbala, the enmity between the Shiites and Abdul Wahhab. To Druff, already lost, the whole thing sounding a little like the feud between the Hatfields and McCoys. She'd delivered the information neutrally, with a sort of willful dispassion, though Druff guessed at once—the *chador* was a clue—she was full-blooded Shiite.

"Well," Druff said when she'd finished and looked toward him for a decision on the merits, "it all sounds to me like your typical power grab. We see it time and again down at the Hall."

"Really?"

"Time and again. Year in, year out."

"Is that so? Really?"

"Oh yeah. Sunrise, sunset."

(Well, Nun of the World. She'd been standing during her discourse, backlit by a low-standing chrome high-intensity lamp. He could see her shape where it came away from her garment as if the *chador* were an X-ray photograph. She wasn't wearing underwear. He saw Shiite snatch. Mikey beamed, and the commissioner wondered if his son might not have had a hand in that, too.)

"Perhaps you'd care for some candy, Su'ad," Rose Helen suggested.

"No," she said. "Thank you, but it is forbidden. There are often liqueurs in American candies. A Muslim may not eat them."

"This is a Hershey's," his wife said. "All it has is almonds."

Su'ad smiled but shook her head. Indeed, she seemed to take a sort of delight in turning down *all* the Druffs' hospitality, declining whatever was offered as if it were a snare. She turned down their fruit, refused their supper. And, though she agreed to take tea—which she made no move to drink—with them in the living room, she rejected the comfortable armchair to which his son had shown her and sat instead on a kind of stool.

They talked (Su'ad drawing him out on the issues) about the national interest, world affairs, the big geopolitical stuff. He tried to tell the girl he was merely a humble City Commissioner of Streets. Su'ad would have none of it and dismissed his demurrers as if his modesty were only more Druff hospitality—— poisoned grapes, tainted chocolate. There was just so much Druff would take, but when the young Lebanese rose from her stool and, looking like some feral Mother Courage, resumed her plantigrade in front of the lamp, he relented and agreed to take a few more questions. Druff, his mind on automatic while his glands took notes—he thought he could make out thighs, bush, and, when she turned, the heavy, flowing principle of breasts—drew upon the various white papers of his imagination for his answers, from the presidential trial balloons he'd floated on taxpayers' time in his office, from his appearances on "Meet the Press," "MacNeil/Lehrer," "Face the Nation," diplomatic, vague as the best of them, forceful as any, evasive as most. While discussing some options which might lead to a possible solution to the problem of the West Bank, he felt an unaccustomed erection stir in his pants and sit in his lap and Druff brought the press conference to an end.

Mikey was beaming at all of them now, at Su'ad for her tricky questions, at Druff for, well—— who knew? It could have been anything—— the hard-on insinuated into his dad's pants or the way the commissioner had sidestepped Su'ad's earnest inquiries. He might even have been beaming at Rose Helen for the drama he'd introduced into their living room. (All three had ringside seats at the shadow show.)

The second time his son brought her over she stayed the night, sleeping with Mikey in his bed. Druff made a mental note about the gaucheness, the erratic behavior of foreigners on the other guy's turf. (This might turn out to be useful, he thought, the next time he scheduled a summit conference.) No, but really, he thought, there *is* something disproportionate and inept about her actions. Su'ad (maybe the kid had said something to her), so suspicious and reticent about accepting anything from them when she'd been there the first time, now made outright demands. "Excuse me," she said, coming into the living room and passing before the low lamp—now off—where she'd paced and posed her angry questions on the occasion of her first visit, "I stripped these off Michael's bed. Where do you keep clean ones?" She held out some sheets and pillowcases like a soiled laundry. "Tell me, I'll change them myself."

"The nerve," Rose Helen told Druff later that night. "Did you hear her? 'Where do you keep clean ones?' I changed that bed yesterday."

"Sure," Druff said, "I agree with you. She calls our Mikey 'Michael.'"

"Hi, Mom. Morning, Daddy," his son greeted them, grinning, when he came into the kitchen with Su'ad for breakfast the next day.

"No coffee," Su'ad said. "American coffee is always so weak." And wouldn't touch the juice Rose Helen poured because it was frozen, not fresh. Did they have Raisin Bran? Oh, good, but that was too much. Yes, that was more like it, but could Rose Helen skim off the raisins with a spoon?

Mikey beamed.

"Enjoy, enjoy. Our tent is your tent," the commissioner wanted to tell her, if not on his own then on his wife's poor behalf. "Just don't push it." But checked himself, didn't, because he was curious, wanted to understand the sheer logistics of the thing, how she would handle it, see how it was actually done, be there when the food was brought to the veil, introduced into her mouth. (She unhooked the thing was all there was to it.) Sure, thought the City Commissioner of Streets, it attaches. I should have known. If it'd been a snake it would've bit me. And he marveled (who would have tested the municipal waters for safe chlorine levels and pulled the stop signs where they weren't needed and permitted folks to pay their fines by mail, who discovered the Fourteen Points and *should* have known) at the simple savvy instincts of arrangements. And maybe ought even to have guessed, backlighting or no backlighting, the absence of underwear. As he had proposed other important political issues and instances. (Don't hassle the constituency. Be sensible, use common sense, don't stand on ceremony, do the right thing.) As, even distracted, and even while his speechifying was otherwise engaged, his cock had speculated a soft scaffolding of hair above her crotch, surmised nipples, and, last night, beside Rose Helen in bed, before falling away to sleep, he had overtaken his son (because she'd nothing to lose, wouldn't have cared, the few thin, intervening walls between their rooms just so much more backlighting), still counseling caution and patience and wait until the old folks are asleep, worked at it and worked at it and finally managed to pull himself off.

(There was nothing Oedipal about it, no fancy spin, no English on his consciousness. He wasn't jealous of the kid. Not to the point where it caused anger or pain or cost him votes or anything. When she'd thrown him into hard-on that time, it had been soft-core, an honest, old-fashioned, platonic hard-on, one he'd never have to deal with in *real* life, and which, if it came right down, would come right down.)

Only what (this part old Druff, outside his parentheses, wide awake, seeking answers) could Miss al-Najaf possibly see in his beaming boy, unless it was the beamer's connection—God forgive me, old Bob Druff prayed sincerely, my blood heresies, for I *know* this part's a sin—to the mayor's own personal officially designated City Commissioner of Streets? Because if a man—this floated later, after the fact, now, in his office thrown in; Druff, in the wake of the bagman fellow, calling upon himself to think about that dead Lebanese girl, about that dead Lebanese girl *really*—could have spies, then surely he'd have to qualify for them, come equipped with all the secrets, plans, codes, microfiche, whatever the spyworthy MacGuffin paraphernalia was, whatever got slipped into Cary Grant's pocket without his knowledge or Jimmy Stewart picked up by mistake when the girl switched briefcases on him.

But for the *life* of him . . .

And recalled how just then Dick had honked the horn on the limo and Su'ad, glancing up toward the sound, rushed down the last of her de-raisined Raisin Bran.

"That's my driver," Druff had explained.

"Oh," said Su'ad, muffled, the little face bib reattached, her lips, teeth and jaws and other private parts decent again, only the tiny strip of self between her brow and nose visible, "you have a *driver*. Good. I'm late for class. You can drop me off. But first we'll have to stop by my dorm." (Sure, Druff had thought, she has to change her *chador*.)

So, he thought, he'd managed to place Su'ad and his spy together, within—what?—ten or so feet of each other in the long limousine. What have we, what have we, he wondered and, when he couldn't figure it, decided it would be a good time to break for lunch.

Stopping off first at Brooks Brothers to pick up his suit. Reminded of the errand by his driver (though he already remembered and it wasn't necessary) as they left the office. (Well, thought Druff, what a heap of trouble it must be to know your man. Though, he thought, if they *really* knew me—Rose Helen; my spy guy, Dick—they could save their breath. I'm a politico. A politico never forgets a face or a chore.) And reflected on the streak—streak, hell, swath—of laziness that must line his being, recalling the spasm of irritation he always felt under the burden of such chores, his fettered, bothered spirit and all the mucked floors and clutter of his littered personal household.

His suit. His suit was an example.

Druff was a difficult fit. He'd never worn clothes well and now he felt a sort of physical disgrace whenever he saw himself in photographs. Dressed, he put himself in mind of some clumsy, human chimera—a gray, unformed behind and a slack, powerless belly and something off plumb about the shoulders that sloughed his right suspender—he called it his brassiere strap—and sent it sliding off his shoulder and halfway down inside his suit sleeve when he moved. His posture was shot. (It looked, his posture, as if it had taken a direct hit.) Well, he supposed it wasn't his size or weight—he was lighter, even slimmer, than he'd been in years—so much as his time of life, living along the cusp of the elderly, his body abandoning itself and his chest caving and his torso sinking, lamed, skewed, going down like a ship—like a ship, yes; that was exactly the staved-in sense of himself he had—the cut of his cloth leaking lifeblood.

So how could trying on clothes be a chore he'd forget? Because they *don't* know their man, Druff thought. They don't know me, that's why I have spies. Or maybe they know me but just can't find me. Out here on the cusp. Between houses. My neighborhood's changing, thought hopeless Druff.

His salesman didn't recognize him.

"Druff?" Druff said, and spelled it for him.

"Oh yes," said the salesman, "you're here for the overcoat."

"The sun is shining, I'm here for the suit."

"Of course," said the salesman, "I'll see if it's ready."

"I called. They *said* it was ready," Druff told him, already beginning to feel his strange pique and building rage, whatever the flaw was that high-horsed his character and made him unfit to hold office. Some failed democracy in him, he supposed, and understood before the man even found it and brought it out that the suit wouldn't fit.

"Better try it on," the salesman said, "before my tailor goes to lunch."

Druff following him to the tiny, flimsily curtained dressing room with its hard little bench, shallow as a bookshelf, where the man handed over Druff's purchase and left him, the venue suddenly, subtly shifted, vaguely medical now, as though Druff had been called in for devastating examinations, something unforeseen popped up in the blood, the stool. (And this, well, aura, too, like a stall in the gents' in a restaurant. Something he couldn't think of as private property, yet understood— from his jacket on the hook on the wall there, like some flag slammed into enemy terrain in a battle—to be his as surely as if blood had been spilled for it, the front lines of the personal here, hallowed ground for sure, if only because of the men who'd occupied it before him, but not so hallowed he didn't resent them, their collective spoor and lingering flatulence.)

It was like dressing in a closet or an upper berth, Druff's limbs and mood pinched, crippled, hobbled as a potato-racer's in the close quarters.

He stared down the inside of the trousers he had just removed into a cloth scaffolding of seams and tucks, great squirreled-away swatches of excess material, some strip mine of fabric. And, as he traded pants, overheard the proprietary tone of the other customers, men—he'd seen them appraising themselves in front of the three-way mirrors as he followed the salesman to the fitting room—whose salesmen, holding jackets for them, helping them into sportswear, seemed more like trusted valets and aides than actual employees of the store.

"What do you think, Barney? Cuffs on these?"

"On crushed, distressed linen, always. That's just my opinion, Doctor."

"Waist thirty-six," a second tailor said.

"Waist thirty-six for the judge," the salesman repeated.

"The collar rides up in back too much," said the doctor.

"I can steam that out."

"Think you should take the shoulder pads down?"

"I'll steam it out, I take the shoulder pads down I throw off the whole armature of the jacket."

"You're the doctor."

"The doctor says I'm the doctor," Barney said.

"Where do you want the trousers to break? Here? About here?"

"There, just above the top of my shoelaces."

"So what do you think?"

"You'll be wearing this at the club?"

"Sure, yes."

"There's dancing?"

"Some dancing, some sitting some out."

"For some sitting some out just unbutton the jacket. For the dancing I can take a couple tucks in the left side panel."

"Tony, you flatter me," said a man just coming out of a changing room.

"No," Tony said, "no."

"No? Who am I, the Jolly Green Giant? There's enough room in the crotch."

Tony was furious. "That was special-ordered. Do me a favor, Mr. Gable. Talk to the store manager, lodge a complaint. Look, I'll show you the measurements I took. There's no relation. You see? You see these measurements? No, take it off, I don't need to check it. I can see from here. Irreparable, irreparable. There's no excuse. Our helpers in New York did this."

Druff's suit, as his heart had known in advance, did not look good on him. It didn't. (Druff humiliated by his hologram in the three-way mirror, the comings and goings of his balding, frailing self like a body knocked down on an auction block, going going gone. His image there telling as a CAT scan—— of shabby old mortality and downscale being. Slackened fat looked awful on a frail man. Druff bitterly damning trousers that wouldn't hold a crease, sagged buttonholes, his too-small handkerchiefs and scarves and failing zippers. Mourning the points of his collars, rounding, curling in on themselves, collapsed as old petals, fallen socks. Argh, Druff thought, I'd look shitty in furniture even.) What looked swell on the rack seemed—he recalled a Nehru jacket he'd owned, outmoded the first time he put it on—on him, in daytime's available light, already played out. It was part of the humiliation of shopping and purchase. And didn't even get the benefit of salesman-and-fitter talk, the shorten/lengthen arrangements, the tuck compensations and break-of-the-trouser breaks.

Indeed, *his* salesman was checking his watch.

"Tell me," Druff asked gloomily, "you got potholes in your neighborhood?"

"Potholes?"

"Deep pits where the road don't meet the road, breaks in the concrete where the city didn't take it in a couple tucks or never bothered to smooth out the shoulders."

"No potholes, no."

"I'm City Commissioner of Streets," Druff told him, "you call these guys 'Doctor,' you say 'Judge.' Anything wrong with the color of my money?"

(*No,* Druff thought, too late, he's going to call me Doctor, he's going to call me Judge, screaming Dick, Dick, *Dick!* in his head the second the words were out of the commissioner's mouth, because where was it written in the job description that his chauffeur-cum-spy-cum-security guard couldn't scare the bejesus out of the wiseguys who didn't treat Druff's office with the proper respect? Or tailors who didn't fit him properly or salesmen who didn't steer him away from colors and styles unbecoming to a man Druff's complexion and build?)

Though—admirably, Druff thought—the fellow restrained himself, or, rather, went in a different direction and was all over Druff with his salesman's sirs and deferentials. It's just that there was nothing—and Druff, sulkily, agreed—that either the salesman or the tailor could do. The suit fit Druff, Druff just didn't fit the suit. He dressed, he saw, above his station. Good clothes were for the gorgeous, for the athletically trim and vigorous, for these prime got-up guys in their recognizable cloth and leveraged primes.

It was a different story at Toober's, a restaurant in his city's near south end where many of the councilmen, department and agency heads, and very upper—almost civilian—cops and firemen took their afternoon meal along with other of the town's higher civil service and search-committee'd political appointees. Here and there a few patronage types were along, secretaries brought by their bosses for their birthday, a retirement do, even, Druff thought, to show the flag, bring out the vote, demonstrate, he meant, a kind of available, last-ditch force like Lear's whittled retainers. ("Missy," he'd told his driver, dismissing him, "won't be needing the car for an hour.") In a way he might never have left the clothing store. He could have been taking his lunch—the place seemed *that* male—from his shallow, déclassé bench in the changing room.

It was a different story anyway. Here he looked fine, jim-dandy. It was recognizable cloth on the diners in the lunch house, too, only theirs didn't lie on them as it did on the successful young men Druff had seen in the store, like well-kept hair on their well-kept heads. Here he, the pols and dependents dressed in a sort of dim apparatchik mode, one size fits all. No cuffs on their crushed linen, and even the color of their fabrics, no matter how expensive, a vaguely unfashionable shade of grime. Some principle operating here like the one that drove the city to stencil seals on its limos, that spoke of the company suit and, Druff supposed, was intended to ward off the voters by a kind of sartorial poor-mouthing. (Though he knew, of course, that the upper reaches of even democracy had its cutting edge. There were occasions when mayors dressed up like governors, governors like presidents, presidents like kings.)

He'd been too long trying on his suit. They were very busy, they hadn't been able, Toober said, to hold his table.

"That's all right, I'll catch a sandwich at the bar," Druff said, testing. Toober considered half a beat too long before he nodded, agreeing to the arrangement. "*Et tu,* Toober?" Druff said.

"Commissioner?"

"What, has Vegas sent in fresh odds on me? Is the new dope sheet out? D'ju see polls?"

"Commissioner?"

"Nah, it'll be all right. I'll catch a sandwich at the bar. I'll inquire about the catch of the day. I'll ask about soup."

"Anything, Commissioner," said the owner. "You want birthday cake and a slice of pie and a malted, say so. It's not on the menu, ask." There was a rumor Druff wasn't ready to believe that the restaurateur was interested in becoming sheriff, and would run for the office in the next election. Druff didn't put much stock in the story, thought Toober a familiar enough type, one of those men—there were women too, of course, plenty of them, but these tended to attach themselves to in-dividuals rather than political parties—who were political groupies, Jack Ruby types, drawn to, charged by, some homeopathic "juice." There was a rough equivalency, he supposed, between the innkeeper and power trades. Both had their backslappers certainly, both worked their respective rooms and loved, if not ceremony, then outright pomp, intriguing circumstance. (Why, Druff wondered, did all restaurant own-ers make such a big deal about detail, fly into rages over ever-so-improperly set tables? He'd seen Toober fire a busboy just for having spilled a drop of coffee into a customer's saucer.) Why were they always hounding the customer with their smarmy ingratiations and is-every-thing-satisfactories? Why, he meant, were they such bullies? (Druff, Druff felt, was no bully, and that was just what might have been wrong with him as a public man.) And why, he meant, did so many pols of his acquaintance share these same instincts, managing merely to smother them with their greased diplomacy? And why, he meant finally, oh why, was everything so political, as laced with motive as the goblets and china service of a poisoner? MacGuffins and plots everywhere. The world was all MacGuffin, one to a customer. (Saving one's grace, perhaps. He didn't think MacGuffins were in him. *He* had no plots, yet found himself to be not entirely displeased with this new—if it didn't turn out to be paranoia—not unpromising dispensation in which he felt himself to be, as they said in the grand juries, the "target" of others'.)

He found a place at the bar and plunged almost immediately into conversation with a woman he'd never seen before.

"Are you," she'd asked, "a politician too?"

Druff, who hadn't been able to judge people's ages for years now (since, in fact, he'd begun to lose "force" and become a hero of anec-dote, his personal golden age before people started to make allowances for him, and not just conducted but sometimes actually flourished his spirit through their wide-opened doors; that time, he meant, when they were still wary of him and he had their ages, indeed, all their numbers), had a particularly vivid notion of this one's. He thought the woman to be a few months shy of her forty-fifth birthday and curiously amended to himself that he didn't think she looked it. She was attractive—she looked, Druff thought, very smart—and was as openly blond as an au pair girl. Seated, the line of her back held almost militarily straight and her long, somewhat heavy legs reaching even farther down the bar stool than Druff's, she seemed quite tall, and Druff felt a quick rush of intimidated lust.

"Well," Druff answered her question, "I'm more an official than a politician."

"An official," she said, and Druff smelled her light, liquored breath, pleasant drafts like lovely, discrete things boxed, bottled, packaged, wrapped. Sheets, say, banded in boxes, or the stripped scent of perfume on the ground floor of a department store, sealed candy at the confectioner's, unopened cartons of cigarettes at the tobacconist's. Pungencies, the sweet, substantive zephyrs of bakery.

Uh oh and uh oh, thought Druff, and placed a few loose coca leaves onto his tongue from the stash in his pocket.

"Well, tell me," said the tall, blond stranger, "how official are you? Could you have me arrested?"

"I could get you a 'No Parking' sign for the front of your house, or 'Quiet Please, Hospital Zone.' 'Slow. Children Crossing.' " Then—perhaps it was the additional coca leaves kicking in—he said, "You're here on the tour, right?"

"The tour?"

"You're between planes. You saw notices for the city's hot new 'Change planes in our town and we'll show you a time' campaign. You had a four-hour layover and figured, 'What the hell, I'll go for it' and hopped on the free luxury tour bus."

"This happens? I pay taxes for this boondoggle?"

"Well," Druff said, "it's still in the planning stages. I'm trying the idea out on folks, getting their reactions, taking a straw vote. *Vox pop.* It's not very scientific, I don't suppose."

By the time Druff's turkey club came, the coca leaves had taken the edge off his appetite and he thought they were on easy enough terms to offer the woman his sandwich. She refused, but accepted the pickle and agreed to eat some french fries, which Druff spread out on a napkin for her. He asked if he could pick up her bar tab but she declined. He told her his name and identified himself as City Commissioner of Streets, and she told Druff she was Margaret Glorio, a freelance buyer of men's sportswear for some of the city's chain department stores. She worked for herself. They exchanged cards, and he undertook to identify many of the people in the room for her. He'd actually turned around on his bar stool and was pointing.

"Nobody, no one, nobody, no one," Druff said as if he was counting. Several of Druff's best friends in the world looked up and waved.

"Oh," Druff said, "the little unassuming fella in the corner?"

"That one?"

"That one."

"Oh."

"Curator of the art museum."

"Really?"

"They're cold. What you have to understand is I'm happily married thirty-six years. Nothing that happens between us is going to change that. You ought to know that going in. Want some more fries?"

"No thank you."

"As it happens, I've just come from doing some shopping myself. Brooks Brothers? Oh, I suppose you get weary of hearing that after you've just told folks you're a buyer for the major chains, but do I look like someone who'd lie about his haberdashery? Besides, it's not sportswear I've been looking at anyway, it's a suit. Not even your field."

"Are you really the street commissioner?"

"Sure as Langello there's the county coroner," Druff told her, indicating the man Toober had placed at Druff's table.

"He's county coroner?"

"Like to meet him? Want to shake his hand?"

"I see no need," Miss Glorio said, adding she'd never been much of a voter in the local elections and that if a suspicious transmission on her automobile hadn't caused her to bring the car back to the dealer she'd never have discovered this restaurant or known it was a hangout for local politicians.

"Local elections, local politicians," Druff said, "you make us all sound like the Great Gildersleeve. See Superintendent of Schools Carlin? No, over there. Right, that one. You wouldn't think it to look at him but he's in charge of a budget of over a hundred million dollars a year."

She was trying to catch the bartender's eye. Druff, a little belligerent, tendered one superbly inflected cough and the fellow came at once. He presented Druff the checks. She started to object but the City Commissioner of Streets overrode her and handed the man money for both their bills. He wouldn't even let her get the tip, Druff said.

"Look . . ." she objected.

"Nonsense," he said. "Fire Chief, Sewers and Mains, Chief of Police," Druff said, taking her arm and indicating these various public servants as he nodded to them and steered Margaret Glorio toward the door. "Assemblyman, assemblyman, head of the zoo," he said. "You may be an arbiter of taste, but these fellows are the knights and paladins. —Our town," he said. He brought her to the curb where Dick, in his twin capacity of chauffeur and spy, was illegally parked in the limo, and waited while the man came out from behind his driver's seat, touched his hand to his cap to the lady and held the door open for them, crisply shutting it when they were seated. "Women don't usually go for a street commish," Druff confided. "Nine times out of ten they'd rather have an alderman. Blunt, *visible* power's the aphrodisiac in this trade."

"*I'd* rather have an alderman," Miss Glorio said.

"There's a cellular telephone in this limo," Druff said. "Want to call the dealer, see what's what with your transmission?"

"I don't know what I'm doing here. What do you *mean* you're married, that I ought to know that going in? I'm not going in anywhere, you're not sweeping anyone off her feet."

"Look, I'll show you." He picked up the handset and called Time and Temperature. "It's seventy-one degrees," he reported to the woman, "it's two-sixteen." He proposed ringing it again and letting her hear for herself. "Boy that gives me a kick," he said. "Look, I even have call waiting. I don't care, I don't think I'll *ever* get over it. I'm old enough to be from a generation that still marveled that there were car radios. The clarity of long-distance calls astonished us. 'Gee,' we'd say to the people of our time one and two thousand miles across the country, 'you sound like you're right next door.' But this is even better. We're in a moving car, for goodness sake. I can call long-distance, I can call long-distance to someone in *another* moving car."

"Why? What would you say?"

"I don't know, that they sound like they're right next door. It's the idea of the thing. I don't know, maybe I just have a lower awe threshold than the next guy, maybe that's what keeps me feeling young," lied the City Commissioner of Streets, who felt neither awe nor youth, who'd

4 3

T h e   M a c G u f f i n

heard—and at once had registered—Margaret Glorio's remark that he wasn't sweeping anyone off her feet, and whose insistent, meaningless, imperturbable charm rolled off his tongue as casually as a campaign promise and who, by engaging her in conversation in the restaurant in the first place, and paying her check, and by saying outlandish things to her and practically hijacking her into his municipal limousine, had merely meant to keep the MacGuffins coming, though he realized, of course, that it was alien to the form to volunteer, even to intercede, that one didn't go prancing after a fate or it wasn't a fate anymore, only one more misplaced obsession. Still, the commissioner reasoned, adding his driver's admission earlier that morning that the city was talking about transferring him (and Dick's being there, in the outer office, standing in for the regular security guy, soaking up Druff's interoffice communications with Mrs. Norman) and the man's unaccustomed solicitousness (the chauffeur's buttered bushwah about Druff's Fourteen Points) to the coincidence of his son's having kept company with the hit-and-run-over Su'ad, and the city's and university's nervousness about the incident, even the usurpation of his table at Toober's (what had he been, fifteen minutes late? twenty?), even the restaurateur's little hesitation step when Druff had offered to sit at the bar and even (though here, Druff had to admit, he was probably stretching) the treatment he'd received when he went to claim his suit, there was enough circumstantial affront to warrant Druff's aroused suspicions. Well, worse cases had been made. Though, if only to be fair to the rest of them—to Toober, to Dick, to Mrs. Norman, to Hamilton Edgar, to his son and the unnamed co-conspirator hustling alterations at Brooks Brothers—didn't Druff have to wonder that if a little mid-life crisis might not be entirely unwelcome, then how much more agreeably might a bit of actual, flat-out Sturm and endgame Drang strike his fancy? (And wasn't this the true reason most guys didn't hit their tragic stride until they were old?)

And just look who was still sitting there beside him. Who, despite her mild protestations and her delayed take about his being married notwithstanding, and all the usual disclaimers—he supposed usual, but what did he know, a guy on Inderal years?—and the fact of her size— the unswept feet remark, for example, might just as easily have been a simple physical observation as a boast or metaphor—had permitted him to guide her into his car anyway, even if, once she was there, she'd been unimpressed by all the mod cons and was apparently indifferent to his offer to let her use his car phone. Well, she's a buyer for major department stores, Druff thought, a sophisticated lady, a woman on an expense account, a Frequent Flier.

"I know people," Druff said, returning the phone to its housing, "who use these to call home and ask what's for dinner."

"Me too," Miss Glorio said.

"Yes, well," said Druff, discomfited, looking up to catch Dick, his spy, spying on them in the limo's rearview mirror and covering for himself by grinning away like some hovering, hand-rubbing Dutch uncle in films, for all the world as if Dick were Druff's senior and not the other way around, as if, thought age-innocent Druff, Dick were love's advocate, *that* avuncular, *that* European. And suddenly remembered the force of his intimate augury in the restaurant. Then and there deciding to test it, willing to let their affair stand or fail on the accuracy of his presentiments.

"Say," he said, "ask you a personal question?"

"Depends."

"Depends. Fair enough. Depends."

"What is it?"

"I was wondering," Druff said. "How old are you?"

"I'm forty-four, I'll be forty-five in three months."

"Ah," said Druff, and thought, as though their liaison were already assured, this is going to be a sea change made in heaven. And added, as though what was already assured were already over, "Where would you like us to drop you?"

Glorio referred him to the business card in his suit jacket and, when he pulled it out and held it at arm's length to read, she reached over and took it away from him. She folded the card between her fingers, slipped it into her purse, leaned forward, and called out the address to Dick. "What," the commissioner said, "I'm a little farsighted? Because I'm not twenty-twenty and have a granddad's vision you're cutting me loose?" He wasn't daunted, didn't think he sounded daunted. He was perfectly aware of how feeble he must appear to the woman, a buyer of men's sportswear, a lady with a gift for inseam, pocket, crotch, detailing, who knew the demographics of taste, the secrets of fashion, what certain colors hid or enhanced, who took men's weights and

4 5

measures as easily as Barney or Tony the Tailor, was probably as knowing about their bodies as a nurse. He took his fragility in stride. He discounted it, discounted it for her, meant his remark about his eyesight to tell her as much, and was assured, moreover, by what he was about to offer her—— his inspired proposition.

Dick, who knew the city at least as well as its Commissioner of Streets, who might, had he wished, have driven them through any of its ancient, gerrymandered neighborhoods without ever hitting a light or stop sign, seemed, old Cupid's hand-wringing fuss-and-ditherer, to want to draw out the ride, to aim them at traffic, scenery, affable and smug as a hackman with newlyweds. Though they rode in silence, and the glass that separated the front of the limo from the back was shut, Druff felt covered in lap robes by the man, and he leaned forward and tapped on the window with his wedding band. "Step on it. Don't spare the horses, please, Dick."

"Oh, aye, Commissioner," Dick said, and in minutes they were there. Then came around, opened the door for Druff's lovely passenger. "Mademoiselle," he said, inviting her into the world, a faint smarm on his middleman's lips, and would have closed the door on his boss had not that frail, feeble old man pulled something out of his buried old alacrity reserves and reached the pavement at almost the same moment Miss Glorio did.

"Wait for me," he told his chauffeur and grasped the lady's arm, drawing her apart from the entrance to her office building. "Will you be my mistress?" he asked her suddenly.

"What? No, of course not. I don't know you. You're old, you're crazy. You're married, you're not a sharp dresser. What do you mean, will I be your mistress? My share of that check came to just over five dollars. Tell me the truth, are you really a public servant? I mean I saw the seal on the side of that ridiculous car, but maybe that's what people are into nowadays, renting police cars, fire trucks, limousines with official-looking seals. So yes or no, are you the street commissioner? Because if you are, I'll tell you something, mister, it's the decline and fall all over again. *No,* I won't be your mistress! I never heard anything so nuts." She was furious with him, not actually shouting, too furious for rage, and Druff took advantage of what was still a lull in the noise levels to ask his question a second time. "Do I look hard up?" she demanded.

Druff turned and waved Dick back into the car. "Look, I'm no spring chicken, I admit it, but I'm probably twenty years *your* junior."

"Fourteen," Druff said.

"Fourteen, right. I stand corrected. Fourteen. How could you, how *could* you? *Do* I, *do* I?"

"Do you what?"

"Look hard up?"

"No, of course not."

"Because I'm not. I do okay. I have a job that takes me all over the world. My passport has stamps in it from the four corners. I meet men. Even married men. Where do you get off? You don't even know me. I certainly don't know you."

"Ah," Druff said.

"What?"

"Just listen to what I'm suggesting. You *don't* know me. I intend to do the right thing."

"The right thing," she said.

"Wait," he said, "hear me out. Give a guy his day in court a minute. Hear me out. Didn't I hear you out when you said I was old and crazy and that I'm just a little married nutso old slob who doesn't know how to dress? Didn't I listen patiently to your side of the story when you questioned my credentials as a civil servant and stuck an additional half dozen years onto my age and called an official, bona fide limousine of this city a ridiculous gimmick and accused me by veiled allusion of trying to buy you for an outlay of something less than six bucks? Well, didn't I? Fair's fair."

"Fair's certainly fair. You sure did."

"All right," he said, "here's the story. I won't try to kid you. I *am* old, I *am* married. And I *know* my clothes hang on me. Even expensive Brooks Brothers. To tell the truth, I dress above my station, and would probably look better in open hospital gowns than I do in street clothes, but I'm City Commissioner of Streets all right and the limo's legit. That's the absolute truth, a matter of public record. You could look it up."

"Listen," Margaret Glorio said, checking her watch and edging toward the entrance of the office building, "this is ridiculous."

"Is it?" Druff said. "I hope not. I hate looking foolish and haven't much patience with loonies or even time to be silly. I'm not physically attractive but I'm not a particularly stupid man. I don't look it, I know, but I'm something of a man's man, actually. Men enjoy my company, I mean, and from what I understand that's supposed to be a plus with the ladies."

"You're annoying me."

"All right," Druff said, "forget all that. You're a busy person and none of this is part of my pitch anyway."

"What *is* your pitch? I'm curious to know."

"That you could do worse."

"That I could do worse? That's your pitch? That I could do worse?"

"Of course. Sure. You spelled most of this out yourself. I'm married. That protects you, you're protected."

"Oh, right," Margaret Glorio said.

"Boy, you don't know beans about blackmail, do you? Well," he said, "call me old-fashioned, but I find that attractive in a woman."

"Blackmail?"

"No, of course not. Your innocence of it. I guess what's slowing you down is your suspicion I'm not really a public man. Well, you have my card, but that could be counterfeit. There are dozens of ways to check me out. Find out who authorizes snow removals in your neighborhood. You drive a car in this city, next time you come to a detour look at the chap's name on the bottom of the legend apologizing for the delay and thanking you for your patience. *I* know. Are you on the tax rolls? The city sends out a calendar with the names of its officials and little photographic insets of what we look like.

"Listen, Margaret, I know you're anxious to get back to work, I don't want to hold you up. Check me out. If I'm who I say I am, you'll know it's all right for us to get it on. Once we start sneaking around together I'll be buying you gifts, we'll be checking into motels. I'll be laying down a paper trail Hansel and Gretel could follow out of the woods in the dark better than crumbs. Oh, way better. (Birds peck up crumbs quick as snap.) Don't you see? I *love* public life. You'd have me over a barrel. You'd *have* my old ass."

"Why are you standing here saying these things to me?"

"I've reason to believe," Druff said reasonably, "that my limousine is wired, that my car phone is tapped."

"They keep a record of your calls to Time and Temperature?"

"They stoop at nothing." She laughed, Druff taking her hilarity as the first good sign for his suit's success since his confirmed presentiment about her age. Then and there he would have pressed her to make an assignation with him but she continued laughing. "What," Druff said, "what?"

"Nothing," she managed. "I was just wondering, what are they going to make of your telling some guy with a car phone in Massachusetts or Texas that he sounds like he's just next door?"

"That was a heart's confidence, Margaret," he said, pretending offense. "I was letting you in on something," he said stiffly, stooping at nothing in his own right and, then, drawing himself up, asked again if she would be his mistress.

"No."

"To me you're beautiful, Margaret, well above the usual normal, but face it, you're a woman of a certain age. All right, it's no secret. I'm not exactly your customary foot-sweeper, but you think I don't have needs? If not, tell me, what do you think dirty old men are for?"

"Please," she said, not smiling anymore, though forced to maintain a sort of ceremonial cheerfulness by the proximity of the various men and women, colleagues, supposed Druff, coming in and out of her building, an early cast-iron skyscraper in what was left of the city's garment district, with huge windows and even more fretwork ornamenting it than the iron script that ran along the sides of City Hall like a kind of reductive Arabic.

"Tell me, yes or no, will you be my mistress?"

"No."

"I mean to pursue you then, Miss Glorio. You haven't heard the last of Bobbo Druff."

"I'll report you," she warned as Druff turned and walked away from her. "I'll turn you in."

"Hah!" Druff barked without looking back. "You haven't got the goods on me yet."

This is what he thought about while he went up to the limo and climbed in: that he'd come on. That he'd come on strong. Like a fool, but strong. That however ineffective he may have been, he *had* come on. That was the thing. He discounted his foolishness, his ineffectuality, his age and marital status, his awry, skewed dress, as, earlier, he'd discounted his fragility. He had come on. His cards on the table. On the table? All *over* the place. It was the *strength* of his appeal that mattered, that gave at least a little of the lie to what he'd felt in the changing room at Brooks Brothers, before his devastated reflection in their three-way mirrors, within hearing of other people's kibitzing, other men's flatterers. And how about that quickstep when he hopped out of the car, when he scooted after Margaret in double time—*double time*—drawing off energy from those threatened old alacrity reserves? He meant it when he said what he'd said about the paper trail, about buying back a little relented life at the expense of scandal. Do all men feel as innocent as me, he wondered, when they've had it with their honor? Do they strain so against the laws of their MacGuffins? And I wonder, he wondered, if it's love, time or only the threat of death that's got me hopping?

And now, back in the limousine (which *was* ridiculous—and why hadn't he acknowledged *that* one when she was drawing up her bill of particulars against him and he was conceding to her accusations right and left; what would it have cost him?—and not only ridiculous but an environment whose charms he'd tired of long ago, charms that had, quite simply, worn off, worn out: the mystery of the controls, the appeal of the electric toggles for the windows and door locks, of the sunroof, the lights and air-conditioning and heat; the novelty jump seats he couldn't remember anyone ever having sat in, the recessed armrests and all the straps and sequestered little lamps, all the hidden niches where the ashtrays went, the substantial, cumulative candlepower of the concealed cigar lighters, the tucked-away speakers for the radio, the secret drop-down desktop, and all the rest of the wet-bar, cable-TV-ready built-ins, the whole thing bristling with as much expendable latency as a hotel room or a compartment on a train), Druff contemplated old Dick suspiciously, trying, as neutrally as he could, to stare the man down in the same rearview mirror in which his driver had bullied *him* earlier, spying and smiling down on the cute couple they made, in his old-timey all-the-world-loves-a-lover mode.

"Women," Dick offered as if the word were the concluding point in some telling, elegant argument.

Druff determined to stay the course, decided to stare him down by drawing him out.

"Women?" Druff repeated as if he were unfamiliar with the term, as though Dick had called out the name of some strange creature spotted in the road, the commissioner actually turning his head for a moment.

"Sure," said *his* man to *his* man. "They'll say anything. Even when there ain't anything in it for them, even when they don't stand to gain. 'I'm forty-four,' she says."

"She *is* forty-four."

"Yeah?" said the chauffeur. "Mikey said she's fifty."

"Mikey said?"

"Well, wasn't she a friend of that Arab who died? I thought I recognized her. Ain't that why we gave her the lift?"

Who's drawing out whom here, wondered the City Commissioner of Streets, and found the switch on the control panel which sent the glass partition window up. "Here I go again," his driver had just time enough to say before he was shut away, "off to Coventry."

It was a cheerful enough remark but Druff could have slapped the side of his own head with the heel of his own hand, mentally cuffing himself in abrupt, classic realization, stagy awareness. (Actually seeing himself do it, the self-deprecating code gesture, the slammed clarity of his damning *Dummkopf!* theatrics, and even time to wonder why it was that for all their direct, stripped meaning, efficient, he supposed, as cursing, one rarely observed—and never executed—such things in real life. All one's performances—he was a pol, close to government, privy to the high dramatics—— blackmail, bribery, kickbacks and fraud, of course, but the hard-core rough stuff, too; the fires, he meant, the betrayals and anguish for which government, which made the laws and set the rules, had all the hottest tickets and best seats—— all that devastating hard stuff, the gossip, rattling bones and smoking guns they did for each other, and which, he'd come to see, was a kind of professional courtesy, a sort of common currency, their mutual, collective corruption not only leveling the playing field but, by piquing each other's interest, actually mining it—held in refined check not because one was naturally refined but because it just never really occurred to a fellow that these gestures were available to anyone but actors. So, at least till now, he'd never rubbed his chin to draw forth his thoughts, never torn at his hair or thrown up his hands in despair, couldn't recall when he'd last touched thumb and forefinger to the inside corners of his eyes to ease fatigue. Nor had he ever sighed or touched the back of his hand to his forehead and brought on a swoon. He'd never swooned.) It was too powerful a vocabulary to have been deprived of. Now, possessed by his MacGuffins, and handed things to think about, he was aware of himself performing several of these gestures at once, caught out in some frenzy of squirming and thrashing, and actually administering those hard, initial, thumping salutes to the delayed consciousness that slept in both temples, pummeling them, right temple, left temple, as though he had water in his ears. (While meanwhile, back inside the transparent overlays of his parallel parentheses, he was suddenly appreciative of what he hadn't appreciated before—— that it was no mere showy false modesty which brought on these blows, that the Sherlocks who usually took them must usually have meant them, that it all *had* been plain as the nose, that if it'd been a snake on their face, it *would* have bit them!)

That window was *closed.* Druff had deliberately shut it himself when they'd entered the car. (Wasn't that just what he'd been referencing moments before when he'd referred to the "mystery of the controls"—— the queer, international graphics for limousines he'd never quite mastered? Sure, he remembered fumbling for the switch, recalled that it didn't go up at first, moving it so it did only on a second or third try.) So it was closed all during their—well, his—sexual banter on the ride out to her office. What did he *mean,* " 'I'm forty-four,' she says"? They'd been speaking softly in the rear of the big, ridiculous car. How had Dick heard her? Unless what he'd told her outside her office building was actually so, that the limo was wired, that partition or no partition their voices came across to the dirty little spy fuck like people's on a radio call-in show. It must be so. The bug just some additional municipal mod con add-on he hadn't known about. (*"Glasnost glasnost glasnost,"* mumbled President Druff in a language du jour.) Which meant, Druff, groaning—gestures of humiliation here: thrashing, squirming—knew, Dick had probably heard it all, everything, his plaintive pleas and come-on, his absurd claims about his low awe threshold, even his solemn invitation to be blackmailed by her, though he was sure that that proposition at least had been delivered out on the street, beyond the range of his city's—his party's?—high-tech doodads. What the hell? It all was it all. His ass was in the wrong hands. Dick and the operatives had it.

"Something wrong, Commissioner?" Dick had lowered the glass partition a couple of ticks.

"What?"

"I see you wriggling around back there is all. Anything wrong?"

"Just easing my piles."

"I didn't know you had piles, Commissioner Druff."

"Yeah, well, there's a lot about me you don't know." Sure there is, he thought. My best color, my favorite song.

In the mirror the son of a bitch was smiling. Was he smiling?

And, troubled, considered going for the coca leaves. What would that make it, three times today? Four? In for a penny, in for a pound, he thought, and then and there would have stuck in his thumb and pulled out the plums but Dick was watching him narrowly in the mirror. He folded his hands in his lap and sat up straight. What a good boy am I, he pleased, then wondered abruptly, What's wrong with this picture? And was reminded that the glob of spit was gone, vanished from the floor of the limo as if it had not been. Unless the lady had spiked it on the heel of her shoe and taken it with her, Dick—he was a plainclothes policeman after all—had probably tweezered it up and stuck it into one of those clear little evidence baggies cops always seemed to carry around with them. He could have done it when Druff was off in the restaurant with Glorio the enchantress. Hell, he could've done it when he dropped Druff at City Hall that morning. Most likely Druff's saliva was off even now being tested for steroids, HIV shit and coca leaves in some special, same-day-service spit lab. Can they do that? Don't they have to tell you first, wondered the man from UNCLE.

Then this in his head, who was on a roll: "Mikey said . . ." (And just who was and who wasn't going by the book now? Was Dick moonlighting, was he hiring himself out? Because Druff was damned if he could recall the boy ever saying, "Big date tonight, Pop" and asking for the keys to the limo. *He* didn't even have keys to the limo, had never actually driven the damn thing.) And was really steamed now, not with his son, or even Dick, so much as with Margaret Glorio. What was she, toying with him, playing him for a fool? Listen, she was a grown woman, he was pretty much a non-chauvinistic, macho-neutral, fairly progressive sort of fellow—what, he wasn't? someone with *his* Inderal levels?—and understood she was perfectly within her rights to spurn him, even to scorn him. That was one thing. It was another entirely to mess with the signs or crap on the karma. She must have seen how he'd lit up when she'd said she was forty-four. Surely she had. And fifty—if that's what she was—wasn't out of his love range. It was what he said. Or thought anyway— that if he had somehow managed to get hers right—whose judgment in that area normally extended only to whether or not people were old enough to vote—it would be a major auspice, magic's happy green go-ahead. (He didn't mean to seem ridiculous, he *didn't*. He *despised* absurdity, the absurd. He wouldn't split hairs, but this was a MacGuffin thing now, out of his hands.) Steamed. Outraged, in fact. So much so he was tempted to pick up the car phone and call her. Just let her have it. Right there in the limo, Dick's bugs and satellite dishes notwithstanding, or even his snoop's eyes working Druff's moving room in the rearview mirror. And might have. (Anyhow, what goods could they have had on him? He'd never been a *chazzer*. He honored sealed bids, and if he did a favor now and then it was rarely for cash. Oh, when he was a councilman, a few bucks here and there for the war chest maybe, but he was cleaner than most on that score. Your average traffic cop did better business.) So if he managed—*just* managed—to stay off the airwaves it had to be the humiliation factors at work, merely your normal, good old old-fashioned pants-down, open-fly apprehensions. But it was a struggle. How he longed to ring her up. "Look," he'd say, "are you forty-four years old or what? Don't lie to me, I could run a credit check on you like that. I'm a public official. I could punch up your Social Security file, your IRS one. Forget confidentiality. I have my own personal sunshine laws. I could bring the FBI in on this, the driver's license people. Does the name Su'ad mean anything to you?"

Which *was* pretty much what he said when he finally managed to reach her at her office late in the day.

"Are you calling from your car?"

"No," Druff said, "why?"

"Ship-to-shore?"

"Of course not."

"Don't tell me, you're in a pay phone."

"I'm in my office. I'm down at the Hall. Why?"

"Nothing," Margaret Glorio said, "I was just wondering. You said you'd pursue me, I like to know what I'm up against. Are you connected? Some old-timer with consoles, a finger on the button of devices that lower other devices, projectors that shoot out from the walls, screens that come down from the ceiling—— stuff with zoom capability, freeze-frame, special enhancement features that dim the background and highlight only what's important like a Magic Marker, that can bring out the pores and go in so tight you can make a positive identification of a subject by his dental work? Tell me," she said, "do you have a code name? Are you one of those guys who can pick up a telephone and have another of those guys killed?"

Was this flirting? Was she flirting with him? Gee, earlier he had come on and now maybe there was possible reciprocal flirting. It was up to Druff, Druff thought, to keep it going. "Fifty's not out of my love range," he blurted. "Fifty's still in my ballpark."

"What?"

"Ha ha," Druff said, "that has to be special-ordered. Getting someone killed has to be special-ordered. How about a 'No Parking'? How about a 'Tow-Away Zone'?"

" 'Su'ad,' " Margaret Glorio said suddenly, "isn't that a restaurant? Are you asking me to have dinner with you?"

"Yes! Sure am, yes!" committed hurriedly the City Commissioner of Streets. "What's good for you? Sevenish, seven-thirtyish? Eightish? Your ish is my command," joked the man, in the grip of his MacGuffin, who hated to appear ridiculous and despised absurdity. And agreed upon a restaurant and arranged about a time.

So you can just imagine how Druff felt when he finally got home that evening.

Well, it was a good thing he had no appointments that afternoon. That was on the plus side. (Because he'd have been no damn good to the city streets for the remainder of the day if he had.) Fortunate for the commissioner, too, was the fact that when Dick dropped him back at City Hall at around three, he left the car for Doug and asked if he could take the rest of the afternoon off (and wasn't it interesting that even spies had lives of their own, that they weren't merely these dedicated automatons interested only in their mission, but, like any civilian, were subject to the toothache or maybe even found they had to lie down for a nap once in a while?), his absence freeing Druff up to make the reservations, get down to the automatic teller—he counted out the money in his wallet, decided the fifty-or-so-dollars wouldn't be enough if they drank wine or if Margaret was particularly hungry that evening (so far as he knew she'd skipped lunch— a pickle, a few french fries spread out on a napkin, and she was a good-sized girl) because, despite what he'd told her about paper trails, he intended to pay for the evening in cash, and to consider the rest of his plans. The business of the condom, for example.

The thing about safe sex. It was all over the papers, radio, TV. (Those people always had to have something to scare you with. They'd just come through a winter. All right, it had been a particularly bitter winter, lots of snow, plenty of ice—didn't Druff have the almost archaeological evidence of his potholes; hadn't he seen for himself that very day?—but the way the media carried on about windchill factors, hypothermia, frostbite, you'd think they lived at the North Pole. If you weren't wearing gloves and the temperature outside was fifteen degrees and the windchill was minus twenty-two, in two minutes you would lose all the fingers on both hands. Hypothermia was even worse. Ninety-three per-cent of your body heat escaped through your head. If the temperature was seven degrees and the windchill was minus thirty-five, and you didn't have a hat on, your skull could crack open in under five minutes and you could get gangrene in your brain. They were like the sworn political enemies of winter, these weather terrorists. Once, in Detroit on city business inspecting snow-removal equipment, Druff was without his hat and had become so worked up by the weather terrorists on local TV that by the time he was ready to go out to see the people with whom he was meeting, the balding Druff had gone into the bathroom in his hotel room and found the clear plastic shower cap the hotel left for its guests in a little wicker basket along with the soaps and shampoos, conditioners, shoehorns and sewing kits like a hamper for some odd picnic of grooming, and put it on his head. It was the windchill factor's final factor. In four seconds you looked like an asshole.) So he wasn't concerned for himself, or for Margaret, or even Rose Helen. He'd been

faithful for years, the perfect husband. Hell, it'd been years since he'd
even lusted after anyone in his mind, let alone his heart or other organs.
(Well, that wasn't entirely true. There'd been Su'ad—the woman, not
the restaurant—that time she'd lectured them in front of the high-
intensity lamp, and Su'ad again when Mikey had been preparing to boff
her right there practically next to their bedroom. All right, so once with
his eyes and once with his ears. Such lust patterns didn't make him Jack
the Ripper. No jury in the world.) And forget needles, he didn't share
coca leaves. If anything, his concern about the condom wasn't a courtesy
to any of them so much as a tribute to their times. Speaking for himself,
he was clean as a whistle, and doubted—oh, he knew what they said
all right, that it cut across class lines, but that was just more windchill
factor if you asked him—that the tall, snappy-dressing, frequent-flying
Margaret Glorio was any more an Apple Annie of the venereal than he
was an Apple Andy. Besides, he didn't expect they would even get to
mess around. This wasn't any just-in-case scenario he was running
through here. (He hadn't been a teenager for thirty-nine years.) And it
wasn't his credentials as a man-about-town (who'd come on with her,
come on strong) he was protecting. He didn't have to show the flag.
(Indeed, he'd be tempted *not* to show it, even if she asked.) No. It was
that windchill factor again, the terror anyone could be talked into, the
promise he'd made himself in Detroit after only his third second under
the shower cap—— *that he'd never again voluntarily permit himself to look
like an asshole!*

And he didn't. Not to Dick the spy, who, as luck and the gods of Farce
would have it, had asked for the rest of the day off. Nor to Mrs. Norman,
his secretary/receptionist (and if he was paranoid, tell him what was
that all about then—— the idea that someone could be assigned not one
but two—count 'em, two—chauffeurs and security people, actual armed
men with real bullets in real guns standing by in the outer office, and
have stripped from him—all in the name of cutbacks and economies,
of course, but tell *that* to the Marines—sufficient office help, the clerks
and administrative assistants and gofers, just your ordinary roster of
deserving civil service and spoils appointees like those symbolic elevator operators who still rode up with him in the building's self-service
automatic elevators just, so far as Druff could tell, for the company of
the thing, the sociableness, so he wouldn't have to pass his remarks

about the weather or the ball scores to strangers or the empty walls, tell him, *what?*). Certainly not to Doug (not Druff's second driver so much as Dick's backup man), who, in Druff's humble, would not have recognized an asshole if one were sitting on his face.

The man was talking with Mrs. Norman but snapped to a smart attention when Druff appeared.

"Oh, hi, Commissioner," Doug said agreeably enough, but in odd opposition to the starched formality of his stance, "it's nice to see you."

"It's nice to see you, Doug."

"Thank you, Mr. Commissioner. How are you, sir?"

"Fine, thanks. Yourself?"

"Oh, it's not my nature to complain, Commissioner Druff, but I'm all right."

"That's good, Doug. That's good."

"Are you going out, sir? I'll bring the car straight around."

"No, no," Druff said, "it's too nice a day. Don't stir yourself, Doug. I'll walk."

"It's *absolutely* no trouble." He carefully studied his commissioner. "Of course, it *is* a fine day, and a brisk walk sets a man up. I understand that. I'd only want to make sure you're not doing this to save *me* effort."

"Doctor's orders, Doug."

"Oh?" said Doug, who, despite the clipped-sounding youthfulness of his name, Druff knew to be his own age, a fellow (clearly a cop, though he had vaguely about him the ingratiating air of a somewhat sinister doorman, an unindicted despoiler of male children, say, and an aura of one already vested but still building his pension, a man always on overtime, whose activities belied the sense one somehow had of him that there was money there somewhere) who seemed to know things about him he'd been at pains to learn. Druff liked him. Probably the man was only a passive-aggressive, a nurser of secret grudges, but Druff had the idea that the city was missing a bet here, that he'd have been a better operative for it than Dick (though he believed all Doug's oleaginous loomings and hoverings would, in the end, come to nothing, that there'd be no September surprises from that quarter, the guy a classic case of mistaken identity, more a type, finally, than a man).

"I don't mean *my* doctor's orders. Your generic doctor's generic orders. Me, I'm fine. My clothes don't hang right is all," Druff reassured.

And Doug, considering, measuring Druff, sizing him up, apparently bought it. "Have a good walk then, Mr. Commissioner," Doug said in his cop-cum-doorman's negligibly effacing and commanding way, putting Mrs. Norman on hold, putting, Druff suspected, *everything* on hold; so long as the commissioner still sauntered to the door, not permitting, as if it were in his power, even a phone to ring. Druff had the sense that he was being safely conducted across a street while traffic waited.

Not even to the pharmacist in the drugstore a good three blocks from City Hall from whom Druff bought the condoms. Or at least any *particular* asshole. Who you would think ought to know better. I mean, Druff meant, a fifty-eight-year-old guy with an ill-hanging suit on him and probably plenty more just like it home in the closet, who wasn't even trying to appear casual, but simply, quite casually appears and bellies up to the counter requiring a packet of condoms? That was the word Druff used, "packet." Meaning to imply by his carefully chosen diminutive just that. No in-for-a-penny-in-for-a-pound largesse here, only the smallest quantity that could possibly be purchased, as if whatever fling the fifty-eight-year-old type was contemplating was just that, too. A fling and, judging by the size of his order, possibly his last? Not even, mind you, as any high school boy would, specifying a brand? What, this *isn't* an asshole? Just selling the so apparently hopeful last-flinging old-timer the generic packet of condoms he asked for, and maybe (because Druff would in his place if Druff were the pharmacist and the pharmacist the customer in the ill-hanging clothes) hoping that the condom would hang better on him than the clothes did. But then again, Druff knew, the man was a professional, and a professional—his license was right up there on the counter like a framed picture of the wife and kids—keeps his feelings to himself. So he could be wrong, Druff thought. Maybe he *did* look like an asshole.

But (if you didn't count the druggist) only to himself. And not because of the couple of condoms safe in his suit pocket next to the coca leaves (the condoms he knew he would not have a chance to use once even, and then throw away, throwing them away first, before they were used, *or* seen, like the flag he knew he not only didn't have to show but wouldn't even if he'd had to; *hey,* he was a guy who covered the bases, even if, not quite respectably he *did* have a spy, even if, he not only had a spy but maybe a MacGuffin, too, and certainly plenty of humbug in his heart) but because of the FTD flowers already on their way to Margaret Glorio's home address.

So you can imagine how he felt. You can just imagine.

On the one hand anticipate, rampant with a kind of self-regard. In a way, he was already half in love with Miss Glorio, not for her per- ceived qualities (which he didn't know about yet anyway) so much as for those which the contemplation of a relationship induced and re- leased, or induced and released again, in Druff. Why, love, even half- love, was heady, hearty stuff, like the drugged aromatics of chemical flowers or the recovered toxins of adolescence. Thinking of it that way, years wilted from him, he filled his suits. He felt a sort of strutting potency and would have liked to get another gander at himself in Brooks Brothers glass. Love, contemplated Druff, was good for the gander, and the commissioner, like some world-class cuckold, had a temporary respite from the ordinary anxieties of ego, self-consciousness, was even enough liberated from himself to permit himself to regard—it was a festival of regard—some things which might please Margaret. Would she go to the fights or enjoy a day at the track? Was she a good sport, he meant, some down-and-dirty lady, the kind who would appreciate the unraveled arcana of a dope sheet? Because he could go that way, teach her the Racing Form, coach her in the codes of a low art, the stats, weights and measures of a compromised metrics, then tell her to forget all she'd learned, and to learn something new—— that all bets were sucker bets, that the ponies in this town were fixed, that it was as well to know who was into whom—better!—than all the histories of all the horses in the field. And wasn't this thrilling information too, to have this lowdown, this insider's window on the world? He was sure it was the same in Sportswear, he'd tell her, and that he would be just as surprised to have *his* assumptions challenged, all the old warrants. Wasn't it, wasn't it thrilling? And then he would take her with him to the paddock for some private discussions because, he'd confide, you didn't dope the horses so much as bet on those already doped. He longed to bring her along, a girlfriend like the son he'd always wanted.

Oh, thought Druff, let it begin, not just the touchy-feely but the

philosophy parts too, all the shared sentimentals they sought to hook
you with in the love classifieds. He'd been hooked years, reconstructing
hypothetical dreamgirls from the tiny bytes of smuggled, implied tastes
revealed there, played out like line to kidnappers. Oh, he thought, let
it! Wanting to trade on special theories—— that you'd make a killing,
if you bet the professional wrestling, as fixed, everyone knew, as the
stars. That all you had to do was to be willing to offer high odds and
depend upon turnover, or find out when the champion agreed to stand
down and the belt was about to change hands. You bet, he meant, the
practicals in life, only first determining which these were. Only then did
you stand to gain. (Was this too poetic? Not for *his* dreamgirl! She, no
matter what she said about the love of a good fire after a walk in the
woods on a drizzly, overcast day, would take such things in like
aphrodisiac, or what did one talk about around those fires?)

Oh, thought Druff, surprised to be made to feel so male—those
ponies and percentages, his cryptic dreamgirls in those classifieds—
pleased by what he felt, some ballsy, weighted swagger of a vain regard,
his discrete maleness urgent as mercury, forceful as magnetism, like
some phantom erection paraded in a bath towel, seduced by his hanker-
ings for all the tutorials of love, the thought of those shared *pensées* of
a street commish.

On the other hand . . .

His hopes that afternoon were hedged all around by what he would
tell Rose Helen.

It wasn't that he was stuck for things to say. What, an old campaigner
like him? Trippingly on the tongue. He'd qualms, but he didn't doubt
his ability to lie, even his ability to lie to Rose Helen. He just didn't
want to be caught out in a campaign promise. He rarely made them.
(Because he knew he was a goner. For whatever reason, what he'd said
to her, to Margaret Glorio, was true. He'd thrown his hat into the ring.
He *would* pursue her, had already started.) It was what he would tell
Rose Helen if his suit was successful.

They'd been married thirty-six years, after all. What was he, twenty-
two when he married her? Just a kid. And Rose Helen, sixty now—
sixty, Jesus!—had been twenty-four. Jesus! too, as far as that was
concerned. Because hadn't a deep part of her attraction been, as, God
help him, it was something of an aversion now, those two extra years

she had on him, as if she lived in a distant, telling time zone, coming to him, it could be, from alien geography, bringing alien geography, the covered flesh she'd not permitted him to see until their wedding night and teased him with—only it was nothing near so playful as teasing—denying him its light even then, granting him access to her only beneath the sheet and thin cover in the darkened room? The mysterious functions of her moving parts as much mysterious. Allowed to bring away with his eyes, like some impinged victor of guarded rewards, only what he could make out in that hobbled, weighted light. Only what he felt on his lips, the moistened tips of her powdered, perfumed nipples in licked conjunction with his moving, frantic tongue, a thick, yielded chemistry of a clayey, bridal milk. The source of her sweet and sour odors protected as the upper reaches of some under Nile. And what Druff was able to take away with him on his fingers, lifted like fingerprint from that dark and solemn scene.

Things were different then. At least for Druff. Well, give him credit, for others too. This was the earliest fifties. A time of girdled sexuality. (Poodle skirts were a sort of Su'ad's veil.) If you knocked someone up you married her as much to make an honest man of yourself as an honest woman of the girl. Guilt was champ. He hadn't thought the belt would ever change hands.

Now he knew, too late, it had all been just so much magic, the superstitious flimflam of conspired, agreeable fears. There'd been no especial power in her, he'd fallen through the net was all, squeezed through the cracks by his times, assigned, like others of his generation, high-flown attributes to what was mere rumor, the prose of innocence, guilt, the hype of "upbringing." It was as if—truly—he'd lived by almanacs, "fun facts," lore, raised in weathers controlled by swallows punctually returned to Capistrano or Puxatawney Phil frightened of his own shadow. He'd bought into such notions. It was like someone deciding to flesh out his portfolio because the NFL had won the Super Bowl that year, or someone pushed into buying or selling off because hems were high or low. (He didn't remember the formula and reminded himself he would have to ask Margaret about that one when they were around the fire.) Well, why should he chastise himself, they *all* did. For who gave blowjobs then, who took it up the ass? Poor Druff, Druff thought, who was new to self-pity, a man who'd missed his season, who'd—you can imagine how he felt, you can just imagine—wasted ripeness and mourned girls—dreamgirls, indeed—he not only had never had but had never even dreamed about in dreams.

Sixty, his wife was sixty. Rose Helen was a golden-ager. Who'd dyed her hair since the first gray appeared in it in her late twenties, and had begun to let it go gray on her fifty-fifth birthday, and allowed the gray to go white, gradually turning the color of house salt. His golden-ager, his silver citizen.

And now recalled how he'd met her, how it had been on just such an almanac occasion as those he'd lived by years. On a pseudo-holiday, Sadie Hawkins Day, named for a character in a comic strip, a day of suspended decorums, when the girls chased the boys, were permitted to ask them on dates, make first moves. (Only even *that* didn't happen, or happened only timidly, some vouchsafed mistletoe indulgence which would never stand up in court, all of them playing a Mardi Gras in the head.)

In some gymnasium now forgotten. (Who'd forgotten so *many* details, his life chewed by remoteness and Druff left standing there holding on to a big bag of first impressions which hadn't lasted, just some gray overview, and him a guy, this latent pol, whose stock-in-trade it was to recall everything, everybody's facts and figures, who seemed, here at least, to have misplaced his own.) But, though this may only have been his politics speaking, instincts of the retrograde enhanced, he seemed to remember bunting. (Perhaps it was a function only quasi–Sadie Hawkins, some student council thing, or even a do where Republicans asked Democrats to dance.) Well, it was gone. But in a gym at the state university. And Rose Helen, already twenty-two, already at her roots' roots the melanin fading, a chromosome snapping in her aging hair. Sure, he remembered now. The only Sadie Hawkins part to it—for them, he meant; it really had been Sadie Hawkins Day—was that both of them had agreed to be there. A friend of his from her graduating class in high school had given him her name, had given her his, who'd never mentioned either to the other before, was not fixing them up but only supplying on some mutual demand (though he couldn't, in truth, conceive of Rose Helen's ever having asked for it) this unwritten letter of introduction, the names like a sort of reference—— To whom it may concern, say.

His friend had told him Rose Helen was a cripple.

"She's crippled?"

"What are you, Druff, planning to enter her in a footrace? She has this minor deformity. Some hip thing you can't even notice. It's no big deal, don't be so narrow. She's very insecure. I think she has an inferiority complex. My mother plays cards with her mother. She's very self-conscious, that's why she started college late. If I were you, I'd call her, Druff. It's the crippled-up girls with the inferiority complexes who are hot to trot."

"How come *you* never took her out?"

"Hey, don't you listen? Our mothers are friends. Though, personally, my mom would love it. She keeps giving me this shit about her beautiful skin. Druff, I don't know how we ever got born at all. To hear my mother tell it, you'd think clear skin was a secondary sex characteristic."

And, really, you didn't notice it, and after he met her the notion of her invisible physical deformity was vaguely exciting. It was a mild scoliosis, the slight curvature of her spine lifting her left hip and thrusting it faintly forward, providing a small shelf where she characteristically rested the palm of her hand and lending her the somewhat hard look of a dance hall girl in westerns. ("Miss Kitty," he would call her later.)

But on the Sadie Hawkins Day in question they almost missed each other. He looked for a girl with a deformity. He looked for a girl with clear skin. And, though he found no cripples, two or three clear-skinned girls actually agreed to dance with him when he went up to them. He said his name, they told him theirs. Then he bowed out. (Jesus, Druff thought, do you see what I mean? I was this shit-scared guilt avoider! They could have *sainted* me, for Christ's sake! Because it was only the knowledge that somewhere in that bunting'd, made-over gymnasium there must have been this shy, suffering Rose Helen lurching around looking for me that spooked me. Not just that her ma knew the ma of my friend, not even that my friend's ma could connect me to the scene of my friend's ma's friend's daughter's shameful stand-up, but that *I* made the connection, *I* did, that these particular two or three clear-skinned girls were not that *particular* clear-skinned girl, and how would *I* feel if *I* were a crip and told, *urged,* Come on, Sadie Hawkins Day falls on a weekend this year, you can sleep in Saturday, come on, whaddaya *say,* how about it, come on, we have a mutual friend, and then get caught dancing with two or three girls who weren't even deformed? No thank you. Thanks, but no thanks. Jesus, he thought, I was, I was—— this *Mikey!*)

And found her, of course, where he should have looked first, along that wall of wallflowers, which isn't always a wall, or even a partially occupied row of chairs, but often as not just an area, some dead space in the room which, occupied or not, busy or not, is something set aside, set off, a kind of sanctuary, as necessary to the practice of civilized life as flatware or toilets. Asking as soon as he saw her, "Are you Rose Helen Magnesson?"

"Yes, I am. Are you Robert Druff?"

"Yes. Happy Sadie Hawkins Day. Would you care to dance?"

Dancing wasn't his specialty, even a simple box step, though now he thought that if it had only been a few years later, when people first began to dance to rhythm and blues, it might have been a different story. He could have handled the fast stuff, accommodated the large motor movements of funk. It was going in close that clumsied him, moved him, that is, toward unearned intimacy, pulled him, he meant, toward love. Dancing with Rose Helen that evening, moving his hand to rest casually on her left hip when she suddenly started, bolted, pushed it away, as if he'd grabbed her haunch.

Assuming he'd found it, accidentally touched her invisible deformity, whatever secreted, hidden-away thing it was (running on instinct here, believing, without knowing he held such beliefs, in some compensatory system of synergistics, of absolute justice, the up side of eye-for-eye) that, wounding her in one place, fixed her in another, cleared her skin, say—it *was* beautiful, remarkable, radiant in fact, incandescent, burning with the pearly collagens, moisturizers and organic steams, the mossy herbals and chemical brews of flush, full pores, all the natural cosmetics of, at once, a shining virginity and devastating pregnancy— and transfigured self-consciousness into a sort of shy, suffering charm.

Druff blurting, "Did I hurt you? I'm sorry, I didn't mean . . ."

"No," she said, "I'm not a good dance partner. I think I'd like to sit down now."

"Oh sure," he said, "but I'm the one who's the lousy dancer. I'm sorry if I hurt you."

"You didn't hurt me," Rose Helen said, "I'm not hurt. My dancing's okay, I'm not a good partner."

They were having coffee in the Union Building. Rose Helen guessed their friend had told Druff all about her. "All there is to tell," she said. "I'm not a good partner," she said, "because, well, I don't like it when a boy touches me there."

"I wasn't trying anything. I mean all he said was it was some hip thing, that it isn't even noticeable. It really isn't."

"I'm sitting down."

"I didn't see anything when you weren't."

"A full skirt covers a multitude of sins."

He thought it a wonderful sentence. He believed she was clever. The synergistics again, the very thing which had driven her underground and caused her shyness, had given her wit. He actually laughed out loud.

"Look, I'm sorry if I loused up your Sadie Hawkins, okay?" Then *she* laughed.

"What?"

"Nothing."

"No, what?"

"Well, look at me. Sadie *Hawkins!* I mean did you pick the right girl for Sadie Hawkins, or what? I guess I'm just not the Sadie Hawkins Day type."

"Why do you say that?"

"Well, I mean I'm too nervous to dance, aren't I?" She looked at him. "I'm two years older than you, you know." Sure, he thought, *his* deformity. Their friend was a good reporter. He'd spilled the beans about both their deformities. (Druff as self-conscious about his age as Rose Helen about that raised left hip.)

They discussed their majors. Rose Helen said she enjoyed being around kids and thought she would become a teacher, possibly declare a minor in English since, counting this semester, she would already have six hours of credit in that subject. Druff confessed he was still undecided, that he hadn't realized until this year how important it was to have a plan since you'd probably be stuck for life with whatever you chose, adding that it wasn't fair to expect someone only nineteen or twenty—not, he amended in deference to that two-year difference in their ages, that being nineteen or twenty was anything of a handicap (that was the word he used, "handicap")—to lock in on what he wanted to be doing fifteen or so years later. It was a serious business, and sad, really, when you thought about it, that you had to start your life off on the right foot or otherwise you could wake up when you were thirty-five and find out that you weren't where you thought you belonged. Because how many times were you alive? Once, right? He thought, he said, that to waste your life was the worst thing you could do with it. It was like self-murder, suicide.

"This is very depressing," Rose Helen said.

"Well, it is," Druff said. "That's why I don't think that just because someone has six hours of credit in a subject that's a good enough reason to say, 'Yes, I have six hours of credit in this subject, I might as well make it my minor.' You have to be interested in it for its own sake." (You tell her, Mikey, thought Druff inside a judgmental parenthesis.)

"Yes, but did it ever occur to you that the reason a party already has six hours in a particular subject just might be that the person is already interested in it?"

Then she said she thought he was being pretty sarcastic for someone who didn't seem to know what he was going to do with his life and talked about self-murder a few years down the line. And now Druff remembered exactly what an attractive, tragic, brooding figure she had made him feel at the time, recalling, who hadn't forgotten so much after all, though they were seated inside the Union Building—*"La Mer"* on the jukebox was playing—how he had had this vagrant image of himself, how he must have looked in her eyes—— this windblown, tempest-tossed guy, collar turned up against the elements, cigarette smoke rolling like fog up the side—it wasn't that many years since the war had ended—of his doomed resistance-fighter's sharp features.

"I'm interested," he said, "—to the extent that I'm interested in anything—in politics." To fulfill his social science requirement he was taking a course in civics. Monday there might be a snap quiz on the bicameral legislature.

"Really? In politics?"

"I'm like you," the future City Commissioner of Streets confided offhandedly, "I want to help make sure that future generations of children will have, well, a future."

They met for coffee, they went to the movies, they went to concerts. They'd become enthusiastic about certain of their professors and from time to time would sit in on each other's classes. They were the only couple they knew who did this on a date. Though they really didn't know all that many couples. Rose Helen was a sorority girl. (Yes, it surprised Druff too.) There was this rule that sorority girls couldn't date Independents. Well, it was an unwritten rule actually, enforceable only while the girls were still pledging. Though even after they were initiated it was strongly discouraged. "They wouldn't want to be hypocrites," Rose Helen told him. "That's what they say, that they wouldn't want to be hypocrites, the hypocrites. That it would set a bad example for the pledges, that what would *we* think if *we* were still pledging and found out one of our sisters was dating someone who wasn't a Greek?"

That's why they didn't know too many couples. That's why they met for coffee in various cafés on campus, that's why they met in front of certain movie theaters, and managed to be on line when the tickets to particular concerts—Odetta, Pete Seeger, Theodore Bikel—went on sale. That's why they sat in on each other's classes.

Because the pressure was on her not to date an Independent, because she couldn't bring him to her sorority house (and because the landlady in Druff's boardinghouse was as strict about men socializing with women in their rooms as the sisters were about fraternizing with Independents), couldn't and wouldn't, she said, even if she could. Because she didn't want any brooding, tempest-tossed, *"La Mer"*-whistling, tragic and sarcastic friend of hers subjected to the silly remarks of a bunch of spoiled, malicious, superficial girls. Though Druff felt he could have held his own with the best of them and wouldn't have minded. He told Rose Helen as much.

"No," she said. "Why stoop to their level?"

"Well, why did you?" he asked in turn.

Which was just exactly the wrong question. They were in one of their coffee shops again, or, no, he remembered now, this time not in one of their coffee shops at all, not even on campus, not even in campus town anymore, but in the town proper, in a diner, the sort of place they might drop in on after one of those folk concerts they went to but which they ordinarily avoided, because they were both clearly students, and as much resented by the townies who went there as Druff was by the

Greeks or Rose Helen by Druff's landlady because she was a woman. Where no one they could possibly know would recognize them, except for the types they were. (And maybe he *was* interested in politics, maybe he *was.* Just maybe all this bi- and tri-cameral apartheid of ordinary life was beginning to have an influence on him.) But which was just *exactly* the wrong question. Because she was crying now, Druff's little poster girl dissolved in tears, and not because she couldn't answer his oblique reference to her own hypocrisy but because she could. Because she knew herself *that* well.

"I'm two years behind my year," she sobbed. "I should be graduating in June. Instead I'm only this sophomore. Don't you know anything? Because why did they rush me if it wasn't to show off how liberal they are? Not only a cripple but a relatively presentable cripple, and not only a relatively presentable cripple with this almost sanitary deformity, but someone older than they, and aren't they sisters, and don't sisters have *big* sisters? So what does that make me if not an intermediary somewhere between an older sister and their housemother? Someone who not only can do for them—make last-minute adjustments on their hairdos, go over their lists of French and Spanish vocabulary with them, help with their mending, give them a hip to cry on—but who looks good on their record too. Don't you know anything? I wasn't here three days before they spotted me and rushed me. They didn't even give me a hard time. I wasn't even hazed."

She was telling him—though of course the terms for all this hadn't been invented yet—that she was their first affirmative-action, primal status token project.

He persisted. "You didn't answer my question. Why? Well, why did you?"

"Don't you know anything? You don't know anything, do you? I told you, they made it easy for me. All I ever had to do was pose with them in the front row when the group picture was taken. I wasn't even hazed."

If she was their first affirmative action, Druff was their second.

Rose Helen said she'd told them about him and that they couldn't wait to meet him. He was invited to come to dinner Tuesday night.

"Well, yes," he said, "I'm an 'Independent.' " This was in the living room. (He supposed it was a living room, though it might have been a drawing room or a music room or even a library, even, for all he knew, the boardroom of some fabulous, oak-paneled corporate headquarters. There was a huge crystal chandelier, there was a concert-class grand piano. There were leaded glass bay windows and cushioned window seats. There were lacquered wooden tables and tall freestanding lamps. There were shelves packed solid with books in leather bindings, golden titles mounted in layered frames set into their spines like seals. There were long leather sofas and wing chairs upholstered in what looked to Druff like fine Oriental rugs. There were fine Oriental rugs.) He'd never seen anything like it. It could have been a manor house in the family generations.

"No," he said, answering another girl's question, "I have nothing against the idea of fraternities, *qua* fraternities. I guess I just never bought into the notion that one could have instant 'brothers,' or the odd, exclusive idealism of fraternity life."

"Rosie tells us that you intend to be a politician," said another of his hostesses.

"Well," he said, "I'm not *running* for anything, if that's what you mean. My eye isn't 'out' for any particular 'office.' " That's how he spoke to them all evening, in the living room—if that's what it was—and, later, at the head table at dinner, attempting aphorisms by stressing individual words or setting them off in what he hoped would be understood as quotation marks, sometimes punching up everything, addressing them in a kind of oral Braille. When they were informed that they would be taking their coffee and dessert by the piano that evening, Druff rose, wiped at the corner of his lips with his napkin and thanked the president of the sorority for having him over for dinner. "Really," he said, "though I'm this, quote, bred in the bone, unquote, quote Independent unquote, I have to admit that the dinner was excellent, and the evening was *fascinating*, and I underscore fascinating. You're very kind, all of you. As a would-be, quote, public man, unquote, I have to confess to a certain, quote, interest, unquote, in the dynamics of your organization. I find it's all rather like some loyal politician's allegiance to, well, *'party.'* Quote party unquote underscored."

In that living room again, Rose Helen and he were directed to seats on one of the leather sofas and offered coffee and cake by a waiter. (Druff recognized him. They lived in the same boardinghouse.) There was some general conversation. Then the waiter went around the room taking up their cups and saucers, their cake plates, their forks and spoons and paper napkins. One of the sorority sisters walked over to the piano and sat down at the piano bench. She was joined by the rest of the girls who ranked themselves about her in what even Druff recognized as a formation, a kind of musical battle stations.

"Oh no," Rose Helen groaned.

"What?"

"Oh no."

Two or three of the waiters had come in from the dining room and were leaning against a wall in the entrance hall.

The president of the sorority was speaking directly to Druff and Rose Helen on the sofa. "Robert," she said, "the women of Chi Phi Kappa are proud of all their sisters. Rose Helen, however, whose maturity and unselfish generosity have been an inspiration to all of us, holds a special place in our hearts, and we do not wonder that she should have found one in yours. Now, Rose, in your honor, and in honor of your interesting new friend, the ladies of Chi Phi Kappa house are pleased to honor you this evening with a serenade, one of the most beautiful and cherished of our traditions.

"Your sisters smile on you tonight, Rose, and wish you all the happiness you could wish for yourself. We delight in *your* delight. We support you, we love you, we bless you."

They sang the Chi Phi Kappa song. They sang the school fight song. They sang love songs. They sang "Rosie, You Are My Posy." They sang *"La Mer."*

Of course they were embarrassed, of course they were. All that drilled attention, it was like having the attention of a firing squad, a little like taking, at close range and at full force, a blast from a fire hose. Of course he felt patronized, of course he did. Nevertheless (maybe he *was* a politician, maybe he *was;* maybe at nineteen he was already developing the politician's thick skin, or at least a willingness to deal, something *quid pro quo* in the nature; if they hadn't actually given him a girlfriend, why at least they had endorsed him; and all he ever had to do for it was eat their dinner, submit to their questioning, good-sport his way through their silly patronage), he felt he had made a good impression.

He had, Rose Helen told him, he'd confirmed all their misgivings, was everything they thought an Independent would be.

"Didn't you feel it?" she said. "Didn't you feel any of it? Didn't you? Don't you know what that was?" They were in one of the small study rooms—two small typing tables, a couple of desk lamps, two chairs, a narrow cot—at the back of the sorority house. The door to the study room was open. Rose Helen was standing with her hand on the little shelf above her damaged left hip, the akimbo elbow and forward thrust of her body giving her her familiar, faintly bold air, and a suggestion about her mouth (though if this was there at all it was something Druff had penciled in himself) of the pursed pout of some saloon cupid.

"Rosie, you are my posy," Druff said, reaching for her hand and lifting it from her hip to pull her gently toward the cot.

She held her ground. "If I scream they'll come running."

"Why would you scream?"

"Listen, it's almost ten-thirty. Males have to be out of here by ten-thirty."

"Why would you scream?"

"We came in here to study. We're supposed to be studying."

"Isn't this the passion pit? Isn't that what they call it?"

He stood up and kissed her.

"The door's open."

"I'll close it."

"It's supposed to be open. You're not allowed to close it."

"The door across the hall is closed. That one over there is."

"Girls are studying in those."

"Sure," he said.

"They are," she said. Then she went over to the door and closed it herself. Druff stood waiting to embrace her. "They are," she said, "but even if they're not, even if they're in there with boys, even if they're slow dancing with their hands all over each other's behinds, even if they're French-kissing. Even if they're quote doing it unquote, I wouldn't let you touch me. I wouldn't even let you hold my hand."

"Why? My God, Rose Helen, why? They're your sisters. They serenaded us. Isn't that like piping us aboard? Didn't they just practically marry us at sea?"

"Don't you know what that was? Don't you? They as good as made

you their mascot. They brought the waiters up from downstairs as
witnesses."

"Come on," Druff said, "I don't care about them."

"You don't?"

"Listen, Miss Kitty, we're like men without a country."

"Don't call me that."

"Well, we are," he said, "just exactly like men without a country.
Except for those coffeehouses, this is the first time we've been alone
since we met."

She was crying again, and Druff suddenly understood that that was
why she'd closed the door, because she knew they were going to have
this conversation. And why she'd extended their invitation in the first
place, because it was exactly the conversation she'd wanted to have with
him from the beginning. Understood she was permitting him something
far more intimate than just the groping he had anticipated, showing him
a glimpse of her turf, an unrestricted view of what her cards looked like
on the table.

He tried to comfort her. "Oh, Rose Helen. Rose Helen, oh."

"Don't you?"

"Don't I what?"

"That was it. That's what they were saving. That's what they were
waiting for all along."

"What are you talking about, Rose? What were they waiting for, what
were they saving?"

"That was my hazing."

"No," he said, "you've got it wrong, Rose. They're your sisters,
they're on our side. Really. All the happiness we could wish for ourselves, remember?" (Druff taking her in his arms—maybe he *was*
political, maybe he *was*—and working his own agenda, wondering,
marveling: Don't they know? Don't girls know it's all a line? All of it?
Don't they see how it is with us? Don't they know what we want to do
to them, what we want them to do to us? Are they fools, or what?)

And astonished to be stroking her breasts beneath her sweater, to slip
his hand up beneath her skirt, to negotiate the rind of stiff corset and
feel the damp silk of her panties.

They were seated on the edge of the cot now. He tried to draw her
down, to get her to lie beside him, but she resisted. She struggled to

a sitting position and started to rise. "All right," he said, "all right," and she sat back down again. (Of *course* political. Political certainly. Bargaining actual territory, dividing physical spoils, making these Yalta arrangements, so that it was somehow agreed without one word passing between them that he could do this but not that, that but not this. Though he was not, for example, permitted to blow in her ear, he was allowed to feel her nipples. Though she would never hold his erection in her hand, she might touch it here and there through his trousers.)

Druff astonished, astounded, amazed now by her bizarre terms, terms, he realized, roughly equivalent to the restrictions imposed by the Hayes Office in regard to sexual conduct in films. (One foot had to be on the floor at all times. They could kiss with their mouths open, but only one of their tongues could be moving and, if it was his, he could touch her breasts but was not permitted to go under her dress.) It was to become the source of what weren't so much arguments as vaguely legalistic, quickly abandoned disagreements, like appealed line-calls in tennis, say, or a batter's brief, abrupt flash of temperament about an umpire's questionable called strike. ("I don't understand," he might tell her, "I let you nibble *my* ear." "You *like* it when I nibble your ear." "Of course I do, the ear's a very sensitive area. I'm surprised you don't like it too." She said she didn't object to the feeling, it was the wetness she couldn't stand.)

And touching her hip, of course, was out of the question.

As out of the question as the flesh and hair beneath that chartered, licensed, two- or three-inch strip of damp silk or cotton underwear, the tolerated, *nihil obstat* elastic piping that edged her drawers and which he worried with his finger like a lock of hair.

So maybe she was political too. A born legislator, some negotiator of the physical being. Because she was right, it *was* almost ten-thirty, almost time for him to leave, gratefully disappear with the other males—she was right about that too; his presence in that house of females had altered him; he was "male" now, his sexuality some new state of chemical excitation, simmering, charged, changed, like the cooked properties of solids melting to vapors—and she'd somehow managed to arrange all this in the last quarter hour of that first night.

(But why was he grateful? He was grateful for the same reasons he'd been relieved, the shit-scared avoider, to learn that the clear-skinned beauties of the Sadie Hawkins Day dance had been the wrong clear-skinned beauties. He was grateful because he'd been this, well, Mikey. It's not true, Druff thought, that we ultimately turn into our own parents; we're our own children long before they're ever born. He was wrapped in a cocoon of stupidity, innocence, inexperience. Not virtue, but its simulacrum, what virtue did while it bided its time, until it sloughed fear and all fear's hiding places in the cosmetic folds of guilt. *He was grateful because he was a virgin and he didn't have to fuck her and get it all wrong was why!*)

Now at least they had a place to go.

Though they still didn't know that many couples, didn't double-date, were there—at least, as her legacy, Druff was—on sufferance, like a guest of a member of a country club, say. Now they didn't have to meet outside movie houses. These days he could pick her up at the sorority. (Gradually they stopped sitting in on each other's classes, stopped going to coffeehouses; gradually they even stopped going to movies.) And if, collectively, they were novelties to the girls of Chi Phi Kappa, the girls of Chi Phi Kappa were even greater novelties to Druff. Rose Helen was a novelty to Druff. Indeed, *Druff* was a novelty to Druff. (It was strange—that simmering maleness, his ballsy, newfound exhibitionist's swagger, his vain regard, his simmering chemical privilege and liberties—but these days he always went about feeling as if he had on brand-new clothes.)

Even though he knew no more people now than he did before, even though, except for Rose Helen, he had no friends there, only, here and there, a few people he could nod to—the waiter from Druff's boarding-house, three or four of the pledges—Druff had become a sort of fixture around the place. The fact was they rarely left the sorority house. On weekdays he came there to study with Rose Helen and, if one was unoccupied, they would go into a tiny study room. (Since the night of the serenade when she had gone to the door and closed it herself and then negotiated with him the unspoken rules of their relationship, the study was never closed when they were in it.) At ten-thirty, however, he was the first male out of the house. Even on weekends, when the curfew was extended until midnight, he was always the first to leave.

It was as if he understood their sufferance (he did), their combined weight on the thin social ice that supported them. And if he was political, he thought, it was a strange way to practice his politics, lying low, muting, as it were, his own horn, making himself scarce on the very dot of the curfew hour like a frightened Cinderella. Not like him, not like his position, or his presence during what he had almost come to think of as their office hours, the sorority's, his own—he was there more often than any of the fraternity men who dated these girls, longer than the waiters who set their tables, served their dinners, washed their dishes—a position and presence which had become obsessive.

He could not keep his hands off her, their almost surgical, circum-scripted petting as complicated as the careful, delicately drawn lines of a contended geography, treatied borders; obsessed (not just Druff, Rose Helen too) with the endless diversity, variations, interpretations and all the fine distinctions available to them within compliance. So that he became, *they* became, respective Casanovas, very Venuses, geniuses of foreplay.

He was never there during scheduled house meetings, secret rites, restricted practices. He was fastidious, meticulous with their curfews, and lived, like many fabulous criminals, by the letter of the law, as if he sought to keep his nose clean by always paying his taxes, going about like one shoving change into parking meters, or each day dropping by the library to show the librarian the due date on a still-not-overdue book. He kept, that is, his accounts with all of them, Rose Helen, the girls of Chi Phi Kappa, the frat boys who visited them, the housemother, Mrs. Post.

Yet it was no game he was playing, neither with Rose Helen nor with her sisters. He was not seeking to test the limits of their patience. He *knew* the limits of their patience. He didn't observe their curfews out of any of the old olly-olly-oxen-free impulses of his childhood, but because he was quite terrified of them really, afraid of having his privileges stripped from him.

Because those privileges were large, new, rare, immense. It wasn't just what happened between the two of them in the study (and much, despite the unimpeded view they afforded anyone who happened to be passing that open door of their strange love gymnastics, the compulsory Olympic figures they cut, *did* happen), but the incredible feeling he had at those times. It was exactly what he'd said when he'd first gone in there with her, that they were at last *alone*, his sense of their privacy somehow fed by the curfew he was forced to observe, by his knowledge that the door was open, that their exciting, dangerous gyrations were, well, almost—living on the edge, pushing the envelope, you can just imagine how he felt—adulterous, anyway risky, anyway more intimate than even what her cards looked like on the table—— Druff permitted all.

The feeling, if anything, amplified on weekends when they never even got close to one of those studies. (It was understood that on weekends these rooms were reserved for upperclassmen and their dates.) Then they went out into the big music- drawing- living room-cum-library, whatever the architectural equivalent was for that commodious, luxurious center—— the house's real passion pit, he supposed. And there, in that crowded space—there might be upwards of a hundred people in it, girls returned with their dates from campus beer gardens, from dances, from parties, flicks, pep rallies, concerts, basketball games, celebrations—a strange thing happened. He melded in with them, felt that he had somehow become invisible, though the others were plainly visible to *him,* what they did—— he heard sweaters sliding up over cotton blouses, glimpsed underpants, cleavage, flesh, erections—he brandished his own, less self-conscious, finally, than he might have been in a communal shower, a public bath—all about him could hear girls groaning, boys coming. ("Our comings and groanings," he joked to Rose Helen.) Not a voyeur. In the scene. Of it. Could feel, hear, see, taste the mass dishevelment, some sense of the undone and awry, of smeared lipstick and smudged face powder, of colognes gone off and all the fired chemistry of naked pheromones. A passion pit indeed, a steamy, cumulative sense of the stuff growing, of love cells dividing, multiplying, building in the room like weather, rain cloud, say, electric storm, thunderclap, passionate waves sweeping over them, a kind of heavy sexual traffic, his hip at their haunches on the long, crowded window seats, so that what he felt was not just his own passion but his passion added to the passion of everyone else, his passion compounding, earning interest on the passion of both sexes. (As his own, he felt, increased theirs, all their activity and somber, solemn concentration conjoined, benefited, a public privacy, like the serenade Rose Helen thought was hazing but Druff understood as encouragement, warrant.) A great joy in this, like the joy in a marvelous parade. (Maybe he *was*

political. *Sure* he was political! Oh *boy*, was he political! Necking with
Rose Helen at Rose Helen's sorority no orgy but a democratic manifes-
tation, great island chains, archipelagoes of feeling, some republic of
sexuality. Druff thinking, no wonder I was so horny when Mikey was
screwing Su'ad that time, it was *the proximity* again, only my fatherly
good Americanism. Thinking, no wonder *he* was, because if we're our
own children before they're ever born, maybe they're as childish as
their fathers before the fathers have had a chance to grow up. And
feeling this anachronistic unity with his son.)

So you can just imagine how he felt, you can just imagine.

His precious invisibility different in kind from the invisibility he so
carefully cultivated at the curfew hour, or the invisibility they sought
out on those lines outside the picture show, or in the coffeehouses, or
could have used in that diner in town, the invisibility not only exciting
but comforting—— a *shared* invisibility. And for the first time since he
met her unconscious of resentment, all resentment—his, theirs—dissolved or maybe only absorbed in the mutual, protective clouds of sperm
that were a sort of collective atmosphere in the fancy room.

He was in his element. He *loved* Friday and Saturday nights, he *loved*
e pluribus unum, and would willingly have traded four weeknights alone
with Rose Helen in a study room for just one additional half hour of
extended curfew on the cushioned window seats, long leather sofas,
upholstered wing chairs, or stretched out with her in the sexual traffic
on the fine Oriental rug in the big ground-floor room.

Which is just where Mrs. Post, the housemother, found them on the
one night out of the eighty or so since Druff had been coming to the
Chi Phi Kappa house, on the single occasion when he was not the first
one out the door. A fixture indeed. And not only a fixture, but someone
whose habits were so well known by now it was said that you could set
your watch by him. He had simply lost track of the time. Or no, that
wasn't quite true. As a matter of fact it was time he was thinking of at
the time, how this was only a Friday, how they still had all Saturday
together. (Because he loved her now, had discovered in just the last
month, the past few weeks, that there was something there beyond the
simple fact of her availability, the damaged-goods advantage he thought
he had over her because of her two-year seniority and scarcely legible
limp, which, if it was not completely put on, she had at least to take

the trouble to memorize; a limp which wasn't, he'd begun to realize, entirely natural, as a dance step is never entirely natural, but had always at least to be a little studied, like a runner's stride or swimmer's kick turn. Because he loved her, because no one could hold his tongue in someone else's mouth for eighty out of the last hundred nights without developing a certain fondness for the head as a whole, the neck and everything it rested on. Teeth were just not that interesting—— palates, gums, inlays, lips. Because he loved her, because he had come to appreciate her savage resentment, enjoy her outcast representations of herself, his own accreditation in the drama—he'd never played an outcaste before, had gotten by on his innate Mikeyness and good-boy behaviors; now they were in it together, Rose Helen, himself, could almost put Greek letters of their own beside their names—appreciate Rose Helen's marvelous mimicry of the sisters and frat boys, even of the waiter from Druff's boardinghouse. Because he loved her now, her fastidious dignity and rough, playful ways with her own rules. She had qualities. Also, she let him put his tongue in her head.) Thinking, this is only Friday, there's still Saturday. Then thinking, Sundays we go our own ways, then it's Monday and we'll have all those ten-thirty nights in the study. Isn't it peculiar, he thought, we do so much more to each other in the study than we ever try to do out here (where the rules were house rules, liberal enough, astonishing really, but ultimately table stakes), but to tell the truth (and he knew what was probably going on right now on the cots in those studies) he preferred it out here, though— they hadn't talked about it, it was just, knowing her qualities, something he felt—he didn't think Rose Helen did. Thinking all this (because you can't do two things at once, you really can't, not if you were to give each the attention it deserved), and meanwhile letting up on the very things he so loved about these Friday nights—— the collective concentration, that mutual chemistry of fired nerves and cumulative, conjoined hip-to-haunch loving, at the same time that, though he didn't realize this, he failed to hold up his end of the bargain—— one hand on R.H.'s breast and the other starting to lift her dress while, absently, he nibbled her ear (not even aware of her squirming until later) in direct violation, though he was woolgathering, lollygagging, oblivious of all her Geneva conventions, not even excited, in his content mode, thinking, it's only Friday, there's still Saturday.

Mrs. Post was standing over them.

"What," Druff said, startled, "what?"

She laid one finger across the face of her wristwatch.

"Is it curfew? I'm sorry, I mustn't have been paying attention. Is it curfew already?"

Though here and there there were people about, the room had begun to thin out. The bays and window seats were cleared, the piano bench. No one cuddled in the wing chairs, the sofas were all but vacant.

Rose Helen sat up and, to Druff's chagrin, immediately began to lay into her housemother.

"How *dare* you?" she demanded. "He's not the only one left." Pointedly, she named names, not only indicating a few of her sorority sisters still lingering with their dates, but ticketing indiscretions, citing violations of dress codes, some general dishevelment of human decency.

"I'm sorry," Druff mumbled, "I guess I must have lost track of the time."

Rose Helen interrupted him. "You've nothing to apologize for, why are you apologizing?" And turned furiously to Mrs. Post. "Have you looked in the study rooms? Is everyone out of the study rooms?" She tugged at his sleeve. "Let's just go see for ourselves."

"I'm sorry," Druff said, "I wasn't paying close enough attention, I guess. I just didn't hear that bell you ring in here ten minutes before curfew."

"Stop saying you're sorry. No one else says that. Do you hear anyone else saying they're sorry? It's not your job to be sorry, it's not your job to listen for the bell. It isn't your job to have people set their watches by you." She was furious with them both, Rose Helen. And though it was Rose Helen who did the shouting, it was Druff and Mrs. Post who got all the attention. The girls, their dates, looked from one to the other of them following their flabbergast silence. Druff felt an odd connivance with and sympathy for the housemother. It occurred to him that her heavy, almost powerful hair, its immaculate sheen, so at odds with her wan, brittle features, must have been a wig. "Well, come on," Rose Helen said, "let's just *see* what's going on in those study rooms!"

"Most of those people are pinned," Mrs. Post defended. "Many are already engaged."

"So," said Rose Helen, "they're in there. They *haven't* left! They're in there, all right."

"Please," Druff said.

"No," snapped Rose Helen, but not at Druff, at Mrs. Post, at her sorority sisters, at the fraternity boys, "I *won't* please. Rules are rules. I'm going to empty out those study halls for you!" And then began exaggeratedly to limp about the now silent, curiously passionless passion pit, circling the big room and gathering, it seemed, a sort of momentum, and went out into the hall, going past the big staircase and continuing on toward the studies at the back of the sorority house.

He heard her roughly opening doors, heard her shout *"Curfew, curfew"* like a hysterical town crier.

"I'm going," Druff called. "I'm leaving now, Rose Helen."

"Curfew in there! Curfew!"

"I'll phone you tomorrow," he called. "Would you tell her I'll call her tomorrow?" he appealed to Mrs. Post.

But she called him. It was almost three in the morning. It was the waiter from Druff's boardinghouse who came to fetch him to the phone.

"It's your girlfriend," he said.

"So late?"

The waiter shrugged. "They ask for ketchup when it's right out there on the table in front of them."

"I hope nothing's wrong," he told the waiter.

"Sometimes, if it's chicken cacciatore, or meat in a heavy gravy, they ask us to cut it up for them in the kitchen so they don't dirty their hands or get grease on their clothes."

"Rose Helen? Are you all right, Rose Helen?" He expected her to be crying. She wasn't, though he could tell she seemed excited, even pleased. She didn't scold him, didn't even mention that he'd left without saying good night.

"I threatened to resign," she said. He didn't understand. "From the sorority, I threatened to resign from the sorority."

"But why?" Druff said.

"Mrs. Post was there when I told them. Though you know, Robert," she said, "I don't blame Mrs. Post. She doesn't make policy, she takes her signals from the girls." Druff was uncomfortable. If any of this was on his behalf . . . "I've only just left them," Rose Helen went on. "It could have been, I don't know, a beauty parlor in there. You should have seen them. All those girls in their curlers and face goo . . ." He thought of her own soft, beautiful skin, oddly backlit, pearly from suffering, maybe from grudge. "Except for the few of us who were still in our clothes, it could have been a giant slumber party, all those girls in their shorty pajamas, some still clutching their teddies, the goofy, outsize turtles, froggies and stuffed kitty cats they take to bed with them. It was really rather touching."

"You woke them? You got them out of bed?" (He thought of the ketchup right out there on the table in front of them, of the cut-up chicken cacciatore and of the meat in heavy gravy.)

"I called a special meeting," Rose Helen said. "I had charges, I had witnesses. You can call a special meeting when you have charges and witnesses."

"Charges against who? Mrs. Post doesn't make policy. She takes her signals from the girls, you said."

" 'If I resign,' I told them, 'your room and board goes up. You've already lost Jan and Eileen this semester. Rachel's on academic proba-tion and may flunk out.' "

Druff thought of the furniture, of the grand piano, the Oriental rugs. He couldn't imagine that whatever few dollars Rose Helen's leaving might cost them could make a difference. He thought them rich enough to take up the slack by themselves. He didn't want her to resign. He'd grown quite too accustomed to the furniture. Besides, even after he heard her speech, the good arguments she'd presented to get them to keep her from resigning (the money it could cost them if she quit; the straight-A average she maintained and which—"A rising tide raises all boats"—helped keep the Chi Phi G.P.A. just about where it needed to be in order to remain competitive and continue to attract prospective pledges—"Because supposing," she argued, "Rachel *doesn't* flunk out, supposing she just manages to keep her head above water and drags along with a D-plus or even a C-minus average, then losing all those A's would *really* mean something"—throwing even her deformity into the argument, that limp that made her look so bad and them so good), he was still uncertain about her reasons. If this had anything to do with Druff . . . And what *about* Mrs. Post, who *didn't* make policy, who took her signals from the girls? And what about the girls with their stuffed animals and face goo, and who were really rather touching?

"Charges?" Druff said. "Witnesses? Has this anything to do with me? Am I at fault here?"

"Why, against the girls in the studies, silly. And my witnesses against them were those boys I rousted."

"Was Rachel there when you said these things? Were her feelings hurt? Did she cry?" he wanted to know.

Now she was more interesting than Druff.

She was political, certainly. It was those two years of seniority she had on him, had on most of them, plus all those other years of pure physical outrage, the one or two before they actually knew that anything was wrong, then the fifteen or so when she had to wear the successively larger braces to make the correction in her spine, to bring it to the point where it was barely noticeable, except possibly to Rose Helen, and which left scarcely a trace, unless it was to those who picked up on the tiny shelf she had made for it above her left hip where she could rest her palm. Because all that kicked into the seniority, too. Plus things he could have only a guesswork knowledge of. (Prosthetic bathing suits perhaps, prosthetic evening gowns.)

There were more meetings. Nothing, of course, was done to the girls Rose Helen had brought her charges against. She was political, perhaps she didn't intend anything to come of them more than the apologies—which she got—and pleas to stay with the sorority, which she got.

In the end, however, she determined to resign from the sorority.

She told him she didn't even want to live in a dorm, the fine new women's residence hall the university had put up, that she'd prefer a room in a boardinghouse.

"A boardinghouse," Druff said. "What's so great about a boarding-house? You live in a boardinghouse, you have a landlady. I've told you what mine is like, Rose Helen. They're all like that."

"It just seems," she said, "I don't know, romantic. You know what I really think? I think they won't be around much longer. Those big old wood houses. They're a piece of Americana. All those old landladies and landlords will die out one day. Their kids won't take them over. One by one they'll burn down, or the university will start buying them up and turn them into queer little departments—— meteorology, Asian studies. Or they'll just raze them altogether and put up big new build-ings. You're lucky. You already live in one. You know what it's like. I want to live somewhere they put your whole supper down on the table in big serving dishes and you have to ask someone to pass the mashed potatoes, pass the string beans, the water pitcher, the rolls and bread. It's like missing out on vaudeville. Al Jolson, Fanny Brice, Eddie Cantor. All those people I know only from listening to on the radio who lived in boardinghouses and used to be on the 'circuit.' No," she said, "when I resign from Chi Phi Kappa I'm definitely going into one."

Because she was definitely more interesting than Druff. Falling for her now at second-per-second rates. As stones fall.

But who tried still to talk her out of the boardinghouse. Uncertain whether he'd be welcome once she moved. Knowing there'd be no more study rooms, no passion pit worthy of the name (not, as it were, after you'd seen Paree), forced again to think of those long lines at the movies, big public rooms in the Student Union, even of the classrooms and lecture halls where they'd spent the early weeks of their courtship.

They didn't quarrel exactly—she was too high-strung, he was a little afraid of her—but he took the position that it was mostly their own fault.

"I was woolgathering," he told her, "lollygagging. You know what the first thing was I thought to tell her when she caught us stretched out there on that carpet and I saw her standing over us? The very first thing? 'Both my feet are on the floor, Mrs. Post.' That's how out of it I was. 'Both my feet are on the floor.' No wonder she wanted to throw me out." (And would have added, if she'd been less high-strung, that it was probably Rose Helen's squirming when he nibbled her ear that called Mrs. Post's attention to them in the first place.)

"She had no right," Rose Helen said. "She was out of line."

She refused to hear anything more about it, declared the subject closed and even stopped talking about her plans to resign from her sorority. (She told him she was still looking, however, though she thought it unlikely she'd find anything suitable until after midterms and the students who were failing saw the handwriting on the wall and pulled out.) Meanwhile she denied him access to the sorority house, insisting it would be too humiliating for them (who, for his part, was hard to humiliate, who was perfectly content to accept serenades at face value, content to have watches set by him, to be the first out the door, content to eat shit, Mrs. Post's, Rose Helen's) to be seen there together.

He asked the waiter from his boardinghouse to keep his eyes open, to tell him if anything was going on.

"You want me to spy on her?"

"No, of course not. Look," he said, and took the waiter into his confidence, told him the story till now. "I'm not asking you to spy, I'm not asking you to do anything you're not already doing. Just keep an eye out. If they're still talking about what happened, if there's any more discussion about her giving up the sorority—— if she's seeing someone else. Edward, I think I'm getting the runaround." (Because he was in love now, because she was more interesting than he was, because he thought they thought his lapse, his failure to leave on time, was a violation, like the nibbled ear Rose Helen forbade him, of the conditions of his probation. *Because he was in love now*—the girls were touching, she'd said; she didn't blame Mrs. Post; he recalled her talent for mimicry—*and couldn't trust her.*) And revealed all the intimate details and actual physical logistics of the complicated, astonishing foreplay they practiced in the study. He made mention of her hip.

Druff didn't regard any of this as a reward or payment for information, or even as bragging, but as simple, heartfelt confidence, one heartfelt guy in a boardinghouse to another. All that detail, are you kidding, if anything, it was as if he were the waiter's spy and not the other way around.

"Well?" Druff said when Edward returned one evening.

"She didn't take the soup, she refused dessert. I think she's on a diet."

"So," Druff said the next night, "what do you think?"

"I was the one who said about the boardinghouses. This was before you were in the picture."

Rose Helen called on him at the house. She was standing outside. It was Edward who came to his room to tell him she was there. (If we ever get married I'm going to have to ask him to be my best man, Druff thought, then felt misgivings go through him like a bullet. For all he'd made him his confidant, Druff didn't like the waiter very much, regretted his soiled, spilled beans.)

His landlady climbed the stairs and was waiting for him on the landing. She turned and went down beside him. With Edward, there were three of them on the steps now. Druff had a ludicrous sense of convoy, of imposed escort, a vague impression he was being handed over into another jurisdiction.

"That's your girlfriend out there, the one you used to go see, the one who calls at all hours?"

"She called at all hours only once," Druff said. "She's a nice person, Mrs. Reese."

"I have keys to all the rooms," his landlady said darkly. "I know who is and who isn't a nice person."

Then they were standing at the screen door. It was already spring. The weather had been mild for two weeks now. The rooming houses up and down Druff's street all had gardens—— glowing, spontaneous flowers, grass the bleached, light green of Coca-Cola glass, parrot feathers. But here there were no crocuses, no daffodils, no hyacinths, no tulips, no forsythia. There were no trees or ornaments at all. Mrs. Reese's scant, grudging yard was all surface, a kind of scrubbed earth. It seemed tracked, neutral as a path. It wasn't even scuffed. There were no chairs, no porch swing on the crabbed front porch, no place to sit, not even steps, a proper stoop.

Rose Helen was waiting for him on the ramp which, in lieu of steps, led up to the porch. Druff had heard explanations about the ramp. Mrs. Reese had had it built after the war for paraplegics and quadriplegics, all the veterans in wheelchairs she hoped to attract to her rooming house. Word in the house was that she was the first, at least the first landlady, to understand the implications of the G.I. Bill. The war hadn't ended yet, only in Germany, when she'd made her plans, when she realized that if returning veterans were to be paid a handsome allowance to go to school, then it was only reasonable to suppose that disabled veterans would be paid an even more handsome allowance—the greater the handicap the greater the allowance. It wasn't the extra rent she'd be able to charge for their rooms that had held the appeal for her, it was the handicap itself, the tamed, chair-bound presence of the soldiers, the wild oats they'd probably be too depressed to sow even if they still could. They said she closed the house after the '45 graduation to have the ramp put in. They said she'd already hired an architect to design modifications to the house itself, interior ramps, special bathrooms, special tubs, workmen to install them. It was the atom bomb. She hadn't counted on the atom bomb, they said. The war was over before anyone expected. There just wouldn't be enough casualties to justify the costs. This was what Druff heard. He didn't believe a word of it, but it was what he was thinking of when he saw Rose Helen on the ramp, leaning invisible inches into the incline, her height and weight evenly distributed.

Druff looked at each of his escorts and opened the door. It hadn't even closed behind him before Rose Helen began to speak.

"What's different about me? Can you say, can you tell? No, don't look at my hair, it isn't my hair. Why do boys always look at your hair when a girl asks that question?" She was addressing the two witnesses at his back behind the screen door. "Come on," she said, "I'll give you a hint. It's something you wear but it isn't clothes." He examined her scrupulously. "Oh, Robert," she said, "you're so *dense!*"

"It's your pin. You're not wearing your sorority pin," the waiter said.

"Who's that, Edward? Good for you, Edward. You're absolutely right." She suddenly sounded to him like the schoolteacher she would one day be. "Well, I've done it," she said.

"They make you turn those things back in if you resign?"

"Please," Druff said, "we're having a private conversation."

"Sorry," the waiter said, injured, "sometimes it's hard to know what's private and what isn't." Druff remembered he'd once tried to describe to Edward the taste of her breasts, the smell of her damp pants on his fingers, the odd feel of a particular softness here, the compensatory muscularity somewhere else from the exercises she continued to perform for her hip, her spine, stretching and bending herself, he supposed, like one doing farm work, forking hay, maybe.

"So," she said, "I've voluntarily deconsecrated myself. I've left the Chi Phi's. I'm an Independent now, too."

Now they were sunk, he thought. She didn't sound sunk, but now they were sunk. He wouldn't taste those breasts again until they were married. (At least it wasn't the furniture, he told himself. I'm not *that* bad, at least. At least most of my disappointment has to do with the fear of not being alone with her.)

She started to come the rest of the way up the ramp but Druff went to meet her. He began to walk with her toward the Student Union.

"Here," she said, when they had gone about half a block, "you wear this." She took her sorority pin from her purse and pinned it to his shirt.

"So," Druff said, "they don't make you give them back."

"Nope, that one's bought and paid for. It's free and clear. I burned the mortgage on that pin when I quit the Chi Phi's."

"Usually," Druff said, "when pins are exchanged it means you're going steady."

"It means you're engaged to be married," she said. "It means you have children together. It means forsaking all others. It means till death us do part."

"I don't have any pin," he said.

"Hey," she said, "you're this quote Independent unquote. You've probably your own weird customs. You'll teach them to me."

He gave her the waiter, he gave her Edward (as he had given parts of Rose Helen to the waiter). They still didn't know any other couples, they still didn't double-date, but they had a sidekick now, a squire, a retainer, a factotum, this best-man-in-waiting, this in-the-wings witness, their sworn fifth wheel and interested second party, someone to back-stage for them and legitimate their love, make it interesting enough, dramatic enough, their own personal second-banana man, Edward R. Markey, with his name like a clerk of the court or some high-up in the Motor Vehicles Bureau, the man who signs the driver's licenses, or the State Treasurer, say. (Druff enjoyed believing that the waiter was a little in love with her himself, or even with Druff in some safe, charming, companionable way which didn't threaten anyone, even the faithful retainer. He thought of him, early on, as he would have thought of a devoted theatrical manager, some mysteriously womanless, childless, unfamilied—unsibling'd and, for all he knew, motherless, fatherless, perhaps even cousinless—bachelorly man whose only interest was that they—the two principals—not ever suffer.)

She'd taken a room off campus, in town, in enemy territory, behind the lines, near the railroad station, not far from that diner where they'd gone the time Rose Helen had sobbed to him, confessing her suspicion that she'd made Chi Phi Kappa because of what she called her "sanitary deformity," something between a pledge and a housemother, who did for them, a kind of dobbin, a sort of Edward herself, the patron saint of their vocabulary lists, of their mending and hairdos, Cinderella

without the fairy godmother, a fairy godmother herself, theirs, or at least their fairy good sport.

She'd taken a room off campus.

Strictly speaking, it was an illegal address; unauthorized, non-university housing, not the apartment that undergraduate girls weren't permitted to lease, and not even the boardinghouse—no meals were served—about which she entertained so many fancy, romantic notions, but a furnished room in what wasn't even a rooming house for an exclusively female clientele. The house where Rose Helen stayed had as many men living in it as women—— railroad employees, conductors and engine drivers, switchmen and gandy dancers. The women in the house were mostly students at a local college for beauticians; some were wives from the nearby air base whose enlisted-men husbands, still receiving their training, were permitted to leave the base only on weekends. Two or three Druff recognized from the Student Union Building, cashiers, food handlers.

"What do you think?" Rose Helen asked him.

"How did you get this place? You're not allowed to live here. They could withhold your credits."

"I never gave the university a change of address."

"Suppose they have to get in touch with you?"

"Why would they have to get in touch with me? I lived at Chi Phi Kappa almost two years, they never had to get in touch with me."

"What about mail?"

"Edward's there for lunch, he can bring it to me."

"It's beautiful," Druff said. "It's really nice."

It really was. His standard was the rooms at Mrs. Reese's, his own, Edward's, the three or four others he'd visited since coming to the university. His standard was the small study rooms with their typing tables and desk lamps, their wooden chairs and narrow cots.

There was a double bed with a pale, flowered spread across it, a small sofa, a ladder-back rocker, a stripped dresser with a pitcher and washstand on it. There was a closet. There was a painting, a pleasant landscape, not a reproduction but an actual oil. There were lamps, plants, hooked rugs, lace curtains on Rose Helen's two big southern-exposed windows.

He heard someone coming up the stairs.

"Am I supposed to be in here?"

"It's Edward," Edward called, "with the rest of your things."

"That was a close one," Druff said to Rose Helen.

"Why a close one?"

"Well," he said again, "am I supposed to be in here?"

"The landlady never said anything about visitors," Rose Helen told him. "All she ever said was that the railroad workers come in at all hours, that they sleep when they can. All she said was that I have to be considerate of my neighbors, to play my radio low even during the day."

Her room was beautiful, it really was. Still, he felt he was a thousand miles from a grand piano, big stately furniture, Oriental rugs, civilization. He felt like an outlaw.

The stairs and hallways, the rooms and shared baths, even Rose Helen's landlady's—Mrs. Green's—apartment (where the television was which they were invited to watch with her: it was an early color set, an experimental model Mrs. Green's boyfriend, an electrical engineer, possibly a married man, had given to her; only a handful of color transmissions a year were sent out at that time, and Druff remembered seeing the first lecture ever televised in color, the first-ever color telecast of a polo match, the announcers reporting all this solemnly, the commissioner reminded—now, not then—of those other almanac occasions to which he'd given credence, the Groundhog Days and leap years, Sadie Hawkinses and the various solstices, of all bloodless, neutered history) always smelled of pork chops, frying meat. (Mrs. Green permitted tenants to store food in her kitchen. There was a hot plate in Rose Helen's room but she used it only to boil the tan beef and pale, mustard-colored chicken bouillon cubes and black coffee she drank, and to heat up the food, the almost untouched leftovers Edward stole from the Chi Phi Kappa house and gave Druff to bring to her, or brought her himself, and on which she lived.)

It was like being married. It was and it wasn't. They studied there. They necked there, did all their heavy petting there. Because despite the sofa (to say nothing of the double bed), they still played for the same relatively low table stakes that they had played for in the study rooms and in the big, crowded, luxurious central passion pit at the sorority house on those Friday and Saturday nights deconsecration ante. He even observed the same curfew. Maybe it was only Edward (or Rose Helen or even himself) who was landlady or housemother now. Maybe it wasn't any of them, maybe they didn't need a housemother, maybe they didn't need a landlady. Maybe it was merely the Zeitgeist which protected (if that was the word) them, or maybe they were really these collective, dedicated virgins (though technically he wasn't a virgin, he'd been to the whores; so had the waiter), or maybe it didn't finally matter where they conducted their white, unconsummated courtship. And maybe, despite what they'd told each other, it *was* a game, or a sort of a game, but something loftier, higher, more important. Maybe though they weren't there yet, they were still honestly striving to become the respective Casanova and Venus of foreplay, sexual-stimulation savants. Maybe foreplay was their event. Because these were the days of mag*nif*-icent foreplay, the student prince, his education-major consort. He could remember times when he'd gone around packing blue balls like kidney stones. Other times Rose Helen, who often sensed his pain before it reached actual critical mass, would bring him off.

She brought him off, he brought her off. But always in the dark—because there was a daytime curfew too; Rose Helen wouldn't let him touch her while it was still daylight, and sometimes he had to sit like an Orthodox waiting for the last light to quit the two big windows with their southern exposure—and always between the mutual, prophylactic cloth of each other's clothing—— beneath coats, towels, laundry, things grabbed out of the closet, on the always-made double bed.

They grew closer. Not just he and Rose Helen but he and Rose Helen and Edward as well. Who broke stolen bread with them, increasingly shared in their diminished, doggy-bag suppers, and whom, and not as founder of the feast (which even Rose Helen, who'd been on the sorority's housekeeping committee the year she pledged and so had actually had a part in hiring him, had interviewed him, had been there when he'd sworn his male employee's Chi Phi Kappa solemn oath that not only was he not to fraternize with the girls he would be serving twice a day six times a week but was not to speak of to other men or discuss with them what they discussed, how they comported themselves in their housecoats and lounging pajamas, what they looked like without makeup, or with their hair up in curlers, the slumber-party coze they affected when no men were around, never acknowledged him to be, preferring to think of herself as its founder, who still held that grudge against her sisters for singling her out—or no, not her so much as just that part of her which constituted the "sanitary deformity"—not to haze, and whose dues and room-and-board at the time of her resignation had been paid up in advance for the rest of the school year anyway), they regarded as their invited guest, despite the fact that he was the one who always served them whatever happened to be reheating itself inside whichever pot or pan he had placed there for them on the hot plate.

. And not just eating warmed-over supper, but some shared sense, certainly for Rose Helen and Druff, and quite possibly for the waiter, too, of a picnic occasion, of roughing it, or, if they were sitting by the window near the plants, a vague notion of actually being outside, dividing foraged food.

"So," Rose Helen would occasionally remark after Edward had cleared away their dishes, "how's *your* life?" This was the signal for him to start his strange commentary, as if it were not enough that he had just brought them their supper and prepared and even served it, but must now sing for it, too.

"I don't know how any of them expects to make it in the real world," he might begin. (And now it was *exactly* as if they were outdoors, in dark woods, beneath the stars, or like tramps in hobo camps alongside railroad tracks, Edward's voice lulling, almost musical, his gossip like some postprandial accompaniment to their digestion.) "Do you know what Anita Carlin had the nerve to ask me to do for her tonight? Her soup was too hot. Instead of waiting for it to cool, she told me to take it back to the kitchen and bring it to her again when it was safe enough for her to eat without scalding herself. Just who does she think she is, Goldilocks? When I asked how I was supposed to know when it was the right temperature, you know what she said? 'Edward, do I have to do all your thinking for you? Just pour off some in a cup and sip it.' Now how will someone with an attitude like that ever raise children? Or Jean Allmann? Last night she complained the milk was sour. It came from the same pitcher everyone else's came from at her table. No one else thought it was sour, but she made me go back and open up a bottle just for her. 'Where's the ketchup, where's the salt?' " he grumbled. " 'Is there cream on the table?' When it's right there in front of them. 'Edward, my napkin's disappeared. Would you be a darling and get me another one?' 'Edward, there are too many bones in my fish. See can you find a piece that doesn't have so many bones in it.' I mean it, the average Chi Phi expects there's always going to be someone around to wait on her hand and foot, cut her meat up for her, blow on her soup, recommend her dessert. 'Which is better tonight, Edward, the German Black Forest or the chocolate mousse?' Then light her cigarettes as if we were waiters in some fancy four-star restaurant instead of just students trying to get an education like everybody else. How *will* they? I mean, really, how *will* they? Make it I mean, in life, in the world?"

And, in the wake of his voice, as if they had all the time in the world, as though all the night sky were above them, over their clubhouse in the treetops, they contemplated his question as if it were the profoundest ever posed.

"But the one who gets me, who really gets me, is that Lorraine. Who does *she* think she is? The other day at lunch she didn't like her sandwich. She took a bite of it and spit it out on the plate. Then she hands it to me and says 'Taste this.' Well, I don't want to taste her sandwich, but Lorraine has other ideas and says, 'Go on, Eddy, taste it. This ham is spoiled. They serve us spoiled ham and expect us to eat it. What, and get food poisoned? Taste it, Eddy. Am I crazy or what?' Oh," he said, "and Rachel?"

"The one who may flunk out," Druff said.

"Well, that's the thing," the waiter said, "you know how worried she's been about her classes?" His remark was to Rose Helen, who Druff realized the waiter never directly addressed by name.

"She never studies," Rose Helen said dreamily. "How can she pass? She never studies."

"Well, that's the thing," Edward said, "that's what everyone thought. But you know, the last couple of weeks, she's been eating like a horse. She asks for second helpings on everything. Seconds on soup, on the main course, seconds on salad."

"Rachel doesn't even like salad," Rose Helen said.

"Seconds on salad."

"She doesn't *like* salad."

"Well, that's the thing. She never particularly liked soup. She never *particularly* liked anything. Now she wolfs *everything* down, she can't get enough. She eats, pardon my French, like she's got two behinds.

There's this running joke in the kitchen. The dishwasher can always tell which dishes were Rachel's. Because they look like they've already been washed."

"Is she fat?"

"She's getting there."

"Poor Rachel."

"She has this really scruffy bathrobe. There are cigarette burns all over it."

"Rachel doesn't smoke. She comes down in her bathrobe? Mrs. Post doesn't say anything to her?"

"Her fingernails are a mess, she bites them to the quick."

"Rachel doesn't bite her nails. Poor kid, she's so worried about her grades."

"She's pregnant."

"She isn't," Rose Helen said.

"She is," the waiter said, "she's pregnant all right. She's had the tests."

All Druff could think was Where? How? She was an underclassman herself. On weekend nights she hadn't any more access to those study rooms than they had, he, Rose Helen. She was pregnant? She'd *done* it? She wasn't a virgin? And if she wasn't a virgin, he wondered, then who was the guy? Not the mouse, the little Gamma Beta Sigma shrimp she dated, it couldn't be him. And if it was him, then how many times did the runt get to poke her before he knocked her up? And who, finally, were Miss and Mr. Foreplay on this campus anyway, and what was the point of having a girlfriend with her own private room in her own unauthorized, non-university housing with a landlady who apparently not only lived and let live but was this high-rolling high liver herself, if all he ever got to show for it was, pardon my French, the goddamn blue balls he went around with all bent over so he was never any higher than the little runt Gamma Beta Sigma son of a bitch himself?

"Oh," the waiter said, "by the way, I won't be seeing you guys Saturday. It's Alumni Weekend and they're putting on a special banquet. Mrs. Post wants the waiters to come in two hours early to serve drinks and pass around hors d'oeuvres. Then we have to be there for the banquet part, and by the time we clean up it'll probably be midnight or later before we get out of there. So you'll have to fend for yourselves about dinner."

But he'd stopped listening, and Rose Helen was probably fixing to call curfew on him anyway.

Which, because of what the waiter had told them, had suddenly become a question between them. Because, though it was true, it no longer mattered to him that she was the more interesting. He had begun to discount her seniority, the damaged-goods factors, her recovered cripple's way of walking, her defiance and resentment and pride, even the outlaw housing where, in the dark, in their nest there on the double bed, beneath all the queer hodgepodge of their coats and towels and laundry, all the odd, invisible motley of what, for warmth and style and texture, might just as well have been a housepainter's drop cloth, she was even more inventive than he was. He had even begun to discount the fact that he loved her. Because he was jealous now. (This was the old days. This was the old days and somehow he already knew it was the old days, had this prescient sense of a soured nostalgia, realized they lived in a magic conspiracy of flimflam fears, knew the times were shoving them through the cracks, shucking them, jiving them, feeding them the prose of innocence, the hype of upbringing. For who gave blowjobs then, who took it up the ass? Poor Druff, Druff thought. Because evidently somebody did, and why did he have the feeling that it might have been him? Because maybe they weren't the Dutch and Duchess of foreplay at all, maybe they were only the floor show. He would, recalling his old, presumed invisibility and warm, comfortable *e-pluribus-unum* ways, the fancied atmosphere of mutual absorption and the cumulative, conjoined hip-to-haunch of those Friday and Saturday nights in the Chi Phi Kappa passion pit, wince.) Because he was not only jealous now, he was furious.

Furious (and not just on poor, pregnant Rachel's behalf either), and not just at the mouse, the little runt shrimp Gamma Beta Sigma son of a bitch, but at all single men and women everywhere, particularly at every unmarried undergraduate or graduate student, coed or otherwise, who was getting it, regularly or otherwise, anywhere in the jiving, shucking, civilized world.

And not only furious either. Regretful as well. For all his bent-over trials by erection, his excruciating stalled blood and stopped-up sperm.

They quarreled. Or Druff did, Rose Helen just said no. *He* quarreled. Or cajoled and wheedled, rather; fawned and flattered, soft-soaped, pleaded and begged.

He argued.

"There are less attractive guys than me. The Gamma Beta."

"No. I'm sorry. No."

There were less attractive men, he argued, plenty of them, but it wasn't the flukes he cared about. "Really," he told her, "good *for* him, good *for* the Gamma Beta son of a bitch! Good for runts-of-the-litter everywhere!" Because who he really resented, if she wanted to know, were the non-runts, the idea of simply *ordinary* fellows taking their pleasure was the *really* galling thing. If she wanted to know.

She didn't want to know.

And now they really quarreled, really went at it.

We never do this, he told her, we never do that, naming acts for her, citing specifically denied sexual frictions, indicting the five-or-so months they had known each other now, almost, as lawyers do, fixing dollar amounts to his pain and suffering (so much for each blue ball, so much for going around all bent over), and assessing his mental anguish (so much for frustration, so much for the personal humiliation he felt when he'd learned that even a little runt Gamma Beta Sigma mouse had knocked someone up).

"Don't I let you touch me down there?" Rose Helen said. She might have been close to tears. It sounded that way, but he couldn't tell. They were on Rose Helen's made bed. It was too dark to see. "Don't I?" she repeated. "Let you touch me down there?"

"Sure, through layers of underwear."

"Haven't you kissed my nipples?"

"Oh come on, Rose Helen, you practically make me brush my teeth first," he said irritably. "And when did you ever let me even touch them with your brassiere off?"

"Don't you get to hold my behind?"

"With gloves on, mittens, through goddamn snowsuits."

"Don't you go under my dress?"

"I have to get past all the dry cleaning first, all the clothes and shower curtains on the damn bed. I have to prick my fingers on the pins in your Ship n' Shore blouses. It's a regular obstacle course!"

"All right," she said, "haven't I kissed you down there?"

"Through my trousers!" Druff yelled.

"Don't raise your voice to me!" she raised her voice to him. *"And if this bed's such an obstacle course, why don't I just get out of it and remove one of the obstacles?"*

She got out of bed, smoothed her clothing down. She turned the light on.

"Fine," Druff shouted in the now bright room, "and why don't *I* just remove the rest of them!" He ripped the bedspread off the bed, scattering it across the floor along with all his and Rose Helen's intervening protections, the various towels, washcloths, throw rugs and clothing.

"Pick all that up!" Rose Helen said.

"I won't do it," Druff said.

That was when Edward came up with their dinner.

"Hey," the waiter said, "what's going on here? It looks like a cyclone hit the place. What happened?"

"A cyclone hit the place," Druff said. "All that crap ended up on the floor."

"Here," Edward said, "let me help you get some of this stuff up," and started to bend down.

"Leave it alone," Rose Helen shouted. *"Don't touch a thing!"*

Which was when Mrs. Green, startling them all, came into the room.

"What's this shouting?" she demanded. "Didn't I tell you about the railroad workers," she said, "the irregular hours they sleep? How are they supposed to get the rest they need if you people are so inconsiderate?"

She looked from one to the other, taking in the mess on the floor, taking in Rose Helen's *Butler's Principles of Basic Education,* Foerster's *American Poetry and Prose,* and Druff's *Civics,* taking in the big cellophane-wrapped dinner plate with Rose Helen's supper on it that Edward still held.

"You kids aren't students, are you? That one, he isn't a waiter sneaking food in from some sorority he just stole it from where he sets table and serves the sisters their lunches and dinners, is he? Because

I run a respectable house here with railroad workers, beauticians, cashiers, Air Force wives and food handlers. This isn't any authorized university housing I do here to baby-sit for a bunch of all-grown-up kids on the excuse that they're here for an education, while the truth is that the male grown-up kid is mostly just interested in finding some agreeable female grown-up kid who's willing to take his pecker and hold it inside her for a while."

"I don't steal it," Edward said.

"What's that?" Mrs. Green said.

"The food," he said. "I don't steal it."

"Well all right," Mrs. Green said, "so you don't steal it. That's still no call to go shouting at each other at all hours of the day and night and make the kind of mess I see here on the fl—"

"They give it to me themselves. I'm no thief. I don't steal it. They make up the plates themselves. For her, for Rose Helen. 'Here,' they tell me, 'you're friends with them, you know where she's living, why don't you go on and take these scraps to her? We won't miss them, we'd only have to throw them out. Why should they go to waste? This way we'll know that at least she's eating well. She was one of us, after all. We took her in once and made her feel welcome. Just because she thinks she had a falling-out with us why should she go hungry? She's had a hard enough life as it is.' So I didn't steal it. The Chi Phi Kappas give it to me for her themselves."

"The *hypocrites,*" she shouted, "the *hypocrites!*" She started to cry.

Druff didn't want to leave. Rose Helen said no, he had to. She said that once he picked everything up he'd tossed on the floor he could stay for a while but that she expected him to observe the usual curfew.

That night she tried to kill herself. Mrs. Green and one of the railroad workers saved her life. They called the authorities and, afterwards, Mrs. Green had the decency to call Druff at Mrs. Reese's to tell him what happened.

She was still being held for observation when he proposed. Both of them understood that his proposal of marriage and her acceptance had nothing at all to do with forgiveness, or mercy, or their sorrows.

So they still didn't know any couples, and now they no longer had even Ed with them, good old Edward R. Markey with his name like a clerk of the court or some high-up in the Motor Vehicles Bureau, their

friend downtown, could be, and who may have been the real politico
here, who knew where the bodies were buried, their whys and whats,
their names and addresses, and whose own bodies, his, Rose Helen's,
he would keep in his files long after they ceased to bother with his.

So you can imagine how he felt.

Even after all his careful arrangements for the evening, making the
reservations at the restaurant, withdrawing two hundred dollars at the
automatic teller, sending the flowers, purchasing the condoms he knew
he wouldn't be using, evading Mrs. Norman, sidestepping Doug, Druff
had still to call Rose Helen to explain why he wouldn't be coming home
for dinner that night. It was the thing he most dreaded, and he put it
off till last—unless, as he feared, calling Margaret Glorio and canceling
out altogether (a distinct possibility) were to be his final "arrangement,"
allowing the flowers to stand as a sort of olive branch—because he
didn't have the slightest idea what he would tell her. He'd had few
occasions to lie to Rose Helen, so few, in fact, that he was sure she'd
catch him out the minute he opened his mouth. The times he *had* lied
to her had always been in the line of gallantry, and even then never
volunteering, only if she asked, insisted. (Even after almost forty years
he was afraid of her because she wouldn't be patronized, his proud,
up-front, warts-and-all wife.) And then the furthest he'd go might be to
tell her that he liked a dress he didn't particularly care for, or approved
a hairdo to which he'd not yet become accustomed, Rose Helen not only
reading his reservations, reading his mind, reading his instincts, but
putting her finger precisely where he'd have put it himself if he'd known
enough about fashion or coiffure to be at all articulate about them.

So they didn't lie to each other. They never made excuses for Mikey,
or for each other. If anything, Rose Helen was even more honest with
Druff than Druff was with Rose Helen. She told him, for example, that
she'd rarely voted for him. Only in three of the elections in which he'd
stood for office. She wasn't even of Druff's political persuasion. More
than once, if she felt strongly enough about his opponent, she'd shown
up at his rival's campaign headquarters on election night to help him
celebrate if he'd won, to console him if he hadn't. And maybe it was
something about their disparate franknesses—perhaps both were politicians finally, though of different orders; Rose Helen, at sixty, a Young
Turk; Druff, two years her junior, this, well, pussy-whipped City Com-

missioner of Streets—which bleakened the prospects for the phone call he was so reluctant to make. She would see right through him. Even over the telephone she'd be able to tell he was blushing, hear his voice toeing in with lame excuse. He couldn't think of a thing to tell his wife. Better forget it, he thought, he hadn't a hope and, deciding to cancel, looked up Margaret Glorio's number which he'd been at such pains to obtain only hours before. He slipped a coin into the slot—because she'd been right, he'd called from a pay phone the first time, too—and, looking at the number he'd so carefully copied down, he started to dial.

Rose Helen picked up on the second ring.

"Yes?"

"Howdy, Miss Kitty. I hope you haven't gone to the trouble of baking my favorite pie or doing up some difficult recipe you've been meaning to try for years only the ingredients were always out of season when you finally found the time," the commissioner said breezily.

"I thought we'd eat out," Rose Helen said.

"Yeah, well," Druff said, "that ain't gonna happen."

"What's wrong? Is something wrong?"

"Not a thing."

"Your voice sounds funny."

"I'm at the airport, I'm at a pay phone."

"At the airport? What are you doing at the airport?"

"Well, I'm meeting a plane."

"Who's coming in?"

"Bert McIlvoy. Irwin Scouffas. But their plane was over an hour late getting out of Denver. It isn't scheduled to arrive for another twenty minutes yet. I got here at four-thirty. Can you imagine holding a plane because the heating element in the galley isn't working? Airlines, Jesus!"

"Who are Bert McIlvoy and Irwin Scouffas? I never heard of them."

"They're from the marathon. They reached me in the limo this morning. I finally actually got to take a long-distance call in the limo! They sounded like they were right next door."

"Well, who are they? Why are you meeting their plane?"

"I told you. They're from the marathon. You know how long I've been trying to get a marathon going in this town. Well, if they approve the routes I've marked out—it's a big if—and if the city's willing to meet their terms—*another* big if—these two guys can make it possible. I'm going over the routes with them tonight."

"In the dark?"

"Certainly in the dark. Of course in the dark. In the daytime there'd be much too much traffic. They can get a better idea on a relatively empty street."

"When will you be getting home?"

"Gee, I don't know. Not till late, I guess. Long past your bedtime. Hell, long past mine. A marathon is twenty-six miles three hundred eighty-five yards. I've drawn up three possible routes for them. This McIlvoy character is supposed to be a real stickler. We'll probably have to go over each of them. I only wish they'd have come two or three weeks from now when the potholes will all be filled in."

"Well, have fun," Rose Helen said.

"Yeah," Druff said. "Oh, and Rose Helen?"

"What?"

"You know what they're bringing with them?"

"What?"

"Well it seems there's this brand-new gadget that not only measures linear distance but gives you the precise gradients, and then totals the whole thing in feet and inches. This was specifically designed for marathons. That way they can tell whether a Cincinnati marathon is longer than a New York marathon. The damn thing factors the basic twenty-six miles three hundred eighty-five yards and determines the exact degree of difficulty."

"That's really something," Rose Helen had to admit.

"Yeah. Irwin Scouffas was telling me about it. He says it isn't any bigger than an ordinary stopwatch," said the man who couldn't lie to his wife.

They met at the agreed-upon restaurant at the agreed-upon time. Druff hadn't been at all sure she'd show up, but there she was in the bar waiting for him, big as life, beautiful, and, just for a moment as she rose up off the stool and called out to him in greeting, totally unrecognizable, someone he not only could not remember ever having seen before but a person whose name he knew he would not recognize even if she were to say it for him. He began to go through his City Commissioner of Streetsmarts grab bag of ploys to please, his airy, insubstantial token talk.

"Maggie Glorio," she interrupted. "Your dreamgirl?"

"Pardon?"

"Your date for the evening?"

"Sure," he said, "don't you think I know?"

"You're at a loss," she said.

"Well I am," he admitted, "I *am* at a loss." And took her into the dining room—he had selected a restaurant in a small, "continental"-style hotel; it was already nine o'clock; this was the second seating—making conversation, explaining Rose Helen, finding his theme in his family, neither boasting nor complaining, merely giving away the store, talking to the woman as if she were already the one person in the world to whom he could bring his life, at ease, almost offhand, no more self-conscious, really, than if she had been a professional, his doctor, say, his tax accountant, someone accustomed to peering at his private parts, having inside info on his bottom lines. Shipboard romance was written all over his conversation, some no-holds-barred, strangers-on-a-train immediacy to their—well, *his*—speech. It was as if they had been in combat together or knew—well, Druff; Meg gave away nothing—that they would never meet again. (Well, he *was* at a loss, set adrift. This was merely a reckless hand-over-hand he was doing, some Theseus/Ariadne routine to locate himself for her, to locate himself for himself. There was, he thought, nothing personal.)

"For example," he said, continuing now that the waiter had gone off to fetch their drinks, "from time to time I'll talk in my sleep. Nothing very interesting, nothing of much importance. Nothing compromising, I mean. No secrets divulged or lives jeopardized—— just this old, aging guy small-talking in his sleep.

"Where's the harm? What damage do I do? But, you know? It drives Rose Helen crazy. No kidding, it's the cause of some of our biggest fights. *I* don't know why she gets so upset. It can't just be because I woke her up. Hell, you think it would interest her to tune in. It would interest me. It *does* interest me. That's why I get so mad at her when she cuts into one of my monologues. Because once she starts shaking me I lose my place and it's all over, you can forget it. There I am trying to find out why I'm so exercised about whatever it is I'm so exercised about, and Rose Helen is swinging on my pajamas telling me I'm asleep, I'm sleeping, and to wake up, I'm talking like a fool.

"Well, I'll tell you something. I'm *not* talking like a fool. Dreams are nature's way . . . Well, any psychiatrist will tell you. Besides, I enjoy it. Some of my best speeches occur in dreams."

"She's probably a light sleeper," Margaret Glorio said.

"Wake up, I'm talking like a fool?"

They were eating their steamed mussels now, the commissioner going on (when he was not going on about his wife) about his city's elaborate appetizer arrangements, the ancient New Orleans trade routes. "It's important that a town's restaurants have some juice with the established Gulf Coast shellfish interests," he told her. "I mean, take away prawns, take away shrimps, crabs, clams and lobster tails, and what have you got? You've got bush league wineries and dineries, that's what you've got. You've got a strictly one-horse, non-starter sort of a town where no one entertains and there's half an inch of dust collecting on the credit cards and nobody knows what to do with a wedge of lemon except set it down in a cup of tea. You can forget all about your Astrodomes and zillion-square-foot convention centers. You can forget about your combination concert hall–cum–opera house slash shopping mall–performing arts centers. All that shit's for naught if nothing's cooking with the influential dory-and-trawler water interests. It all starts with crustaceans and mollusks," said Druff, speaking of dreams, speaking of dreamgirls, and plying his date with all the inside info he could think of.

"Well," she said, "you seem to have it down to a science."

They were eating their greens. They were eating their roast potatoes. They were eating their crown rack of lamb for two.

And now he'd stopped talking. Had said almost nothing since he'd asked the waiter if he would check with the chef to see how their fruit soufflé was coming. It took forty-five minutes to do a soufflé, he explained to Ms. Glorio. If it didn't go into the oven at just about the time the diners were served their main course it could be a disaster.

"Yes," Margaret said, raising the side of a fist to her mouth and lightly tapping it against her teeth by way of a yawn. "I'd heard that."

"Then there's nothing more I can teach you," the commissioner said.

"I've hurt your feelings."

He pooh-poohed the notion with a wave of his napkin.

"I have," she said.

He brushed away the idea with his knife and fork.

"Well, I mean," she said, "why are you so nervous? What do you think you have to be talking for all the time? What are you so afraid of? I don't bite. You didn't act like this this afternoon. Oh, you were out to impress me, but that was cute—— a little. I mean if all you want is to get laid, there's no reason to go through all this rigmarole. Just get on with it. My place or yours, Commissioner?"

"I've always had this heavy sense of decorum," the commissioner said.

"Oh, de*cor*um," Margaret Glorio said negligently.

"It's what separates us from the bears and giraffes," Druff said.

"It's what pries us from where our bread is buttered," said Margaret Glorio.

Again with the love? the commissioner thought. Again with the thing for the interesting ladies? Aiee, aiee, thought Druff, and—you can imagine how he felt, you can just imagine—helplessly, once again began, though even less at ease now, to bring Rose Helen into it. (As if she'd ever been out of it. Indeed, she might, gone off to the powder room or to make a phone call, have just left the table. Margaret Glorio might just as easily have been an old pal, not seen in years, in town on business, Druff filling her in on the flora and fauna of his married ways, his picturesque local color, the tricky state of their life's economy.)

"Oh yes," he said fondly—they were over their coffee now; Margaret had taken out a cigarette, Druff two or three coca leaves which he slipped into his mouth like after-dinner mints—"she claims she hardly ever voted for me. She says she did it out of principle, but I tell her I regarded it as good luck. That's true, I'd become almost superstitious about it, like a ball player who keeps using the same handkerchief to blow his nose in because the team's been winning.

"Well, that's not felicitous, but you know what I mean. Still, a wife *shouldn't* vote for her own husband when he stands for office? Come *on.*

"I'll tell you something though. I don't care. I really don't. Well, I've never been particularly ideological, and I had a pretty good winning record, election-year-wise. I don't suppose I *had* to deliver my own wife's vote, though it's something my opponents picked up on. But, you know," he said, "in the long run I think it actually helped me. Well, you can see where it would. It's good for the image. What the hell, it humanized me—— that I couldn't even get my own wife to vote for me. I'd be willing to bet that in a close election—believe me, they're never that close; this is pretty much, at least on the local level, a one-party town—something like that could actually make the difference. And Rose Helen's pretty sharp. Now I think about it, I'm not entirely certain she didn't do it on purpose. Of course, now I serve at the mayor's pleasure, but I don't really think it makes any difference. I mean what are we talking about? City Streets Commissioner? How much could she care? Rose Helen doesn't even drive!"

"So what do you say," Margaret Glorio said, "my place or yours?"

"I guess," Druff had to admit, "mine's pretty much out of the question."

"I guess," said the buyer. "I mean those are some heavy burdens you've got on you there, Commissioner. Rose Helen, your statecraft. And I only have this little studio apartment."

"That's because you're out of town so much," Druff said.

"Why yes," she said, "it is."

"That's good," he said earnestly. "It is. That helps us out. Oh, shit," he said, "I'm not good at this. I'm like some dummy kid."

"Well, you're certainly not good at it," she said. "What was that you put into your mouth? Coca leaves?"

"No, of course not."

"Yes," she said, "they were coca leaves."

"No," Druff said.

"Don't try to swallow them, for heaven's sake. You'll gag and ruin your beautiful dinner."

Druff, coughing helplessly, eyes watering, nose running, choking on all the acids of his contraband, was ruining his beautiful dinner, his ancient, comfortable marriage, his brilliant career. Margaret Glorio had come around the side of the table. She pressed a glass of water into his hands. Diners rose at their different tables, waiters came running from their various stations. "No CPR," he managed, sputtered. "I'm fine, I'm fine now," he said, fiercely waving them off. "A bone," he explained, recovered, "a bone in the fruit soufflé. My fault. I should have seen it.

I *did* see it. I thought it was a stem. It looked delicious. Well," he said, "no harm done, praise God, thank you Jesus. All's well that ends well."

"Rue Glorio?" Margaret said when everybody had returned to their places. "Margaret Street? The Boulevard de Margaret Glorio is a bit grand, but it has a ring. What do *you* say, Commissioner? They're your streets."

"This would be about the blackmail then? A little to-do about the little to-do when I scarfed down what you apparently thought were coca leaves?"

"If I blackmail you," Margaret said, "it won't be over the coca leaves so much as the soufflé bones."

It turned out to be her place after all. They were in bed now, over their brandy snifters, over Meg Glorio's astonishing—to Druff astonishing, who'd never seen anything like it—clinging, red—silk? satin?—nightgown. (Anyway glowing, flushing anyway, some bright raddle of soft, luxurious, idealized skin, of flesh perfected beyond the condition of flesh, of flesh transcended, raised to some new plane—to Druff new—of tidy, sweet, unappurtenanced harmony— realized, hypostatic lovematter.) Just looking at her now he almost fainted. And the thought that they'd just made love near killed him. She had finished him, he was a goner, some polished-off shell of his former self. She would blackmail him? She wanted streets named after her? He would give her esplanades, parades, entire arrondissements! He'd been a politician more than thirty years. He'd call in his markers, see to it they changed the name of the city.

"Margaret Town," the commissioner said. "Gloriville. Meg Glorio City."

And wasn't entirely kidding. At least a part of him serious, at least in his inclinations, in his good will serious. If not in his baggy boxer shorts. Oh, but they were mismatched (he'd be the first to admit it), he in his big boxers, she in her red silk or satin, flesh-transcended, lovematter nightgown.

And even if the actual lovemaking, though fine, and even several steps up from his usual performances, hadn't been anywhere near the standard of your normal, average blockbuster, history-making, place-namer fucks, face it, it was plenty good enough and, for Druff, better than good enough, something which at fifty-eight, or even at forty-eight, or at thirty-eight even, he would never have expected to have happen to him again. (Or he might even name a street after that nightgown, he thought.)

"You know what would be okay in my book?" the commissioner said. Ms. Glorio ran a finger around the bottom of her glass and raised its sweet, bronzy dregs to her mouth as one might lick frosting from a pan. "Sleeping over tonight."

"Oh, but wouldn't Mrs. Druff worry? And the fuss and bother you'd be putting her to with all those cold, tired policemen." He had spoken of Rose Helen's conscientiousness, how she often greeted visitors with mugs of coffee in her hands. "Anyway," she said, "you'd never get away with it."

"I would," he said. "I'm covered." He was thinking of those race routes he was supposed to be covering with whatsisname and whatsisname. "I'm telling you, Ms. Glorio, I could have danced all night."

"Well, your driver then. Didn't you say he always picks you up in the morning?"

"Nuts!" Druff said. "I forgot about my driver. But don't you have an alarm clock? I could set your alarm clock. Even if I can't sleep over, then just sleeping *with* you, even if it's only for an hour, would be okay in my book, too."

"I don't know," she said. "It's awfully late."

"Oh, I know," he said. "It is. And I'm pooped. I am. But all I need is an hour. One hour, then I'm up, dressed, and out of here. I'm City Commissioner of Streets, I know where I can call a cab. I wouldn't even have to use your telephone. No telltale, embarrassing taxis need ever show up at your door. Dick wouldn't know a thing."

To give you an idea how far gone he was. Not even nagging at him. Not even nagging at him all evening, though it had occurred to him. What Dick had told him in the limo—— that the driver recognized her, that she was known to her son, known to Mikey, to Su'ad. *None* of it nagging at him or ruffling his feathers. Though he was as conscious of it as of her ash-blond hair, conscious of it as of that elemental red nightgown, the soft silk or satin lovestuff that might have passed for her skin. That's how far gone. To give you an idea.

Had there been a love potion in the soufflé? Not bones at all, not even coca leaves, just some out-and-out love philter? Enchantment-monger-

ing juices in the fruits and sugars, magic heart sesames and all obsession's amorous fee faw fum? The bell, book and candle therapies and
dowser gravitationals, could be, the wand of that ashen hair and all the
red sorcery of her nightgown.

"May I? May I then?"

"It's your funeral," Meg Glorio said and, lying down beside him,
switched off the light.

Almost at once she began lightly to snore. She lay on her side, facing
him, her mouth putting out little sour puffs of brandied air, breath
bubbles of systemic gall and, somehow this struck Druff as the most
erotic—well, in a way erotic, in a manner of speaking erotic—thing that
had happened to him yet, as though his fly-on-the-wall relation to her
now, to her intimate cheeses and bitters, were some signal of absolute
trust. (He thought of Rose Helen's small, inaccessible shelf, of her *real*
private parts.) Breathing in Margaret Glorio's miasmas and off-limits
climates not as a tourist, say, wandered and lost to the beaten paths,
but as some hardened native of the place, acclimated, adapted, who
lived light, who went without the frills and didn't bother with repellents,
sun blocks, the sissy amenities. This is what the Chamber of Commerce
didn't tell you about, thought the drifting-off, civic-minded public man.
This is what didn't get advertised or written up in brochures. This was
what the sourdoughs knew, what the squatters wouldn't share with you,
what the founding fathers and first families kept to themselves.

"Well," said Druff, speaking from his sleep, "I, of course, won't
breathe a word. No, a lady's breath is her own business. What goes on
in the guts is a matter between her liver and onions. When in the course
of privates events she chooses to leak on a lover, that lover, or so it
seems to me, is sworn to secrete."

Druff giggled.

"No," he went on, "but seriously folks, this is the case with me here.
I happen to need this MacGuffin thing because otherwise just about all
I'm good for is to think about myself. Now, admittedly, this ain't news.
I've been thinking about myself just about all my life. Well *somebody*
has to, *n'est-ce pas?* Do you leave such a thing to amateurs? Old pros
like Dick, the paid professional? They'd hand you your head, fellows
like that. The down side is your hat would be missing.

"Because what it is essentially, I think, is that the world is getting

away from me, I think. Like I was telling Dick in the car just this
morning, it's whizzing past us, the world. Just look at me you need an
example. I've served as a Republican, an Independent, a Democrat, you
name it. I've sat on all the committees. I've gone for an assemblyman,
a streets commissioner, and one time for mayor. I've been this utility
infielder of a pol, and what did it get me? Where's my constituency?
Will I ever be in a history lesson? It's tough to be an old-timer, I'm here
to tell you. You know why? Because you've got to take it sitting down!
Well. I suppose you'll say I'm just falling into the nostalgia trap, but
there's a lot to be said for the old days. (I was beautiful then.) (Oh, not
me. I don't mean me. But me too.)

"You know what I never see anymore? Just as an instance? Slo-mo
movies of chicks hatching out of eggs. Plenty of queer larvae and
nameless life forms emerging from the damnedest stuff, even human
babies straight out of their mamas' kootchies. But no chicks. Nothing
even remotely edible slouching toward breakfast! Why is that, I wonder?"

Margaret Glorio moaned.

"I know," Druff said, "I know. Ain't that just what I've been saying?"

She moaned again. She shuddered and issued a great exhalation of
bad air, covering Druff, who was under the impression that it came from
himself, a mournful accompaniment to his sad complaint. He waved his
hands in front of his mouth to disperse the fumes. Jolting himself and
opening his ears so he could actually hear what he was saying, making
the words manifest, drawing them forth to a kind of consciousness, a
sort of flagrance. (Rose Helen should have shaken him by now, tugged
at his pajamas. The fact that she hadn't, encouraged him to continue.)

"I'm pleased you're sitting still for all this. It's good to get such stuff
off the chest.

"I don't know," Druff said, "it's a different world. I see people
walking around in malls, wearing the styles and noshing on foreign
finger foods, and colored lights blinking beneath the flight paths of
aircraft on the tops of tall buildings. Jesus, how organized it is! It's all
crowd control these days. Well, it has to be, I guess, or they'd mug you
just for your junk bonds and clean out your Swiss accounts. But where
are the bosses going to come from? There ain't any places for your

Pendergasts and Tweeds and Daleys to break in their acts today. If you can't talk Greaser and don't do hand jive you might as well pack it in.

"So I need it. I *need* this MacGuffin thing!

"*I* know I talk about myself, I *know* I do. Sure! This is my subject now. This is the case. But you know? I don't particularly love myself. Really. I don't. It's just all that's left over when you've burned up your power. I feel, I feel," he confided, "like little bits of the British Empire!"

And, Rose Helen or no Rose Helen, was now another few hundred feet up the side of his consciousness, breathless, outraged in dreamland, stifled in the rarefied places between sleeping and waking, though he was almost sure, roused by the sound of his voice, stung by the spice of his tears, that he was almost certainly awake.

He wanted her to hear this next part, insisted she must listen, was prepared, had she raised an objection, to shout it down.

"Do others have themselves so thoroughly? No," he said, "I wonder. I *do* wonder. Do they work themselves up like a foreign language, have they their parentheses and footnotes? Their grammar and . . .

"Well," Druff, cutting in on himself, observed craftily, "of course we must suppose old Su'ad may certainly have let down her guard. I've a few theories about that at least." He waited for her response, got none—to be perfectly honest he hadn't expected he would as a matter of fact if you wanted to know to tell you the truth; also, the air in the room had suddenly cleared, sweetened, as if a rain, say, had laid the summer dust (this would have been the held breath of her attention)—and went on. "Just feel free to shake me whenever you want," he said. "Just break in anytime."

There was nothing. Excellent. It was a hell of a way to do business, he thought. It was a *hell* of a way! Forget your TV spots, your "messages," dumb debates, campaign stops, being there at the gates to press the flesh when the shifts changed, and all the rest of it. Just give him ten minutes alone in bed with the voters, and let him go! Well, he thought, now that I've got their attention, I'd better get on with it. He got on with it.

"One," he said. "Mikey ran her over.

"That's not as farfetched as it sounds. They could have had a lovers' quarrel. Who knows? Here's this young girl from a broken, war-torn homeland. She's fond enough of my kid, but maybe she's got a fella back in the old country, a sweetheart in the sand, some PLO type with a five-day growth of whiskers under the head drapes. Or maybe there *isn't* any boyfriend. Maybe—'Two different worlds we live in, Mikey. Your ways are not my ways. You say potato, I say potahto.'—she's just homesick. Who knows? It could have been anything. Maybe her green card's run out, or she can't stand our Mikey. They quarrel, she calls him a name and he gets in the car and runs her over. Maybe they *didn't* quarrel. Maybe they were having a race, Mikey in the car, Su'ad on foot. They're neck and neck. He steps on the gas, she lengthens her stride to pass him and takes the lead. Mikey's humiliated, a little slip of a girl hobbled by a *chador* passes a guy in a powerful, American-built car. Say what you will about him, Mikey's a pretty patriotic kid. He guns it, *really* guns it. And he's getting it up there now—ninety, ninety-five, a hundred ten, a hundred fifteen miles an hour. He's catching up to her. He's catching up to her and he's getting excited. Hooray! Hip hip hurrah! Three cheers for the U.S. of A. But as I say, he's excited, *too* excited. His hands are sweating. He makes a mistake, his hand slips on the wheel, he loses control. Bingo bango! He hits her, runs her over, and it's good night nurse.

"That's one way of looking at it.

"Two!" he announced.

"Which brings us to the traffic signal on Kersh Boulevard. (How does Meg Glorio Way strike your fancy?) Oh, yes, the fatal stoplight itself. That pedestrian-activated 'attractive nuisance' about which we've heard so much, and that anyone, particularly anyone who's just spotted a lone, obviously foreign, obviously Arab-looking young lady, could just step up to at will and activate with the same casual and discretionary ease with which one turns on a radio. Recall the conditions on the night of the so-called accident. Was it raining? Were the streets slick? Was there fog? What was the phase of the moon? (Someone's going to have to look this shit up.) And if the person in question happens to be of a different religious or political persuasion from the Shiite Muslim in question, what's to prevent him or her not from pressing the button on the fatal stoplight, but from *not* pressing it? What's to prevent such a person from holding Su'ad back when the light was green in her favor, or from throwing her to the wolves when the light was against her? And suppose such a person had an accomplice? Now this is a big city, a major market. The accomplice could have been anyone, of course, but let's say for the sake of argument it was Mikey. He hits her, runs her over, and it's good night nurse all over again!

"Farfetched? You think so? Let me remind you it was once far-fetched to think we'd ever have the scientific wherewithal to put a man on the moon!

"Normally, I might rest my case, but these are not normal times.

"Three!

"The traffic signal was itself at fault.

"Lookee here. The timer inside the box was defective. One of Su'ad's Sunni enemies tampers with the signal so it can't change colors, the critical wiring on the doodad for Go becomes entangled with the critical wiring on the gizmo for Stop. Your green won't turn green, your red won't turn red. It just hangs there on amber. It's rigged so that both the driver's and the Shiite's patience run out at exactly the same time. Mikey starts up, Su'ad starts out. Know what we're talking about here? Talking about the fatal conditions for bingo bango, good night nurse.

"Oh, I don't have to spell it out for you. There are hundreds of possibilities, dozens, several.

"Four!

"She was a terrorist. Mikey finds out about it and doesn't like the idea of becoming involved with someone who spills innocent blood. He runs her over. Open and shut. Prima facie b. b., g. n. n.

"Bear with me. Five and I'm finished.

"Because so far all I've presented, no matter how persuasive it's seemed, has been circumstantial. But five. What about five?

"Suppose as I've suggested that Su'ad and Mikey *didn't* fight. Suppose they didn't race, the one on foot, the other in the car. Let's further suppose that no one noticed her at the light and pushed her out into the street and under the wheels of some oncoming car driven by an accomplice. Let's even suppose that Mikey didn't run her over. Are you with me so far? All right then. What if there wasn't even anything wrong with the traffic signal and nobody's patience ran out, what then? What if she didn't die at the hands of either mischief or mischance? What if she wasn't even a terrorist? Or what if she was but Mikey didn't know it? What if she was a terrorist, but, in the course of reading the

American press saw the error of her ways and became so upset with herself that she settled into a deep depression and determined to take her own life? What if she enlisted the aid of our simple, smitten, good-hearted Mikey to help her do herself in?

"What, I ask you, if it was self-murder? What, that is, if it was a case of simple *Su'adicide!*

"Think about it. *Think* about it!"

"Wake up, Druff," said Margaret Glorio, "it's time to go to school."

Only he was awake, of course. Had been, sort of, since somewhere between his second and third arguments. Even if he didn't immediately understand who was shaking him, even if, in his confused, hypnagogic wakefulness, he didn't always understand where he was, or knew only that it was somewhere dreadfully, disgracefully off-limits, he was awake. Awake enough, at any rate, to recognize his clothes at the foot of the unusual sofa bed, the stylish sheets, awake enough as he stepped into his pants and put on his socks and shoes and buttoned his shirt and tied up his tie and arranged his jacket around him to comprehend where he was, even as he recognized Margaret and recalled their evening together and blew her a kiss, mouthing "Good night, Margaret dearest. I love you, darling. You've captured my heart, my heart, and I'll call you in the morning," and took in the long, splendid red nightgown that only two or three hours earlier he'd helped to take off her and held as she stepped back and let him behold her glorious ash-blond bush and firm, trained, unforgettable all. Awake enough, even in the dark, to have registered finally what, excited as he'd been by all the stir and jiggle of his glands and all the bumps and grinds of his unprepared imagination, he had not even seen in the light, some tentative, on-trial, thirty-day, money-back guarantee texture to the decor, or, no, nothing on-trial or thirty-day or even guaranteed to it at all, so much as—see how awake, see how fine his fine distinctions—experimental, some run-up-the-flag-pole quality, a feel in the furnishings almost of demographics, of cus-tomer-satisfaction surveys, almost, that is, as if the buyer, like some hero of science, had first to work out on herself the exact dosages and precise indications of these surroundings, some environment of the new and venturesome, of the questionable and dangerous, he was able to guess at, anxious and hurried as he was, and in the dark, remember, and only from the dark's graduated, particular finishes and thicknesses,

1 1 3

the bold colors of the walls and carpeting, drapes and slipcovers, working up even the studio apartment's queer lamps and appliances from what appeared to him—or, rather, didn't even actually appear to him— not even as black shapes finally so much as almost sonar interferences and encumbrances. That's how awake, that's how alert! Even as he stepped, intuiting where it would have to be from the room's dark, almost invisible silhouettes and pitchy mass, directly up to the designer telephone and dialed, by terrible, instinctive, ruinous rote, Dick, his driver, the spy.

"Hello?" came the worried, sleep-ridden voice, so thickly accented with semiconsciousness that Druff almost couldn't quite recognize it at first and paused, waiting for it to go on. "Hello? Hello? Who's this, who's there?" Gradually the cop's voice came into rich, angry focus. "Is that you again? Give me a break. How many the fuck times I have to tell you don't call me. You know what time it is? Hello? Come on, what is it? What shit did you get into now? All right, all right, I ain't mad. If you're calling this time of night you probably got a reason. What is it this time, you dent a fender, scratch the paint, run a stop? Man, they're gonna lift your license one of these days. They're gonna strip you of your privileges."

Druff, furious, said calmly, "It's your employer, Bobbo Druff. It's your City Commissioner of Streets." He gave Margaret Glorio's address, even the number of her apartment. (See how awake? See how alert?) "But I'll wait in the lobby," he said. "Stop by the canopy at the front of the building. Don't leave the car. I'll see the limousine and come out."

Ms. Glorio had turned on a freestanding leather lamp beside the sofa bed.

"Gee," she said, "and here I thought I was under no obligation. No salesman would call, or telltale, embarrassing taxis show up at the door. Here I thought my reputation was all safe and sound and that Mary Sally—— what's your wife's name again?"

"Rose Helen."

"And that Alice Nancy wouldn't have a clue about what's going on in our sordid little lives. Oh well," she said, "I guess Mother was right. It'll have to be heaven that protects the working girl, after all. Because God knows the gentlemen callers don't seem to have a handle on it."

"I got a little confused," Druff said. "I called him by mistake."

"Hey," Margaret Glorio said, "we make mistakes. Who's perfect? Any volunteers? It's just that at this point in my life, maybe just a couple notches up from the last thing I need, right around, oh, bad news from the Pap smear, say, or a failing score on my mammogram, would be an embittered wife hanging around trying to scratch my eyes out, throwing acid onto the drapes and furniture, making scenes."

"That won't happen."

"No."

"It won't."

"I know that."

He was afraid she was telling him she wouldn't see him again. It was a terrible time to press his case. "I'll call you in the morning," he said.

"It ain't the romantic dinners," she said. "It isn't the flowers. —Oh," she said, "that reminds me. I never thanked you." Druff body-Englished it was unimportant, that there was nothing to thank him for. "No," she said, "it was sweet. An orchid corsage. I might even have worn it. It's just that I thought the prom wasn't till next week. —Where was I, what was I saying? Oh yes, it's not the dinners, it isn't the flowers. It's not even the lovemaking. It's always that damn extra hour that gets us into trouble. You sweet-talkers with your 'hour, up, dressed and out of here' routines. That's where you do us in."

She liked him. She did. Otherwise, why would she waste time on him with *her* routines? She liked him, all right. Druff could tell. He guessed it was as good a time as any to get going. He let himself out, but turned first in the doorway. "I have a feeling," he said, "I may have talked in my sleep. I hope I didn't disturb you."

And desperately hoped he hadn't, that he'd dreamed his hypnagogic state, only dreamed he wasn't entirely dreaming. It was very important now to clear the decks, get on with his grace period, be rid of his MacGuffin.

"Disturb me? Of course not. It's that Mikey's pants you seem to be in, who you're giving the hard times. You'd best leave," she said. "Your man will be waiting."

In the lobby, Druff waited for Dick in a comfortable armchair near the night doorman's station. He didn't, of course, intend to rouse him— the fellow was dozing in front of a bank of closed-circuit television monitors—but for reasons he didn't entirely understand would have welcomed his attention. He glanced about to see if there might not be one of those logs even employees had to sign when they entered or left a building after hours.

Now he was entirely alert. Really. He would probably pay for it in the morning but he didn't see how he'd be able to sleep tonight. Indeed, he was so excited he thought he would probably wake Rose Helen when he got home. He would never deliberately hurt her or say anything which might cause her a moment's anxiety, but he didn't see how, after a day and night like this had been, he could be expected just to go home and get into bed as though nothing had happened. Whatever else, they were friends, even best friends—whatever happened between himself and the Avenue of the Boulevard of Margaret Glorio Street, nothing, at least so far as Druff was concerned, could change that—and best friends were there for each other. They clipped each other on the chin and rifled each other's pants for car keys if one was sober and the other too drunk to drive. That was the nature of friendship, he thought. All real buddies were drinking buddies finally. Intoxication investigators, they stood guard, kept this hold-hand vigil at each other's bedsides, or over each other's sprees. They were the fail-safes of tipsy hearts. Of pie-eyed heads.

So of *course* he would wake Rose Helen. Of course he would. He needed the company. And out of good, simple reciprocal fellowship give her details of his evening with Scouffas and McIlvoy, the one, of all things, a clubfoot, the other, for all he'd practically invented the degree-of-difficulty device that marched around through the city with them and that poor McIlvoy had trouble adjusting in the dark whenever his clubfoot pal, Scouffas, who actually wore it, was thrown too much off the track by his hobbled leg, making the loyal companion's loyal deferentials, resetting the damn thing, factoring in all the dipsy doodles of friendship and love. Who knew? Perhaps they were lovers. Who knew? (See? See what Druff meant? Druff meant. There for each other. Joining the divergences, the pal Scouffas's couldn't-be-helped, staggered meanderings, McIlvoy at pains—he had severe astigmatism, you should have seen his glasses; Coke bottles? try ice cubes, why don't you, you want an idea—to make the fine, tight Kentucky windage corrections and allowances that crippled-up old Scouffas caused to be required to be made whenever he took six or seven steps forward and went half, or one, or one and a half steps to what wasn't even always the side, but more often than not some even-more-difficult-to-figure bias.) Regaling her, his best friend, Rose Helen, with tales of his evening, giving as good as he got, possibly even better than he got because old Rose Helen, the wife, the best friend, rousted from sleep at whatever the ungodly hour was, maybe—possibly probably—wouldn't even know that she was on duty.

So regaling her, giving Scouffas the clubfoot and McIlvoy—this detail a surprise because normally you'd expect it would be the other way around—the thick Greek accent you couldn't cut with a knife. What the hell, these extra flourishes, they were what best friends did for each other. Considerations no different in kind, really, from McIlvoy's for Scouffas when the former—not permitted, friends of that order of magnitude don't "permit"—encouraged the latter to tramp about, pacing off the marathon with the delicate thingamajig it had taken him years to perfect attached to his old friend's clubfoot. Regaling her— she'd be laughing along with him by now—reinventing the invention he'd invented, perfecting it for Beverly Susan because friendship was a two-way street and, after all, it was really Rachel Joanne's sleep that had been broken into and, appearances notwithstanding, Marsha Sandra who was doing the driving; on good old Pamela Ruth's watch that he'd had the one-too-many that sounded all that red-alert friendship in the first place.

Regaling her. Perhaps not even what you could honestly call out-and-out lying. All the best details true on one level, at least spiritually true, a sort of projected, sublimated truth. That part about the possibility that Scouffas and McIlvoy might have been lovers. This, Rose Helen's attentiveness here, where Druff needed her most. Segueing from the speculation to the possibility, the possibility to the likelihood, the likelihood to the certainty it was so, and Druff portraying in the crudest but most necessary code the validity of every possible detail. Taking her into the studio apartment they kept because they were on the road so much of the year pacing out marathons. Speculating about the high-tech furniture they probably had, their stylish, red silk pajamas. Regaling. Making it clear. Regaling. Regaling and relishing.

"Hey. Hey, mister. There's some limo outside honking his horn."

"What? What's that?" asked Druff, shaken from sleep by the doorman.

"Yeah, he's been making a racket. He's going to wake the neighborhood. I see he's from the city, but my first duty's to the building. Could
you go out and get him to stop?"

So he was already angry, at himself for calling his spy, for the rote
instincts and reflexes that lived in his hands and, independent of his
intentions, pushed the buttons on his telephones for him, at the chauffeur, who, wakened from sleep, had blithely seemed to acknowledge all
Druff's troubled suspicions, at the chauffeur again for having been
indiscreet with the city's limousine.

The doorman was right. Druff could hear the chipper, almost larky
soundings of the limousine's horn. Not leaning on it, mind, which might
almost have been extenuated by urgency, pressing business, perhaps—
though this was a stretch—the saving of lives, but the brash, overly
confident *"Who,* who owns this town? *We,* we own this town!" laid-
back, boom-box musings of street punks and gang toughs. Steamed and
double-steamed not because the man was out of uniform—*Druff* was out
of uniform—or because he did not get out from behind the wheel and
run around the side of the car to open the door for him, but because
of the arm, thrown over the seat, across the lowered window partition,
that loud arm that spoke contemptuous volumes, that, well, practically
fucking smirked at him, God damn it, and which, were it longer or not
too much of an effort for the chauffeur to get it to move, might have
doubled itself up at the elbow and nudged him in the ribs. Was he
winking? Was the son of a bitch winking? Was it some sexual high sign
the brute was throwing at him off his fingers?

So, as you can see, he was already angry.

"I," Druff gently reminded Dick when he'd closed the limousine door
after himself, "am a public servant. You are a public servant's servant.
No, don't start just yet. I'll tell you when.

"Dum dum de dum dum, dum dum?" the commissioner asked. "I
don't think I quite care for your way with the taxpayers' horn, Dicky,"
he said. (Caring, despite what he'd just said, for it quite a lot, as a matter
of fact.) "We aren't hunters, kid. You didn't pop by the trailer court
to fetch some chum for a ride out to the duck blind. Dum dum de dum

dum, dum dum? It's three-thirty in the morning. You don't wake neighbors. We ain't fellows in the same car pool years. Dum dum de dum dum me no dum dum de dum dums, Dum-Dum," he said so softly he knew Dick had to strain to hear him. And leaned forward and quite casually knocked his chauffeur's arm from where it still rested along the ledge of the partition.

"Hey," the man said. "Hey, what the . . ."

Druff moved the toggle switch that raised the window. "I don't care to hear it," he said through the intercom.

"You ready *now?*" the spy asked past what Druff—wondering Is he armed, is he armed? Is he licensed to kill me?—supposed were clenched teeth.

"Check the pressure in the tires," Druff said.

"What?"

"There's a pressure gauge in the glove compartment. Check the pressure in the tires."

"What's this shit?"

"Do it," Druff said.

"The hell I'll do it."

"Then get out, I'll drive myself."

"No way," spoke up his MacGuffin. "No way. This baby is signed out in the motor pool to *me*. Only me and Doug are authorized to check it out, and I'm the party that's going to drive it." Druff was already standing at the driver's side. He'd opened Dick's door. "No way," Dick said, "no goddamn way. I ain't turning over any fifty-five thousand dollars' worth of equipment that I'm signed out on and responsible for to some guy who's high because he just got his ashes hauled. No way!"

"Get out," Druff said.

"*You got a chauffeur's license? You happen to be packing one of those?* You may be a big-time City Commissioner of Streets, but I'm the cop in this deal and, honest to Christ, you make a move to drive off in this limo without a chauffeur's license in your wallet and I'll arrest you."

But Druff, reaching into the limousine, already had the car phone in his hands, was already through to the sheriff's office, was already on the line to the dispatcher, when the chauffeur pressed the "disengage" button and broke the connection. "What did you go and do *that* for?" Dick said. "What's the matter with you? Do you *like* a showdown?" He sounded disappointed. "What's to be gained? Nobody wins. All that can happen is that somebody's feelings are going to get hurt and there's blood on the other fellow's hands. That's no way. Ain't you been a politician long enough to know that much at least? I'll tell you something, Commissioner. You never asked and I never said, but all those times you ran for an office, I voted for you. I was in your corner. Maybe you didn't know it but that's true. I did and I was. Because I thought you were onto something. I really did. Hell," he said, "you want to drive, drive." He slid away from the wheel.

Druff made no move to take his place and the chauffeur looked at him expectantly.

"Check the pressure in the tires," Druff said.

"Oh boy," said the spy, "you're really something. I thought we had a moment there, but you're something. Yeah," he said, "sure, I'll check it." He opened the glove compartment and to Druff's surprise actually found a pressure gauge there. (Well, Druff thought, it was the MacGuffin. On overtime. Moving his fingers on telephones, riding his tongue, getting him laid, fighting his battles and, now, mining the rich, inexplicable ores of serendipity and golden, incalculable, long-shot, break-the-bank chance. Despite the fact that not half an hour earlier he'd wished it called off, at least suspended, so that he, together with Margaret of all the Boulevards, might make something out of what was left of his life. But it was the old story, wasn't it? Once out of the bottle you couldn't turn the genie off, call back a wish, rescind a fate or have ever again the boring old status quo ante. It was magic time, not Kansas anymore, and he had better learn to live with it.)

"They're fine," Dick said flatly. "Even the spare. Those guys in the garage," he said. "We get the credit but they keep us flying. You want to go home now?"

In the back the City Commissioner of Streets made assent with his head and the chauffeur guided the long black limousine out into the traffic.

He can talk to me like this, mused the commissioner, because he's civil service. But he's right, Druff thought, push should never be allowed to come to shove. And marveled at how infrequently it did. How civil the civil service, he contemplated. How difficult it is to fire anyone in it. And, oh, the genius of men's imaginings, and was astonished at the world's astute behaviors, the sweet models of its arrangements and gracious systems. We take care of our own, they seemed to say. And meant it. They did. Everywhere a dependent, low-born incompetence, the slow, the dull, the stolid, the vicious, the crass. The foolish and crazy. The soft, flawed and fallible serving the fuddled. The cunning timeserver side by side with the simple drudge, sharing the planet with the sane and sober, with the dedicated, with the seers and masters. We take care of our own. Come one, come all! was life's stirring cry. And offered its generous tit to any mouth that would have it. Sure, Druff thought, that's why he can lip off to me like this. I can't fire his rascal ass and the cocksucker knows it. He knows how many forms I'd have to fill out. He knows all the supporting letters I'd need to get together for his file. He knows all the hearings and committee meetings I'd be calling down on my head!

And just then felt the presence of his own body, a kind of electric thrill. He felt palpitations. His knees went weak and he was momentarily light-headed. Gee, he thought, and I *won* that round, and wondered how his driver must be feeling. Perhaps it was the lateness of the hour, but suddenly Druff felt a sort of tenderness toward his old friend, the constituent in his corner from way back when. Dick the Spy was disappointed in him, stunned. Obviously he hadn't known it wasn't only Druff he was up against, but Druff's MacGuffin too, the jujitsu leverages theatrics gave a fellow. He never had a chance, the commissioner gloated, then suddenly remembered the case of nerves he'd experienced, was still, to judge from the dryness of his mouth and the trembling hands folded in his lap, experiencing. If the chauffeur should come at him now it was Druff who wouldn't stand a chance. The MacGuffin was gone. He was forsaken, abandoned. If he could only get some rest it might return. (Having a MacGuffin took it out of you. It certainly wasn't for the fainthearted, and Druff realized it was a good thing Dick had backed down about the tire pressure thing. Because if he hadn't it would probably be the City Commissioner who'd be driving now, and he knew this was exactly the wrong time for him to be operating heavy machinery.) My God, he thought, returned from his parenthesis and in the world again and, picking up on an idea he'd had in this same limousine that very morning—well yesterday, actually, but since he'd last been home—not only am I going stupid, I'm getting crazy!

He wondered if he shouldn't attempt some rapprochement with the driver, at least lower the window which separated them. Then thought no, it was a bad idea, a sign of weakness, the worst thing he could do. Let Druff sit in aloof luxury, distant, behind bulletproof glass, pulled along his streets like a Caesar in a Triumph. Meanwhile, meanwhile, the dirty son of a bitch could plot to his traitorous, mingy little heart's content. It would keep him occupied.

So, feigning indifference, Druff sat back, inappetent, a commissioner most high, vaguely colonial, almost military, a visiting fireman, a "Guv," any touring, pidgin-English'd muckamuck and grand panjandrum, in fact, who ever showed the flag or put a dinner jacket on in the jungle. Reviewing his Streets and—— What's this? What's this? What's wrong with this picture?

Amazed. Flabbergast. Astonished.

Maybe they'd gone five blocks. It was almost four o'clock in the morning. It could have been rush hour. Well, not rush hour but the nervous edge of it, rush hour's fuzzy, fish-nor-fowl atemporal margins. The traffic of people who want to beat the traffic. And drove with the same jumpy, tailgating, lane-changing abandon. These people might have been refugees, the first to hear news of a disaster on the Emergency Broadcast Band. Were enemy planes on their way to drop the Big One? Had there been an "event" at the nuclear power station? Was it meltdown? Had a freight car been derailed, was it bleeding toxic waste? Druff, attempting to switch the radio on, fumbled with some controls. He touched the eject button on the tape deck. He pressed "open" and the drawer on the compact disc player slid out. Perhaps the driver controlled the radio. Druff lowered the window between them. "Quick," he said, "turn on the radio." Music from an easy-listening station filled the car. "No," Druff said, "change the station. See if there's news."

"News on the hour," the chauffeur said.

"Just *see.*"

It was all music on FM. On AM it was mostly music with an occasional talk or call-in show.

"What's happening?" Druff asked. "Where's all this traffic coming from?"

"Which traffic?"

"What do you mean 'what traffic?' *This* traffic! Just look at these streets. If it isn't bumper-to-bumper yet, it's damn near. I've never seen it like this."

Dick said nothing.

"I wonder where the traffic came from," the commissioner muttered and almost pressed his face against the window. It was as if he were in some principal city he'd heard about but never seen. It was as if he were taking in the sights. He stared in wonder at lines of automobiles stopped at cross streets waiting for the lights to change, at individual cars jimmying their way into the flow, from curbs, from alleys and parking garages. On either side of him he could see drivers and passengers in other vehicles glance his way as they pulled alongside him and tried to make out who was riding in the important-looking limo. He stared back as curiously. It was the middle of the goddamn night. "Jesus Christ," he said. "What's going on?"

"It's a service economy," Dick snapped waspishly. "In case you haven't heard."

"It's the middle of the night," he told the man. "In case you haven't noticed."

"Oh, I noticed," Dick said. "I noticed, all right. I notice lots of things."

"I notice," Druff said coolly, restoring a proper pH balance to their relationship, but then, unwilling to take him on in his condition, added, "I still don't understand about the traffic."

"Well, it's the nurses," said the spy.

"The nurses."

"Changing shifts. The nurses changing shifts."

Druff, no stranger to hospitals—his several pneumothoraxes, his heart bypass surgery—said, "They come on at seven in the morning, at three in the afternoon. They come on at eleven at night."

"That's all changed," his driver said companionably. "They come on at three in the morning, and again at eleven. They come on at seven at night. It's experimental. It plays hell with their menses unless they have the middle shift, the eleven-to-seven one, but the thinking today is that PMS gives them an edge. It's supposed to be good for the patients."

"Is this true?"

"It would be easy enough to check out, wouldn't it?" Dick said smugly.

"Don't you worry," the commissioner said, "I'm *going* to check it out."

"Do that," Dick said.

"They can't all be nurses."

"Of course they aren't all nurses. They're bakers. Haven't you noticed the rolls and bread taste better recently? Sweeter? Fresher? It used to be the bakers came in at two, two-thirty to heat up their ovens, roll out their doughs. Now they go in an hour later, more. It's cutthroat but it's the consumer who benefits. The deliverymen couldn't care less. They get to sleep an extra hour, so the Teamsters got no kick coming either."

He *had* noticed. The bread *did* taste better.

"It's nurses and bakers," Druff said.

"It's nurses and bakers. It's guys who roll up your morning paper and stick them in those little plastic wrappers. *There's* an industry that's tripled in the last few years."

"Tripled."

"Sure," Dick said. "*The New York Times* gets delivered nationwide. *The Wall Street Journal, USA Today.* At *least* tripled. And what about the guys who have to drive their trucks to the airport to pick up those papers when they come in on the flights? And what about the guys who service those trucks? Or the men and women who print up the wrappers or carry them to the distributors?

"It's kids riding home from delivering pizzas, managers of fast food joints from closing up. Sure," he said, "these days it's a service-oriented economy. It's poor saps on night shifts and minimum wage."

The City Commissioner of Streets looked away from the traffic and into the sky for a fireball. It was easier to believe in a sneak attack and a mushroom-shaped cloud than in much of this stuff. It was what he'd only recently been telling someone in a dream, that the world was getting away from him, that all its new amenities were overbearing somehow, and seemed, here, at ground level, under the colored, blinking warning lights on the tops of all those tall buildings, beneath the tangled flight paths of all those planes, guiding them, passing them on, like a kind of crowd control.

Druff thought he could see Dick's eyes watching him in the rearview mirror. He seemed to be waiting for some sort of response. "Well," he said, "it just seemed to me there was a lot of traffic for this time of night."

"Sure," Dick said acidly, "it's chauffeurs driving their playboy bosses home from a night on the town." Using the control in the front of the car, he drove the window back up between them.

Druff, in traffic, a bit fearful, isolated in the false, municipally dispensated coze of his glass and leather booth, confused, puzzled by the bad cop/good cop/bad cop avatars of this bad cop and less-than-civil servant, invoking the MacGuffin with fervid, almost hot Hail-Mary hope, thrown by the loyalties, the suspect, undermined, indeterminate allegiances in the general air and who'd, within the hour, arisen from the bed of a buyer to whom, for nothing, he'd given secrets and promised streets and so whose own allegiances were compromised and perhaps, if the MacGuffin in question was an avenging MacGuffin, should maybe have been a touch more chary about just whom he wanted there in the back seat with him, if only because of the old Let-him-who-is-without-sin proprieties and, if he needed other reasons, because, too, he understood about two-edged swords and the hedged consequences of magic, knowing if for no other reason than that he was a fifty-eight-year-old man already disappeared into his tailoring, six-sevenths, at the *outside* six-sevenths, but, in a guy with his history of blebs and leg stenotics and the long, jammed zippers of his arteries, more likely nine-tenths, more likely ten-elevenths, most likely fifty-eight–sixtieths or even fifty-eight–fifty-ninths gone, that it was easier to spring a rabbit from a hat than to stuff one back in again, but invoking it (Him, Her, the Muse of his plot line) anyway, like some jeopardized Samson shoving the stone furniture around. Because he hadn't slept, see. Because he hadn't slept even if within the hour he'd arisen from the Glorio bed and perhaps even scarfed a wee nosh of a nap in an armchair in the Glorio lobby. Because he hadn't slept and looked like hell and felt like shit and was vulnerable as a chicken to the fox in the front seat. "Cary Grant," he silently prayed, "thou shouldst be living at this hour!"

And shut his eyes.

When he opened them again he felt, though they'd gone only another two dozen blocks, refreshed. Traffic had considerably thinned, but they were stopped four or five cars back at a signal waiting on a green left-turn arrow.

He lowered Dick's window.

"Well," the man said, "what is it this time?"

"I was just thinking," Druff said, "I have more conversation with you than I do with my wife. We do more bickering, too."

"You should take that up with your wife."

"What is it," Druff said, "how do I explain your nerve? It can't just be tenure or the peaceable kingdom standoff between public servants, the lion/lamb sleeping arrangements we lay on each other, our mutual in-it-together durance. Sooner or later something stirs the straw. A smell, a sound, a movement, a look."

"You're really something, Commissioner. Think you can put me off with your one-on-one, you sweet-talker, you? Is a sound made in the forest if the Lincoln-Douglas takes place and there's no one to hear? Maybe we never even had this conversation. I mean, why'd you call me? You got two drivers. Why'd you pick *me* to wake in the middle of the night? You don't even trust me."

"The only thing I don't understand," said City Commissioner of Streets Druff, "is why anyone would go to such lengths. To put a twenty-four-hour tail on me, we never close. There are jobs in this town that make mine look pathetic. And I'm not so bad. Really," he said, "I'm not so bad at all. I'm not greedy. I don't solicit. I *never* hold my hand out. My policy—I hope you're getting all this, Dick—has always been you call me up we make an appointment. We meet for drinks, we ask about each other's kids, we look at one another's snaps. My God, Dick, sometimes we get so caught up we never even get to the point. That's happened. That's happened plenty of times. More than you'd think. Because we're each too embarrassed, if you take my meaning. Because a fellow thinks his innards are a hideous thing, his secret manners, what he does with his fluids. Jesus, Dick, we come on like we were career diplomats, secretaries of state. All of us, all of us do. Like we had silver hair and cards with our names embossed. Like we shower three times a day and speak only after we've tippy-tapped the crystal with our butter knives and have the attention of the table. And even then only to make gracious speeches, to thank our guests for coming and eating up our food. Folks are so shy, Dick. That's why there's actually less evil in the world than more.

"And none of us really thinks well of himself. Though we talk a good game and may try to drive our flimsiness off with our self-importance.

"Jesus, is that light stuck, or what? I have a theory that that Su'ad kid might have been killed because something was wrong with the traffic signal. That it wouldn't turn red on the driver or something, and finally she got impatient, didn't notice the car—maybe he didn't have his lights on, maybe one was out, maybe he was just less than that mile from home where they say most automobile accidents take place—and she stepped off the curb without ever seeing it. That's all that would have had to happen. From then on it's all bingo bango, that's all she wrote, good night nurse. Just look at that one up there if you want an example. Honk the horn, see can we get a little action here. Just listen to me, will you. So impatient, and I'm City Commissioner of Streets, for goodness sake."

"Then why don't you behave like one?"

Rather than sounding rude, the question, at least its tone, had seemed conciliatory, or as if Dick was waiting for an explanation, anything he could mark down as a mitigating or exculpatory circumstance. Well, the commissioner thought, that seemed fair. He would try to meet them— tired as he was, he was under no illusion any longer, if he ever was, that Dick was working on his own; there had to be at least two of them, at *least* two, since Dick himself had said that Druff could just as well have called Doug—halfway.

"Would you really have me behave like one?" he asked in what, playing to Dicky's gallery, he hoped was a sort of wounded wonderment. "I mean *would* you? I mean, look at me. I mean, even if there *are* guys in City Hall with juice and firepower to beat the band, I'm Street Czar here. There are no other gods before me in the greater metropolitan area. Along the byways and highways, at least. On the blocks, at a minimum.

"I mean what about cable? Do you know what a cable franchise is worth to a street czar in a market like ours? What just maybe HBO or MTV is going for these days? We ain't Chicago. Hell, we ain't Detroit or even Indianapolis. Do you have any idea? Well, you could put your kids through college. You could put your kids' kids through and have enough left over to buy everyone a fine dress and a nice suit for all their graduations. And I'm not even counting the buck or buck and a half skimmed off the top from the installation fees, or the two or three cents he realizes off every item on every order filled by the Home Shopping, or the penny for postage and handling.

"There are people who have founded fortunes, Dick, from behaving like City Commissioners of Streets. And I'll tell you the truth—we're telling the truth here, we're telling the truth, we're clearing the air— sometimes I wish I'd been more like them. Sometimes I wish I could have put my scruples behind me and gone for the mink fur with the chinchilla lining and just chucked the good gray Republican cloth or never claimed it again when it went to the dry cleaners. Rose Helen might have been a happier woman today if I had, Mikey a different young man.

"Well," Druff said, "if wishes were horses beggars would ride. What's done's done, right, Dick?"

The left-turn arrow had come and gone and now they were waiting for it again. Only one car was in front of them.

"Oh," Druff said comfortably, "my intention isn't to whitewash my- self. —Someone really ought to make a note of that signal. The timing's off. And that's another thing, one more area a City Commissioner of Streets could clean up, could pull it in plenty, make it worth his while to have his own gnome in Zurich. Because location's what it's all about to the merchants."

"Location."

"I agree with you," Druff said. "If he's on his toes the first thing a merchant does when he opens up in a new location is try and get next to someone like me—— get him to fiddle with the traffic patterns, hold the Right or Left Turn on Green Arrow Only burning forever if it favors his shop, snuff it like that one there if it doesn't. Did you know, Richard, that out in San Francisco, out in San Francisco, Chinatown is where it is today because back in the twenties the City Commissioner of Streets threw in his lot with the egg-roll interests and created it entirely out of traffic flow?

"So behave like a City Commissioner of Streets? Come on, kid, why not tell me to put a patch over my eye, wear my hand in a hook, my leg in a peg, and go for a pirate?"

They were still at the goddamn light, still waiting on the green arrow, almost posed there like racers waiting for a checkered flag, Druff smarting under the pressure of his own blocked flight path. "Jesus," he said cunningly, "there's all the latest wrinkles. There's CDs back here and practically a microwave to boil my soup. Ain't there a damn siren on this thing?"

"There's a siren." The chauffeur in him sounded almost miffed that Druff didn't know the equipment.

"Use it, then," commanded the City Commissioner of Streets.

"Use it? What about Dum dum de dum dum? What about the neighbors?"

"Screw the neighbors. Use it. Step on it. Take me home."

Almost wearily the man made a show of producing a Mars light from somewhere beneath the dash and slapping it on the roof.

"Turn it on. Use it. Let's get out of here." Druff lowered all the limousine's windows. Instantly they were awash in piercing sound, noise.

"So what do you have on me?" Druff suddenly demanded, enraged, furious, startling his spy. *"What do you have on me besides the crap I've been handing you to take up your time and run out your tape?"*

He'd pulled down one of the jump seats and moved into it. He'd leaned his head through the partition opened between them and was speaking devastating, incriminating things in a normal voice directly into his driver's head, decibels beneath the ability of any sound equipment to register it against the continuous crescendo of the siren. "Just what, eh? What? The sexual goods? Big deal. Everyone alive has sexual goods. If they never even raised a hard-on they have them. There are no eunuch hearts. There ain't a pussy living could pass a white-glove inspection. Not inside your maiden aunt in old lace and mothballs. Not under your mommy before she met your daddy. The sexual goods is just what's baked inside all those innards I was trying to tell you about.

"So just what? Tell me what you're looking for, maybe I can help you find it.

"Who's after my job? You ain't the private sector, you aren't the type. Who's after my job? Is it Basset in Parks? Murphy in Hospital Administration? Who are my enemies here? Give me a clue. Sounds like? Is it Roth from Sanitation? Stern out of Water Treatment, De Conde from the art museum, someone on the school board? Somebody else? Is it Lap, the alderman? Yalom, the comptroller? Just who am I up against? What? Because ain't we pals, don't we go back, aren't we thick? *I'd* tell *you.* Honest injun I would. *I'd* tell *you* who you were up against. I will, as a matter of fact. You're up against me. Look for me on the monuments, I'll be waiting for you. Look for me up along the ledges. Down by the railroad tracks where the freight trains live. Among the struts and spars and webbing on the spans above the rivers. Expect me in the cages of the tigers and the bear pits at the zoo. I'll be right there behind you on the newspaper that lines the bottom of the bird cage. We're into melodrama here, turf, putsch and the Higher Bullshit. Look for me backstage, on the catwalks, in the costume jewelry on the heavy chandelier dangling from the ceiling of the opera house."

Despite what the Mars light and siren seemed to be saying, they were proceeding slowly, moving along barely faster than the pace of a float in a parade. The chauffeur seemed cowed and interested. Druff was moved, very excited. Past four, almost into false dawn, after the heaviest date he'd ever had, and him fifty-eight already, practically pushing sixty, and that meal heavy too for a man in his delicate position on the actuarial tables, Druff was feeling and talking like the old Bobbo again. He took another reading of their stately pace, noted its discrepancy with the terrific sound they made, the bewildered responses of what was left of the traffic. This was MacGuffin. This was MacGuffin, too, he thought. These odd displacements, the skewed idiosyncratic angle of their engagement.

Dick said something the commissioner couldn't hear. Druff asked him to please turn off the siren, how did he expect to be heard over all that racket.

"I think you are," Dick said, "if you want to know."

Druff didn't follow him, listened for hints in the tone of his voice, from which, like the stilled siren, all hostility seemed to have been drained. Indeed, they seemed to have exchanged moods— Dick, exhausted, now as worried and wounded as the commissioner had been twenty minutes earlier, puzzling the traffic, parsing the now-you-see-it-now-you-don't essence of his fled MacGuffin. It's what Dick might have been doing, lying back, nursing his abeyant energy, waiting for the proper growing conditions of a fallow strength. His voice was not just polite, it was courteous, almost obsequious. Like the fearful voice of a fallen foe. He would tell Druff anything he wanted to know. What Druff wanted to know was the question to the answer he had just provoked. Dick the Spy, who seemed to know so much about him, evidently knew this, too. "I said I think you are. You asked for an enemies list. You'd have to be on it. In my opinion. Right up there."

"Jeez," said Druff, "out of the mouths of babes."

And, turning around on the jump seat, sat back. Leaning his head against the window between them, closed again, resting his hair, leaving greasy trace elements from Glorio's bed—hair tars, soured breath shellacs, lamb and soufflé resins, love-nest suets—on the rapidly amortizing municipal glass. He was so tired. He couldn't remember when he'd been so tired. And rode braincase to braincase with the driver, only the partition intervening. He could have been more comfortable, of course, if he'd stretched out on the long leather back seat, but it was worth his life to move just then. He just couldn't do it, it just wasn't in him. When, he wondered, did those guys in the movies catch catnaps? Always on the go, on the run, making a moving target of themselves. All that going, going, going, all that stress. Boy, thought Druff, it took a heap of living to make a heap of living. A man his age? Was it worth it? Yeah, he thought, tasting Glorio's glorious gall again, her mouth gone off like laundry. But recognizing the pattern now, the dangerous action/respite pulses of adventure, would not permit himself to drift off. That's why he sat in the jump seat. That's why he pulled himself up.

Right up there? Well, he didn't believe him. A politician, even so peripheral a one as himself, had enemies. The simplest candidacy called them down on your head—— your opponent, everyone in the other fellow's campaign, everyone who would vote against you. And it was a myth that they didn't hold grudges, that everyone came together again after you sent off your concession telegram and read it against the silenced dance band and canceled joy of your disappointed rooters and partisans. Add your enemies to your enemies list, add your rooters and partisans. Well, it was a question of worldview, wasn't it? Of Manichaean divisions. Darkness, light. Of generosity, of the hint in the heart that you don't live long enough to afford generosity. It was ancient political principle, the basis of party. Frighten the demons, fend bears with the fire. Or use it to dance around the light. Joy factions, fear. The there's-no-tomorrows. The waste-not-want-nots. Lo the Democrats, lo Republicans. You had enemies. He had enemies.

Oh, Mikey, Mikey, Mikey, Druff mourned his boy. Whose trouble was that he had no facts. No hard information. Was without data, proofs, lowdown. Chapter and verse. Grounds. Had neither at hand nor on call any of the hard evidentiaries of the world, none of its soft circumstantials. Who was neither learning-disabled—he knew his alphabet when he was three, could read when he was still in kindergarten—nor stupid so much as plunked down in a world he did not take in. (He confused, for example, motels and hotels, always said the one when he meant the other. *Mo*tels, Druff had constantly to remind him, stood for *mo*tor hotels. They were the ones with the swimming pools.) It was as if, at entirely the wrong age for it, he had been moved to a country whose language he did not understand, would never completely master.

Also there was the question of his alarming, unreasonable fears. He lived at a level beneath cause, some constant red-alert life. Druff remembered—this would have been before seat belts came in—that Mikey insisted that all the doors in an automobile be locked before he would let his father—otherwise he would cry, howl, scream bloody murder—turn the key in the ignition.

Well, he was craven. To this day he winced at fireworks, was uneasy in electrical storms, terrified when fuses blew or the phone lines were down. It was as if he'd been raised in air raids, rubble.

It wasn't, Druff knew, so much for his own safety he feared as the safety of his family. "Mom, Dad, I'm back," he'd call when, no matter the hour, he let himself into the house. And if he or Rose Helen didn't immediately respond he would march through the rooms looking for them. Nor was it love that made him call out this way. He needed protection. It was his fear of being suddenly orphaned. He needed protection, he needed reassurance. "Are we rich?" he would ask when he was still a teenager. "We're comfortable," Druff or his mother would tell him. He might mention the name of some friend's parents. "Are we as comfortable as they are?" "Jesus," Druff said, lying on the couch, his head up on pillows, *"I* sure am." "No, really, Dad, no fooling. Don't kid. Are we well off?" Druff estimated the size of his estate for him. "Is that net worth?" "What's net worth?" (He was willing to tell him what they had. He only wanted to make sure the boy understood the term. Maybe, he reasoned, it might be a way of finally bringing his kid into the world.) "After probate. After outstanding debts." "Gross," Druff said. "Does that include insurance?" "Of course it includes insurance." "But you're rated, Daddy," Mikey said, "you can't *get* insurance." "I'm a municipal official. I get term insurance." "Do you have to take a physical for term insurance?" "I get the maximum for my grade. If I wanted to purchase additional insurance I'd have to take a physical." Mikey was uncomfortable. "What about the house? Does it include the house?" "My term insurance?" "Your estate."

So the commissioner began to tell his factless, troubled, finally unreassurable son about certain deals that went down, little fiddles he was involved in at the Hall. He made them seem innocuous, said he was doing only what all politicians did, but made him promise never to discuss any of this with his friends. To a certain extent Mikey seemed appeased, but Druff wondered if he'd made a mistake when the boy started coming to him with questions about how much time his father would have to serve if he was caught. "How long can they keep you in jail if you're found guilty of taking bribes, Dad?" "Oh," Druff said, "if you've *been* bribed, they usually let you off with a fine. If you've *asked* for the bribe they generally give you up to three weeks per thousand." The boy shook his head, concerned. "Oh, don't be such a worrywart," he counseled his son, "you know it's your dad's policy only to accept bribes." "I know that," Mikey said, "it's what all those fines could do to your net worth."

Maybe he was exaggerating. Maybe he made Mikey seem worse than he really was. But he had him dead to rights in the essentials. His factless condition. His craven fear of the world, the frightful picture he had of himself left alone in it. His awful, debilitating dependency.

Though to look at him—— Well, to look at him the word "debilitating" would never have occurred. He'd belonged to the same gym for years. Had been working out since before anyone had ever heard terms like "fitness craze," "health food," "steroids." Even in blazers he looked muscular, even in suits, heavy winter overcoats, sheepskin jackets.

Power giving him neither self-confidence nor ease—he always wore his seat belt, still checked to see that all the car doors were locked before setting out on a journey—taking some weird, limited comfort not in sports heroes but in teams, leagues, as if it was only in the collective that he hoped to find some paradigm of fitness or invincibility to stand in for the pervasive flaws and frailties he saw all about him—Rose Helen's just perceptible limp, Druff's bust blebs and constricted heart; perhaps even a sense of his own naïveté (his ruling passion)—and that so terrified him about the world, his old anxiety that it was haunted and that when his mother and father died only he would be left, forced to spend his nights alone in it.

The city had no baseball franchise. Mikey fastened onto the Atlanta Braves, a ball club whose fortunes he could follow on cable. He rooted for his hometown football and basketball teams.

But it was hockey that consumed him and, of hockey clubs, the St. Louis Blues with which he passionately identified. He'd chosen hockey partly because of its long season, partly because of its intricate, complicated second season of play-offs, Mikey's personal Manichaean system of extended drama, his second-chance, comeback heart. But mostly he'd chosen St. Louis because he'd been there once with his father, been to the Arena to watch them play, sat with him in the owner's box, openly enjoying the privileged, baksheesh arrangement, sucking up power and favor and finding a kind of earnest in them of his dad's license, some tiny, comfortable toehold on childhood and immortality. At any rate, Mikey had cast his lot with the St. Louis Blues Hockey Club. And though, except for an occasional game on television or the even rarer—although he watched for them every night—news clip on the local ten o'clock news—the town had no hockey franchise either—he never saw them play another game, he'd become a sort of whiz at picking them up on distant radio stations.

One night—this would have been when the boy was already in his twenties—they were in their bedroom and heard the downstairs door slam.

"Mom," Mikey shouted, "Daddy? I'm back."

"Up here," Rose Helen called out.

"Dad too?"

"I'm all right," Druff said.

He loomed powerfully in their doorway, huge, vastly troubled. Druff had a sudden vision of burst seat belts, broken door locks.

"KMOX was fading," their son said. "Sometimes, when it fades like that, you can pick it up better in the car. I listened out there."

"Did we win?" Rose Helen pretended to her son she was a fan. You went along to get along.

"Afterward, they were talking to the Star of the Game? He said the owner is thinking of moving the team to Canada. Dad, is that true?"

"I don't know, Mikey. I don't know anything about it."

"He's a friend of yours, isn't he?"

"No."

"We sat in his box."

"We were visiting firemen," Druff said.

"But you talked with him."

"Fireman to fireman. He wouldn't recognize my hook and ladder today."

"But we sat in his box. How'd we get to sit in his box?"

"God damn it, Mikey. I was barely introduced to the man. We had those seats because I was a guest of the St. Louis streets commissioner. He had an in. If he came here he could go out on the snowplows or ride up front in the trucks when they salt for ice."

The boy had developed a curious tic. He closed his eyes when his father became impatient or said humiliating things to him. It was as if by squeezing the light from his vision he was able to hide, go so far the words never reached him. He did that now. It broke Druff's heart, the son of a bitch.

The commissioner softened.

"Even if they moved," he said, "you'd still be able to pick up their games on the radio."

"If they moved to one of those states they only speak French?"

"Quebec is the only province they speak French. Don't they already have a team?"

"The Montreal Canadiens," Mikey said. "The Quebec Nordiques."

"There, you see?"

"What if he took them to one of those far-off places? I wouldn't even be able to pick them up in the car."

"Then when they played in the States. You could hear them when they played Chicago. On the Pittsburgh station. Plenty of places."

"Half their games are at home."

"It hasn't happened yet. These things are complicated. Most of the time they fall through."

The thin reassurance seemed to settle him, but then he found out there was a newsstand downtown where they sold yesterday's out-of-town papers. Each day the kid took their car and fought the traffic and went there to buy the St. Louis papers. He pored over details about the impending sale. Taking hope—more than hope, euphoria—when articles began to appear saying that a consortium of St. Louis businessmen was trying to put a package together to buy the team and keep it in the city. Mikey's moods hung on these delicate negotiations. He followed the proceedings closely. He kept Druff posted. He dragged Druff in.

And Druff—this was what constituted current events for Mikey—almost felt honored, an elder statesman, a good gray eminence. He followed the proceedings himself. He sent Doug or Dick out to buy his own out-of-town papers, special-ordering the Canadian papers, not just the ones in Calgary and cities even farther west with a declared interest in acquiring the team, but the Toronto and Montreal papers, too, where the sale of the Blues was also current events. He went over the information with Mikey, parsing the various accounts and rumors like Americans in a foreign country discussing late-breaking but already outdated developments in the Cuban Missile Crisis, say, as new reports filtered down to the *International Herald Tribune,* and then to Americans lingering in foreign cities, waiting on every fresh detail.

In a way, they'd never been closer, more psychological with each other.

The team had gone into a slump. Mikey suggested they wouldn't be themselves again until the issue of where they'd be playing next year was resolved.

"Most of the players are married," he said. "They have homes, kids in school. In a situation like this they have to be under all sorts of pressure. They have to be worried about what they'll be able to get for their houses. I mean if you're forced to sell your house, doesn't that mean you might have to take less for it than you could ordinarily expect? And I've been looking at the housing ads in the St. Louis papers. It's a buyer's market out there right now. They'd have to sell at a loss."

"That's true," Druff agreed.

"And what about their kids? The players are young. Their children are mostly in grade school."

"That's right."

"It puts a kid in a bad position. I mean, if he thinks he might be in a different city next year, let alone a different country, he's going to have a lot on his mind. His grades are bound to suffer even if he isn't deliberately trying to goof off."

"There's something in that."

"And children can be cruel. His classmates don't always understand that it isn't the child's dad who wants to move, that he's only going where the job takes him."

"So?"

"So maybe they're fans, so maybe they think the team *wants* to leave town, that maybe they took a *vote* on it or something, that they're deliberately betraying St. Louis. All right, they don't know any better. But they could tease the kid, pass remarks. And if the kid isn't mature enough, and doesn't entirely understand the situation himself, maybe he feels the same way. Unconsciously, he could begin to side with his classmates. He could become depressed, even sullen. Communication breaks down. He won't speak to his dad, he's nasty to his mom."

"I see what you're driving at."

"Sure. And meanwhile this is going on in all the houses of all the players. In the defensemen's families, in the houses of the wings. In the home of the goalie, in the home of the center. Even in the coach's house, though his kids are probably older and ought to know better. Pressure's got to build up. There are going to be fights. Things will get said which shouldn't get said. It's in the heat of the moment, sure, but that doesn't change anything."

"I'm certain you're right."

"And aren't we forgetting something here, Dad?"

"What's that?"

"That no matter what we read in the papers, no matter how many

St. Louis and Banff, Calgary, Toronto, Montreal and other Canadian columnists and newspapers we read, we're only getting part of the story. They're there. They're on the scene. They're hearing things we can't possibly know anything about—— talk in the locker room, things they pick up on the road from opposing players."

"I hadn't thought of that."

"The latest rumors about the changing positions and attitudes of the various owners. Gee, if we think *we're* confused about all the mixed signals that come in, you can imagine how *they* must feel!"

"That's a good point."

"So the thing isn't that we've been losing, but that we've been losing by so little. That we've managed to keep from being blown away."

"You've really got a handle on this thing, Mike," Druff ventured feelingly.

And then Mike asked him to use his influence with the St. Louis Commissioner of Streets either to dissuade the owner of the Blues from selling or to see to it that the St. Louis consortium of businessmen that was seeking to buy the team was successful in its efforts.

Because what Druff hadn't understood was that all this talk about the Blues, however distant, however remote from Druff's full blebs, precarious as blown bubble gum, however wide of the mark of his marked heart, was finally concerned with Druff's existence, the flawed ramparts and bulwarks where Mikey crouched, his son's magic, superstitious circle of well-being.

He couldn't even blame him, couldn't cut bait or pare his losses.

Because how old could M. have been during Druff's deathbed speech, nine, ten, eleven?

Dick had come around and opened the door for him.

Druff must have looked surprised, possibly threatened. He may even have thrown his hands up defensively.

"You startled me."

"I thought you were asleep," Dick said.

"Lost in thought."

"You've got nothing to think about, Commissioner." Druff didn't take it personally but the driver thought he had. Dick lowered his voice. "Oh, Christ," he said, "I didn't mean that the way it sounded. I'm sorry. I got this bug up my ass. Trouble at home. Shit with the wife. Like

someone said, we go back, you and me. Thick and thin, long and short.
I know it don't always seem that way, but I got no complaints. It ain't
anything personal. Hell, you've been *good* to me. I know I sounded off,
but we both said some stuff. Here, let me help you. You can stiffen up
pretty good on those jump seats. They're more trouble than they're
worth, you ask me. Hey, sit where you want. Sit where you can keep
an eye on me. The way I've been at you? I just wanted to let you know.
You *don't* have anything to think about. Not from this quarter. Mum's
the word. Mrs. D. don't hear boo from this quarter. Not a peep. Hellfire,
Commissioner, if you could just find it in your heart to let the past forty
minutes' worth of bygones be bygones, you have nothing to fear from
me.

"And I'll tell you something else. Old Doug isn't going to hear
anything about it either."

"Get away from me."

"What did *I* do?"

"Hey," Druff said, changing his tune, "nothing. It's how I tell people
good night."

And let himself into his darkened house, though before he went
upstairs for what little remained of the night, he made, in the dark, his
way to the kitchen where, still in the dark, not bothering with the light
switch, he fumbled about for a few seconds around the kitchen table
where, near the unwashed cereal bowl, the glass in which perhaps an
inch or inch and a half of milk lay souring, hard by the crumbs of toast
and drying smears of jelly, he found, propped against the toaster, where
the thirty-year-old man-child couldn't miss it, the note Rose Helen had
left for him and which, because it had been laid in so cheery a place
as a kitchen, so redolent of his mom's home cooking, against an appli-
ance designed not to reheat the bread she did not bother to bake but
to receive fresh slices of the packaged white bread he preferred, he
would not even remove, reading the signs of the message instead of the
message itself, and which Druff, the adventurer/philanderer neither of
them had bargained for, did not bother to read either, that would
undoubtedly say (there in the dark, so why even bother with a light,
which just might wake him, draw him, concerned, who was always
concerned, who lived in the depths of concern as a fish lives in water
and who, even if he didn't clear tables, had made of himself this

safety-first sentinel, this factless, better-safe-than-sorry son who pulled space heaters from their wall sockets, standing lamps, radios, anything electric which, at least in the estimation of his concerned imagination, could reach the critical mass to draw energy, ignition flame, into the kitchen to check, to make sure their house hadn't been broken into and his parents left for dead in their beds): "Michael sweetheart, I'm upstairs in bed. Dad's not home yet, but called to say that he's with some men arranging about that Marathon he's been trying to get for the city, and not to wait up. I hope you had a good evening at school, or in the gym working out. If you're going to have something to eat, please rinse out the dishes before you go to bed. They're hard to wash when food is left standing in them too long, and they attract bugs. See you in the morning. Love, Mother."

But it was too late, had already been too late when Druff had let himself into the darkened house and, ever so quietly, and with as much care as if there had been a real MacGuffin in his life, made his way into the kitchen to confirm what he should have taken for granted in the first place, which he *did* take for granted. It would have been too late even if he hadn't fumbled about at the kitchen table for those few seconds, even if he hadn't clinked the spoon in the cereal bowl or brushed his arm against the box and shaken the cornflakes in it.

"Dad?" his son stage-whispered from the stairs. "Dad, is that you down there, Dad?"

"I'm all right, Mikey," Druff said.

Down came the boy the rest of the way and switched on the light in the kitchen.

"Why didn't you turn a light on? You could have fallen."

"I didn't fall. I'm fine. What are you doing up so late? And if you're so worried about people falling in the dark, why'd you turn off that hall light Mother leaves on all night?"

Now, in their bright kitchen, Mikey performed his strange, blind tic. He shut his eyes. Druff, who'd picked the tic up from his son, shut *his* eyes. They watched the tinted darkness of their squeezed lids, passed through the waves and breakers of their mutual resentments. Mikey went first.

"So," he said, "how'd it go, Dad?"

Druff didn't realize at first what his son meant, answering, "Fine. I said I'm all right."

"No," the kid said, "I meant with Scouffas. I meant with that other guy."

Hurriedly, Druff glanced down at the note Rose Helen had left.

(So you can imagine how he felt. You can just imagine.)

But Mikey was already speaking. "Jeez," said their man-child, making his queer symbolic associations, working his own ritualized actuarials, factlessly, baselessly, adding years to his father's life, extending by decades the frontiers of his own boundless childhood, "you could have knocked me over and over with a feather. Any city can have a baseball team. Seattle has one, unlikely towns like Minneapolis and Milwaukee. And all those places in the Sunbelt? Come on. San *Diego?* Give me a break. They're jokes, they're just jokes. I don't care how many times they win their division, *or* the pennant. Or the World Series, even. They're just jokes. Or can you imagine a state like Texas having *two* teams? In the Lone Star State? That's just got to be graft. Somebody must have had their hand out big time. You know how that works. I mean I don't have to tell *you!* If it ever came out, the people responsible could get years. *Years!* They'd be put away so fast for so long their kids would never see them again. And how long do you think they'd survive locked up like that? People like that? Privileged people. People accustomed to *giving* the orders. Just the shame and disgrace would kill them if the hardened cons and the bread and water didn't get to them first.

"Don't make me laugh. Those guys would be goners.

"And I'll tell you another thing, Dad. It's one thing to have an NBA franchise, or even an NFL one. Or even your own hockey team in the NHL, but you saw what happened in St. Louis. Well, the Blues came out of that one all right, and no one's more grateful than I am, but what happened in St. Louis could happen anywhere. Let's face it, Dad, the fans are subject to the whims of the owners. And the only thing *those* people care about is the bottom line. That's where *their* loyalties lie. You're deluding yourself if you think otherwise. 'Build us a bigger stadium. Give us a tax abatement, maybe we'll stay. Promise not to go after us in the press to get better players if we don't produce. Let us raise ticket prices whenever we want. Give us a bigger percentage of the popcorn and peanuts and Cracker Jacks. Permit us to keep more from the *Cold beer, cold beer here!'* They're such *babies!* And we're at their mercy. We're at the mercy of people who have no mercy!

"You tell me I should be realistic. Well, I am. I *am* realistic. I'm realistic enough to know that the Indianapolis 500 is locked in, that the Kentucky Derby is, that it'll *always* be run in Louisville. That the Preakness belongs to Baltimore, and the Rose Bowl to Pasadena, and the Masters to Augusta. Those are American Classics, Dad, and no so-called owners can ever come along to try to change the venue."

Druff, fascinated, terrified, thought, he knows "tax abatement," he knows "venue." He's almost eloquent, he *is* eloquent.

"Well, then," the son said, "you can just imagine how I felt when I saw Mom's note. You can just imagine. So how was it? How did it go? What did they say?"

"Scouffas?" Druff said. He took up his wife's note and read in the light all he'd known in the dark would be in it, failing to predict only the additional details of his visitors' names. Rose Helen had managed to get even the difficult *I* in McIlvoy right, a tribute, he supposed, to his careful pronunciation of his absurd, complicated, unpremeditated lie. (Thinking, Why, I'm good, I'm really good. Under the guns of Old MacGuffin I'm really good.)

"Yes," Mikey said, "and that other one. What's his name, the stuffed-shirt one, the stickler—oh, what *is* his name?—McIlvoy. Did you get to see the gadget, the thing no bigger than a stopwatch? Did they let you hold it?"

"The gadget was Scouffas's department."

"Oh," Mikey said, "you'd think it would have been the stickler's."

"Life is strange, Mike," he told his son truthfully. "How'd you even know about the gadget? There's nothing about it in your mother's note."

"I think it was written up somewhere. Anyway, Mom told me about it after I got back and read her message."

"She was in bed. You woke her up? What for, to do your dishes?"

His son's eyes closed tight for three beats. It was as if he was in pained, desperate biofeedback trance. He sniffed the air, opened his eyes, then aggressively asked his father if he'd been smoking.

"What? No. Of course not."

"Maybe McIlvoy, maybe Scouffas," his son said. "There's this funny smell."

"What funny smell? I don't smell anything funny. What funny smell?"

"I don't know. This funny smell. It's not a *bad* smell."

The trace elements, Druff thought. Margaret Glorio's hair tars and breath shellacs. Royal dust from the crown rack. He smelled it himself, tasted it. Love laundry, the stale savories and sweet fetids of their rich, cloyed traffic. Was this a counterattack? Nonsense. The child was fact-less. Yet he'd heard him be eloquent. Could he also be clever? He spooked at the notion of a clever Mikey. Suppose he hated him. Suppose there was malice there, bad blood, evasion like the unsettled soup of magnetic aversion, some call in the bones for revulsion, repugnance, abhorrence, revenge. Suppose there were menace, rancor, all the pledged bitters and solemn loathelies of stalled grudge? Suppose this was the long, slow abiding of crusade, jihad, uprising, holy war? He had always known that his son's fear for Druff's life had little to do with love. But suppose his son's behavior had *nothing* to do with love? Suppose he needed him around to give his hatred something to believe in? What if his dependency had been adversarial all along? Only a campaign? Some Hundred Years' War of Getting Dad's Goat? MacGuffins were abroad in the land tonight. Thick as pea soup. Druff was breathless, he couldn't move. It was MacGuffin gridlock.

Yet when his son began speaking again it was in the same loopy register and tropes of his ancient argument.

"So how did it? You didn't say. Did they give you an indication? I know this was only preliminary, a feasibility study." He knows "only preliminary," Druff thought, he knows "feasibility." "Still and all," Mikey said, "they came all this way. Their plane was held up all that time on the ground in Denver waiting for a heating element to be replaced in the galley!" He knows *facts*. He knows the facts of my convolute lie. "I mean, they *could* have canceled. Important fellows like that! They might even have taken that stupid delay as a sign. And there must be just plenty of cities dying to get a marathon. Every Middlesex village and town, right, Dad?

"So did they give you any indication, did they hold out any hope?"

"It was all very preliminary. It was only a feasibility study."

"Sure," Mikey said. "Those birds have to play it close to the vest. It's how they are. I suppose they wouldn't be where they are today if they didn't. Still, Dad," he said, "I hope you didn't buy into any of their tired old arguments."

"Which tired old arguments?"

"Oh, you know, that there's already a Boston marathon, a New York marathon. That there are marathons in Chicago and Honolulu. All that 'oversaturated' stuff you usually hear."

"Those are factors," Druff said.

"Those *are* factors. They are. But all they're looking for are assurances. It's the consortium of St. Louis businessmen all over again. Just tell them you can get them national exposure, TV coverage. The cable sports networks are out beating the bushes looking for events to cover. You might even suggest the possibility of closed-circuit stuff on the big giant screens, spin-offs from T-shirts, paper cups with soft-drink advertising and the marathon's logo spectators can hand out to the runners as they pass critical points in the race—— Dead Man's Hill, Heartbreak Flats. Or how our marathon could be this really different marathon, open only to serious runners—— no one on crutches, no one pushing himself in a wheelchair or muscling along strapped to a board and doing the twenty-six-plus miles in push-ups or some other simple brute force variation of chinning yourself through space." He knows twenty-six-plus miles, Druff thought.

"Those are some good points," Druff said. "You should have been there."

"I wish I *had* been, Daddy."

And Druff suddenly recalled the strict, explicit terms of Dick's limited guarantees. Mrs. D. wouldn't hear a peep from that quarter, Doug wouldn't. And then his son was nattering away again, but this time in the baby talk of the more familiar mystic Mikey mode.

"Because," he was telling his dad, "an owner can move his franchise right out of a city. I suppose that if he wanted, and had the permission of the other owners, he could even shift it into a different league entirely. Owners can do just about anything they want because this is the United States of America and it's their own private property, after all. They can even let the team stay in a city but ruin it anyway by never spending any money on it to buy better players. But a marathon would

be different. It would always be our city's marathon. And there wouldn't
ever be a way it could have a losing season. I mean someone would
always win it every year, and even if their times weren't as good as the
times in the New York marathon or the Boston marathon, still, since
they invented the gadget that gives the exact degree of difficulty of a
marathon, then even if they *did* take it to another city it would still be
our marathon in all the record books. In a way it would, anyway,
because anything that came after it would have to be judged by our
weights and measures. Do you see?"

He didn't and, frankly, felt relieved he didn't—better the Mikey you
know than the Mikey you didn't—but still, he thought, rising from the
chair in which he'd been sitting, it could be a trap. "Well," he said,
lacing his fingers, pushing them through some rich semaphore, wig-
wagging weariness, beddie-byes, all the studied repertory of his Mac-
Guffin handjobs and shrugs, his shakelegs and stiffness-be-gones, audi-
tioning the full range of his showboat moods from the good-talkin'-to-
yas to his see-you-in-the-mornin's. "I guess I'll be going up," he said.
"Shall I get the light or will you do it?"

"I'll do it, Dad," Mikey said. "Good night, now."

"Good night," said Druff. And then, checking himself before passing
through it, turning slowly around in the kitchen doorway, poised there
for a curtain speech like the vaudeville bang of a rim shot, only tossed
off, thrown away, scored against the pace of the scene, as if to say, God
knows why I'm telling you this, or what made me think of it just now,
but while it's fresh in my head, and before I forget, let me try this on
for size, see how it plays in Peoria, Druff said, "Oh, hey, I meant to
tell you, I almost forgot. In the cab—it's been a long night, Doug was
tired so I sent him home and picked up a cab at their hotel—— Scouffas
and whoozis's—well, I don't know where it came from, but anyway
there was more traffic for that time of night than you can shake a stick
at, and normally I might not have noticed it but it hadn't been there
earlier—and a good thing—when we were pacing off the marathon and,
incidentally, did you know you don't actually have to strap the little
sucker to your leg like some Boy Scout's pedometer, or even hold it in
your hand like you'd find your way through the woods with a compass,
but almost just stick it there in the chauffeur's pocket and forget about
it while Doug or whoever just cruises along as if he didn't have a care

in the world, or the fate of an entire city's hopes and dreams for a
marathon of its own wasn't riding on every little bump and grind in the
road, every pothole and manhole cover, every cobblestone and speed
bump, or forget about it, that is, as long as the guy doesn't have to pull
up short or come to any sudden stops—the damn thing's so sensitive
and is programmed to make every conceivable adjustment and compen-
sation, except, as I say, for sudden stops, and that's why I say it's a good
thing that that traffic wasn't there earlier in the evening when McIlvoy
and Doug and Irv Scouffas and I were doing the dry run of the dry run
of the dry run of the contemplated battlefield or it might just have
played Oh, Well, Back to the Drawing Board with all our plans—when
I happened to notice these long delays on some of the traffic signals,
particularly on the cautious left turn on greens, but on lots of others too,
especially *where the pedestrian activates the signal in order to put the green
light in her favor,* and I say *her* favor advisedly because I suddenly
flashed on Su'ad, on how it might have happened to her, just that very
way, stepping off the fatal curb at just the fatal moment when she
became impatient and the hit-and-fatal-goddamn-run driver slammed all
that fatal second-per-second tonnage and momentum into her frail,
mortal Shiite bones. What do you think, Mikey? What do you think,
kid? Is that a scenario you can live with?"

The father studied the son during all this long speech, carefully
watching his boy's face as, wide-eyed, it bumped along in the eddies of
information then pulled up short, and opened out again into the avenues
of its snarled syntax. Abruptly, when Druff came to Su'ad's name,
Mikey's eyes squeezed shut, but it was difficult to imagine that he was
not seeing her anyway, despite whatever layers of darkness he inter-
posed between the light and his sealed, locked lids.

And didn't wait for an answer, going instead, and at a pretty good
clip, too, particularly for a guy of his advanced age at this advanced time
of the night, up the stairs to the bedroom, tired, of course, but not a
little compensated for his troubles by adventure's and danger's spiced,
chemical buzz, interested, observing himself, thinking, Oh, right, so
that's how they do it. Sure, right, yes, of course. (Removing a shoe,
pulling a sock.) Thinking, I see. Ahh. But of course. Even as you, even
as me. (Taking his pants off, one leg at a time.) Thinking (loosening his
tie, discarding his shirt, in the bathroom fumbling his shorts, peeing a

ton), Well, I have to suppose that the body has its priorities too, and that's why, caught up, we don't require as many pit stops as otherwise. (Thinking "we" now.) Brushing his teeth and thinking, Now this surprises me, it really does. And *this!* (As he bothers to floss. To *floss!*) But *really* wowed, blown away wowed, by what he does next. He takes two ten-milligram Procardia out of their plastic prescription bottle, unscrews the lid from a jar of stool softeners and removes one odd, brown, football-shaped Peri-dos softgel. He takes a Valium, considers his unusual circumstances and decides to spring for a second. (Well, diazepam, actually, since it came in generic now.) (This is amazing, Druff thinks, all those others, CIA glamour boys, or just ordinary, caught-up bystander types, professors, say, businessmen, docs off on medical convenings in Paris, part business, part pleasure, would be dipping into the generics these days. Well, why not? We'd be crazy—he thinks "we," already translated into that distinguished fraternity of fall guys, straw men and stalking horses pursued by blurry, unfocused, maniac furies and enemies—not to. Ain't a chap with a MacGuffin already in enough trouble? Does he have to buy into inflation and the exorbitant prices the big drug companies get for their pills, too?) Well! This has certainly been a lesson for him!

And the lesson is this:

Life goes on. Life goes on even in the chase scenes. Life goes on even as Grant and Stewart and Kelly and Bergman run for their lives. They would have Kleenex in their pocket, lipstick in their purse. In the climates calling for them they would have Chap Stick, sun block, insect repellent. They would have diarrhea equipment. They would need batteries for their transistor radios, stamps for their mail. Life goes on. They would need a place to cash their checks. They would have to get haircuts. Life goes on. They would require reservations, they would have to stop at the gate to obtain a boarding pass. Life goes on, life goes on. If they were religious they would be saying their prayers. They would continue to watch their salt intake and think twice before accepting an egg. They would laugh at good jokes, whistle, hum, wipe themselves, scratch where they itched, obey the laws of gravity and try not to use the strange, immediate pressures of their new situations as an excuse to start smoking again. They would, irrelevantly, dream. A glorious drudgery, life goes on. It goes on and goes on.

Then he moves to the bed and gets in beside his wife, dead to the world. It's—what?—almost five in the morning. It must be a scientific fact, not noted until just this moment, that Rose Helen, whose snores (If I had a dollar, etc.) he'd always been able to extinguish simply by reaching out and touching her shoulder and saying "No Snoring," easy as that, as if the words carried exactly the same municipal weight as his City Commissioner of Streets directives on signs ("No Parking," "No Standing," "No Loading"), doesn't snore at this time of day. Druff is certain he's uncovered a law of nature. It must be something in the five A.M. nasal atmospherics, or that snorers leave off when the birdies start up their songs, some symbiotic sound/silence deal—— din physics.

Druff, moved to the bed, slipped in beside Rose Helen, dead to the world himself, sleeps, putting everything he's got into it, with nothing left over, not even an ounce, with which to dream, let alone make speeches or sketch from the edges of his consciousness his fabled Lincoln-Douglases.

It was almost noon when he woke. He showered and dressed quickly. There was a possibility, he thought, that he might have missed Rose Helen, something, given the nature of his behavior, that was not entirely unwelcome. But he was wrong. She was in the kitchen, rubbing red seasoning into the carcass of a raw turkey. Mikey, beside her, sat on a stool peeling potatoes, pretending they were onions. He drew his shirtsleeve across his eyes, wiping away imaginary tears, pretending to flick them onto the floor. He whined. He wailed. He went boo-hoo. Conjugating noises in a toy grief. Rose Helen was laughing. Druff walked into the room. "Mama, look," said his son, breaking off, "it's Lazy Mary." Rose Helen laughed even harder.

Druff suspected something was terribly wrong.

"You're all dolled up," Rose Helen said.

The times were out of joint was what. Druff suddenly understood it was Saturday. He'd mistaken the weekend for a workday and couldn't have felt more like Rip Van Winkle if all the appliances in his kitchen had been invented since he'd gone to bed. If he'd placed his hands on a long gray beard or seen in the paper that the government had changed hands overnight. It was the weekend and he felt as deprived of time as a jailbird, cheated as any prodigal crying over the spilled milk of a misspent youth, or money down the toilet of a bad husbandry.

"I overslept," he said. (Thereby losing a piece, too, of Saturday.) "Jeez," he said, examining his suit coat, plucking his tie, "I'm dressed for downtown."

"Did you think you had to go to work today?" his son asked.

"Sure did."

"Bank dividend in your favor."

"Error," Druff said. "If the allusion's to Monopoly, 'Bank *error* in your favor' is the quote you're looking for."

"I'll fix breakfast," Rose Helen said. "Pancakes? We have Canadian maple syrup. I'll squeeze oranges."

"It's 'dividend,' Daddy, I think."

"How could it be dividend? A dividend's something already coming to you," Druff said.

Mikey looked down at the potato he was holding, considering. "I should be done with my chores by the time you finish your breakfast. We could play some Monopoly and settle it like men."

"Coffee and toast," Druff said. "Don't bother squeezing any oranges. Frozen's all right. Where's the All-Bran? God damn it, Mikey, I opened up a new box just yesterday. How many times do I have to tell you? All-Bran is not a snack food. It's medicine."

"For God's sake," Rose Helen said, "are you going to start in with him over a box of cereal?"

"He goes after it like it was potato chips!" Druff said irritably. "He puts it away like popcorn! Oh," Druff said, "now I understand the pancakes and syrup bit. Now I see what the fresh orange juice was all about. You knew he'd eaten up my All-Bran."

"Your All-Bran. *Really,*" she said.

"Well, I hope you enjoyed it," he told his son. "I just hope you found it a tasty treat. Because my colon cancer is on your head, young Mikey. My colostomy bag's just one more piece of matched luggage you'll have to learn to live with."

"Fine breakfast table conversation," Rose Helen said.

"Just who does he think he is?" Druff demanded. "Who gave *him* the right to scarf down all the roughage and high fiber in this house?"

"Don't get your bowels in an uproar, Dad," Mikey, deadpan, said.

"Toilet humor, very nice," Druff said. "Thirty years old and he still makes ca-ca jokes. Mikey, do you understand that when Jesus Christ was crucified he was only three years older than you are right now?"

"I don't see what that has to do with it," Mike said.

"No," said Druff, "I don't suppose you do. All right, Rose Helen," Druff said, "I see I'm going to have to go with the pancakes and maple syrup after all."

"Make your own goddamn breakfast," Rose Helen said.

"I *will* then," he said. Then, more softly, "Of course, any idea I may have had of playing Monopoly with Michael here has entirely left me."

"You wouldn't have anyway," Mikey said.

"No? How can you know that?"

"Because you're always trying to fool me," he said.

"Oh please," Rose Helen said, "the *both* of you!"

Well, it was the weekend, Druff thought. He was at an age when weekends spelled nothing but trouble. When they were no longer the big payoff they once had been. Baths, for example. Grooming. There was a time, he recalled, when the jokes on the radio had it that Saturday night was the night universally observed by Americans for taking their baths. Maybe it was farmers, factory workers, people in cold-water flats whose hot water was rationed, doled out on weekends. He wasn't blue collar himself, none of his people had been. His father, a traveling salesman, made *good* money, had been a stickler for the personal hygienes—— shined shoes, soap behind the ears, haircuts and finger-nails. Even dancing lessons—fox-trots, the waltz—had been high on his father's list as a kind of personal grooming, a preparation for feats of business linked in his dad's mind with the *mens sana in corpore sano* of cleanliness and presentability. So he couldn't imagine he'd ever been let off from taking baths on weekdays. Yet it was all a blur in his mind, and he had a sort of racial memory of long, ritual Saturday night baths when he lay soaking in his tub with, in effect, an entire country. Getting themselves up, sprucing.

As he remembered the wonderful *e pluribus unum* arrangements of his Friday and Saturday nights with Rose Helen at the Chi Phi Kappa house. Not only out of the question, gone forever, unimaginable.

Or MacGuffins either. He couldn't imagine being visited by his Mac-Guffin on a weekend at home. MacGuffin's night off.

Where were the museums and zoos of yesteryear, or even the Monopoly encounters of Mikey's blown hope? Druff, down Memory Lane, missed Saturday matinees.

"Truce?" he suggested suddenly, tapping toast crumbs at the corners of his mouth with a napkin, swirling his coffee like a brandy. "What say?"

Nothing, they said nothing. Michael peeled his potatoes, his wife rubbed her red seasonings. Druff sniffed at the neutral, still unroasted air. "Mnh," he said, "mhnn. Something smells good. Company coming?" Without troubling to answer, Rose Helen abandoned the turkey, left the kitchen. Druff stared at the big dead bird. "I don't suppose you've ever heard of such a thing as salmonella then?" he said, raising his voice, calling after her. "I suppose you think salmonellas don't show up in white people's kitchens. I suppose you think they're a respecter of persons. Well, that's just what they want you to think. That's playing right into their hands, Rose Helen. That's burying the old head in the sand. There you go. That's just the opening they're looking for. You hear me? Hey, I asked did you *hear* me? Did you *hear* me, you ostrich?"

"Come on, Dad," Mikey, fingering Druff's mood, his weekend irritability like some virus held in the bones, said. "Come on," he said. "Please?" Managing him, gingerly, like a handler of drunks.

"Well," Druff said grudgingly, "this will just have to be one of those unilateral truces then. It's too nice a day to quarrel and let rip," he said, quarreling and letting rip. "Because you know why Dad's dressed up like this? Not because he thought it was still the workweek. Did you think he thought it was still the workweek? Well, you *are* easily fooled then. No. It's because I thought maybe we'd all go somewhere nice together. Take you to McDonald's, get you a Big Mac, see did their new Care Bears shipment come in yet."

He didn't know why he did it. It had to be more than a moody weekend virus traveling his system, too much time on his hands, nothing happening until Monday morning when he would climb back into his limo again. (Absent emergency, of course, sudden ice storms, something fucked in the infrastructure, the pavements buckling, whole thoroughfares taken out.) His inexcusable behavior. It had to be more than cabin fever. Cabin fever? It wasn't even lunch yet. Though whatever was bitching him, the weekend was part of it, of course. Also, Druff had a MacGuffin. Anything could happen. It had been only twenty-four or so hours, but you learn fast or die when you have a MacGuffin. Basic crash course for a City Commissioner of Streets. (How's that for irony?) Already he was at least a little qualified in MacGuffin technique. No, anything *could* happen. He'd overslept. Margaret Glorio may have called. Perhaps she was taken with him. Maybe he was a dynamite fuck, him this political bigwig and all, this power-play type. She might have been a democracy groupie, some victor/spoils sport. He'd met her at Toober's after all. Car trouble or no car trouble, the City Hall hangout had been her restaurant of choice. (Two meals he'd had with her now.) Who knew? The best defense . . . He slammed back into action.

"Did anyone call?" he asked his son.

"The phone rang a couple of times."

"Well?"

"Mom got it."

"She say it was for me?"

"She didn't say."

"Listen," he told the boy, "go find your mother." Playfully he reached his hands out to Mikey's neck, straightened a pretend knot on an imaginary necktie he made believe his thirty-year-old kid wore down the front of his T-shirt. "How's them eyes?" he whispered. "All better?" It was an allusion to the tears he'd shed peeling potatoes. His eyes were shut now too, guarding against the vision of Druff's slant purpose. He'd spent a lot of time, Druff thought, crouched behind his sight today. All through his father's Monopoly, cancer bag, salmonella and McDonald's riffs. "Say how late I got home, tell her I'm still a little cranky," he instructed his son. "Ask in a nice way if there were any calls while Daddy was sleeping?"

Druff poured a second cup of coffee for himself.

Mikey lumbered off. Well, *lumbered*. Actually, he moved rather gracefully for so big a fellow. It was all that muscle gainsaid his grace, the vaguely armored, vaguely plated, faintly scaly quality of his flesh, skin's moving parts, pads of muscle like a moving man's quilted being, that lent him all the slow, frozen majesty and power of some giant, foursquare reptile. For all Druff's contemptuous swagger, he feared the kid, scared in the rudiments and deep fundamentals, like someone apprehensive in darkness, or held frozen, checked by his atavistic

willies. All that repression, all that hatred. It was maddening, Druff
thought, no day at the beach, no month in the country. He hadn't even
the pie-plate look and sweet nature of the openly retarded, but all the
feral anger and pronounced cheekbones of a psychopath, always wrong,
always belligerently logical. Druff feared the poke Mikey would one day
take at him, the swat that finished, the swipe that killed.

Or suppose, he thought when Mikey went off—it was the weekend,
all that time on his hands—company *was* coming? Druff'd just had his
ashes hauled by a beautiful woman. How could he be expected to sit
through a big meal?

"Why," Rose Helen said, "were you expecting a call?"

"Oh," Druff said, "you startled me."

"Yes," she agreed, "you look startled."

"You surprised me," he said, "your voice surprised me. I was a
million miles away. A shock to the system. Ever take up your water glass
when you reached for your tea? Has that happened to you?"

"What?" she said. "Speak up, I can hardly hear you."

"Nothing," Druff said, "I said you surprised me."

"Oh damn," said Rose Helen. "I *just* put this battery in. That's the
second *time* this week. And now I'm all out. Wait, maybe it's not seated
properly." She removed her hearing aid and laid out its parts on the
table near the remains of Druff's breakfast, his unfinished coffee, the
crusts of his bread. A bit of earwax clung to a side of the stainless steel
battery like jam on cutlery. "I swear," she said, "these things are more
trouble *than* they're worth."

"Is that a zinc oxide?" Druff asked. "Dr. Zahler told you only zinc
oxides."

Rose Helen, vulnerable, missing one of her senses, began to cry.

"Oh Christ, oh Jesus," he comforted. "Baby," he cooed. "Rose," he
said. "Never mind. *Don't.* Aw," said the Commissioner of Streets, *"I
know, I know. So what," he said, rubbing her back, raising her chin
to hold between his forefinger and thumb, "fuck it. Let 'em hear cake."

He took the battery out of her hands and fit it into a little compartment in the hearing aid. (Druff was no expert, of course, but it looked
no different to him from the less efficient, less expensive mercury or
silver oxide batteries.) "There," he said, "see is that any better."

The First Lady of City Streets took the device and, turning away, reinserted it. She inclined her head, she shook it, as if testing to see if water was lodged in her ear. "Oh my," she said, turning back to her commissioner. *"Oh* my, yes. Yes indeed. What a difference. *Day* and night. What a relief. I thought for *a* minute . . . Well," she said, "what were we . . . Oh yes, how startled you looked. Then my *silly* battery went dead on me. *It's* so strange," she said. "I don't think I'll ever *get* used . . . One minute I hear everything they throw at *me,* the next I'm deaf as a post. Well, I can't say he didn't warn me. He said when he first fitted me for the stupid thing not to let the batteries *go* down, to take them out when *they're* not in use. It's a nuisance and really, well, frankly, to tell you the truth, there are times I don't dare take them out. That's why *it's* important I should try to see about getting tested for a second hearing aid, one of those new space-*age* models that practically *turn* you into a spy satellite. Wouldn't that *be* something? How'd you like your wife *to* have such powers? I could overhear everything that goes on, all the plotting. Can you think of a better advantage a politician could have? I thought," she said, "the impression I was left *with,* was it wouldn't happen with a zinc oxide, that it drained down more slowly, *like* the reserve in a gas tank after you're already on 'E.' That's what it's supposed to have over the mercury or *silver* oxide. It's *six* of one, half *a* dozen *of* the other, if *you* ask me. And twice as expensive. Even if I get them *from* Zahler. I bought half a dozen from Zahler. It couldn't *have* been a month ago. He's no cheaper than Williams Pharmacy and they're an *arm* and a leg. But take them out when they're not in use? When aren't they in use? That's a laugh. When aren't they in use? When I go *to* sleep? Could I have taken them out last night? With you gone and Mike out all hours? Suppose there'd been a fire? Suppose *there'd* been a fire and the smoke alarm went off? How would I *have* heard it? I wouldn't *have* heard it. I'd have burned up in my bed. The deaf perish in fires. On a per capita basis more hearing-impaired burn up in fires than people still in control of their sound. *Did* you know that?"

"Come on, Rose. You're not going to burn up in a fire. It's senseless to worry about a thing like that. What are the odds, Rose? More people win the lottery in this town than go up in flames."

But she couldn't hear him, probably couldn't hear herself, her mistaken emphases bumping up the stress on certain words like a hiccup, knocking meaning for a loop, blowing it sky-high, sounding alarms, laying down her insistence and hysteria like a trail.

And then this occurred to the commissioner: This was the same little lady who stepped on his best lines in dreams. This was old Rose Helen. It couldn't have been forty years ago she rested her palm on the tiny shelf above her damaged left hip, posturing buffalo gals, dance-hall ladies, leading him on with the thrust of a raised hip beneath those full skirts, drawing him, luring him, pulling him in with her seductive dip and forward glide, turning her "deformity" into a lewd suggestion. This was old Rose Helen here, the throwback cripple, pouring it on with the skewed iambics, cute as a lisp, of her oddball speech and nervous, loony monologue.

Only suppose she was faking it? Suppose this was only another lewdness meant to arouse in Druff whatever sucker passions he had left to his name? After all his decades in politics he ought to be able to recognize a dirty trick when it stared him in the face. Suppose the batteries still lived in her hearing aid? What a mistake to have thought MacGuffins took weekends off. That's just how adulterers, their guards lowered and their minds groggy from the candles they burned at both ends, from their monkeyshines and escapades and scrapes, had their nuts handed to them.

Aha! thought the City Commissioner of Streets. (Thinking Aha! Thinking its concomitant, exclamatory dagger, too, as, yesterday, in the limo, he could have slapped the side of his head with the heel of his hand.) Had Margaret called? Probably Margaret *had* called. Rose Helen was setting him up with her hear-no-evils, waiting to listen in the minute he picked up a phone.

"Well, no," he said evenly (and getting sore now, too, recalling the silver or mercury oxide thingummy in its tiny compartment in the hearing aid which, for whatever reasons, Rose Helen, some misleading alchemist of the downscale, was eager to pass off as zinc), setting his own traps and thinking two can play this game (having just thought Aha! and into clichés' easy, comfortable rhythms now), turning his head away and speaking into his coffee cup, answering the last question which, on the evidence, he could be certain she'd heard. "It's just that I thought the company you're making that turkey there for might have canceled out at the last minute."

Rose Helen didn't answer.

"Because frankly, Rose Helen," he said, "I was hoping they had. I'm too tired even to go through the motions. Last night really took it out of me."

She didn't say boo. He'd just have to up the ante was all. He turned to face her.

"They marathoned my tail off, those two. Scouffas and his broad." She smiled at him.

"Margaret Glorio," he risked fearfully. Rose Helen nodded and went back to polishing her turkey.

What? he wondered. Does she or doesn't she?

Poor Druff, poor Druff thought, who recognized a no-win situation when it stared him in the face. Because if she really *couldn't* hear him it meant not only that she was deaf and that he was married to her, but that he was, well, maybe just a little paranoid into the bargain, and that his suspicions, so reasonable and even exciting during the workweek, seemed so much blown smoke in the glare of a civil-service sabbath. And as if that wasn't enough, he'd been picking on a little sixty-year-old lady with white hair and a failing hearing aid and a limp. And as if *that* wasn't, he'd been cheating on her, too!

A grown man. Well, he amended, *once* a grown man.

And then, contemplating an endless vista of the long weekend before him spelling nothing but trouble, he was overcome with a sort of bedrock blues. He didn't know what to do with himself. Maybe he could run out for half a dozen nice fresh zinc oxides for Rose Helen's hearing aid. Saying as much, watching her face, testing, uncertain how to read her bland regard, first thinking up and then pulling the old switcheroo, throwing mixed signals, underscoring innocent, cheerful things with sneers and scowls, bad, devastaing ones with encouraging smiles, a jaunty facial merriment.

"I *don't,*" she said, "know what *you're* talking about?"

Well, thought Druff, if Rose Helen was in the enemy camp (if there *was* an enemy camp), she was a worthy adversary.

He fixed her wagon. Neutrally he asked a question at point-blank range.

"Do you expect there'll be an earthquake sometime soon?"

Neutrally Rose Helen shrugged.

"Oh no you don't," Druff said, "no you *don't!*" Making his mistake, as if to shake her reaching out.

She turned away from him, locking, so to speak, her mouth, throwing away, as it were, the key.

Druff, steamed, losing it.

"What is it?" he shouted. "Tell me. What's going on? I demand to know. What are you people after? What's the scam? Just what are you pulling here? Out with it, Betty Marjorie."

Oh, he was fuming.

He didn't even believe the weekend had anything to do with it anymore, and laid down a barrage of piggyback names. Mary Molly, he called her, Annie Mildred. Sonia Eileen. Scandalizing, he figured, an entire generation of Peter Pan–collared women.

"Because it ain't as if there were two sides to this story. I'll tell you something, Beth Jessie—— our lives are short enough as it is. Here we are, down toward the precious few. Toward? *Into!* Does 'bottom of the barrel' mean anything to you? I don't need the aggravation at this juncture."

And hoped like hell there was something to it.

Because as he was just telling Heidi Minnehaha here, he *didn't* need it. Here he'd made an eleventh-hour connection. If it didn't pan out, if his fears weren't real, why then, *that* was the aggravation. He'd become cranky, another fearful old fart afraid in the streets (and him their commissioner), shying at bogeymen who weren't there, at robbers and highwaymen, cutpurses, pirates and rustlers after his cattle, poachers with a blood lust for his fish and his game. If the pillagers and ravagers weren't at the gates, then his suspicions and fears were merely the sure signs of a withering self-regard, the miserly selfishness of the craven aged.

"You lied to me about the zinc oxides, didn't you?" he demanded. "What else is untrue? What else are you keeping from me? Are we having company or not? Out with it. What else? Zahler *is* cheaper than Williams Pharmacy, isn't he? *Isn't* he, Rose Helen?!"

And that's how he left it, slamming out of the house, trailing his furious spoor of sabbath anger, leaving her, if she even heard him, cowed, wide-eyed, dumbstruck, amazed, and about the same, he imagined, even if she didn't. (*Damn,* she was clever!) Seeing out of the corner of his eye as he quit his hearth, too, the lurking, hulking, dangerous Mikey, that beamish boy, that piece of work, his son, of whom more later, he thought, and already rehearsing in his head their inevitable confrontation: "There comes a time," he'd say, "when you get frail and your kids get strong. You're afraid they'll hurt you, beat you up, shake you down. It was ever thus. Well, we're old now, Mother and I, living in fear for our lives, blaming the niggers, blaming the Japs, niggers and Japs just water off a duck's back when we were healthy and young and you kids were feeble. So get out," he would say. "I want you out of my tent." Was this legal? he wondered. Could he call the cops? Would it stand up in court? Be perfectly frank, he didn't know. Out of his jurisdiction. He'd ask Dick, he'd take it up with Doug. Solons and Solomons of law, Doug and Dick, angels of arbitration.

And was outside, outraged and angry in the streets—*his* streets—and had walked as far as a good few blocks before he caught a calm breath, was outdoors in the groomed spring weather, the tactile, sensible air, fussed, clean, scented as shoreline, making as much of itself as a kind of primped, laden, reversed fall, Commissioner Druff clomping along the unaccustomed sidewalks like someone needing an address, a reporter or lawyer in the neighborhood, a fellow with appointments. Commanding—he'd quieted down enough by now to notice—a sort of curiosity, a kind of respect, some thin, hospitable deference anyhow, whatever it was, thought the commissioner, that a competent, assured citizenry owed its strangers and outlanders. This was puzzling and at first he thought, why, of course, the limousine (or its absence, rather), accepting, smiling, surprised, the tribute of his admirers and well-wishers, the shy smiles and unblown kisses of his constituency.

And who only then, wheedled down from his dudgeon by the curious amiability of their attention, understood it, took it in. Recognizing the truth in their windbreakers and comfortable old-shoe ways, in the holes in their sweaters and the stained sweatshirts they wore, their patched trousers and cotton drawstring running pants, all the lazy weekend mufti of their relaxed civilian stances. Or, looking up at him from the broken concentration of their jogging, their jammed athletic traffic, as if he, respectably dressed, rather than they, clothed in their juices, in all the garb of their flushed selves, their soaked shorts and sweaty T-shirts, curiously revealing and intimate almost as the furious metabolism of violent lovemaking or of bodies in fever crisis, was the street's odd eyeful. Or stooped, looking up at him from the level of their spades and shovels and trowels, all their trident tools and modified hoes, pausing over paper packets of spinach and pea and lettuce seeds to brush the hair out of their eyes or knock away excess dirt with the Mickey Mouse fingertips of their enormous, rough cloth gardening gloves, taking, he now realized with some embarrassment, not the pleasure of recognition so much as the quick profit of a small amusement at the sight of their commissioner—only he knew better now, even if they didn't; they wouldn't know he was any kind of commissioner let alone "their" commissioner—in full dress, in the workweek's suit and tie on an early Saturday afternoon. Well, he was stunned to discover himself so set apart from his fellows, *stunned!*

Feeling, by virtue of his spick 'n' spans and all the tailored accountability of his respectable three-piece suit, caught out, like a man nude in dreams, a comical figure, someone in pajamas, say, accidentally locked out of his house. Forced thus to bluff, to carry it off, vaguely go "through" with it, and wishing meanwhile for props, pamphlets perhaps, or that he might represent himself to the neighborhood as a canvasser, or, *of course*, a *candidate*, introducing himself, pressing the flesh, seeking their support, begging their pardon for interrupting their Saturday (though in their shoes, his shoes, he'd probably have welcomed the interruption, even embraced it, pulled the poor guy indoors, offered him coffee, sat him down, invited him to discuss the issues) but wishing to leave just this little bit of campaign literature with them to look over (the pamphlets with their smeary block letters and their blue photographs of poor resolution) when he'd gone. (And feeling, who felt so much, quite out of it, nothing there save a soft nostalgia for the vanished old hurrahs.)

But the heart had its fingerprints, and old Druff, who either knew better than to wage war against the forensics of character, or understood that there wasn't all that much diff between a political war-horse and a political appointee, that a City Commissioner of Streets needn't know any more about macadam or cobble than a Commissioner of Parks and Playgrounds did about landscaping and sandboxes, that power was its own information, gave up, almost volitionlessly—he hoped disarmingly—one of his City Hall, downtown, really blockbuster smiles. Smiling his way, this way and that, down the boulevard, a cheerful, for-a-Saturday-dressed-to-the-teeth, dressed-to-the-nines, suited-up fellow of parts showing the flag. (Was he still troubled? Did he still have the blues? Always up for a bluff, he thought rather not.)

He'd thought neighborhood, but he'd left *his* neighborhood long ago, was in a different neighborhood now, a good, upper-middle-class neighborhood, just the sort of precinct—if he lived to be a hundred he'd never understand it—a pol had to win if he was to take the election. America was a well-meaning, go-ahead country. Yet even in America more people were poor or lived on the edges the break-even life than in places like these—— doctors' houses, lawyers', with wide lawns and a suggestion of property hidden away behind their homes like inner courtyards in architecture. If the poor couldn't keep up with the Joneses, then maybe they felt they must at least vote with them. It's true, he thought. Politicians squandered resentment, it was the emotion they least understood or knew how to use.

So Druff smiled away and was smiled away at in return. A suited-up guy in a one-man parade. What did they make of him all dressed up, anachronistic by a mere day but as out of style for all that as if he wore the fashions of a bygone age? And had them all over again. The blues. Could even put a name to them now. Stopped smiling and *put* a name to them. —The All-Dressed-Up, No-Place-to-Go Blues.

And now was passing one of the city's tonier synagogues. Wooden horses had been set up to close the street to traffic. Druff read the temple's name, black, transliterated, stenciled across the bright yellow planks of the barriers. (B'nai Beth Emeth, it said, and Druff, feeling lost, momentarily flashed on the old Chi Phi Kappa sorority house of his and Rose Helen's youth. Sure, that had been about weekends, too.)

A young man in his mid-thirties, a sharp dresser in a knit skullcap like a tiny area rug, lounged, chain-smoking cigarettes, in the middle of the street against one of the temple's yellow sawhorses.

"*Yontif,* Commissioner there," said the man.

"How are you?" Druff said, smiling widely and greeting the man as if welcoming someone invited to an open house. (It was the way he saluted people sometimes, not voters so much as folks vaguely in the political trade themselves, not even cronies exactly, but precinct work-

ers, laborers in the vineyards. A human professional courtesy he extended, was how he thought of it.)

"Hamilton Edgar," the man said, lazily raising the cigarette hand he
rested on his left shoulder, vaguely posing, and looking more slender
than he really was, and oddly taller than his height, like a young man,
it struck the commissioner, out of the Jazz Age. "We had a meeting in
your office yesterday."

"Hamilton Edgar, Hamilton Edgar," the commissioner said specula-
tively.

"The lawyer from the U. You turned me down. Held out the bid I
brought you all arm's length and little pinkie finger like somebody'd
pissed on it."

"Hamilton Edgar?" the commissioner said.

"What's *that* supposed to mean—— 'What's a guy with a moniker like
yours doing under the headgear?' "

It was exactly what it meant, thought the commissioner who, though
he couldn't always put names together with their faces these days, felt
he still had perfect pitch for the demographics. "Oh no, of course not.
Not at all," he flustered. "No no."

"Because *I* didn't change it," the young man said. "My old *zeyde*
did."

Druff nodded.

"Hey," Edgar said, "speak of the devil, lookee *there* who's coming."
Druff followed the fellow's arm as he uncurled it once more from his
shoulder, flourishing it like a magician's assistant.

A third man in a suit, maybe two or three years Hamilton Edgar's
senior—ballpark figures—came down the wide temple steps toward
them.

"Who?" Druff said.

"Is that who I think it is? Is it? Is it?" the other suited man was
saying. "Is that City Commissioner of Streets Druff that Ham 'n' Eggs's
been telling me so much about? He *said* you two were thick, he *said*
he took meetings in your office, but darned if he mentioned he was
inviting you. Ham 'n' Eggs," the fellow scolded, "you really should have
said something about this. Listen," he addressed Druff, "you're too late
for services. You're even too late for the *kiddush*. The aunts and old

uncles were mopping up the last of the wine and sponge cake when I came out to fetch Ham." He turned back to Hamilton Edgar. "We're starting lunch up soon. The *klezmers* have gathered. Don't you think it would be nice if you got with the program? I mean if you'd *said* something. Now—excuse me, Commissioner—I don't know where we could even fit him in."

"Dan, he's City Commissioner of Streets. These are his sawhorses closing the street off to traffic. How do you think B'nai Beth Emeth got them? How do you think it ever got its one-way street? Who gave us yea and nay over the flow-control patterns?"

"I *know,*" the Dan one said, "I *know,* but tell it to the caterers. You don't draw blood from a stone, Ham."

"Isn't this ridiculous?" Hamilton Edgar, winking at the commissioner, said. "What are we talking about here, an extra place setting? No big deal, I'll pay for it out of my own pocket. Here," said Ham 'n' Eggs, pulling a twenty-dollar bill out of his wallet.

"Twenty dollars?" Dan scoffed. "You think twenty dollars would even begin to cover it? Filet mignon? Fresh vegetables? Wine? Strawberries out of season? *Klezmerin* with embouchures on them that go back before the sounding of the first *shofar?* You're living in the past there, kiddo. Rosebird! Rosebird!"

"It's not enough? It isn't? Here." The Jazz Ager held out his wallet. "Take whatever you need."

"An extra place setting," Dan said scornfully, taking the twenty and lifting additional tens and fives from Edgar's billfold.

"Look," said Druff, finally intervening, "there's been a mistake. He didn't invite me to your son's bar mitzvah."

"*My* son's bar mitzvah, *my* son's? Is that what he told you?"

"What's going on?" Druff said.

"What I'd like to know," Dan muttered, pouting.

"Speak of the devil," Hamilton Edgar said and looked again in the direction of the temple steps.

"Oh yeah," Dan said. "Yeah. This is a guy," he told the commissioner out of the side of his mouth, "you really have to meet him. Wouldn't you say so, Ham?"

"A 'must.' A definite 'don't miss.' "

"Don't let on, Ham. See if the commissioner catches it."

"Even money says he names that tune in three."

Were they high? It occurred to the commissioner these two were high. They *sounded* high. Amused by their own rash slapdash. Into the wine and sponge cake deeper even than the aunts and old uncles. (A judge in these matters, a fine distinguisher—— the ground-up coca leaves, he supposed, white against his gums as toothpaste, the fine, frothy hydrophobics of his own hooked rabidity.) And turned to where a new man, another, Druff, who was no judge, judged, baby-boomer came coming—— a man (this one suited too, but in a style more deliberate, the belted back of his suit coat seeming to flourish material, throwing out pleats like a kind of sprayed fabric, vaguely reminiscent of the accordion reserves and expanses of backpacks, garment bags) with a raised, forward-thrusting smile he seemed to carry balanced on his chin like a Roosevelt.

"Jerry," said Dan, "do you know who this is here?"

"It's City Commissioner of Streets Robert Druff," Hamilton Edgar said.

"Gosh, is it? No *fooling?*"

"Pleased to meet you," Druff said.

"Jerry Rector," said the baby-boomer and took the commissioner's hand. He pumped it. "It sure is swell to meet *you,* sir."

"Yeah, well," said Druff, "I got in late last night. I set the alarm but slept through it anyway, wouldn't you know? When I finally got up I was totally disoriented. I shaved, showered and dressed just as if it were an ordinary workday. That's why I'm wearing this suit and tie instead of the more casual clothing you might expect someone to have on on a day City Hall is closed."

"What I think," Jerry Rector said, "is he looks mighty yar."

Hamilton Edgar, giggling, politely covered his mouth.

"Well, he *does,*" Rector said. "Doesn't he Dan?"

Now the two of them were giggling, covering their faces like conscientious coughers.

"Just ignore them, Commissioner. My chums are a couple of stinkers."

Druff shrugged.

"That's just bunk, Ham and Dan," Rector said. "That's just bunk and hooey."

"Oh Christ," Hamilton Edgar said. "The man breaks me up. With his yars and bunks and hooeys. He sounds just like Jimmy Stewart in *The Philadelphia Story.*"

"More like Katharine Hepburn, you ask me," Dan said.

"Very nice," Jerry Rector said, "very nice indeed." Then *he* grinned. "I happen," he explained to the commissioner, "to be an admirer of the screwball comedies of the thirties and forties. It was a more gracious time. I mean anyone can say fuck or call some asshole a cocksucker. I'm sorry," he said, "but that's just not my style."

Him too, Druff thought. High as a kite. The drugged Jews of B'nai Beth Emeth. It was a good thing the street was closed to traffic. Otherwise it could have been all chaos and fender benders. Like in an ice storm before the salt trucks responded.

"Well," Ham said laughing, wiping his eyes, his amusement damp now, run to mucus, settled in his chest and nasals, "I say it's about time we tucked in to that filet and those berries. Commissioner?"

"Ham has to have his grub."

"Grub!" Dan exploded. "Did you ever? This is some guy, this guy."

"Commissioner?" Ham said, taking his commissioner's arm.

"Is he joining us?" Jerry Rector wanted to know.

"That's very kind," the commissioner told Hamilton Edgar, "but I guess I'll take a rain check. My compliments to . . . the guest of honor."

"That might be you," Hamilton Edgar said levelly, all traces of his moist hilarity gone.

"You told him guest of honor?" Dan said. "Guest of *honor?*"

"Come on, fellows," Jerry Rector prompted, "let's get going. It isn't as if we had all the time in the world."

Gently, the commissioner withdrew his arm. "Please," he said, "let's have a little separation of church and state here."

Jerry Rector laughed.

"Hey," Druff said. "Israeli lobby or no Israeli lobby, Bobbo Druff wears no man's beanie. There ain't an ecumenical ounce in my entire body."

"Yeah," Dan said, "we respect that in you."

There wasn't, he thought. (Who couldn't *really* have been thinking. Their high must be contagious.) That ounce of the ecumenical. Or of the ethnic, either. Not for Druff *scamorza,* lox, green beer. All the holies

and high masses, kissing this one's prayer shawl and that one's ring.
If these Jews had his sawhorses in their pockets, they must have gotten
them as out-and-out gifts, his perfectly civic charity, his skimmed,
no-strings, up-front influence. (In this way he must, over the course of
a year, have saved a week, a week and a half of his precious time. Just
yesterday, who was it Dick told him had died? Marvin Macklin? He'd
already dictated the condolence letter. What had it taken him, ten
minutes, fifteen? And the family had gotten a letter out of it. Signed
by the commissioner on his office's official stationery. If he'd gone to
the chapel or called on the family at home he could have been tied up
for hours. And who, in all that grief and distraction, would even remember he'd come? No, a letter was better. The solace that kept on giving.
The separation of church and state wasn't just sound public policy, it
was good business.) So spare him the lunch invitations, please. Though
there were lunch invitations and lunch invitations. He was, he had to
admit, drawn to these guys. There was something about them. They
seemed very yar guys. Even old Ham Edgar, whose first impression on
the commissioner, let's be frank, hadn't exactly been a good one. Druff
thought: I believe I thought he was a bagman. *And* he was hungry.
(Denied his All-Bran, his fresh-squeezed oranges, the pancakes and
maple syrup of his just desserts. Nothing to show for his quarrels all
day but toast and a cup of coffee on his belly. He could almost smell
it, his hosts' catered goodies—— the fruits out of season, their mignon,
fresh veggies and wine.) *And,* well, he was in the mood. (High, anyway,
peckish and primed by his special Andean mouth appetizers.) *And* they
seemed like folks from whom it was possible to learn a thing or two.
If only they didn't stick him at the head table with the heavy-duty
relatives, the parents and grandparents, the bar mitzvah kid, his brothers and sisses. (Although no one, come to think of it, had actually ever
said bar mitzvah. For all Druff knew it could have been a wedding going
on in there.) He'd mention his head-table aversions, make it the condition of his attendance.

Dan slapped his temple with an open hand. "You told him there was
a head table?"

Even Druff had to laugh.

Even when Ham 'n' Eggs said, "I told him fucking nothing. He's out
of the loop."

"Hey don't," Jerry Rector said. "Talk like that's a lot of hooey."

Druff understood that Rector couldn't really speak the language, that he dropped his few measly words into the conversation like a tourist, like someone who knows how to ask the time, say, or directions to the toilet in French. It was the screwball vocabulary of a screwball. Yet he could not rid himself of the notion—he couldn't account for this—that these men were sympathetic, that running into them like this was a boon, some omen of endowment, vaguely—they were at a place of worship—heaven-sent. Druff, tossed and turned in his sleep, drugged as a schoolboy on the glamour of a Margaret Glorio whose magical availability had been the cause of his ablutions, his grand investiture, suddenly saw his weekend salvaged. He could talk to them. They would get down.

And found himself leading the way, onwarding up the synagogue steps like a Christian soldier.

Not, now he'd taken things into his own hands, so much hurt by their cries—"Hey, hey man, where *you* going?"—as instantly aware of several sudden, even conflicting urgencies—— to call Margaret, to do something about Rose Helen's batteries, to pee, to come to terms with his understanding new pals. Leaving them behind, beneath him on the sidewalk, calling out and waving like people farewelling passengers on steamships in one of Rector's screwball comedies. Wondering why they were calling him off and, to win them over, to show his good nature and, turning to face them, and not for the first time, turned the tables, welcoming them, signaling them aboard, urging in semaphore that they join him before the synagogue sailed.

"Come up, come up," he called down.

And pushing open one of the temple's big doors let himself into a vacant lobby.

"Gee," Druff said, "where's—— ?"

"All gone," said Ham 'n' Eggs.

"Split," said Dan.

"Where's that darn old poop think *he's* going?" Jerry Rector muttered.

But Druff, too, had seen some movies, and was at once put in mind of an old one, a classic, a goodie. Cary Grant was a legionnaire. He'd stumbled onto a cave, a great, mysterious space. There'd been chanting, wicked prayers sent into the interior of the earth by savage assassins, cultists' blood commitments, the dark, assured fanaticism of an immense pep rally, evil, awful. There was to have been, the commissioner sort of remembered, a virgin sacrificed, a white woman. The daughter of the regiment? Cary's own sweetie? And what had put him in mind— this in the few seconds left to him (a moment like a fragment of precious time one speaker yields to another in a debate) before the others caught up with him—was the sudden, unexpected silence of the big empty lobby. (If "lobby"—he wasn't sure—was what you called these bits and pieces of religious architecture, not "nave" or "narthex," not "sanctuary" or "baptistery." Not, he meant, its working, moving parts.) Wondering because—the doors were open—no one was in the sanctuary. Surprised by the absence of excited children, running, chasing one another in the halls, the sprung shirttails of the boys and collapsed stockings of the little girls, all the loose asthmas and hysterical elsewheres of their unruly attention. (He flashed abruptly on wild Mikey, on his ancient, disorderly holiday encounters with his fleeing cousins. He could have wept, Druff. He remembered wanting to kill the snob assholes, their under-control, son-of-a-bitch parents.)

"Excuse me," Druff addressed the three spacey Jews, "but isn't Saturday your day of worship?"

"Is that a crack?" Jerry Rector demanded.

"Jerry, please Jerry," Hamilton Edgar was saying. "Commissioner here is a trained politician, a pro. A pro's pro, even. Would such a man pass gratuitous anti-Semitic remarks if he didn't have to?"

"Wait a minute," Druff said, "I meant I thought it was a day of holy observation. That you set it aside for—— 'services' do you call them?"

"Services, that's right," said Rector, upset. "That's what we call them, all right. That's *just* what we call them. Who wants to know?"

"Well, no one wants to know," said the City Commissioner of Streets. "I'm here," he said, pointing to Dan, pointing to Ham 'n' Eggs, who'd extended his open wallet to his friend like a submission signal in nature, "as their guest. I come in good faith. No one wants to know," he repeated. "All I meant is, where's the festivities? Where is everybody?"

"Jesus!" Jerry Rector said. *"God!* A sink of the lip slips ships! Does no one here understand that?"

"Someone bring that man a drinky winky," Dan said, giggling.

"A dry martooni," said guffawing Hamilton Edgar.

"You're their guest? You're their come-in-good-faith, invited comrade?" said Rector. "I'm hep. All right. That's all right. Nobody tells me anything, but what the heck? That's jimmy-fine-dandy. Maybe we're into Plan C or something and someone simply forgot to inform me. I can live with that. You think I can't live with that? I can live with it. I can live," the screwball-comedy-dialogue admirer informed them coolly, "with anything you silly fuck wads can throw against me. Follow me," he said. "The 'festivities,' as my new friend here calls them, are in the rabbi's study."

It's cumulative, thought Druff. Whatever they're on. He already *knew* it was catching.

"Jerry, man," Dan said.

"Rector!" said Hamilton Edgar.

"Well, as a matter of fact," said the commissioner, reminded of that film again, of its holy killer thugs, "as it happens, I am. A politician's politician, I mean. I define that as anyone in public office who can make news with his mouth." He was following Jerry Rector. The two other guys were following *him*. New surroundings were generally a maze to him, not a big plus in the City Commissioner of Streets department, he had to admit. For Druff it was the sewers of Paris all over again, new surroundings. And that went double, he thought, when what was at stake was at once as comic and interesting and possibly dangerous as he only just now understood his situation potentially was.

They went up stairs and down corridors, doing, he felt, these mysterious stations of the Star of David, hearing nothing, passing no one, Druff nervous in the strangely abandoned building (in their odd single file like the forced, time-honored defile of guards with a prisoner) like someone locked for the night in a shut-up office building. (His mazy new surroundings, *all* the queer, devious landscape and uncharted sewers-of-Paris quality of the apparently vacant temple now somehow powerfully familiar to Druff, as recognizable as the prescriptive tactics of their captured-prisoner maneuvers.) Primarily what he felt was watched.

So he could either catch up with Rector (clearly point man here), seize the cat's cradle and perhaps change the pattern of the forced march, or he could distract them, as time-honored and in-the-tradition as anything he'd seen yet.

He began to talk.

"Well, I am," he said. "I do. Make mouth news, I mean. It's what us pol's pols are all about. Really. Your kings and your queens, your go-ahead heads of state. Empress to alderman. Lowly streets czars like myself, even.

"Once, would you believe it, it made the papers just because I said I didn't think it was fair that the City Commissioner of Streets in Tampa–St. Pete had a bigger line in the budget than I did with all my added responsibilities of weather to worry about—— snow clearance, ice storms, pothole repair, the wear and tear of a cold climate. You wouldn't *believe* what that started! It was good copy for a week. 'Oh yeah?' This was my opposite number, the other pol's pol, the Tampa–St. Petersburg one, answering back through Reuters, United, the Associated Press. 'Just ask old Jack Frost for me what he'd do after a hurricane hit and he had to lift all that soaked sand up off the highways and push it back on the beaches where it came from? Maybe our budget's so high here on the Sun Coast because snow melts and sand don't!' 'Snow melts!' Can you imagine? He had me with the ball in my court. Hey, they could have asked for my resignation. Mouth newsers go right into the doghouse when the cat has their tongue. They were really after me for copy now, the Reuters boys and A.P. people. 'Tell him,' I told them, 'all that talk about the so-called Sun Coast must have gotten in my eyes and blinded me. I forgot Mother Nature had so damn much weather down there that they had to keep giving it names, as if all those storms and hurricanes were like so many children they had to keep track of before it all got away from them.'

"Well, that brought their Chamber of Commerce into it, which was just what I hoped would happen. I took the issue away from him, the pol's pol guy, and now they were issuing actual denials, putting out that they hadn't had an out-and-out hurricane in thirteen years, putting out they didn't expect one for another ten years. They're quoting the god-damn *Farmer's Almanac,* for Christ's sake, and I'm out of it and live to fight another day.

"Well, it's the tourism thing of course, their bread and butter. Come back to Jamaica, mon.

"It's *not* farfetched," Druff said. "This is the way they think. What would be water off a duck's back in any other country changed in ours to landscaping, fountains, the dancing waters.

"Are we there yet? Are we even on the right floor?"

What he'd told them true, never mind he was stalling. Already contemplating other of his mouth campaigns. His newsmaker's noise-making. Bobbo Druff's Greatest Hits. Willing to feed them to them, who would not, he finally understood, be feeding him. (Appetite whetted, peckish as ever.)

Wafted through—because he couldn't keep track, was loose, without landmark—these featureless halls, at once burdened and more light than was his ordinary nature. Airy, breezy, dangerously glib. And spotted the congregation's Negro shammes (recognizing him even if he didn't know the word for him), identifying by the number of keys he wore on his belt who must have been the factotum here, recognizing him for what he was by the little Hebe beanie, the whaddayacallit, *yarmulke*, on his spiky hair, which, except for the black man, only Hamilton Edgar was wearing.

"*Shabbes*," said the black man, greeting them, talking through his hat for Christmas gifts a mile off, and in a different theological venue.

"*Shabbes* your own self, Richard," Jerry Rector said.

Druff, edgy, punchy still with his glibness, his touch of fear, having to admire him for that, admitting as much. "That's right," he told Jerry Rector when the man had passed them, "I see *you're* no pushover. I'll tell you the truth. Any workman can strike fear into my heart. Whenever one comes to the house it throws me off. I feel I have to justify myself or something. Whatever it is, I don't care what it is. It could be anyone. Anything. Telephone repairmen, the guy who reads the meter, the gas, the electric, the man who works in the garden or puts in special trees. It's emasculating, it pulls on a fellow's balls. '*I* work,' I want to tell them. '*I* work. *I* have a job.' "

"You *do*," the Commissioner of Streets heard Dan humor him. "Doesn't he, Hamilton?"

"I'll say."

"Are we there yet?"

"We're just now pulling into the station," Jerry Rector said, and with a key he took from the breast pocket in his suit coat, he opened the door to what Druff supposed was the rabbi's study.

Which was, well, really something. Better, oh far better, he could see, than his own dusty accommodations—— the little theatrical agent's office beyond the low wooden fence around his own poor municipal digs. Druff, catching Hamilton Edgar's grin, just perceptibly lowered his head, a submission signal, a vague acknowledgment to a man who'd seen the commissioner's offices firsthand, that, nerve center for nerve center, the rabbi outclassed him—— Druff's empty good sportsmanship.

"The private sector," said City Commissioner of Streets Druff, nodding and swallowing (who might have anticipated the trim modern furniture and spiffy light fixtures but never the crisp, rich Oriental rugs), a little miffed that a man of God, under, presumably, all the renunciative vows and dictates of the spiritual, could lord it over a man of Caesar like himself. Someone, Druff figured, was not living up to his end of the bargain. Not bothering to wait until the others arranged themselves—Druff, awarded pride of place, shown to the rabbi's chrome and leather chair behind his big glass and wood desk, still in a mood and not, removed as he was from the streets he commissioned, yet rid of his nervousness, anxious to make a good impression before men who hadn't known him when and despising himself for it, despising *them,* not just for their vigorous primes but for their blatant mockery, Ham 'n' Eggs' languid Jazz Age impressions, Rector's odd profanity—the commissioner began to speculate, idly to make more mouth news.

"Impressive," he said. "He's political, your rabbi? A captain of industry? He knows about downtown, I betcha, the colorful tantrums of Mafia and all the haunted houses where the bodies are buried? He knows who is in whom's pocket? What the grand jury said?

"Is he up on all he needs regarding the other guy's gridlock and monkeyshines, the kickbacks and setups and inside jobs, who was it hijacked the salt truck?

"Well, it's common knowledge. Everything's common knowledge these days. Hey, no offense. I mean to take nothing away from anyone, but there's child porn stars on Phil, cousins of drunks on Geraldo. It's as if everyone feels he has a duty to open up everyone else's eyes—girls who make it with ponies, with ectoplasm in the fruit cellar.

"I think, you want to know, that everywhere there's less than meets the eye. All that fooling around, all that graft, it's only business. Making a living, enterprise. Somehow, well, frankly, there ought to be something personal, something malevolent."

"Well, Commissioner," Rector said, smiling widely, "sometimes there is."

"You're really something, Jerry. You know that? Wouldn't you say so, Ham?"

"An absolute 'must,' a definite 'positively,'" Hamilton Edgar said. Then turned to the commissioner. "It's wonderful you came along today," he said. "That you happen to have happened by."

"It is. I did," Druff said. "That's how it happened."

"Sure," Jerry Rector said, "pure serendipity. This could be a break-through here. We could almost be discovering penicillin, finding AIDS serum."

"We'd like to clear up this Su'ad business," Dan said suddenly, startling the commissioner. "There might be some new terms for you to consider."

"Oh, Dan," Ham 'n' Eggs said, "shame on you. You'd trouble the man with business on the Shabbat?"

"Bunk and hooey," Jerry Rector said. "Bunk, bunk, bunk. He's the one talking malevolent. Dan was just reminded, is what."

"Gentlemen, *please,*" said Ham 'n' Eggs.

"Just hold on a darned minute," Druff said. "Let's just hold our horses. You," he said, indicating Hamilton Edgar, "I thought you were the one authorized to speak for the university. How many of you guys are there? You're *all* lawyers?"

"Ham's the lawyer," Jerry said.

"I'm a banker," Dan said.

"Well, I am *too,*" said Jerry Rector.

"Bankers," Druff said. "What bank are you associated with?"

"You don't have to tell him anything," said Hamilton Edgar.

"Hey, I've nothing to hide."

"We're with the Bank of B'nai Beth Emeth," Dan said, giggling. "We're bankers in the temple."

"Money changers," Jerry Rector said, winking.

"You guys," said Ham 'n' Eggs.

"Yar," Rector said, "I'm yar." If this were an era other than the one in which he pretended to hang out, he could have been saying I'm cool. Beyond that, Druff had an impression that all these guys, but particularly Dan and Rector, would hate themselves in the morning.

"All right," Ham 'n' Eggs said, "but you'll see. You're just making him nervous."

"That's silly," Dan said. "You said it yourself, he's a trained politician. You heard him carry on about the rabbi. Shock a with-it guy like the commish? There's just no way. You think he was born yesterday? *This* old man? He's got bodies stashed in high places. He knows where the bimbos are buried."

"New terms?" Druff said, who, to be frank, had only an unclear memory of the old ones. Not, as you may imagine, because—this he did recall—nothing had been in it for him—he really *was* a civil servant and executed, within the decent parameters of sanity, all the functions of his office without thought to private gain or personal favor—but because he hadn't been able to make much sense of what he remembered of Ham 'n' Eggs' earlier proposition. Druff's impression, post–M. Glorio and all the knockdown, drag-out of a MacGuffin with which he'd lived on and off (counting from lunchtime to lunchtime) going on two days now, was that the university had made rather a point of its indifference to matching the expensive, distinctive campus limestone in the covered walkway Druff's department was to build (this rather a point, too) above Kersh Boulevard. The poor old city's point was that while it would pay its share of the costs, it refused to pay for anything put up on university property.

"Anything we can do," Dan said, "to give the Su'ad kid's soul some peace, a little belated quality time."

"Dan!" Ham 'n' Eggs scolded.

"Steady there, Dan," even Jerry Rector put in, "steady as she goes."

Now he was alert. Perhaps he'd given Dan the wrong impression, shooting off his mouth, sending his with-it type signals, merely extending a tongue, which Dan, at least, had mistaken for a hand. Showing off for him, for all of them, not out of hubris—hubris? him? what did he have to be hubrid about?—but from mood and nervousness. But how were they to know? He'd been led by his doubts to meander along the margins of entrapment. It was good strategy.

"Funny your talking new terms," said the City Commissioner of Streets. "Mr. Edgar practically blamed us for the accident. He said the city's pedestrian-activated signal was an attractive nuisance."

"*Darned* attractive," said Jerry Rector, wriggling his eyebrows and pretending to tip an ash off an imaginary cigar.

"I guess I can only hope," said Druff, "that you folks aren't wired and that this ain't some kind of sting operation. New terms?" he repeated.

"Well, he's right," Ham 'n' Eggs said. "We *would* like to clear things up."

"I'm all ears," the commissioner said. "Where's the TV cameras? Is my hair all combed, is my tie straight? What do I look into?"

"You think we need cameras?" Dan demanded angrily. "You think we keep our goodies in a safe-deposit box? Live it up for once. Throw caution to the winds. *Political scientist! Big public man!* Go public, why don't you?"

"Sight unseen?" Druff inquired coolly.

"What's he mean now, I wonder," the one playing Jerry remarked to the others.

"Quid pro quo, I guess."

"The terms of the terms."

"If he'd get out from behind that desk for a minute he'd practically be standing on them. Jeesh!"

"Dan?"

"What?"

"Shut up."

"Hey, *he's* the one suggested there should be something personal, that something's missing from your average evil."

"You argue like a child! I suppose if he told you to jump off the roof you'd go out and do it."

"Of course not. I'm only pointing out."

"Well, just be careful where you point," Ham said.

"I am," Dan said. "I *am* careful. Hey, if he thinks this is about devil worship or anything like that, he's got another think coming. Profits, incentive. It's still America, what do you think?"

"That's what *I* say."

"Right on."

"Don't he know that blood's been spilled, don't he understand there's a girl dead out of this? Ain't that good enough for him?"

"Yeah."

"That's what *I* say."

"Gents," offered Druff, who knew when he was being triple-teamed,

"I'm elsewhere expected." And, rising, came out from behind the desk.

"He's warm."

"He's *very* warm."

"Very *warm?* He's very hot!"

"You've got to give him credit," said Ham 'n' Eggs.

"Credit, hell," Jerry Rector said, "you've got to bribe him outright."

"See," said Dan, "what did he tell you? Downtown isn't just fixing tickets, moving the dates around on your court calendar like three-card monte, or getting the man from the Health Department to look in the sink but not under the stove. It ain't only always money changing hands."

"Of course not."

"No way," said Rector.

Druff walked over the Oriental rugs scattered through the rabbi's study, moving across one and onto the next as though they were beautiful stepping stones in a gorgeous river.

"The U pays the costs on its own property. What the hell, it picks up the tab at the city's end, too."

"To get the unpleasantness over with."

"To put the nastiness behind."

"*To sweep,*" said Dan in a low, meaningful, carefully inflected voice which stopped Druff cold, *"it under the rug."*

"Come on, boys," Jerry Rector said, "let's leave the commissioner alone a few minutes. Let's give him a little time to consider the bank's latest proposition."

They filed past him and were heading out the door before Druff knew what was happening. Hamilton Edgar paused and turned in the doorway. "I'll shut this for you," he said. "Don't worry. I won't lock it. We'll be just down the hall if you need us."

"Ham?" Druff said.

"Yes, Commissioner?"

"Is there a washroom? I have to pee."

"Just in there," Ham 'n' Eggs said. "Behind that door. It's the rabbi's. Help yourself," he said, and walked out with the others.

Druff sat on the toilet (because peeing was the least of it) and thought: Now isn't this just what I've been telling myself? And wondered he hadn't, at the time hadn't, understood the implications of what was now so apparent. All this pursuant (grunt, squeeze, release) to his observation the evening previous that life goes on even in the chase scenes. Even character did, *its* old autonomics. Wasn't his lie to Hamilton Edgar about needing to pee a testament to his system's urgent modesty? The body had its own agenda and would not be caught up in the desiderata of even an engaged will. Hell, it couldn't even be bothered. Brushing and flossing and following—he recalled, among his other meds, the stool softener he'd taken between the time he'd committed adultery and the time he'd gone to bed—doctor's orders. Even as you, even as me. Your Juicy Fruit in one pocket, your stamps for your letters in the other. He recalled thinking that no matter how hot the pursuit, people with MacGuffins would still need batteries for their transistor radios, and suddenly remembered the zinc batteries for Rose Helen's hearing aid, making a mental note to pop into a store, if he got the chance, to see if he could pick some up. Life goes on. Speaking of which, hadn't he told Margaret he'd call? He'd do so now, as soon as he finished his business. While he still had the chance. Amazing, thought Druff, his notions borne out. And the upshot (what he *hadn't* realized) was *this:* that if something as fragile as one's life could go on, if one, even under duress, could continue to count calories, why then how much *more* procedural were the general comings-and-goings and business-as-usuals of the universe, all its tidals and opportunities, all its knockabout upheavals and the explosive, piecemeal degradation of the earth and subordinate stars?

Thinking, as he washed up and examined himself in the mirror: This rabbi has some terrific deal going. Not only a swell study in which to do the holy contemplatives of his trade, but a private, humdinger john any fellow could really be proud of. The latest fixtures and even a nifty, beautiful Oriental rug.

Now why, wondered the City Commissioner of Streets, would *that* be?

This particular question catching him off guard. Quite rocking him. So much so, in fact, that although he'd heard no one reenter the rabbi's study he was a bit chary about going back in there quite yet, lest they return before he was ready for them. He pulled the lid down over the toilet seat and sat. Dizzily, he contemplated the figure in the carpet. Contemplated having (and in something under thirty-some-odd hours) rediscovered his old, idling intelligence. (Idling no longer. His bright ideas sudden and received, as ready-to-wear and off-the-rack as Commandments. "Call Margaret," he's commanding himself.) In the rabbi's toilet of the rabbi's study contemplated, fearfully, his brand-spanking-new braveries. Not least, he contemplated Coincidence.

Those guys, he thought, Ham 'n' Eggs, Jerry Rector, the Dan guy, couldn't have known I was coming. *I* couldn't have known I was coming! I overslept. So much had happened. I woke up confused. I didn't even know what day it was. I dressed for the office. Downstairs we had words. I stormed out of the house. I don't go for walks, I don't have routes. No one, no one ever, really set their watch by me. What's the deal? I happened by. I just happened by. No one could know. How could anyone know? So life goes on, so character does, so we brush, floss and tune in to catch the news on the hour. So time marches on, tra la. So what's the deal? So I didn't know I even *had* a MacGuffin until yesterday. So I didn't have spies or a girlfriend, either. There's always the random. There's always absentee ballots, late returns, and another county heard from. Things happen at sea while stars fall on Alabama. Who's to say that isn't a cooperation, a conspiracy of engaged, invisible gears? There's chance, back channels and fucking farce. There's this and there's that—— stuff going on all over the place, at all hours of the day and night, rough-hew them as we may. Why *shouldn't* those boys have been waiting for me? She'll be comin' round the mountain when she comes, *n'est-ce pas?* So don't tell *me* hold your horses, old fella. Yes, yes, I know. I appreciate the powers of paranoia. They are surely considerable. But before you go rushing off to find a shrink, consider, I'm a politician. Trained in the random, in the chance remark and glancing blows of everybody's mouth news, in on all the late returns and other counties heard from, in absentee ballots and the planetary swing vote, in the graciousness of concession speeches lived through twice, once on the phone from my hotel, then in the ballroom. Trained, when it comes down, in the thick skin of the professional politician, his water-off-a-duck's-back bathing habits and almost Christian bygones-be-bygones vision. So, sure, I'd have spies. Of course I'll have enemies. An odds-on favorite, for God's sake, a hell of a bunch more likely to have a MacGuffin of my own than that there'd ever be, now I see its tight weave and, to judge by the Chinese water torture it'd probably have to put up with in here, the colorfast qualities of its terrific, mysterious dyes, its rich fringe and intricate design and peculiar shape, what is almost surely a Muslim prayer rug right in the rabbi's crapper!

So coincidence? *Coincidence?* You tell *me*, what's more outrageous, that someone like myself should go along, la de da, minding what he's still got left for business in what he's still got left for life, doing, dum dum de dum dum, his job, suddenly stumbling over conditions' cooked books, or that, as anyone with an ounce of sense will tell you, it's in the nature of books to be cooked, the nature, Christ, maybe even the *duty,* like evolution or natural selection, for people to wear themselves down and wear themselves down to a point where they have an actual edge, some in-tooth-and-claw arrangement which not only enables them to pull the shit they pull but actually drives them to do it! What's more outrageous, eh? That I should step in a mess in the street or that so many messes should be left in the street that I can't help but step in one?

"Oh, Su'ad, oh oh! Su'ad, Su'ad oh," conjured and softly moaned the City Commissioner of Streets, as unready and ill-prepared to step out of the holy sanctuary crapper as when he'd first stepped into it.

But determinations had been made.

He let himself out of the toilet. (Thinking precisely that way now—as one who "let himself out" of things, leaving bathrooms as you'd slip ropes, negotiating ordinary rooms as if they were obstacle courses, some land-mined aspect to the scenery, some *scenery* aspect to the scenery!), thinking of his life as having a "look" to it now, all the authentic fine detailing of a movie set, his clothes, Dan's, Rector's, Ham 'n' Eggs', even the colored shammes's, as real and up-to-date as on the first day of principal photography. It was, all of it, faithful to Druff's times and circumstances, everything *le dernier cri,* organized, arranged as an illusion of environment in a zoo, Druff preserved in the perfect poisoned amber of his ambience.

All right then, he had thought, upon unlocking the door to the W.C. and peering cautiously out. *Action?*

He moved to the desk and tapped Margaret Glorio's number, which he had called only once before but hadn't forgotten, into the phone. She picked up on the first ring.

"Margaret, darling, it's Bob Druff. I have to talk fast because under certain circumstances a fellow in my position not only has to be on his toes at all times but has to have eyes practically in the back of his head. Without going into detail, suffice it to say this may be one of them."

"What do you want?"

"Just to tell you I haven't forgotten last night."

"For a man your age you've a remarkable memory."

"Ha ha, Margaret darling."

"Where are you calling from? Are you calling from home?"

What was left of the decent man in him told him there was no harm in the question, but the fellow straining tiptoe with his eyes practically in the back of his head warned otherwise. "Yes," he said, "that's right."

"I'm glad your wife gave you my message."

"My wife?" Druff said, alarmed. "No no, my wife and son were out when I got back from my errands. We didn't have an opportunity to speak. Er, what, um," asked the City Commissioner of Streets, *"was* your message, Margaret dear?"

"Why didn't you tell me you have crabs?"

"That was your message? You said I had crabs?"

"You don't think she has a right to know?"

"Ha ha, Margaret Glorio, you had me going there for a minute. That's probably one of the reasons I like you so much, you playful devil scamp, you. You didn't even call my house, I betcha. Well well."

"Look," Margaret Glorio said, "I'm expecting a call. You said you'd make this fast."

"You're expecting a call? There's someone else?" said Druff with great feeling. The City Commissioner of Streets was astonished. If he sounded even half as melodramatic to her as he did to himself he must indeed have seemed the fool. It was because she'd picked up on the first ring. Well, he'd been there, hadn't he? Had seen all there was to see of her studio apartment, its cunning furniture and unusual lamps, all that experimental decor, her buyer's bold environment, the strange matte finish of the furniture, of the walls and carpets, the drapes and slipcovers, the designer telephone on the designer table of exotic wood. He'd been there, knew she'd have to have been sitting with the phone practically in her lap to have answered so quickly. Was that kind of anticipation ever *not* love-related on a day not part of the workweek? "Not, I mean, that you haven't every right, of course. Of course you

have. Certainly. Hey, I don't own you. What makes me think I *own* you?
I don't own *anybody.* I'm not some jerk who has it in his head that just
because he sends a girl a bucket of flowers on the night of the big dance
or shares a crown rack with her, that that gives him some right——
Maybe the guy whose call you're waiting for thinks that way, maybe
he feels he owns a piece of you, but not me. I'm just a lowly public
servant. Where would I ever get off?

"No no, I'm just calling to pass the time of day. As I might with any
close personal friend I don't particularly own. Hell no. You're free,
white and twenty-one, as we used to say in the old days. I just called
because I promised I would after our one night of love, and to shoot
the shit."

"Well," Margaret said, "it was good hearing from you."

"Well," said the City Commissioner of Streets, at a loss. "Look," he
said, "I know I caught you at a bad time. I just wanted to tell you what
a swell time I had last night, and how much I admired your pad, how
you fixed it up."

"My 'pad'?"

"Did I misspeak? You think I'm talking above my station, age-wise?
No no, you misunderstand. I meant it as a compliment. You've your
whole life ahead of you, young lady. You go call real estate whatever
you please. But hey, I'm the old-timer in the outfit, what do I know?
You don't like 'pad'? Showplace, then. How much I admired your
showplace."

"Thanks," Margaret Glorio said, "I hope next time you see it you still
like it."

"Next time I see it," Druff said. "Hubba hubba."

" 'Hubba hubba,' " Miss Glorio said. "Where do you get this stuff?"

"Me? This stuff? I'm a gentleman of the old school. I speak a sort
of gabardine, like a man in a hat."

"I don't exactly understand why," she told him, "but it's kind of cute.
Charming."

"Like your lovely pad."

"What's with you, Commissioner? Why do you keep bringing the
conversation around to my apartment? What are you enamored of, me,
or the fact I'm convenient to the good schools, churches, transportation,
water and shopping? It's my *business* to have nice things."

"That's right," said the man with the MacGuffin. "I forgot. You're this buyer, you have important contacts with wholesale. You get the urge, you call you want the furniture moved, and interior designers do you for nothing. You don't lift a finger."

"More or less."

"Boy oh boy," he said, "what perks! Oh, hey," he said, "would that go even for Oriental rugs?"

"Oriental rugs?"

Because he was trying to remember if he'd seen one last night. A little like the rabbi's, bigger than a throw rug, smaller than a flying carpet.

"What are you—"

"I'll get back to you," Druff said.

"Hey there!" said Jerry Rector.

"Will we see each other again?" Miss Glorio asked.

"I'll get back to you. No, really. I will," he said, and replaced the telephone.

"An offer is on the table here," Dan said.

"Are you giving me to understand I can't leave? That I haven't your permission?"

"No, of course not," Ham 'n' Eggs said.

"What, are you kidding us, you big lug?" said Jerry Rector.

"Jerry's right," Ham 'n' Eggs told him. "Aren't I the party who warned against conducting business on the Sabbath?"

"Ham's got something there, bub," Jerry Rector said. "There are certain things that just aren't done."

"Which reminds me," said Ham 'n' Eggs, switching sides, "there are psychiatrists in this town who'll write you prescriptions for dinette sets, bedroom suites, expensive cars."

"For custom-made suits," said Jerry Rector. "Bespoke trousers of cavalry twill."

"For 'round-the-world cruises," Ham 'n' Eggs said. "You take it to your travel agent to be filled. She sells you a ticket, and you just take it off your taxes."

"There are bugged confessionals," Dan said, joining in. "Certain priests will sell you tapes."

"And lawyers," said Ham, "who go into the tank for the sake of the look on their clients' faces when the jury counts them out."

"Yeah," Dan said, "they love that look."

"Will you listen to us? We're giving a City Commissioner of Streets civics lessons."

"What you can get away with," Ham said. "What the traffic will bear. Testing the limits. Pushing the envelope. When there are no more frontiers, you make them up. You strive, you stretch, you reach for the stars."

"I heard him say 'rugs,' " Dan said. "I distinctly did. Clear as a bell. He could have been in the next room."

"He *was* in the next room, silly. That's when we walked in on him."

"But I can leave," Druff said, just checking. "I'm free to go."

"Dan," Jerry Rector said, "there's still an offer on the table."

"Table it," Dan said generously.

"Where's his hat? Did he have a hat? Did you have a hat?"

"No." (Feeling humiliated now, glad his girlfriend wasn't there to see this, glad Rose Helen wasn't, Mikey, Dick the Spy, Doug the Passive-Aggressive, his cronies and cohorts, the loyal opposition. More than a little downcast, in fact, to be himself on the scene. Well, he was out-gunned. Three against one. Four, if you counted the black beadle with his keys to the closets where the brooms were buried, the mops and pails and wringers. Wondering where his powers had fled, the old MacGuffin confidence, backed, he would have thought, by just ages of tradition. Or perhaps *his* MacGuffin was merely magical, of the self-limiting kind, subject to conditions, stipulations, 5/50 arrangements like a warranty on a car. Subject, that is, to a commitment never to abuse the privilege of just *having* a MacGuffin, honoring his obligations to it, holding up his end. Maybe he wasn't worthy of one. Maybe he wasn't noble enough. Maybe Miss Glorio was a test he had failed. Having sweet truck with her not only a betrayal of his wife but, in a way, advantage taken of one already on her uppers physically, a little old lady practically, hoary-haired, a woman who almost couldn't *keep* a battery in her hearing aids, of recent oddball speech patterns and edgy, jumpy attitudes and with a touch, too, of this just perceptible chronic limp. So a question of honor, finally, a matter of morals, of having—quite literally—been found wanting.

(But whatever. His courage was gone. He felt the absence of his breezy insouciance, the wisecracks and eloquent sort of gabardine he'd claimed to speak—— and that they spoke better than he did. The universal language of toughs: "Where's his hat? Did he have a hat? Did you have a hat?" Well, he wasn't surprised. "No," he had told them. They'd taken it from him. Ball in their court now, hat on their head.)

So what was he supposed to do with the leftovers? (That's about what he asked himself now, that's how he felt, as if he'd completely overestimated the appetites of guests at a party.) What *was* he to do with the leftovers, the leads and clues and flashy circumstantials, if he'd come to the part where his energy flagged?

Ol' Bob Druff. Livin' the Tammany life now. Routine, laid back, MacGuffinless. Yet what a way he'd come!

Here it ain't been but a day, he thought, since he'd first surmised the MacGuffin and just *look* where it had taken him. His first tentative suspicion confirmed, connected to his second tentative suspicion, that one to a third and that to a fourth and so on. By God, he might have been hooking a rug! Because everything was linked, everything. If he had a sidekick (just about all that was missing here) he would tell him so. Begin with an initial observation. Make an observation, would tell him, any observation, any observation at all. Like one guy leading another through a card trick. Everything inevitable and conjoined in the vast, limitless network of things, merged in the world's absolute ecology. There was, it seemed, no such thing as a loose end. Not in this life, there wasn't. The universal synergy. In the end, thought our City Commissioner of Streets, *all* roads led.

And because they did, Druff, on the street again, who'd just been thinking, hadn't he, of a sidekick, and what he might pass on to such a fellow if he had one, found himself—because hadn't he been promised lunch (filet mignon, fresh vegetables, wine, strawberries out of season), which had never materialized, incidentally, and could it have been even three minutes ago he'd been thinking what could be done with the leftovers?—going into this little coffee shop where he sat in a booth wondering while he waited for his food to come—his rare hamburger, his order of fries, his coffee and pie à la mode—whether he should use the pay phone in the entryway to call Dick.

He signaled his waitress.

"Miss," he said, "do me a favor, will you? There's this guy I have to call, but, well, to be honest, I'm a little concerned that if I get up and phone him you'll bring the food while I'm gone and my burger and fries will be cold and all dried out by the time I get back."

"No problem," she said. "I'll watch you through the glass. I'll wait until I see you're off the phone before I bring your order."

"Oh, hey, thanks, that's very kind," said Druff, perfectly sincere, on his own turf again, back, that is, with folks who'd never tag him, who couldn't lay a glove on him, touched, actually moved, by the kindness of shockable, susceptible people. "I appreciate that. I really do." (This part of the universal synergy too.) And with difficulty leveraged himself out of the booth (the quarters always too close in these places—even for a chap dropping into his clothing—their shallow seats and steep backs, the unyielding Formica tabletop in its wraparound metal trim) and made his way to the pay phone between the lunchroom's heavy inner and outer glass doors.

"No, I'm sorry," the woman said, "you must have the wrong number."

He quoted the number he'd called.

"I'm sorry," she told him. "There's no one here by that name."

Surprised, he checked it in the directory. Though he knew Dick's number. He *knew* Dick's number. Hadn't he occasion to call it a hundred times a year? Sure enough. It was Dick's number all right.

The waitress smiled at him. She waved. Druff, grinning, nodded acknowledgment.

"But this was an operator-assisted call," he explained to the woman. "He dialed it himself. It *has* to be the right number."

Druff could actually hear her turn away from the phone, hear her place her hand over the mouthpiece and, though he couldn't make out what she was saying, he had a pretty good idea. Get in, he thought, the part about how the operator was a man. Though untrue—he hadn't gone through any operator—it was, Druff felt, an absolutely telling detail.

She was back on the phone. "Dick says to ask who is this." Without guilt at having been caught out, or shame, or the slightest indication that her pride had been in any way compromised. Fucking typical, Druff thought.

"This isn't Polly," Druff said. "You're not Dick's wife."

"*Nolo contendere,*" she said.

Through the glass Druff's waitress threw him a friendly high sign.

The commissioner graciously, broadly, winked. "Tell him," he said, "it's his boss."

He heard her transmit the message. "What," she said, "what's that, Dicky? Oh, okay." She was speaking to him again. "Dick won't come to the phone on the weekend. He told me to tell you that drivers get days off, too, and that you wouldn't even be calling him on a Saturday if he was an Orthodox Jew."

"What," Druff said, raising his voice, *"what's that? What's he say?"* He looked up. At her station, the waitress, concerned, was staring at him. To reassure her, Druff barely shook his head, like a pitcher shaking off a sign. "Listen," he said, looking to make friends with the woman in Dick's apartment, "Miss—" And broke off, paused, waited for her to take the bait. She didn't. "Won't he come to the phone *really?* It's rather important, a matter of quite some interest to him. It won't take much time. I know it's Saturday. Of course I do"—and this goes on too, he couldn't help thinking, that spies get days off—"and I don't expect him to come fetch me or drive me places. If I had anywhere to go, either I'd drive myself or I'd call a cab. Honest."

"Oh sure," she said, "assume I'm not married, just some limousine driver's tootsie. 'Miss' and 'Mademoiselle' me. Just go ahead and make out your stereotypes. If it's convenient for you to think so, you just make up in your head I'm not a respectable mother of twins. Well, my name is Charlotte, incidentally, if you're so all-fired interested. No, I'm not Polly. I'm not Dick's wife. Only I don't know where a person like you would get off. A married man, so-called, traipsing around at all hours of the day and night."

While she spoke, Druff gazed placidly through the coffee shop's glass outer door to the quiet, empty, late-afternoon street. It's like a decompression chamber in here, he thought. With a pay phone and a cigarette machine. When she'd finished, Druff said, "Just tell him it's a snow day."

"Wise guy," Charlotte said.

"No, wait," he said. (Because he was new at this and didn't know when to play what he still wasn't even sure was his trump card. Because City Commissioner of Streets or no City Commissioner of Streets, Druff didn't even recognize the neighborhood he was in anymore. He was a politician. He knew about fixed elections, what could be done, if necessary, to a voting machine, how any even only decent mechanic could compromise it like a one-armed bandit or rigged roulette wheel. What had any of that to do with MacGuffins? With anything as important and down-to-earth as genuine evil? Because he was new at what he hadn't even yet begun to understand, and he couldn't wait. Not that he hadn't as good a sense of timing as the next man, only that he was impatient, and maybe a little too anxious to have everything done with.) "No, wait," he repeated. "Ask him if he ever heard of any international rug rings?"

Impatiently, she relayed his question. Then their connection was disengaged and he heard the burr of the dial tone. Saddened, his good name shot, he went back into the restaurant. At his table the hamburger and fries had already been laid down, his coffee. His sandwich, its meat and juices congealed and gray as brainfat, was cold, his saturated fries limp. The ice cream was melted on his pie like a thin white soup. When he was dead none of this would mean anything.

So he set off to buy Rose Helen's batteries.

It was, as he'd noted, an unfamiliar neighborhood. He was Commissioner of Streets. Of course he recognized the place names. He remembered signing purchase orders for practically every avenue and street he passed, and remembered having authorized the dispatching of crews to probably each of the four corners of this place—— to investigate ruptures in the paving, make determinations about the suitability of street signs citizens had requested, to paint white lines and double white lines in the road. Yet he couldn't say with certainty he'd ever actually been here. He passed commercial districts filled with what were obviously chain stores whose peculiar names he'd never heard before.

And at last came to a place he knew. Indeed to the very pharmacy where only the day before the very pharmacist who served him now had sold him a condom. (From here, he recalled, he was only three blocks from City Hall. He had virtually drifted across the city, doing, it could have been, some rude, off-course, straying, swerving caricature of last night's false marathon, making good the elaborate lie he had told to his wife, and repeated to his son, about his heroic walk with McIlvoy and Scouffas.) Maybe it was only the fact that he was on *terra firma* again, but he had, too, the same distinct impression of safe conduct he'd had yesterday in this place.

"Do you stock batteries for hearing aids?"

The man, who had a sort of mechanical but, on the whole, rather soft hospital-corners way of moving, turned lightly away from the commissioner and disappeared down an aisle crowded with an assortment of miscellaneous boxes. Druff felt rekindle his old admiration for the pharmacist's tight-lipped professionalism and efficient, silent ways. (I, he thought, reminded of Charlotte's bill of particulars, could use me a little of that.) And in moments was back, a variety of batteries extended on a kind of jeweler's tray for Druff's inspection.

The City Commissioner of Streets, ignoring them for the moment, attempted to make eye contact.

"You have a choice," said the pharmacist. "Mercury, zinc, or silver oxide."

"Three delicious flavors," Druff said. (Sure it was unwarranted, but maybe the man felt superior. And supposing the druggist's professionalism wasn't sincere? Suppose there was something judgmental in it? Maybe the pharmacist even remembered him from the day before? "Yeah," he could imagine him telling some cop, "that's him, that's the one. That's the old man who came in and bought a rubber off me." Though Druff, still only on the edge of crime, could not really imagine the circumstances. And, anyway, it was better to needle and do one's riffs of fluent gabardine than to be brought down—— Ham 'n' Eggs, his pals; the cold, spoiled food he had left untouched in the coffee shop. It was better to dish it out than receive.) Again he attempted to engage the druggist's eye. "Too bad you have to work on a Saturday."

"We keep the same hours as the department stores."

Druff nodded, then went up practically into the guy's face, backing off only after it occurred to him that the pharmacist might think he was fishing for compliments on the basis of his purchase yesterday afternoon.

Nah, he thought, he doesn't remember. Maybe, Friday nights, they get a run on old fuckers. I must be a type. But a type who'd spring for a French letter one day and come back the next for help with his hearing aid? Druff was furious.

"It's not for me," he said. "It's for another party. Look. See? Nothing up this ear, nothing up that one."

"Sir," said the pharmacist.

"Or maybe you think I left it in my other suit. Is that what you're thinking? Turn around then. No, go on. It's all right. Go on, turn around," demanded crazy Druff, the political liability. "Say something in your softest voice. See if I don't pick it up."

"Siir," the pharmacist, still facing him, protested.

"No, really. Go on." Sighing, the druggist started to turn. "You *sighed!*" Druff jumped in. "There. You just sighed. I *heard* you. Would a deaf-o pick up on something like that?"

"No, I suppose not," the druggist said quietly, his back to the commissioner and looking, in his strictly cosmetic white lab coat, like an actor in a holdup. Catching Druff off guard.

"Oh hey," the City Commissioner of Streets said, "I'm sorry. Look, turn, face me again. It's not what you think. I'm not normally like this. I'm under a strain. It's a long story, but don't worry, I won't bore you with it. There's no excuse for my behavior. None whatsoever. Well, there *is,* but there wouldn't be any excuse for me unloading it on you. There could never be any excuse for that. Let's just say I'm off my feed. And I am, too. Waitress in a coffee shop deliberately brought me my hamburger and fries after I specifically asked her to wait until *after* I'd placed this call. Then I got hassled about the call (which, incidentally, was totally unsatisfactory) and, when I got back, there it all was, everything I'd asked her to—— I sound a little nutso to you, don't I?"

"No, not at all."

"Well, you're humoring me. In your place I'd probably do the same. Well, I *would* do the same. No probably to it." (God, Druff was thinking, how do I get out of this? I'll probably have to send this guy flowers to make it up to him.) "Now," he said, "about those batteries . . ."

The druggist held out the tray and Druff touched one of the batteries, tumbling it with his finger as one might roll diamonds on a black cloth. "That one's a mercury," the pharmacist said and Druff snapped his hand back.

"Jeez," he said, "mercury. That's the shit fucks the tuna fish, ain't it? Imagine what it'd do if it leaked into your ear." (Thinking this is how I make it up to him, not how I get out of it.) "I guess the zinc," Druff said. "Half a dozen."

The pharmacist nodded. "They're a little more expensive, but they drain down more slowly than those others when not in use."

Druff sorry to have gotten off on the wrong foot with him. Admiring, if not exactly liking him, his command of the hardware, his vast inventory, better than Druff's. Who barely recognized the names of the streets and was lost altogether in the neighborhoods. And who now, the zincs locked into three blister packs inside the pharmacy's little plastic tote he carries in his hand, aimless and feeling vaguely abandoned on what have proved to be his rambling, roved and drifting highways and by-ways, a mite dizzy from all the unexpected topspin of his swerved, off-course tangentials and the almost random eccentrics of his wide, bent bearings, his sideslips and compromised trajectory, his mangled yaw and imperfect pitch, what he's increasingly come to think of as the open itinerary of his private detective's route on what he cannot stop himself from thinking of as a late, MacGuffin-forsaken Saturday afternoon, realizes he has to choose. What's it to be then, eh? In the absence of Ol' MacGuffin, come, he supposes, to represent the spirit of narrative in his life (sort of), shut down for the weekend (more or less), nothing was pushing him, slamming him off the dime. There was, that is, no gun at his head just now. And so, unless he's to go home (not, he's sure, such a bad idea, and doesn't he, incidentally, have Rose Helen's hearing-aid equipment right there on his person to turn his divagations into at least the look of an errand?), he is suddenly faced (if he doesn't count the batteries) for the first time today with the problem of destination.

Druff (influenced by hunger, the pull of the turkey working in the oven, the built-ins and add-ons of Rose Helen's robust fixings) examined his options. To his mind he had three. He could go home. Two, he could pay a call on Margaret Glorio, maybe kill two birds, pitch a little woo if he was lucky, and pull a surprise carpet inspection. Or he could drop in on Doug, his backup limo driver. Where in God's name, he wondered, did *that* one come from? And determined at once, since he couldn't answer this perfectly reasonable question, to get his ass over to Doug's. Well, why not? It was out of his hands now. He was working on instinct. Surrendered, handed over, going with the flow, which, in the absence of MacGuffin, was all he could use for narrative spirit, a gun at his head, the wild tumult, the pushing and shoving at the top of his dime.

And, hailing a taxi, read off Doug's numbers to the cabbie from the book of useful addresses he kept like any old-timey salesman in a pocket of his suit coat. Thinking—he was Streets Czar, he was known to the cabbies—how nice, how pleasant it would be to be lectured, called to account, shoptalked, man-to-man'd. Though Druff didn't think much of his chances. The town, with its high concentration of private cars and its network of interstates—over time, the city had become this sort of trade route—— window to this, doorway to that, "The Nation's Threshold," according to the Chamber of Commerce—wasn't the best place in the world to set up in the taxicab business. Street cabs didn't ordinarily do well here, the only decent franchises being those at the airport and hospitals. And his driver, an immigrant, some refusenik type from the Eastern bloc, didn't seem particularly interested. Druff examined his photograph, read the thick capital letters of his difficult name from the laminated hack license posted above the taxi meter. (And that's another thing, Druff, fifty-eight years old, fifty-nine his next birthday, thought. Did they rig those things? On one of his father's cars, a big, green 1947 Hudson after the war, he remembered a button right there on the floorboard. All you had to do to change the station on the car radio was press your foot on the button. Why couldn't such a device be placed in cabs to jump the numbers showing in the little fare windows? Or maybe do something to the gears in the meter? The steady ticking that already sounded not like seconds clicking off but almost like the accelerated buzz of time itself? It was an ancient mystery to the City Commissioner of Streets. Like what geishas would do for you, whether they went down. Or the degree to which wrestling was fixed.) And sighed. And felt the tickle of his powerless old stupidity like the first symptoms of a chest cold.

And for the hell of it announced himself, pronounced his title. To see where he stood, to see what good it would do him. Willing to entertain questions. To take complaints, suggestions for his suggestion box.

The driver was not forthcoming. Druff pressed him.

"So what do you think?" he said. "As a country, do we live up to your expectations? Nationhoodwise?"

"Are you talking to me?" Edouvard Mrentzharev said.

"Yes," Druff said. "I'm a public official. I'm trying to get a picture. I'm looking for input. Admittedly, I'm strictly Streets. I ain't across the hall, or even just down a few doors from the hack bureau. Tell you the truth, I'm not even sure what floor they're on. But what the hell, eh, Edouvard? Say I'm on a fishing expedition. Say I'm on a fishing expedition looking for input from the people, and, incidentally, don't forget to give me a receipt for my taxes for the cab ride. But I'll tell you one thing, if I'm to serve the public at least I ought to know what it's thinking." He dropped his voice. "Edouvard, I want you to know, this isn't the way I usually come on to people. As a matter of fact, usually I don't come on to people at all. Say I'm in a mood, say the blood sugar is low. Say what you will."

Druff's back sank into the cab's plush, port-wine upholstery, his knees, compromised in the taxi's close quarters, pressed almost gynecologically toward his chest. He didn't weep or sob or cry out. Just felt himself awash in the deep sads, bobbing there in his loneliness and melancholy as if it were the universe.

"Of course," he went on, "you don't have to tell me a thing. I'm City Commissioner of Streets. Does that make me your ruler? It's just, I don't know, your name or something. Hell," Druff said, "I can't even *pronounce* your name. You could be a Sid in a suit. A dad from the thirties poking around in the back of a radio checking the vacuum tubes with a flashlight and duct tape. A guy whose kid is going to remember him fondly.

"Do you have any idea what I'm talking about? Tell me. Don't try to humor me. Don't even bother. Don't count on my being a good tipper. I haven't been in a cab in this city for ages. I probably tip for shit."

"What do you want?" Mrentzharev said.

"Your blessing, little Father," Druff said, somehow, even if Mrentzharev thought him nuts, even if he took down his statement and ran with it to the rest of the city's taxicab drivers, meaning it, every word, all of it. A blessing, a peasant's good word, a benediction from the salt and bread and garlic. Admiring this Edouvard Mrentzharev immensely, even envying him. His bravery, for one. For picking up and making a new life. For learning the language. For crossing the time zones to Druff's city. Manifest destiny generally over now, a closed book, a done deal. Shut down with the heart's and spirit's white flight of the nineteenth century, a decade or so of the twentieth. Mrentzharev was a straggler, with boat people mixed, with *Marielitos,* all the forced marches of all the exiles from all the losing sides. "Hence, buddy," he might have told him, "these tears ripe for the picking, and all the low, blunt blood of my fate's mood swings." Such boldness, Druff thought, examining Edouvard's picture, imagining him throwing in his lot with other oppressed and ordealed folks as easily as a traveler in Oz. There had to be wisdom and the deep abidings in this fellow.

And debriefed him. Getting the goods. Comparative shopping digs in Mother Slavia against what was available here. What Mrentzharev thought of America's stocked shelves, of the number, not counting cable even, of its TV channels. Warming up, practically rubbing his hands, feeling the return, just from fucking talking to the guy, to old Edouvard, of his energy. Of course, of course, Druff, nodding, agreeing, could barely keep up with him, with Mrentzharev's volunteered, exuberant information, his won-over trust.

"Yes, yes, of course," acknowledged Druff, a born-again sucker for the human-spirit thingy, "I understand about the curriculum, how every schoolboy is obliged to know English, but to learn how to drive? Professionally? At your age? This is something special."

The cabbie looked at him.

"What?" Druff asked.

"What so special?" Mrentzharev said. "Is everywhere traffic." And, laughing, began to boast to the City Commissioner of Streets of the small scams, what one did about tickets in the old country. "Oh," he said, breaking off, "please excuse me." And abruptly lifted a receiver. "Yes?" he said. "Yes?" And repeated numbers. Jotting them down with the stub of a pencil. "Fifteen minutes," he said, and replaced what turned out to be his car phone. "You were saying?"

Who wasn't saying anything. Who had lost interest. In the human spirit. In the black-and-blue marks on his own low melancholy. (Because this happened too. Life goes on. Indeed it did. It wasn't only the brushing and flossing, the taking of pills and making sure you had stamps. It wasn't just buying batteries for your wife's hearing aid, or carrying a handkerchief, or any of the rest of the light housekeeping of existence. It wasn't only coincidence or chaos or the scrambled random's unbroken code. It was this. *Mostly* it was this. The deep, hidden peristaltics of mood. Its tidals, its sink or swims. Life goes on. Saving a specific threat to the system, its pull on adrenaline, there was no such thing as priorities. Life goes on. Having a MacGuffin didn't change that. Who thought otherwise was a chump.) Who wished the ride over and was as good as his word about his shitty tipping.

Who hadn't kept up, what it came down to. Simple as that. Not *even* stupidity. Who still operated by the outdated laws of an older dispensation. Well, damn me, Druff thought. Well, fuck me and damn me. Well, kiss my ass. Well damn me and fuck me and lick my wounds. Whose premises had collapsed like a bridge. Who in the back of a cab had suddenly awakened to discover that all of it was real, *all* of it, everything, each and every worst-case scenario, that disease wore you down, that death actually happened, that the goblins *would* get you, and that though everyone was expendable not everyone was expendable at exactly the same time. This was what made all tragedy inconvenient, inopportune. The world happened piecemeal to people. The best parts, the worst. Bad timing was what got you in the end. Not knowing what others knew when others knew it. Thus spake the philosopher king. He had traveled miles on fools' errands on the streets he commissioned. And mourned his lost chances, his blown hope.

Changing his mind, turning back superstitiously to slip Edouvard Mrentzharev a few extra dollars. But it was too late. The fellow was already turning the corner, on his way to pick up a customer who had the number of the émigré's car phone.

Well, here we are then, Druff thought, no longer sure why he'd come, and saw he'd been let off in front of a rather substantial-looking apartment building with two distinct wings angled to a central pile, vaguely Tudor, with a courtyard, and wide, tall stone urns on either side of each of its three entrances. It was, he realized, astonishingly like the buildings he'd grown up in himself, and he was disarmed, not nostalgic so much as bewilderingly at ease, as if he'd been given nitrous oxide by the dentist. It was in this mood (another reversal; this didn't escape him) that he rang Doug's bell and could almost have danced chipper in place while he waited for the answering buzz that would admit him.

"What is it? Who's there?" Doug's voice hummed and gruffed from the perforations in the dull brass speaker alongside the mailboxes.

"Druff," Druff said. "Jeez," Druff, usually not, waiting for the beep, at his best on answering machinery, the long-distance telephone, on intercoms (but this was different, he was at ease now) said, "what's it been, a hundred years in the development and the bugs ain't all worked out. Still sounds like we're talking to each other out of our respective caves and sawmills."

"Commissioner?"

"Mrmp mrmp. Nhhh. Mrump nhh mrmp."

"Commissioner?"

"Because crackle there's crackle phht crackle cellular even in taxis these days. I just drove over with a guy who has one. A simple immigrant. Two lines, little pink Princess speakerphone, answering machine, the works. Is this the dawning of the Age of Aquarius, or what? You say, Doug. You tell me."

"Are you a little tight there, Commissioner?"

"Mrmp phhtt."

"Hold on. I'll buzz you aboard."

Thinking as he climbed the two flights to his driver's landing (since he really hadn't any reason for coming here, that it was just some buying-time thing, not in his game plan, that he was running on instinct now, less than instinct, hunch, less than hunch, bald, gut-level opportunism, serendipity, chasing down his casual, pig-in-a-poke fate) that perhaps Doug had an idea there (since Druff had none of his own and it occurred to him that for an old campaigner—and this happened too: adventure, the whole MacGuffin thing, maybe even heroism itself, volitionless as a knee jerk—he was rather at odds with himself, with his very nature, what with his having no strategy and all, or even the paraphernalia of one—— bumper stickers, campaign buttons, position papers, even positions, and, though he didn't, he should have felt uneasy) with that drunk bit tossed in his lap, a ploy he could use. Sure, he'd play along. Doug wanted tipsy, he'd give him tipsy. Why not? He was already punchy.

"Ah, Commissioner there," Doug, outside his apartment, called hollowly, leaning down over the railing at him. Sending his voice like a signal, some directional thing in the fog.

"That you, Doug?" Huffing and puffing. Laying it on.

"It is, Commissioner." A broad smile in the guy's voice, hearty as brogue, suspect as the good will of an announcer on the radio. Beaming all his heavy deferentials, chippered for the occasion as shined shoes.

"Where are you, Doug?"

"Right up here. Second-floor landing. Could you use a hand? I'll come down and give you a hand."

"No no. Just keep talking. I'll find you."

"Well then, to what do I owe the honor?"

"That's it, you're coming in clearer."

"Careful there. Just a few more stairs."

"My God, we could almost be in the same building, your voice is so clear. Huff puff, huff puff. What's that? What did you say?"

"When? Nothing."

"Thank God. I thought I'd lost you."

"Very funny, Commissioner."

"Crackle nhhh nhhh. Mrmp buzz. Snap crackle pop."

"Here. Give me your hand."

Druff, feeling like an asshole, put a finger to his lips. "Run silent, run deep."

(He hadn't playacted in years, he'd rarely bluffed this way. It was exhilarating, but it made him nervous.)

They shook hands. Doug, who was also in a suit—what was it today, the Easter Parade?—clapped an arm about the commissioner's shoulder, and Druff, who liked him, suddenly remembered all the old conflicted vibes that seemed to collect about the fellow like a turbulent human steam. The doorman cop was a confection, a complicated candy, a bachelor more mysterious than a priest. Druff, still in Doug's protective embrace, felt a sort of alarming reassurance, almost fatherly, as encouraging and skillful as the touch of a pederast.

"Oh," Druff said, pulling away and indicating Doug's spiffy clothes, "you were on your way out."

"No I wasn't."

"Yes you were. I'm interrupting."

"No you're not."

"Yes I am."

"Not at all."

"You're all dressed up."

"Well, so are you. Quite handsome you look."

"Well, I was collecting my rents," Druff said. It was an allusion to what Druff assumed was a general impression, that sense Doug gave off of an overtime heart. It was true. He wore his suit as if it were another uniform. How is it, Druff wondered, I like this agreeable, oleaginous hoverer? The commissioner risked the sweetest, lightest of hiccups, taking Doug in. Who, in turn, guiding him by the arm, covering his elbow like a leather patch, took Druff in. To the apartment. The commissioner attempted a soft stumble like a kind of stutter step and Doug, the blood of generations of crossing guards coursing through his veins, pulled him up quickly. He thought he knew what it might be about the guy. Then Druff, his boss years, who'd never been in Doug's place before, or, for that matter, spent social time with him anywhere, whose habit it had never been to host picnics for the people in his department, or attend their weddings and baptismals if he could help it (and sometimes even their funerals), who had played his political career by some almost Draconian severity of the separation of powers, was helped into a soft, deep chair and smiled up at him sweetly. And Doug smiled back. And Druff put his finger on it. What he liked about Doug. It was the man's asshole blindness. So much for it-takes-one-to-know-one. On the contrary, he thought, and realized he could continue in his assumed role forever, take it as far as he wanted, pull any stunt, go the distance with his act, that Doug would never challenge him. And this made him more nervous than ever.

Stop this, stop this, he commanded himself. And said to Doug, "Stop me. I'm putting you on. With my alcoholic vaudeville. I'm playing you for a sucker. You mustn't believe a word I'm saying."

"That's all right, sir."

"Mrrt phhht."

"Perhaps the commissioner could do with a nice cup of strong coffee? Shall I put some up?"

"Crackle shnarl buzzblat," Druff whispered.

"Sir?"

"Put some up your behind, that means."

"What about a cool cloth for your head?"

"No no no no no. You don't know fuck-all about sobering up tipsies. You've got it all turned around in your head. First you throw me into the shower with my clothes on. Time is of the essence. Don't even bother to empty my pockets. The water's got to be hot. Hotter than human skin can stand. And never, *never* sit a drunk down in a chair. You walk him around. Keep me moving. I've got to keep moving. Break my ass if I even *look* like I'm going to use it to sit down. Then, if there's time, then the strong coffee. Stick the cool cloth in it."

"Ah," humored Doug.

"I'm making a fool of you. You know that, don't you? I'm rubbing it in. I come, uninvited, to your apartment on a day you're off duty. I seem to interrupt you at a time when you're about to go out. And then, because I've apparently nothing better to do, I proceed to abuse you by pretending I'm drunk."

"Strictly speaking, sir, I'm an officer of the law. I'm never off duty."

"You've no shame, have you?"

"What would I be ashamed of?"

Druff studied the man, a fellow he knew to be his own age. Up there. An AARP card in his wallet. No doppelgänger, no alter ego. Just a humorless, unattractive, bachelor, jokey sort of man. "Well," Druff said, "there's been some talk."

"Talk, Commissioner?"

"Not so much talk as rumor, chitchat, idle gossip."

"What is it that's said?"

Druff, slumped in the chair, straightened up. "I'm no tale-bearer, sir," he said.

And then was talking away, spilling the beans. A mile a minute. But not about Doug, about the other one, dark Dick. "I've reason to believe," he said, "the two-timing son of a bitch is tripping on his wife, making nice-nice with persons he never had no license to move on."

Doug shrugged.

"What's that? A sign? Wind sock for 'That shit happens'? *I* know it happens. What do you think, I fell off a turnip truck? But no one bothers to lie anymore. In the past it was different. In the past people clung to their bits and snippets, their scraps and threadbare. But today, today the first thing to go is the fig leaf. It's all ta-da today.

"Shameless. It's shameless. Not like when you and *I* were young, Maggie. You know what she said to me? Dick's chippie? (Charlotte, incidentally, by her own report, and a mother of twins.) You know what she said? *'Nolo contendere.'* Can you imagine? *'Nolo contendere.'* Well, I ask you!"

"And this was after she lied to you," Doug said sympathetically.

"What?"

"This was after she lied to you. After she told you no one by that name even lived there. That you had the wrong number."

Druff perfectly understood that it was entirely possible that today

The MacGuffin

might be the day he would meet a violent death. He rated his chances at less than likely, but it certainly wasn't out of the question. Put it this way, he thought—— I wouldn't be surprised.

Because it didn't even occur to him that he'd caught Doug out, that Druff's drunk act, or any of his subsequent tirade, had sufficiently disarmed the man to a point where he would offer up information involuntarily. It would have been a waste of breath now to spring any traps, launch his devastating accusations. ("Aha! Who said she lied? Who ever mentioned wrong numbers?") Of course the old-timer had said it intentionally. Of course he had. Doug? A suspect old shady for as long as Druff knew him? But that was all it came down to finally. Suspicions. Smoke but no fire. Rumor and chitchat. Nothing ever proven. A man with no goods on him. Without goods. Goodless. Druff would not trouble to give Doug the lie. He wouldn't give the shithead the satisfaction.

So when the commissioner finally shouted at him and threw his challenges in Doug's face, it was for his own satisfaction. Not to see the sucker sweat so much as to hear what the old no-good rat bastard had to say. A matter of simple human curiosity.

"Well, you're our boss," said Doug.

"Your boss."

"We take an interest."

"In?"

"Your comings and goings."

"I see."

"It's only natural."

"So?"

"We keep an eye open."

"And?"

"An ear."

"And?"

"We call each other up."

"This could be it, all right. This could be the day."

"No," Doug said. "Don't talk like that. Don't be so fatalistic. It's too depressing."

"Well," said Druff, "I guess I'll be going."

"You don't have to."

198

"Yep. I'm on my way."

"Where to?"

"Oho."

"No, really."

"Aha."

"See you Monday, then."

"Your mouth to God's ears."

"Please," Doug said.

But the City Commissioner of Streets was standing now. They both were. "No," he said, "don't bother," giving himself the satisfaction, enjoying the words, anticipating the pleasure—this in split seconds, it was all split seconds on the special days—of the rest of the phrase, their melodramatic heft, "I'll let myself out." And just about did, was already at the door when he turned, giving himself still more satisfaction. "Does the name—" he said. And stopped.

"What?"

"Never mind, it's not important."

"No, what?"

"See *you* Monday," Druff said, and left Doug's apartment, moving carefully down the stairs and waiting for the S.O.B.—Druff sensed his presence at the railing—to rain names on his head, dropping them over him like water balloons, a shower of accomplice. Expecting him to. Margaret Glorio, he might have said. Mikey. Hamilton Edgar, Jerry Rector. Whatsisname, Dan. Su'ad herself, even. Or broadening the variables altogether, introducing new, devastating names, hush-hush high-ups from the inner workings, people so powerful your need to keep them out of it amounted to a kind of prurience, a sort of rut. Thinking what one of these might sound like, resonant, reverberant in the hallway as a shout in a shower.

No? Nothing? Off we go, then.

And now he's on his rounds, like a guy in a detective story. On his toes. The rhetoric of Q and A. The rhetoric of wheat and chaff. Sifting, sifting. Bobbo Druff, the truth mechanic.

Except now the jungle telegraph was onto him. They took an interest, Doug said. In his comings and goings. Well, what did he expect? They were professional chauffeurs, these guys, it *was* only natural. They called each other up, kept each other apprised. Administered apprisal advice. Like weather fucking forecasters. (He could talk this way. Who better entitled to use the rhetoric of the streets than their commissioner?)

What gave him pause was that he might not ask the right questions of whatever suspects he could yet run into on his last sweep of the day before he went home to eat his supper. Though that wasn't all that gave him pause. Not if this was Doomday. (He still handicapped the chances for this at less than likely, though they were up a bit since his conversation with Doug. Put it this way, he thought, it's safer than riding in an automobile, as the aviation people liked to keep reminding you. Yes, or being struck down by one, as Su'ad might herself have said. Poor Su'ad.) This could be the day.

He was hitchhiking.

It had been impossible to hail a cab in Doug's neighborhood and by the time he'd left his driver's residential streets for a busier district it had already begun to get dark, the beginning of twilight.

A guy in a pickup stopped for him.

"I seen the suit," he said.

"Hitchhiking," Druff said. "A man my age. It's quite extraordinary. One of those things—I'm fifty-eight—you figure will never happen to you again. Like going skinny-dipping or getting a piggyback ride. You know?"

"Sure," said the guy. "You don't have to be fifty-eight for them to start turning out the lights in your rooms. All the time stuff that might not ever happen again occurs to me, and I'm not even out of my thirties."

"Oh? Like what?"

"Well, when you put me on the spot like that . . ."

"I'll never be a father again," Druff said wistfully.

"You don't know that."

"I do," Druff said.

And then the two of them—the early Saturday evening traffic had begun to move out into the streets—— folks on their way to claim six-o'clock dinner reservations in restaurants, people headed for the rush-hour movie, girls from junior high chauffeured to friends' houses for sleep-overs—started their curious confidings in earnest, intimate as strangers. They bid up their famous last-this lists, their famous last-thats. Charles—that was the man's name—said his prom days were over, but Druff disallowed that one, not on the grounds that they weren't, but that the category, by its nature singular, was meaningless. "You might as well tell me you'll never have your first haircut again."

"I won't."

"Of course not," Druff said. "That's not the point. You can't have any feeling about that one way or another. It passed you by right when it happened."

"I'm told I threw a fit I was so scared, that the barber had to wait until I wore myself out crying and fell asleep in my mother's arms before he could come near me."

"You see?" Druff said. "It passed you right by."

"Oh sure," Charles admitted, "in that sense."

"Well, that's not what we're talking about, is it? We're talking about things we'll miss because they can't happen again."

"Hey," Charles said, "that's how I feel about my prom."

"All right," the City Commissioner of Streets said graciously, "I take your point."

"I can never lose my cherry again," Charles said.

"Well, Jesus," Druff said, "see what I mean? You could go on forever. Tell me, did you ever have mumps?"

"Sure."

"Well, you'll never get them again. You're through with mumps. Mumps are out of your life. When I mentioned that about hitchhiking it was with some awe, a certain sense of wonder. No," Druff said, "I'm not going to sit here and tell you I ain't going back to Capistrano. I've never been to Capistrano, and if I ever do get there it will be as a tourist. It'd be another thing altogether if I were a swallow."

"Got you," Charles told him agreeably. "You give me the prom but I have to take back my cherry."

"Well, it isn't a contest," Druff said. "As I say, what I offered was by way of wonder and wistfulness. I was catching my breath, I was rubbing my eyes.

"I mean it's more than likely I've made my last move. I mean Social Security is practically around the corner, but I won't be retiring to

Phoenix or Florida. Whatever happens. Of course I could always end up in a home, or die in a hospital bed, but it's a surefire, lead-pipe cinch we won't be selling our house and moving into a condo."

"You have a house."

"A nice house."

"A nice house," Charles said. "Kids?"

"My share," Druff said neutrally.

"And you're telling me that with grown, settled kids, probably raising families of their own by now, you and your wife are willing to go on living in a house way too big for just the two of you? I don't believe it."

"I'm sorry?"

"What do you need all that responsibility for?"

"It's comfortable," Druff said. "Living in a big house is comfortable."

"It's a lot of work."

"I'm not talking about Buckingham Palace. I'm talking about a nice, comfortable house."

"More than six rooms?"

"Living room, dining room, kitchen, den. Three bedrooms, screened-in breezeway, two and a half baths. A finished basement."

"Is there a garage?"

"Sure there's a garage. There's a swimming pool."

Charles looked at him. "Aboveground?"

"No. In-ground."

"It's too much."

"We have a small garden. Well, my wife does."

"It's too much."

"It's not too much."

"All that upkeep?"

"She could get a high school kid to come in once a week to do the gardening. We could close off a couple of bedrooms. We can shut down the dining room and take our meals in the kitchen. We could drain the pool, let the backyard reclaim it. And we don't actually *need* the den or that second full bath. We don't use them that much now, if you want to know. And let me tell you something else. When it becomes too much for us to drag ourselves down to the finished basement we'll probably be finished ourselves, and a sure thing for the home anyway. So you can forget all that crap about upkeep. Upkeep's the least of it. Upkeep is trivial. It's *upheaval* kicks your ass."

"Well," Charles said uncertainly, "I don't know."

"Because you're young," Druff said. "When you're my age, you'll feel differently about it. Not so quick on the trigger to make major, irrevocable changes."

"It's sure possible," Charles said.

They'd had a good talk, Druff thought. He'd settled important things with Charles that he and Rose Helen had yet even to discuss. Of course there was a certain flaw in his logic—— the fallacy of the unmentionable middle or somesuch. He hadn't said anything about Mikey. That they might just have to move out on him in the middle of the night when the kid wasn't looking. Even so it had been a good talk. A wonderful talk. This was the stuff people without MacGuffins talked about. (This happens, too, thought the man with the MacGuffin.)

Becalmed, they drifted awhile longer in the slow, heavy traffic. (People coming back from beauty parlor appointments, from high school sporting events, from visiting relatives in hospitals, from errands, from shopping, from making arrangements, from returning things to department stores, too small or too large, stuff which on second thought they didn't really want to own, that was too expensive, too much trouble to maintain.) Druff gazing lazily into the traffic from the height of the cab, staring down into the laps of women. His ride as abstracted as himself, becoming engaged with the traffic, alternately pressing his gas pedal, his brakes; rapt as someone fishing as he touched his pickup's controls.

And Druff, who couldn't get over it, trying to recall the last time he'd had a conversation that didn't sound like dialogue in a book. He couldn't do it. Well I'm a politician, he thought, I have enemies. I'm an enemy myself. Enemies can turn just about anything into a federal case. We're all Sturm and Drang, enemies. We're too excitable by half. We make life a big deal. And had to admit it was pleasant, doing the time of day with Charles—— all that real estate chat, his dining room plots and plans. And wondered about the laid-back life. Nah, he thought, it ain't good enough. I couldn't live like that. Hey, I am what I am. A fellow has to give in to his fiction.

"Awfully considerate," Druff said. "You picking me up like that back there. You saved my life."

"No problem," Charles said, "don't mention it."

"No, really," Druff said.

"That time of day, that kind of neighborhood? I won't tell you you could have called your shots a little better."

"There wasn't much I could do, really," said Druff, opening his book, finding his place. "I don't use my limousine on weekends."

"Maid's day off?"

"Maids is right. There are two of them."

"*Two* maids," Charles said.

"Well, chauffeurs."

"Yeah," said Charles, "chauffeurs. That's what I meant."

"It's pretty ironic. I was just coming back from paying a call on one of my drivers. We had words. Or anyway *I* did. He tried to pretend nothing happened. To be perfectly frank, I didn't think of it, but even if I had I was in no frame of mind to ask my chauffeur if I could use his phone to call a cab."

"No, of course not."

Druff understood Charles thought he was crazy, he understood none of this was any of his business. He didn't care. He didn't hold with secrets. And anyway, if something untoward really did happen to him, he was marking the trees, laying a trail. "So thanks for picking me up back there."

"I told you," Charles said, "I slowed for the suit. I didn't see *you* in it. I didn't see anyone in it."

Right, Druff thought, that's just what I was telling my tailor. "Anywhere around here will be fine," he said.

"You sure? Because this isn't the sort of place you described. I mean it's all elevator buildings. It don't seemed zoned for neighborhood."

"Oh, I don't live around here."

"No."

"Thought I'd drop in on my mistress."

Charles stopped his pickup at the curb and Druff carefully let himself out. Before shutting the door he turned back. "Charles, listen to me," he said. "I'm not naming names because maybe I've got it all wrong and I'm in the clear. *Habeas corpus,* know what I mean? I'm fifty-eight years old. A lot of this could be glandular, a figment. Maybe all of it is. Nobody followed us. Now I know *that's* not worth the paper. I mean, you don't actually have to follow people. Not when you can phone ahead. Shit, Charley, I'm fifty-eight. *My* itinerary ain't hard. Limo guy number one, limo guy number two. My kid, my wife, and a lady who makes it with ghosts.

"It's just I've got this feeling today could be the day I buy the farm. Fill out the forms, pay the points, do the closing. It's only a feeling. I'm not really scared. It's a little erotic, even. Catastrophe is required sometimes, the death-dangers. A touch of the apocalypse. You know, a lick and a promise."

He could tell Charles was anxious to get going, that he wasn't in the mood. (No, thought Druff, he ain't? And was suddenly reminded of last night, of the cars stopped at cross streets waiting for the green.) The commissioner hung on to the pickup's open door for dear life. He was still talking, making his impressions, marking his trail, territorial as an animal.

"It's just I'm closing in on these guys," he said.

"Which guys?"

"Well, as I say, I'm not at liber—"

"No no," Charles said, "don't give me that. You're at liberty. You're at liberty all *over* the place. I've never seen anyone at so much. So *which* guys? Come in, sit down, feel free. *You,* easy rider, I know all about you—— your age, your contingency plans for when the house gets too big—— which goes first, your pool or your dining room. I know which toilet you piss in. So don't tell *me* you're not at liberty. Ain't I been sitting here like limo guy number three, listening to all your harum-scarum? Which guys? Which goddamn guys?"

"You've been very kind," Druff said softly.

"Too right."

The City Commissioner of Streets let go of the door but did not shut it just yet. "It's true," he said. "I'm not at liberty."

"Hey," Charles said, "are you going to be all right?"

"I'm not at liberty to say am I going to be all right," said the City Commissioner of Streets, thinking it could be so, what's there to stop it. There was something to his vague, titillative misgivings. There had to be. Knowing your chances and fate was at least as possible as knowing your body, your own most intimate, physical perceptions of the world. Once burned, twice sorry. If he lived *another* fifty-eight years he'd never mistake a heart attack for indigestion, could, with his telltale left arm tied behind his back, identify the singular pain that shot through it as clearly as some high, burning astronomical event over a quadrant of sky. He would forever recognize the particular stitch in his side, in his back, of a collapsed lung, the strange, sudden heaviness in the groin that prefigured a kidney stone. One minute nothing, asymptomatic, his personal weather like a day for flying kites, the next clouded over with squalls from nowhere.

Charles was all right, Charles was probably as clean as a whistle, clean-as-a-whistle-wise, as it was possible to get in a compromised age. Yet it was almost all he was worth not to ask what he hauled in the truck bed, not, as official commissioner of the city's streets, to demand to see invoices and manifests. Druff knew from their conversation the man was married. He knew he still had kids young enough to be driven in a car pool. He knew he worked as a projectionist, a kind of on-site inspector, in one of those automated multiplex cinemas with enough theaters radiating out from beneath its roof it could almost be a video rental service. (The sewers of Paris, he thought, each time he went to see a movie in one of those places.) Well, for a car pool they'd have to come up with something better than a pickup truck, so if he didn't use it as the family car, and didn't need it in his business, then surely the truck must have been used, at least partly, for hauling a certain amount of contraband. No? Not? These days?

And old Druff still standing there staring at old Charley, sizing up his benefactor. For plunder, smuggle, loot, the sacked and secret booties.

Feeling these vibes, getting this picture, imagining the puzzle coming to a head like a pimple. Thinking like a gifted clairvoyant now, some canny working for the cops, on the city's actual payroll, possessed, running for daylight, inspired, bursting with intimation, sensing the aura of what was, damn near almost seeing the big picture, where everything went, how they put it all together, not the trail he'd been marking so much as that other one, all the trampled green places in the woods others had done for, something as material as hunch, dizzying as odor, Druff at once exhilarated and crazed, chipper as a hound, in it for the luscious bloods and dirts, high on this stench of the hunted, until Charley, in consultation with vibes of his own, intuiting what Druff was up to could be, leaned all the way over and across the cab of his pickup and slammed the door.

Druff stared after the little truck, in the street now but still snagged on pieces of traffic, until the scent gradually cooled, faded, was gone.

So anyway. Even if he didn't buy the farm, even if it wasn't even for sale, something was up. The commish on the cusp of things heavy-hearted. We'll see what we'll see. But no longer in touch with his wiped impressions, these scattered as the shards of a dream.

Remembering only the grander outlines of his bozo itinerary. Margaret Glorio, check. Naming her name in his heart and, opening the plastic sack in which he still carried a half dozen batteries for Rose Helen's hearing aids, he removed the three blister packs and distributed them discreetly about his person, placing one in the left inside pocket of his suit coat, another in the right, and shoving the last deep into the jacket's breast pocket. Running on zinc now, thought the City Commissioner of Streets, his energy up, or on some fillip of shit more likely, what he felt trembling his gut now he'd left the pickup and was out on the wide sidewalks of Meg Glorioland, a jolt of the high school juices gathering, adrenalizing him and giving him, for all he knew, the zits altogether.

Oh, he thinks, taking in the prospect, high rises with their addresses scribbled across their canvas canopies like meticulous signatures or the lettering on expensive invitations; discrete, iron-fenced trees sunk into the pavement like extravagantly potted plants; impressed as always by the tony, handsome upscale of the neighborhood, adjacent, it occurs, to the very park where he and Dick, searching out potholes, had encountered the mounted policeman—has he come full circle? he wonders—only the day before.

Though from here he can't even see Margaret Glorio's building. He had deliberately passed it without saying anything—for Charley's benefit—two blocks back. Nothing wrong, Druff thought, with a little camouflage. It was simple courtesy to lay down a trail. Nobody said it had to be a U.S. goddamn geological survey.

Druff went into Margaret's lobby, started toward the elevator.

"Hey," someone called. "Hey, hey."

It was the man from the night before, the fellow dozing at the television monitors, and who, awakened by Dick pounding on the horn, had then roused Druff.

"What?" said Druff.

"Where you going? You can't go up unless you're announced."

He didn't want to be announced. He didn't want to give her an opportunity to refuse to see him. (He remembered the call she said she was expecting, her initial rush to get him off the phone.)

The doorman insisted.

Druff wondered if the man recognized him, but couldn't tell. (Though he'd made the limo, he recalled, had known it was from the city.) To keep him off the scent a while longer, he offered Margaret's apartment number, not her name. (More lore from the woods, the higher camouflage studies.)

"What's your name?"

"Druff," Druff whispered.

"Wait, I'll announce you." He went to say something into an intercom and was back in less than a minute.

"Margaret *has* a visitor," he said.

"I see."

"She says what do you want."

"What," Druff said, "you think I'd tell you and blow my cover?"

"You'll just have to wait then," he said. "You can sit over in that armchair you fell asleep in last night."

"I wasn't here last night."

"Got ya," the doorman said, and winked.

"Well, I wasn't," Druff said.

"Right."

He was probably supposed to tip him but had no notion of what was appropriate in these circumstances. He had no clue what these circumstances even were exactly. "You know," Druff said, "for a man my age, I have no idea what's proper here. I mean, what are you? A working stiff, same as myself." He glanced at the fellow's elaborate uniform, at his epaulets and ornate, cursive braid. "Just another gold-collar worker doing his job the best he knows how. I wouldn't want to embarrass you," he said. "I mean, you're the expert here. Tell me. What's fair? I want to be fair."

"Forget it," he said. "My treat."

"Well, I appreciate that. I do. But just for the record."

"Well," said the doorman, "just for the record, it depends on who's being protected, some married party, or bachelorette number one."

Druff casually placed a hand over his wedding band and leaned in toward the doorman. He was going to ask about Margaret Glorio's visitor when someone, moving past his peripheral vision, waved to the doorman, who called, "See you, sir. Thank you very much, sir," and waved back.

"That was him, wasn't it?"

"Who?"

"Miss Glorio's visitor."

"Was it?"

"Come on," Druff said. "I didn't get a good look."

The fellow shrugged and Druff produced a twenty, which he extended toward him. Well, *produced.* Which he *fumbled* out of his wallet. Which he was first at some difficulty to remove from the rear pocket of his pants, and was then at some more to unfold and open (the exact amount having been determined in advance, in an instant, less than an instant, and even then not really determined, finally, so much as known, almost—had he believed in such things—inspired), and then tried to hand over. (He was new at this: not bribery, not the fix; he was a political after all, he knew his baksheesh, the cost of doing business; but this kind of business? intrigue business? after years on Inderal?) And, well, for that matter, a *twenty.* A five, a ten, and five singles, actually, which, even at that, he had to practically fucking study, for Christ's sake, looking into the wallet, examining it at close range, reading the goddamn bills like some auditor going over the goddamn books!

"Sorry," the Supreme Allied Commander–looking chap, declining Druff's seven pieces of paper currency, told the City Commissioner of Streets, "that one's under my protection."

"Everyone seems to be under your protection."

"I got de whole worl' in my hands."

(And doing comedy, Druff thought, *this* happens. Comedy is what they do to you when there's nothing you can do, when there's nothing doing.)

"May I go up now?"

"Who's stopping you?"

"Aha!" Druff, a beat or so behind the rhythm of the conversation, said, meaning it had *too* been the guy, forgetting he already knew as much, and had since the doorman told him the man who'd just brushed past his peripheral vision was under his protection. He felt a sort of pity for Miss Glorio at this moment. Being ridiculous, he made her look bad. It was a good thing the doorman had her in his hands.

"Announce me," he said, chastened, and a little resentful, too. Even angry. Because the guy wouldn't take Druff's fistful of dollars, because no promises had been made, and the commissioner was high and dry in the lobby. It was as if he'd been denied membership in a not very exclusive club. "Tell her Druff's on his way up. Give her a chance to put her face on, fix her hair. Maybe slip into something a little more uncomfortable."

And stepped into the elevator and pushed "11," vaguely proud of what he anticipated would be Margaret's view: of the park, of the city, Druff's streets. And for the second time in as many days struck his temple with his open palm. He wouldn't get to see it. Any more than last night. It was dark out. Here, in the elevator, atemporal as Las Vegas, the lateness of the hour so abruptly revealed to him—Druff's vaudeville truths, his dunderhead dumb show—was oddly disconcerting. He was frightened of this particular dark, of Margaret's eclipsed views. What, he wondered, am I doing here? What in hell's going on, just? It isn't enough, he added obscurely, I have no friends in the lobby? It was Saturday night. Now you'd be able to find suits all over the place. But he'd been wearing his all day. It was no longer fresh. There was fear in its cloth. It could use a press. He cursed his bollixed timing. In various pockets, Rose Helen's expensive batteries, not in use, drained ever so slowly. Near the eleventh floor he seriously considered going back down again, skipping Margaret, dropping all charges, returning home. And held his course only because of the vagrant, concupiscent itch in his used, fearful pants.

Or something like that.

And then Margaret, like a landmark, was standing outside her open door in the carpeted hallway when the elevator doors opened, and Druff was lured out. Something hospitable about her presence, gracious, old-fashioned, by-the-book. She could have been his hostess, welcoming him to a dinner party.

"I *thought* you'd show up."

"Is this a bad time?"

"I expected you earlier."

"A contributing factor is potholes," Druff said. "Potholes slow a guy down."

"What is it?" she asked.

"I came," he said, "about the one-night stand."

"You came about furniture?"

"What? Oh, right. Very funny."

"You never heard that one before?"

"No."

"It's buyer humor."

They were inside her small apartment. Druff didn't recognize it. "You've done something to the furniture," he said.

"They came today to dress the windows," Margaret Glorio said.

Druff nodded. "So I see."

"You like it, though?"

"It's different."

Margaret Glorio belly-laughed.

"What?"

"You topped me," she said.

"What?"

"Guy walks into a flat he's been in it can't have been fourteen or fifteen hours earlier. Overnight all the furniture's been replaced. He's asked what he thinks. Guy says 'It's different.' You topped me."

"Well," Druff said, "that was unintentional."

"Sure sure," Margaret Glorio said.

He couldn't get over what had been done to the place. Overnight. As she'd said herself. It could have been a sting operation, or early evening, a week later, a parlor suite in a luxury hotel in a large city, in the second act of a play. He was looking for the bed. Surely Margaret's pricey brocade sofa did not open out.

Miss Glorio, darting her eyes everywhere Druff's settled, matched him glance for glance. Except for the fact that her face registered a certain amusement, it could almost have been a tic, as if she were one of those people whose lips move with your own, silently repeating everything you say.

"Come here," she said, "I'll show you something."

She took Druff's hand and led him up to a mahogany highboy, opening one drawer, then another, in the tall chest.

"What's wrong with this picture?" she said.

"The drawers are empty?"

"Come over here," she said.

Behind a high, silken, vaguely Japanese folding screen was a small Pullman kitchen. She pulled open the cupboards and cabinets.

"Poor Mother Hubbard?"

"There you go," Margaret Glorio said.

Druff nodded and Miss Glorio—she was still holding his hand—led him out from behind the screen and back into the living room.

"So tell me," she said when he was seated on the rich brocade couch she had invited him to share, "you see what things mean to me, how unattached I am. We could go into the bathroom and I could show you my medicine chest. A bottle of generic aspirin, toothpaste, a few hotel soaps and shampoos. There aren't any monograms on my hand towels. I haven't any appliances, not even a microwave. I eat out of cartons from Chinese restaurants, white paper bags. From cardboard boxes the pizza guy brings. Off Styrofoam china from the fast food, trays wrapped in cellophane around airline meals I never touched. So tell me, what was all that about Oriental rugs?"

"I don't understand."

"Oh please," Margaret Glorio said.

He *didn't* understand. There were Oriental carpets in the rabbi's study. In the rabbi's study's crapper even. They'd reminded him of Su'ad, suggested some Middle East connection which had seemed important at the time. He remembered, but didn't understand. Seeing whether there was an Oriental rug at Margaret's had seemed a good reason to come here today. Now he wasn't so sure. MacGuffins were mind-boggling things. They were seductive, they threw you curves, they fucked you over. With the fleeting, now-you-see-'em-now-you-don't appearances they put in on weekends? He could only conclude they weren't dependable, MacGuffins. They were a trip, MacGuffins, but hardly money in the bank. Druff had lost sight of his reasons. Even though he saw that there were small Oriental rugs everywhere. The one behind the folding screen in the Pullman kitchen. The one over by the wing chair. Another practically under his feet. Three he could account for without even taking her up on her offer to show him the bathroom. But he couldn't even find her bed, for heaven's sake. How could he tell how many carpets there could still be?

Was it even important?

Seeing everything changed had thrown him off, the new decor.

"They're nice," Druff said. He meant the rugs, and tapped the one nearest him with the toe of a shoe. He indicated the one over by the wing chair with his jaw.

"Are you all right? What's wrong? Don't you feel well?"

"Well, I'm hungry," he said, "is there somewhere I could lie down?" (This was so. He required food. His breakfast had been botched. And he never got that lunch he'd been promised—— his filet mignon, his garden fresh vegetables, his wine, his strawberries out of season. His hamburger, his order of fries, his coffee and pie à la mode had proved inedible. Margaret was no help. She had no utensils. Even if there'd been the makings for tea there'd be nothing to drink it from; even the brandy snifters seemed to be gone. He could hardly be expected to lick tea out of her cupped palms. Tea wouldn't have satisfied him anyway. What he really needed was a good solid meal. Though he had no appetite for it.)

"Why don't you put your feet up?" Margaret said.

"But it's silk," Druff said.

"You won't hurt it."

"It's silk," he said.

"Wait. I'll help with your shoes," she said.

She was rubbing the commissioner's temples, massaging his neck, touching his hair. She was drawing her nails down his cheek. Her hand was in his lap. He had an erection.

"We should both lie down," she said.

"Where?" he said. "How? Does this sofa make up? You think we ought to do it on the sofa? I don't know, I don't have a rubber," he said. "I could stain the brocade. You think that stuff comes out of silk? Maybe you have rubbers. Could you lend me one? I'll pay you back."

"I don't have soup bowls, why would I have rubbers?"

"Maybe the man I saw in the lobby left one with you."

"Dan?"

"You know Dan?"

"You're such a worrywart."

"Dan doesn't worry me."

"Nothing should worry you."

"I'm no kid," he said.

"What's that got to do with it?"

"A man old enough to be my age takes things into account."

If they were horses they'd be walking. It seemed to Druff the gait of their conversation had slowed.

"I'll make up the futon," she said, easing his head from her lap. She brought a thin mattress and two pillows out of a closet and spread a clean sheet across the futon.

"I'm not sure," Druff said. "I don't think I could get down on that."

"I'll lower you."

"Once I'm down I might not be able to get up again."

"I'll raise you."

He felt foolish undressing in front of her, just as foolish removing his suit coat, shirt and tie as he did taking off his pants. He was no beauty, Druff. He looked even worse in his scarred body and toneless, troubled flesh than he did in clothes. He tried to place himself onto the low, distant futon, only two inches or so from the bare floor. He bowed from the waist, recovered. Feinting, he made as if to lean into a kneeling position, then straightened up again. Seeking various body leverages, this lone, unopposed wrestler.

"I've got you," Margaret Glorio, sitting up, pronounced from the futon. One arm was wrapped about his leg, the other held him around the hip. She was in her underwear, her flesh tones bright as perfectly adjusted color on television. "Go on, don't be afraid to put your weight on me. Lean on my shoulder. I won't let you fall."

Using her back and shoulders for handholds, he carefully rappeled down the side of her body. "Whew!" he said, beside her at last. But his hard-on was almost gone. And he couldn't properly maneuver on the futon, on its sheet like a picnic cloth set down on hard, stony ground. He thrashed away, but the floor, which he could feel through the scant, paltry mat, hurt his knees and dug into his elbows. He at last abandoned her and fell uselessly away. How, he wondered, did Japan manage to repopulate itself? "Well," Druff said, out of breath, "that was pretty humiliating for me. How was it for you?"

"What are all these scars?" she asked, running a finger down the incisions from his bypass surgery and other invasive procedures. Where they'd cracked open his chest. Where they'd taken a vein from his left leg and placed bits of it about his heart where the woodbine twines. Where they'd punctured his side and run a tube through it to his lung to blow it up again after it had collapsed.

"Maybe," Druff said unhappily, "I should have stained the brocade. I could have tried to induce a nosebleed."

"It's odd. I didn't even notice these last night," Margaret Glorio said.

"Well, you wouldn't, would you?" Druff said. "I didn't have them last night."

"Oh you," Margaret said.

"Could you reach me my suit coat?"

"Are you cold? I'll get us a blanket."

"Well, yes, as a matter of fact. But I need something out of one of the pockets in my suit coat."

Effortlessly, she raised herself to a standing position. She was a big woman, tall as the diminished Druff, and not, he imagined, all that much lighter. He could only guess at the source of her agreeable strength. Maybe it came from the luxuriant hair that grew at her luxuriant pudendum. From his spectacular worm's-eye view as she moved away from him, he stared up at her stirring, eloquent ass, at her sparkling snatch, glittering like facets off some hairy diamond as it vanished and appeared in league with her long strides. Anything doing? he wondered. Nah, not much. Nothing at all, in fact. Still, he thought, he was privileged to see this. If they didn't kill him, he'd have to try to remember what it looked like.

"You poor guy," she said, "was this what you wanted?" She held out one of the blister packs.

"That's not mine," Druff said with some indignation.

"It's not?"

"No," he said, "of course not."

"I thought it might be the battery for your pacemaker or something."

"I don't have a pacemaker."

"Well, that's good," she said. "I thought maybe you did. What with those scars and all. You poor guy."

"No," he said. "Those are my wife's. She's deaf."

"You poor guy."

"Could you hand me my jacket?"

She handed over the suit coat, then started to pull her underwear back on, panty hose, a brassiere, white and plain as a kid's training bra. Druff was surprised. He would have imagined teddies on this woman, garter belts holding silken hosiery. "What have you got there? Oh," she said, "your coca leaves."

"A little fortification," he said. "I could use the euphoria right now. Also, it gives me energy and cuts my appetite. Inca Indians use this stuff in the highest Andes. A few of these leaves in their jaws, the little fellas can keep going for days. They're so wired, some of them walk up to work from their homes down at sea level."

"You're not going to share?"

"Here," he said, extending the pouch. "Chow down."

"No thanks," she said. "The way it works is I blackmail *you,* not the other way around."

In minutes his hunger had gone, his weakness. He'd forgotten his humiliation. Waves of well-being moved over him. He wondered if it was too late to try something even though she was dressed now. Nah, he realized, still nothing doing. Years of Inderal chemicals and ages of controlled agricultural substances fighting his libido to a standstill. Last night had been a gift. (Margaret Glorio would have to try to remember *that.*) "Women are damned good sports," the City Commissioner of Streets said from his new, dreamy energy.

"Oh? How's that, sweetie?"

"Well, *you* know . . ."

"No," she said. "I really don't."

"Well, my performance, for example."

"You call that a performance?"

"Right," Druff said, and clammed up and, spreading out his suit jacket, covered his genitals and surgical scars and, pulling the sleeve of his coat over it, tried to hide what he could of the long zippery scar where the surgeons had removed the vein from his leg.

"Come on," she said, "don't be that way. Suppose your face froze like that?"

"Another weather terrorist heard from," Druff mumbled.

"What?"

"I was making the point," he said, "that women were good sports about these things, but I guess no one is, really. Sex is the *hardest* thing to get right. Please," Druff put in quickly, "say nothing unworthy." (Because he realized there was a streak of vulgarity to her. An air, despite her buyer's smarts and chic, à la mode wisdoms, of rough inelegance which cost her points. This, well, jungliness. Her blatant body was an example, her telegenic flesh tones, or just the forwardness of her pronounced strength. Summer vacations, for kicks, on a lark, she might have done stints with the Roller Derby. Oh, he was a *fastidious* asshole. Still, she told jokes like a man—— "Guy walks into this flat . . ." Besides, she knew he was a married man, and had slept with him anyway.)

"Who do you think you're talking to, 'say nothing unworthy'?"

"The performance remark? Then when I said that about the 'hardest thing to get right'? You're not that innocent. I could see double entendre in your eyes practically. I set myself up."

"Oh sure," she said, *"up."*

"I shouldn't be here," he said. But he meant something else. (He'd changed the subject, he meant.) He talked about love now. About what was permissible. Love's dead-center telemetry, blind Cupid's locked-in coordinates. Propinquity was nothing, vaunted chemistry, all inexact dead reckoning's girl-next-dooriness. Likewise Fate, the Kismets. Statistically, Druff figured, the odds of Fate coming through in matters of the heart were up there with hitting the Lotto. So if chemistry counted for nothing, propinquity, fate, what did? However did people end up in bed together?

"It's demographics," the City Commissioner of Streets said.

"The girl next door is demographics?"

Druff spoke up from the Japanese pallet and made a speech, wooing her, wooing himself, chasing her vote, his own, laying a little of the old Lincoln-Douglas on them both. "No," he said, "she doesn't exist. She's like Betty Crocker. Not even. She's a hairstyle, a skirt length, a size six or so shoe. When I say demographics I speak as a politician. Colored or white, combined household income, highest degree earned. Did your mother come from Ireland? Margin for error two points plus or minus. We're fixed, I mean. Set in cement, chiseled in stone. Everyone who isn't denied us is denied us. I mean it. It's the demographics that require a fellow to forsake and forswear. We live by a finding, nature's negative fiat. My Christ, think of the ways screwing is out of bounds—— all God's and custom's disparate dasn'ts. The incests of family, the inside-out incests of class. All the sexual holdouts. When A declines B because B don't measure up. Hey, just fear of trespass or a failure of nerve. An act of adultery's a miracle when you stop to think. I don't care how in synch with the times a man thinks he is, you can't just knock 'em down and pull 'em into an alley. God fixed his canon 'gainst that sort of thing. Let alone the decorums—— this one protecting her cellulite, that one a failure of sheer damned inches. Or holdouts of the head or heart when character's a consideration—— all love's and sexuality's crossed fingers. I talk through my hat if I tell you it's natural. It ain't natural. It's the most unnatural thing in the world. The shortfall in opportunity, in the alignment of inclinations: 'SWM, athletic, non-smoker, social drinker, interested in movies, music, dancing, dining, books and laughter, sitting around the house on rainy Sunday afternoons reading the *Times,* seeks relationship with attractive SWF with similar tastes.' Oh? Yeah? You think? 'SWM looking to get it on with MBF alligator wrestler. Must be able to make her own shoes and handbags' is more like it. C may screw D but he's dreaming of Jeannie with the light brown hair.

"I tell you, Miss Glorio, there are drifts and tendencies and pronenesses. There's kinks and fixations, bent and bias. There's yens and itches. And if the lion ever lies down with the lamb, or the goat with the otter, it's dollars to doughnuts they're dreaming of Jeannie with the light brown hair, too.

"Because love has to be exonerated, the extenuating circumstances taken into account, the forgives and forgets."

"I love it when you talk gabardine. It fetches me, it really does. It's a shame you can't fuck," Meg Glorio told him.

"There you go again," said the commissioner. But she was right. It was. He tilted his head back and looked to where she sat, dressed, looking down on him from her superior position on the brocade sofa.

She was smiling. Then, quite suddenly, she reached down and plucked the suit coat from his body. She started to laugh.

"Jesus," Druff cried, and tried to cover himself with his hands. Then, just as suddenly as she'd pulled his jacket from him, almost inspired, and thinking, no, *not* almost, inspired out-and-out; by his on-again-off-again MacGuffin sung to, City Commissioner of Streets Druff rolled to his side where he lay on the futon and grabbing the edge of one of Margaret Glorio's small Oriental scatter rugs drew it across his body.

Punching up the two pillows, he propped his head against them, spread his fingers and placed his hands on top of the little rug's soft, silken pile. He smoothed the carpet down over his chest and belly and tucked it in next to his torso and thighs.

"How do I look?" he said. "Luxurious? Like a guy in a deck chair? Like someone preparing to take breakfast in bed?"

"Cute," she said evenly, "as a bug in a rug."

Idly, he turned back a corner of the carpet.

"I forget," Druff said, "is it good or bad if the pattern shows through the back of these things?"

"It's good," Margaret Glorio said.

Druff, flourishing the carpet as if it were a sheet flung over an unmade bed, or he some awkward bullfighter losing control of his cape in the wind, managed to flick the thing onto its verso. There, palely, the carpet's mirror image showed itself, all its obsessed finials and geometrics, all its endlessly repetitive interlacing stems and leaves like some deranged floral script.

"You admire my rug?"

"Olé," said the City Commissioner of Streets.

"What are you looking for?"

"I don't know," Druff said, "washing instructions, a tag, the little whoosie they stitch onto pillows and mattresses."

"I don't see anything like that."

"No," he said, "me neither."

"Get dressed, Commissioner. Put the rug down. Get back in your clothes."

It was the syntax of someone with the drop on you, Druff thought. She'd be pointing a gun at him. Well, well, he thought, he wasn't really old, not even sixty actually, but he was a man with conditions—— his

heart, his lungs with their peculiar tendency to collapse and patched as
worn tires, his impotence, his worn old brains, even the tic that shut
his eyes against scorn and diminishment and that he'd picked up from
Mikey—they were shut now—even his MacGuffin. So if he wasn't, if
one counted actual years, old, he felt like an octogenarian. He could
have been someone in a home, though even with his complaints and
conditions, in no way did he feel he'd led a full life. Not, in spite of
his parapolitical street smarts and City Hall ways, politically, not sexu-
ally, not philosophically. In a peculiar way, he had his whole life ahead
of him. And he was frightened. Well, she had the drop on him. Then
there was the guy in the lobby who'd turned up his nose at Druff's
twenty bucks. In such clear cahoots with Maggie. All she had to do after
she shot Druff was buzz the doorguy on the intercom. If they could bring
an entire apartmentful of furniture into her place and set it all up in
a few hours, they could probably dispose of just poor skimpy old Druff
in minutes. There had to be special service elevators in the building.
There could be God knew what all—— incinerators, tortuous, murderous
laundry chutes.

Think fast, Druff thought. He called on his MacGuffin. What to do,
what to do? he prayed at it. I wouldn't bother you, he prayed, only I
just remembered that premonition I had at Doug's—— that this could
be the day I come to a bad end? What with Margaret having the drop
on me and all, I figure the odds on that happening are up from outside
to about so-so. If this were baseball, say, my magic number would be
somewhere in the teens.

Then, quick as snap, Ol' MacGuffin came through, speaking to him
from some court of last resorts, singing the desperate long-shot odds (of
the plan's success, the feasibility of its proposed escape measures),
figuring them at one chance or something in a million.

She told you to get dressed, she demanded you put that rug down,
the MacGuffin reprised.

Yes, yes, impatient Druff, needing to act quickly but thinking Mac-
Guffin was merely vamping, thought miserably.

Put the rug down, the MacGuffin counseled.

Go along with her.

Put the rug *down!*

Sure, he thought, I can do that. Then what?

Don't get into your clothes.

Seduce her? The woman's got the drop on me. Don't you think it's a little late for that?

You're naked as a jaybird. You think she'd shoot you in here? That she could afford to take that kind of chance? This place is tiny, it's a tiny, cozy little place. You ain't but a couple of feet from that brocade sofa. There'd be blood all over the furniture, the pillows and pallet, inside the drawers of the mahogany highboy, soaking into the wing chair's fancy fabrics and the nifty new lamp shades. And you can't tell me that Jap folding screen wouldn't take a hit. And what about the rugs? All this shit's on consignment. Think. It's demos and loaners, this shit. She probably had to sign for every last stitch.

The MacGuffin was right. He'd defy her. Turning his neck, twisting it awkwardly up and away from the pillows, he was about to make the MacGuffin's argument. It was the first time he dared look at her.

"Darn it, Commissioner, I thought I asked you to get dressed," Miss Glorio said. "Why are you still lying there naked like that? What do you think this is?"

"Oh," said the Commissioner of Streets. (Or oof. Or whoops. Something breathless, anyway, something startled and becalmed, something sucker-punched, something with the wind taken out of its sails.) "Oh," he said again, this doomed, debilitated, worn-brained, impotent, heart-bypassed, vulnerable-lunged, tic-ridden, MacGuffin-haunted, paranoid old man, "you're not even packing a weapon, are you?"

"Come on, Druff," she said. "Put up or shut up."

He understood. She meant his cock. Or all his insinuations about the rug stuff, about Dan. Ol' MacGuffin just sat there laughing.

Druff felt like crying. "Why do you put up with me?" he said.

"For goodness sakes, Commissioner, I *don't* put up with you. I just had to see what you're holding, is all."

"I held you."

"Oh, Lord," she said, "you put too much stock, you know that? You set too much store. Really, Bob, I say this for your own good. You do. You really do. You put too much stock in your love life. Everyone has a love life. Birds do it, bees do it. Even educated fleas. Sex isn't the hardest thing to get right, it's one of the simplest. You're so repressed. You're a repressed tight-ass. Or what was all that gabardine crap you

2 2 1

tried to hand me all about? Sex is a lead-pipe cinch, easy as pie, like falling off a log. Hey, come on, Commissioner, it's simple friction. Cavemen did it and discovered fire. Now, what *you* have, married to Amy Georgina all these years and years, *that's* hard! Don't pout. You're not a pouter, are you? It's not attractive in a man. Stiffen your lip. There," she said, "isn't that better? It certainly looks better. You're our City Commissioner of Streets. You didn't get where you are by pouting and wearing your heart on your sleeve. Are you all right? You're all right, aren't you?"

"I'm all right."

"All *right!*" Margaret Glorio said.

"I guess I'll get dressed now," he said.

"Well, you certainly don't need *my* permission," she said. "I'm all for it."

"It's just I feel a little funny dressing with you sitting there."

"Hey," she said, "no problem. I'll go stand behind the screen."

Passing in front of him, she went around the foot of the futon and took up her position in back of the Japanese folding screen. Druff got into his boxer shorts, as long and high waisted on him as if he were actually a boxer. He pulled on his socks, his pants. Margaret spoke an accompaniment of explanation to him in the background. She didn't come out even as he was buttoning his shirt, even as he was knotting his tie.

"That first night? Well, it was last night, actually, or even if you're counting from yesterday afternoon, it all seems so long ago now. It must to you, too. After the long march *you've* been on? Anyway, when you were trying to talk me into going out with you? I said at the time (at least I'm consistent), 'I like to know what I'm up against,' I said. You mentioned Su'ad? I asked if that was a restaurant?

"So I had to, didn't I? Didn't I just say so? Didn't I just admit it to you—it couldn't have been seven minutes ago—that I had to see what you were holding? How could I know you weren't holding anything but your glands? Christ, Bob, a City Commissioner of Streets *your* age? Coming on like some high school boy. Give me a break. Think if this made the papers. Are you decent yet?"

"I've just put my jacket on," he said, "I'm still tying my shoes."

She waited another minute and came out.

"You knew Su'ad?" he asked reluctantly.

"She got me the rugs."

"Dick said he saw you and Mikey together," Druff said, offering his spy's name and surrendering information as if he hadn't just heard what she'd just told him. "He said Mikey told him you're fifty."

"Mikey's your son?"

"You know he is."

"He told you I'm fifty?"

"He's a kid. Kids don't know people's ages."

"Oh they don't, don't they?" Margaret Glorio said.

This was a blow, though he couldn't have said why. Or, perhaps not so much a blow as the softening of a blow. Maybe it was a last gift to him, that if he thought she was fifty he wouldn't make so much of losing her. She was being kind. But her kindness, if that's what it was, had backfired. It only fed his useless, oddball lust for her. And fifty, Druff thought, there was something awfully sensual about a fifty-year-old woman. She'd be menopausal, her secondary sex characteristics less classically articulated perhaps; no longer working off her woman's juices and estrones, all femininity's biologic perfumes, but the moving parts themselves, the sourish organ meats and tainted dairy, her powerful spoiled essences and lurid cheeses. What, oh what, moaned Druff, is being sacrificed here?

Hey, scolded Druff's MacGuffin, bringing him up shortly, stay on task, will you?

"You were saying Su'ad sold you these rugs?" Druff offered automatically, doing a Q and A rag in the detective mode.

"Don't put words in my mouth. I never said sold. They're here on consignment. Like everything else in my showplace. Who's Dick?"

"Hah!" said Druff.

"Is Dick your chauffeur? Is he the one drives you around in that silly limousine?"

"Who's asking the questions here?" the City Commissioner of Streets said.

"All right," she said, "you've got me. What do you want to know? Just ask and I'll tell you anything you want to know."

Whoa, thought the commissioner. Wait up a sec. Hold my horses. Don't let's jump the gun here. Do I really want to take her up on this?

Let's look before we leap. Do I really want everything unraveled just yet? He was on a cusp. The timing was wrong. Was he properly prepared? Did he need anything as final as truth? Did he appreciate the cost of precipitate knowledge? What about all those old fools in tragedy? Didn't curiosity kill their cats for them? What, would he let a MacGuffin egg him on? Old Druff stood his ground.

"Gee," he said, "are you really fifty?"

"More or less."

But it was hard work. Maybe the hardest work in the whole business. It wasn't clear to him how he could put it off much longer.

He closed his eyes. Bringing up the family tic like a belch.

"So you know Mikey," he said offhandedly.

"I sure do."

She sure did? She *sure* did?

Then it came to him how he could manage. Instead of looking for secret information, he would provide it. The MacGuffin told him so. All he need do to forestall the devastating would be to utter it himself.

"Well," he said, "then you understand my position. I mean, I'm sorry to have to say so, but that boy's my cross. Well, you've seen him, you have some idea. He's my personal white man's burden. I know this isn't the way dads normally talk about their children, but damn it, Margaret, the kid's a kid. Thirty if he's a day and still a baby. Big as he is, scared of his shadow. Scared *shitless* of mine. That I might die on him before his time. Which has bloody fuck-all to do with love. Love? He hasn't enough love in him to sustain a thank-you note. We still support him, did you know that? He still gets an allowance. We buy his clothes for him. His mother picks out his suits, she takes him for shoes. I pay his speeding tickets. *All* his moving violations. Sure, I could have them fixed, I suppose, but if it ever came out? I could have another wife, what he costs me. I give him dough for the movies, for tickets to games. He's too old for me to carry on my Blue Cross any longer, so I pay premiums on health insurance that's not even group. And his birthdays? Every year he makes out like it's his sweet sixteenth. He expects a big check. He likes us to take him to dinner, Happy Birthday sung to him by waiters in restaurants. He blows candles out on his cake. He makes a wish. Every year we have to remind him it's the other way around. We give him money for gas, lifetime memberships in gyms that could close in a year. He nickels and dimes us. My son, the kid. If I weren't at least a little corrupt you think I could afford him? In a pig's ass.

"I'm Commissioner of Streets, recall. I've offered to get him jobs. Nothing illegal, mind. Nothing sub rosa or under the table. This would be outside the spoils system entirely. He could day labor streets. He could drive the salt trucks, redirect traffic or handle the signs. 'Detour,' 'Men Working,' 'Bridge Out Ahead.' But he won't deal with the public, he tells me, and I can't bring him into the Hall. How would it look it got out he's my son? You tell me you know him. Well, he's stupid. You've seen the confusion on him, his brow when it furrows like terrace farming in China.

"*We* talk. I take him into my confidence. I father-to-son him. Every chance I get, if you want to know. 'The riddle of the Sphinx ain't no knock-knock joke, Mikey,' I tell him. 'Who goes bare-handed in the morning, holds Mace in the afternoon, and won't leave his house after dark?' I ask. 'It's Man, son,' I answer. 'There's no reason to be so alarmed. You're no needier than anyone else.'

"He is, of course. He's in the top forty of the hundred neediest cases. With a bullet.

"Well, you know him. You tell me, do you think there's any confidence there at all? Because I've never seen such a combination of raw, bleeding need and nutty fatuity. It's outside my experience.

"And he has these ideas? Well, *ideas.*

"He takes this art course at the U? You knew about his art course? This studio thing? That he attends once, twice a week? He doesn't even take it for credit. Well, he can't. It's offered at night but it's not part of their Continuing Education program, just some hobby-lobby deal the university offers to take the business away from the Y. (I buy his supplies—— his canvas and brushes, his stretchers and colors. His alizarin crimsons, his manganese blues. His cadmium yellows and terre-vertes and oxides of chromium. All his raw umbers and titanium whites.)

"So last semester he was working on this project? Very hush-hush? And one day he comes to me and says he wants money for pinking shears, he needs these pinking shears. I don't ask. *Usually* I don't ask. They say the heart has its reasons, and I pretty much go along. But why pinking shears? It's not as if I *had* to know, it's just that I had this hunch. The bill for his art supplies was costing me more money than all the books in all his regular courses combined. The cockeyed advanced meteorology degree he's taking because one time he thought maybe he wanted to be a weatherman on TV. For the disasters? For the cataclysms and catastrophes that that could put him next to, would give him a leg up on the rest of us for the ten or fifteen minutes before they happened, the hurricanes and storm surges and killer twisters. Before they made landfall or touched down in the trailer park. For the inside info it provided him and which he could pass on to the public, the tips and helpful hints. What corner of the basement they should stand, how low they should lie they're caught in a field.

"Well, he wouldn't need pinking shears for that. I knew that much. That much I knew. And, anyway, he'd lost interest, his heart had gone out of the meteorology trade. When he learned that earthquakes and volcanoes weren't weather, that any bozo stringer on the scene could handle them, make the body counts and pass them on, that they couldn't be foretold—the volcanoes, what it would say on the Richter scale—not even in those ten or fifteen minutes he thought he would have on them, and so weren't pure science and he was wasting his time.

"So I asked him. 'Why pinking shears, Mikey? What have you got into now?'

" 'Oh, Papa,' he says, 'that was my surprise.'

" 'Which surprise was that, Mikey?'

"You know what he said? You know what he told me? 'I'm no good. I'm silly this way because I'm no good. I'm not the man my father was. You're too big for my britches. I can't make my way.' "

Druff had trouble speaking.

"Would you like some water?" Margaret Glorio said.

The City Commissioner of Streets shrugged, then followed the woman into her small Pullman kitchen where she rinsed the stale, tinny dregs of tomato juice from a clear plastic airline cup and filled it with tap water.

"What were the pinking shears for? Did he ever say?"

"For cutting canvas. For serrating the edges around his paintings. That was his surprise, his idea. He knew he couldn't paint, that he wasn't any good. He needed a gimmick."

"I don't under—"

"He'd glue the backs of the paintings and stick them in the upper right-hand corner of white, rectangular canvas 'envelopes' that he'd covered with primer. They'd look just like stamps. He'd paint in the purchaser's name and address in Mars black if he made a sale. If it was a gift he'd put in the name and address of whoever it was that was supposed to receive it."

"That's wild," the buyer said.

He wasn't *her* son. Druff ignored her. "I tried to explain," he said. "I told him he couldn't base his future on a gimmick. I warned about the prohibitive costs of his idea. Why, just the canvases alone. I showed him on an actual letter. 'Look, Mike,' I said, 'just consider the ratios. See how much larger the white area of the envelope is than the stamp. What is that, nine to one? Ten? That's on the horizontal, the proportions would be more favorable on the vertical but we're still talking in the neighborhood of four or five inches to one. Now an ordinary first-class postage stamp weighs in at about something under an inch by a little better than three-quarters of an inch. You carry those dimensions over to anything that would be meaningful on a full-size piece of mail art and you're talking of a piece in excess of, oh, nine or ten feet by five feet. That's not counting the frame. Then, even if you find someone willing to pay for all that blank, unpainted area, it would still be too big to go over a sofa. And you're still stuck with the problem of your painting.'

" 'I could make wavy lines,' he says, 'I could cancel the stamp. I could put in a postmark and a return address.'

" 'Too busy,' I said."

"How do you know the size of a postage stamp?" Ms. Glorio said.

"I'm a politician. I used to be a collector. FDR was a collector."

"I interrupted you," she said. "Go on."

"Well, that's about it," Druff said. "I brought him around. I told him it was all very well to come up with original ideas, but that speaking in the main the world didn't much prize what was original, that it already knew its needs and it was the business of successful men to discover what those were and then go about trying to prepare themselves to fulfill them. I reminded him that there were probably already more people studying to be meteorologists in his classes at the university than there were weathermen on all the local news shows on all the television stations in the city."

"Did he answer you?"

"Well, I told you," Druff said. "He'd pretty much lost interest in meteorology. What he said was pretty crazy. He talked about having to go where there wasn't so much competition. Maybe learn to fish, build fires, become this hunter/gatherer. Live on the range off the land.

" 'Ontogeny recapitulates phylogeny?'

" 'What? Oh. Yeah. I mean it, Daddy,' he says. 'I don't think that would be half bad. The benefits of fresh, unpolluted air, of sweet, cold springwater. Hunkering down with nature, learning to watch and appreciate the seasons. Does that seem so terrible?'

"Well, he was making me mad. I'm talking survival, he's talking the quality of life.

" 'Damn it, Mikey, what are you talking about? You don't even know what buffalo look like.'

" 'I do,' he tells me. 'They look like old nickels.' "

"That's where they met," Meg Glorio said.

"I'm sorry?"

"Su'ad and your son. That's where they met. In that night-school art class."

"She was a Shiite Muslim," Druff said. "Very devout, very pious. Into that stuff like a terrorist. Wasn't drawing from life against her religion or something? Even a landscape, even raw fruits and vegetables, bread, a goose on a table with its neck wrung?"

"She painted geometry. Interlocking angles and rhomboids, configurations and patterns."

"Oriental rugs," the commissioner put in.

"Iranian carpets, yes. The Iran-Lebanon nexus. The Iranian-Lebanese-Syrian one."

"Su'ad was a smuggler?"

"Su'ad was a genius," she said. "She not only managed to bring carpets out of her country but got commissions for those designs she worked out in night school and managed to get them back in to her weavers."

"I don't believe this. If she was so good why did she have to take
art classes at night?"

"She used the place as her studio. She used their light. She used the
paints and swatches of those canvases you paid for."

He'd seen it coming, of course. Sometime between the lunch he'd
been promised but which had never been given him and the lunch he'd
ordered but hadn't touched, he'd anticipated that rugs would be in it,
that Dan and Jerry and Hamilton Edgar would. He'd seen it coming.
And had enough of that touch of the gumshoe in him to know, if not
the specifics, at least the broad outlines of what was up. Or, specifically,
that something was. His dilemma now was what to do if he solved it,
put together the pieces of the puzzle. What puzzle? Which puzzle? The
puzzle of how Mikey figured? How Ms. Glorio and Dick and Douglas
did? The puzzle of where he himself was standing and what he happened to be doing on the evening of the afternoon of the morning in
question? The deeper question of the question in question?

And nah, nah, he told himself. He knew which puzzle, all right.
Simply, it was what he would do, could do, if he used the MacGuffin
up before its time. (Because MacGuffins by nature, however it may have
seemed at the beginning, or during one's more anxious moments, were
essentially in your corner, on your side, were these sort of guardian
angels. No matter that they scared the shit out of you. They were tests
from God. Little blessings blown on not-quite-good- or interesting-
enough lives. Holy tremors, sacred seizures before the long, arduous
order of death. That's the way he saw it anyway. That was the view from
Ms. Glorio's apartment. No matter that it was full dark. It would not
do to throw off the spirit of narrative in his life, his sense of closure,
his timing, his all. There would Druff be, compromised, caught with his
pants down in the middle of his muddle if he gave in to the sweet
temptation of a closed case. It was a question of simple good husbandry
and accountable, agreeable stewardship.) Draw it out, draw it out, he
warned. Vamp until ready. But I'm so tired, he argued, I haven't eaten,
I'm lonely and old.

That's why the lady is a tramp, signaled the MacGuffin.

"Wait," Margaret Glorio said, but he was already at the door. "Listen," she called after him in the hallway, but he had already pressed

the button for the elevator to come for him. "Where are you going?" she asked, but he had already stepped inside the little box and was sinking toward the street.

Where it came to him. Not bothering even to check out the building's guardian in the lobby who was checking *him* out, rushing past him, inspired by his destination, the day's one more additional errand which would keep him going, keep him from returning home just yet where he knew he would probably have to fight for his life, hold him on the route along the now quite pointless odyssey on which he was engaged (who could have stepped into a movie theater—the coward's way out— or saloon, or even gone bowling for that matter, or dined in a restaurant, or checked into a hotel—— all, all cowards' ways out). Where, as if it were a scene from the life of a drowner, he was splashed by a memory, not even a memory, Marvin Macklin's name like a clue in a scavenger hunt. The fellow who died, whose death "after a long illness" had been reported to him yesterday by Dick, his chauffeur and spy, during their hunt for potholes in the park. He turned around and went back into the lobby from which he'd just emerged, up to the desk behind which the doorman (for whom he'd have to supply a new job title since he was never anywhere near a door and who seemed to conduct all the build-ing's traffic from his post in the lobby, almost, it occurred, like someone in a war room) sat waiting for him, grinning.

"Say," said the concierge almost pointedly (in light of the puzzles Druff had been putting to himself only moments before), "are you trying to establish an alibi or something?"

"Do you have yesterday's paper? There's something I have to check."

"As it happens," he said. Stooping, he produced a newspaper from some little cubby behind his desk. Druff thanked him and took it with him to the armchair in which he had dozed off only last night. (Only earlier today, actually, he thought. My God, he thought, I'm observing the unities.) He flipped through the paper, found the announcement of Marvin's death. Then, turning to some more neutral page, he refolded the newspaper before handing it back to his old friend, the wise-guy concierge.

"Would you call a cab for me?"

"Sure. Where should I tell him you're going?"

Damn! thought the Commissioner of Streets and, from his less-than-vast knowledge of the city's neighborhoods, named a section of town he thought to be in the general vicinity of his destination.

Almost as if he had other fish to fry, the concierge phoned up Druff's cab and permitted him to leave the building without incident.

The City Commissioner of Streets gave the driver the name of the chapel.

"Wait for me," he said when they'd pulled up to the funeral parlor, "it doesn't look as if anybody's home."

And thought again, *Damn!* Realizing even as he rang the night bell and waited for someone to come and open the door for him that Macklin had died Thursday, that Catholics didn't bury on Sunday, that in all likelihood they wouldn't have waited till Monday, that he'd probably have gone into the ground today. He stood forlornly, conscious of a chill developing in the evening air.

"I'm sorry," he told the man on duty, "I got into town too late for Marv Macklin's funeral. Would you happen to know if the family is taking condolence calls? Would you happen to know the address?"

"It just so happens," the night man told him, echoing the concierge/doorman of Ms. Glorio's building.

He told the cabbie and they drove in silence to Mrs. Macklin's house, Druff chastising himself for his stupidity. And you call yourself a politician! You, City Commissioner of Streets, where's your vaunted street smarts? You're supposed to be this big old-school political figure, a man of the wards with turkeys and gift hams in his Christmas and Thanksgiving hampers, how come you don't know your Catholics? How come it never occurred about Saturday interments? (How come, for that matter, when you got up this morning you didn't even know it was Saturday? A savvy, moxied-up power broker like you? Or is time so jammed up on you you just don't bother to keep track any longer?) Have you forgotten everything you ever knew about the political forks? All those precinct clichés, all that district and ward lore? Names of the wives and kiddies in the prominent families, the not-so-prominent, of deadbeat in-laws with input, of ethnic strivers, the police and fire fairs, hinge events in the inner city, graduations, track meets, barbecues?

Where had he been, oh? What had he been doing that he hadn't had a good idea since the Fourteen Points? (Bringing a marathon to town

was a good idea but he'd only been teasing.) And why, since there was
no doubt about it now, had they bothered to put spies on him? Was it
to discover his incompetence? They could have done that before lunch,
they could have done it in an afternoon. A fly on the wall could have
done it within buzzing distance of Margaret Glorio's pallet. Druff knew
he was in trouble. It was no good asking MacGuffins to play with him,
to go along with him for the ride. But for the life of him, the *life* of him,
he couldn't imagine what he'd done.

Though he knew now what he must do, the only thing he could do.
And that he'd have to wait till Monday *to* do. He would have to meet
with the mayor and turn in his resignation. He'd have to plead for terms.
See could he still get his benefits he resigned in midstream. (Or maybe,
they wanted him out bad enough, they'd double-dip him, carry him on
phantom books, bench him, pay out his contract, debenture his life, do
him up like a human junk bond.) Technically, of course, he hadn't a
leg to stand on. It would all come down to mercy of the court, technically. All his bragging notwithstanding (the buried bodies in the city's
closets), his news was old news. Like John F. Kennedy gossip, Martin
Luther King. Or guys in history—Ben Franklin, Abner Doubleday—
whose claims of discovery were unproven, a matter of folklore their only
standing. Druff's claims had *no* standing. He knew it. Did his old
nemesis, the mayor, know as much? Or was it all, as he now suspected,
just some almost good-natured deference they allowed him, the lip
service convention paid to myth?

And just who, as far as that's concerned, was Marvin Macklin anyway?

Trusting to luck—ha, ha ha—Druff figured it would all fall into place
once he got there.

He paid and tipped the driver. Who, along with almost everyone else
among Druff's encounters that day, didn't know him from Adam. As he
in turn, even as they rode up the driveway, passing the automobiles
parked there (eclectic—— a limousine, expensive German and Italian
jobs, some mid-list G.M.'s, a Ford Tempo or two, a Chevy Nova), and
he left the taxi and went up to knock on the large double doors of the
imposing brick house (quite, he thought, like Rose Helen's old sorority),
didn't recognize it, knew only that he'd never been there before.

The taxi had left. It was too late to withdraw.

A butler came to the door. A butler.

"Macklin's?" Druff hesitantly asked.

"The family is in the drawing room, sir," the butler said. (A mourner's black arm band attached to the sleeve of the butler's uniform surprised Druff, lending to the occasion a quality of a kind of official corporate woe, rather like the players on a professional football or baseball team donning some black badge of collective tribute for a dead colleague.) The man stepped deftly aside for him, almost as if it were a tight squeeze and he were permitting Druff right-of-way in the narrow passageway of a Pullman car.

"That way?" Druff said.

"Yes, sir. Go right on in."

He started in the direction of the drawing room. Well, Druff thought, it wasn't a wake. There wouldn't be clog dancers. All he heard through the room's cracked doors was indistinct voices, vague figures moving dimly about all he saw. Where was he? How did he know that name?

He recognized it, recalled he'd fixed the fellow's given name to the surname Dick had spoken when he'd mentioned the death. Everything else was a blank. It really *was* time Druff offered his resignation. Where was he? Who was Marvin Macklin? Some big contributor? Some old opponent? Or just one of those famous buried bodies Druff's kind so liked to brag about? Well, sure, thought Druff, *now!*

And caught himself grinning and paused to adjust his demeanor. Well, he thought, you haven't *quite* lost it, have you, old-timer? You're still savvy enough to recall you don't march to the muffled drums with a shit-eating grin all over your face. And had this sudden, bleak take on himself—— his worn, now scruffy suit, rumpled from a day in the weather, creased from sitting prim on toilet seats in rabbis' studies, squeezing into tight restaurant booths, from lying in it across a sofa along a lady's lap, strewing its component parts down in passionate abandon, stretching its coat out to cover himself and tucking its sleeves under his body to create some snug illusion. *From getting in and out of it so often!* And his cuffs, his poor shot shirt cuffs grubby with grime, the streets', *his* streets' contributory grease and air. Though on the other hand, he thought, he would almost certainly look more the mourner than any of them. Sure. He was dressed for it, struck just exactly the correct note of stale, unshaven grief, and probably gave off—his unfed breath—some quality of aged, fermenting fruit.

This bleak but fitting take, he thought, and decided not to bother to pat himself down or buff his uppers against the cloth of his trouser legs. Fixing only his expression, neutering it, balancing upon it a kind of shy politeness, he carefully presented himself to the drawing room.

Aiming himself, as best he could determine, straight for the doyenne here, the widow Macklin herself. (Still enough of the politician to do that much at least, following some spoor of bereavement, of hysteria, to pick from a crowded room the one dressed in the most suitable black, the one with the twisted handkerchief, the one—by God, he was still at least a *little* good!—with the palest cheeks, whose makeup had sustained the heaviest losses, whose face powder had been practically rubbed off by hugs and the cheek-to-cheeks as effectively as if soap and water had been applied to them.) Trusting in his on-again, off-again MacGuffin not to trip him up, let him down, not to cheapen things by turning him over to farce, play him for a fool, having him make up to some wracked sister, some distant, dithered cousin. Consoling the maid.

He picked his woman, found his man.

"Paula," he told her boldly (recalling this detail from the little death squib in the paper), "Bob Druff. I'm *so* sorry. What can I say at a time like this?"

"I know," she said, reflexively touching the handkerchief to her nose. "Thank you for coming, Mr. Druff. Marvin would have appreciated it."

"I apologize for not being at the funeral," he said. "I only just found out."

"Yes," she said, "thank you. It was a shock to us all."

"At least his suffering is over."

"Do you think so?"

"Well," Druff said, and broke off mindlessly. He smiled ambiguously, nodded politely from his thin store of boyish reserve, and withdrew. Retreated, he wondered? Routed, he thought. Backing off from the woman who seemed to gaze down at him from the high ground of her power in the room, he made his way to the bar where he poured a drink for his empty stomach, then pulled himself to a neutral corner, the far, unoccupied end of a genuinely immense sofa on which, Druff observed only after he'd joined him, his mayor was already seated. The very man he'd been thinking about it couldn't have been fifteen minutes ago. *Don't tell* me *there's no God!* Druff thought. *Or at least that my life ain't haunted!* Before he was able even to acknowledge him, however, he heard his name being summoned, pronounced in just precisely that curious tone (only reversed) of vocal conjure he himself had employed with Dick when he'd mused aloud, "Macklin, Macklin . . . Marvin Macklin?"

"Druff, Druff. Commissioner Druff?"

It was the widow addressing him. At full room temperature.

"Why yes," said the City Commissioner of Streets.

"Isn't there some scandal?"

"No," he said, "I don't think so."

"I thought there was a scandal."

"No," Druff said. "But I know where the body is buried. Oh," he told Macklin's widow, "sorry."

"No problem," she said, and Druff wondered if that famous hankie he'd looked for and which she'd touched to her nose wasn't perhaps used just to blot a cold or tap the itch of an allergy.

Druff thought he recognized a tentative, amused but sycophantic wheeze or snort.

"Is that Doug?" he said.

"Yes, sir, Commissioner. Top that off for you, sir?" And there he was suddenly, practically up in the commissioner's face, extending the very same bottle of rye from which Druff had just serviced himself, dressed in the suit Druff had seen when he had called on Doug a few hours earlier. This was Druff's thinking: Doug had made a day of it. He'd been at the funeral home, gone on to the cemetery, returned to his apartment to shower and prepare for an evening chez Macklin. Then this was: if Doug had been at the funeral home and gone on to the cemetery, why Dick must have, too. And, if he had, then perhaps he *hadn't* been home when Druff called from the restaurant. Then, frightfully, *this:* the Charlotte person had been left behind. To be there in case the commissioner called. What terrified him now was that whatever it was it turned out they were trying to pin on him, so many were in on it. Not a ring, no conspiracy or compact, plot, scheme, plan, deal or design, but a cabal, out and out. And, indeed, this is exactly Druff's feeling, that he's

stumbled into a cabala. Was it devil worship here? Some soiled, municipal arcana? Whatever, it was certainly widespread. Widespread and
up-front.

"We see each other socially only at funerals, ceremonial evenings
when the family has us in," Doug explained quietly as he filled Druff's
glass. "You sure you don't want any ice, Commissioner? No extra
charge." What he was saying seemed at absurd odds with the man's
take-charge moves, his expansive, liberal ways with their liquor, their
ice. "I'm not saying folks don't kick the bucket often enough for my
tastes. That would be callous. It would be stupid and mean. But there
ought to be a middle ground."

"Death vigils?"

"There you go."

There was a sound of a sort of muted, general amusement throughout
the room. Druff hadn't looked around yet, had still to take a census in
the room, large almost as one of the public rooms on a cruise ship, but
he'd a sense that when he did there'd be many here he already knew.
Mr. Mayor, of course. Dick, perhaps. Dan, Ham, Jerry Rector. The
doorman-cum-concierge, taking some well-deserved time off from his
duties, might even be there. Maybe Mikey, maybe Margaret. Maybe the
colored guy from the synagogue. His waitress. The pharmacist, perhaps.
Edouvard Mrentzharev. The guy who'd given him a ride in the pickup.
Neighbors, joggers he'd passed in the streets. (It could happen. If they
were tailing him, why not?)

He recalled all the fat hints so freely given, the warm, warmer! *hot!*
tips Ham and his pals had been so careful to pass him. (Which was what
troubled him about this caper, that no one connected with it—it was
almost his style with Meg Glorio—bothered to cover their ass.)

So he did, he looked around. He sought out familiar faces, but they
were strangers. Only Doug. Only the mayor.

Maybe Mrs. Macklin was a mind reader.

"It's been a long evening," she said to Druff. "Yours must be the
third wave."

Turnover she meant. A third complement of condolers. (Even now a
few people were making the collective sighs and coughs and peremptо-
ries, all their collected-bundle sounds and shifts preparatory to leave-
taking.)

Druff, still thinking cabal, hated this. It offended him, he meant. His notions of economy. Well, he was old school, was, to all intents and purposes, practically out of it. Which didn't mean it didn't register, that he couldn't object. So many. *Too* many. (Never mind there were only Doug and the mayor. Mrs. Macklin herself had told him as much. His was the third shift. He'd just missed the others.) It was enough to choke a guy. Signaled a sort of gridlock. Something foul was going down in his streets. Was he their commissioner or not? All right, he was a little paranoid, but that only put a spin on his vision, it didn't obscure it. Conspiracies, compacts, plots and plans required decorum. At least a *little* decorum. Druff, who was no snob, had always felt there ought to be standards, that any scam worth its salt should be run rather along the lines of a good country club. The power of the blackball had to be reserved or you'd end with this huge balance of probity deficit. That was bad for business, bad for traffic, bad for crime. Even if they weren't here—Ham, he meant, Margaret, Jerry, Dick and Dan, his goofy son— they'd been by, or would be. And City Commissioner of Streets Druff suddenly remembered certain things said in the synagogue earlier that day—— Dan's and Ham's and Jerry Rector's articles of faith—— *their* Fourteen Points. "Throw caution to the winds," Dan said, and suggested there ought to be something personal, something malevolent. And Ham said he knew psychiatrists who wrote prescriptions for dinette sets, expensive cars. Awful, he thought now, awful, awful, but it was the idea of throwing caution to the winds which had most chilled him. It was as if the world had gone a-wilding.

"Paula," the mayor said, "it's late and I'm tired. God knows you must be too. I think I'll go back to the Mansion. Perhaps I can stop by tomorrow. I'll try to bring Frances."

"Thanks, Frank, for everything."

"Nonsense. But listen, if there's anything I *can* do, anything, just let me know."

"You're kind, Frank."

"Paula, I mean it. Keys to the city, kid. Keys to the city."

"That's no campaign promise, kid. He means it," put in the City Commissioner of Streets, who'd been sucking down the rye.

"She knows I do, Bob," said Hizzoner.

Which earned Monsieur le Mayor the City Commissioner of Streets' studied glance for trace irony. None to empty-stomached drunken Druff there seemed to be. Which oddly reassured him, oddly. For hypocrisy's simply-saked decency of the thing. But, hey, cautioned the remnants of Druff's sobriety, you're throwing caution to the winds yourself here. Is there a full-court cabal on or not? It's your call. If there is, look to your moorings, chuck the footwork. Don't say chuck. Check, it amended.

Druff wanted his MacGuffin.

How did he know that name? Where was he?

Reassured. Hypocrisy of the thing. Check.

Because it was so. The mayor's bland response *was* reassuring. He'd not taken Druff's bait, he'd honored Marv's death. He'd humored the room. He'd shown self-control when all about him were losing theirs. Druff thought that all mankind needed to make a better world was a little deniability, enough energy to establish a decent alibi. It showed respect.

The mayor was standing. He'd taken Paula's hand. He'd leaned down to peck at her cheek, to tell her something.

"Time, gentlemen," Doug said gaily. "Do you again, sir, before I leave?" He offered more rye. Druff, straining to hear, waved him away.

"Good night all," the mayor addressed the room. "May we meet again on a happier occasion," he solemnly said. "Did I have a coat with me, Doug?"

"I don't think so, Your Honor."

The son of a bitch, thought sobering Druff. That limo we passed in the driveway. *He* drove him here! And that other son of a bitch. "Did I have a coat with me, Doug?" That was for Druff's benefit. Grandstanding bastard. He took back his banquets and bouquets, everything he'd thought that evening about Hizzoner's circumspection. "Did I have a coat with me, Doug?" Thinks he can play rub-my-nose with me, does he? Druff could hardly believe it. Whatever happened to discretion? Didn't they know what a dangerous world it was, coming and going, outdoors and in? Did they give no thought at all to appearances? Druff sized up the room, took a deep breath, and only prayed the MacGuffin was within hearshot and sightshot.

He'd considered turning in his resignation Monday morning. He would probably have to spend Sunday not only drafting the letter but typing it up as well. (He was, what he was. He had, he congratulated himself, too much class to drag Mrs. Norman into it.) But why bother? he thought. Why not strike while the iron was hot? Why should he show any more consideration for them than they did for him? Why not run with the flouters and flaunters?

The City Commissioner of Streets stood up. *"Saay,"* he said, "it *is* late. I wonder could you fellas give me a ride home?"

Well, he *was* what he was. *Why* drag others into it? If he was so considerate of Mrs. Norman, a woman he didn't particularly like, why should he be less so to Mrs. Macklin's visitors, people he didn't even know?

He watched Doug, who looked to the mayor for guidance.

"You're one of his drivers, aren't you, Doug?" asked their mayor.

"Oh, on occasion, sir. Yes sir, Your Honor."

"You'd be in the best position to know then. Tell me, Doug, is it well out of our way?"

"Well, Your Honor, you've put your finger on it, sir. The city commissioner lives in the Homan district. Off Overodey, two or three blocks down Page."

"Why, that's all the way across town, isn't it?"

"Near enough, Your Honor."

"Not only in the opposite direction of the Mansion but close to all that new construction?"

"Well, sir, from where the overflow on Edson feeds into the detour on Valor and Hoe."

Druff observed the two comedians. Someone should have gone over to the piano and hammered out rim shots for them. If he'd known any more about the piano than he did of the districts, streets and phantom construction sites in the imaginary city they pummeled him with, he might have done so himself. And now he turned his gaze away from the two municipal clowns working Mrs. Macklin's big room to the audience itself. There were still a number of people in the house, people frozen along the fault lines of their imminent departures—— the scufflers and seat shifters he'd detected earlier but who'd been caught by "Hizzoner and Doug" and their surprise, unexpected floor show like a pop quiz.

Although she maintained perfect control, Mrs. Macklin seemed more amused than anyone in the room. She might almost have been a royal dowager witnessing some slightly irreverent Command Performance.

Well, it was a distraction, Druff supposed. Marv shoveled into the ground just that afternoon, all the holy, highfalutin goings-on at the funeral chapel, her dark clothes and strained graciousness and this not yet even the first full day of her official mourning. So it was a distraction. Druff could hardly blame her.

Well, he was already standing anyway. Looking back in Doug's direction, whose shtick about detours and overflow and made-up streets had closed out the routine. He nodded at his erstwhile chauffeur and turned to the city's chief executive.

"I quit," he said.

"You quit?"

"That's right. I'm resigning. I quit."

"Just like that?"

"Yes."

"That's your trouble, Druff. And you call yourself a politician. You quit? You don't know dust about smoke-filled rooms, do you? You'd just go and give up a plummy job like yours? Snap? Just like that? No quid pro quo? No dealing? No nothing? Well, I never," said his mayor.

He was right, Druff thought. Everyone did.

Sure, prompted the MacGuffin. You didn't even get how you know that name out of it.

A lot you've got to criticize, scolded wounded Druff. Where were you when I needed you?

Within hearshot, sightshot and soulshot, little buddy. Don't worry about me.

So what do I do now?

Did *I* bring you here on an empty stomach? Did *I* pour rye in your eye? Did I feed you coca leaves all day like there was no tomorrow? The *hell,* scorned the MacGuffin. You got yourself into this. You just go and get yourself out.

Beat a strategic withdrawal, is that what you're advising me?

Jesus! contempted old Mac.

Druff tossed a grateful mental wink at his friend.

Jesus Christ Jesus, kibitzed MacGuffin.

While Druff stared down the mayor.

"Gotcha!" he told him. "No, Frank," Druff said, "I'm not quitting. Don't you recognize more floor show when you see some?"

"Well, come along then," the mayor said.

"You'll take me?"

"Does he need your arm, do you think, Doug?"

"Maybe that and some stretcher-bearers, Mr. Mayor."

And made a face as he came within breath range of the still-incumbent City Commissioner of Streets. Who, startled, suddenly recalled his performance that afternoon in Doug's apartment. And willed his imperfectly steady legs into a locked position, conscious of his hip flexion, deliberately straightening his lumbar curve, minding all his orthopedics. In this manner he carefully made his way toward his bereaved hostess. I must look, he thought, like whatsisname, Frankenstein's monster. Yeah, he thought hopefully, but sober.

"What can I say?" he said.

"You're kind," Mrs. Macklin said.

"Me?" he offered. "Nah. Marvin was kind."

"Kind? Marvin was a hardened banker."

Eureka! he exclaimed mentally. And didn't forget to propitiate his MacGuffin.

Oh boy. His MacGuffin was disgusted.

Thinking as they led him off, It's the company I keep, the circles I do and don't travel in. *Of course! Marvin Macklin was a hardened banker!* What's a hardened banker?

It was the first question he asked when he got into the limo. (Asking it through a speaking tube which he took off a hook where it lay on the dash. Because the mayor had instructed Druff to sit up front with the driver. "You're not out of the woods yet," Hizzoner explained through the tube. "You could be carsick. I'm only human, Druff. Well, I'm queasy. It's nothing personal. I just can't stand the sight of blood or the smell of puke." Druff not too drunk to register that Motor Pool One was not as high-tech as his own electronically bristled limo, that its upholstery was not even leather but some gray cloth stuff he could not name but which wore an odor, not unpleasant, of some at once sweet and sour, luxurious mildew. It was a "machine" he associated with the days of lap rugs and tasseled hand pulls, some golden age of "motoring," of hampers and running boards, of spares securely buckled inside round metal forms mounted near graceful, elegant fenders. He doubted that the limousine had a radio, let alone a cellular telephone. Or if it did it would be on the AM band, or shortwave perhaps. It would have vacuum tubes. Static would crackle in its felt-lined speakers. Now he was conscious of it, he noticed that this boat was stick-shift, a banker's car from the days when streets were streets, and that's what reminded him.) He looked at Doug as he lifted the speaking tube from its hook. "How do I work this thing, do I blow into it first or what?"

"The captain blows into it first. You just talk into it."

"It's funny," Druff managed to fish when they'd traveled a few blocks, "I wouldn't have called Marv 'a *hardened* banker.' What do you suppose Mrs. Macklin meant by that, Mr. Mayor?"

"Mind your business," said Mr. Mayor.

"Are you sore at me?" Druff asked. "Don't be sore at me. I've had a rough day. I was only kidding when I spoke of resigning. Those were my nerves resigning, not me. Hey, loyalty is my middle name. You really think I'd quit on you with the streets how they are? I was out in them last night. You wouldn't believe the traffic. The traffic was terrific. The bankers, the bakers, the candlestick makers. Boy oh boy."

"Quit, don't quit," the mayor boomed at him through the tube while Druff was still speaking. "No one's indispensable. FDR's brains blew up on him when he was out on a date with his girlfriend during the War. You think that affected anything? The *hell!* A few weeks later the Germans surrendered." (Hmn, Druff thought, not only the same phrase MacGuffin had used, the same inflection, the same tone of voice!) "And what do you mean, 'the bankers, the bakers?' Why do you keep carping on that?"

"And what do *you* mean, 'FDR's brains blew up on him when he was out on a date with his girlfriend'?" the City Commissioner of Streets shot back.

"This is a ridiculous conversation," the mayor said in a normal voice unaided by the speaking tube.

"It is," Druff replied, too exhausted to trust his voice to an unabetted acoustics, and still speaking into the tube.

"Drop this one off first, Doug," the mayor commanded.

What did he mean "this one?"

He was so tired. Beyond tired, weary really. He'd been on the go all day. It was amazing to him it was still only Saturday night. As that afternoon it had been amazing to him that it was still only that afternoon, as twilight had astonished him, as even now he was surprised not to be able to perceive just a hint in the darkness of even false dawn, time running in place on him, stuttering, skipping, caught like a phonograph needle in a faulty groove, the day's long melody making no progress. It was Saturday, the weekend. On any normal Saturday he would have found some occasion to go off by himself in his house, to lie down, at least to put his feet up, to snooze in an easy chair, perchance to dream. It was the failure of privacy which so tired one, thought Druff, pressed and pooped. If he could just lean back in the old-fashioned, comfortable and roomy automobile, big as a bedroom even up front with Doug, sit back, maybe catch forty winks. Druff gazed sleepily out the window. He didn't quite recognize where they were. There was probably still a ways to go. The mayor had finished speaking. Doug, always a more focused driver than Dick, was concentrating on the road. Druff, lulled by the ride, allowed himself to shut his eyes.

No! Don't you dare! his MacGuffin startled.

"What's it to you?" jolted Druff out loud.

The hypnagogic sleep, jerk. You talk too much, remember? It's already been demonstrated that speaking tube's for show, not for blow. The acoustics in here are better than Carnegie Hall's. They'd pick up every word.

But I'm so tired.

Keep walking, don't sit down. Run a cold shower, drink some black coffee.

Sleepy weepy.

Then *talk,* I tell you! Keep talking. But stay awake! Don't let yourself lose consciousness. Stay in control.

My hero, Druff appreciated.

"Mr. Mayor, why haven't we been better friends?" Druff asked.

That's the way, MacGuffin encouraged. Good shot there, Druff, you wise old pol, you. Frame the argument, preempt and conquer.

Druff beamed. It was the nicest thing the MacGuffin had ever thought to him, and the City Commissioner of Streets felt ever so slightly more alert.

Though maybe Mr. Mayor was asleep. He didn't answer him. It could be a trap, but.

Force his hand, prompted MacGuffin. Take a follow-up.

"Because I've never understood why we aren't closer. I feel no animus toward you. I voted for you, as a matter of fact."

"You voted for him," Doug said. "You're in the man's administration, for heaven's sake."

"It's a secret ballot," Druff hissed. "We go into that booth, the curtain closes behind us."

"Oh, please."

"No 'Oh, please.' We could get away with murder if we wanted to."

"Oh, please."

"Give the man a break, Doug. He's warm. He's *very* warm. We *could* get away with murder."

"I'm sorry, Your Honor. It just makes me angry the way certain prominent officials who serve at your pleasure carry on sometimes."

"It was a fair question, Doug. The man's entitled to an answer. The reason I didn't offer one is I found it hard to believe he didn't already know. I still do. *However*—"

"What do you mean 'drop this one off first'? Where are we? What part of town is this? I don't recognize it."

"The City Commissioner of *Streets* wants to know what part of town this is, Frank. The City Commissioner of *Streets* doesn't recognize it. The City Commissioner of *Streets* is lost."

"Now now. The man's responsible for—— what is it, Bobbo, a few hundred thousand square acres of streets in your jurisdiction?"

"I'm not out of the woods yet, you said. What kind of crack is that? You can't stand the sight of blood, you said. What do you mean, I'm warm? What do you mean you *could* get away with murder?"

And now the City Commissioner of *Streets* was completely awake.

Doug was giggling. He was laughing out loud. He was snorting and laughing uncontrollably.

"You're going to wet your pants you don't watch out," Druff said. "He can't stand the sight of blood, he can't stand the smell of puke. Maybe he's not too thrilled with the stench of wee-wee."

"I like the stench of wee-wee," the mayor said.

Just jump in anytime, Druff addressed the MacGuffin.

"Oh hell, Bob. I said you're entitled to an answer and you are. The reason we're not better friends is I can't let go of a grudge. That's it. That's the long and short of it."

"Against me? What kind of grudge can you have against me?"

"Well, to be perfectly honest, I didn't approve of your negative campaign tactics that time you opposed me in the primary."

"That was a thousand years ago. We were both just starting out. We were only running for alderman! Anyway, what negative campaign tactics? No one used television in those days. We didn't even take out radio spots. Christ, most of my campaign literature was these cheesy, heavily inked fliers, my name on a piece of cardboard up on a stick in someone's front lawn. Debates were held in high school gymnasiums, VFW halls, the American Legion. Out-of-doors in the park on company picnics. Which negative campaign tactics? What negative campaign tactics?"

"All right. *You hired a car!* You hired a car with a great big loud-speaker on the roof and rode all over the precinct playing loud music and crying 'VOTE FOR BOB DRUFF! VOTE FOR BOB DRUFF ON APRIL EIGHTEENTH!' "

"You've got to be kidding. You're kidding me. You're kidding me, aren't you?"

He is and he isn't. You're not out of the woods yet. This one's got a lot of unresolved menace in him.

"Would I kid you, Druff?"

"Doug's right, I serve at your pleasure. If you've so much against me, how come I'm still working for you?"

"I didn't appoint you," the mayor said. "You were appointed by my predecessor. Anyway, that was just politics, that was just campaign promises."

It was true. The mayor had pledged that if he was elected he'd do away with the spoils system. As part of his campaign to break up the machine, he'd promised to retain everyone who'd been doing their job reasonably well. Druff had come in toward the end of the Golden Age of streets and highways, just before the money Eisenhower had pumped into the interstates had begun to give out. It was a brilliant idea. A lot of his opponent's hacks in City Hall either actively campaigned for the mayor, or stayed home. Meanwhile, he'd convinced enough of the voters that he was apolitical to win by a landslide.

He's kidding and he isn't kidding, the MacGuffin warned again. Where there's smoke, in other words, there could be fire. A word to the wise old pol was sufficient.

Who then upped the ante, who took the bull by the horns and raised the conversation from bland schmooze and the cult of personality to bottom lines.

"All right," Druff said, "do I need a lawyer? Am I a target of a grand jury investigation? What do you have on me?"

"Oho."

"You owe me that much, Frank."

"Sure, sure. Tell me another."

"You do. You owe me that much. Whatever you may think of me personally I'm still an important player in this town. I'm a prominent official. Even Doug said as much. I control a few hundred thousand square acres of street. That was your estimate."

"And just how much of that acreage is gutter, Mr. City Commissioner? How much runs over sewer?"

"Listen to me, Frank, I had nothing to do with that girl's death."

"Are we there yet, Doug?"

"Just about, Your Honor."

"Well, step on it then."

Druff listened for a siren. He hoped there'd be a siren. He wished Doug would slap a Mars light on top of the car. He wanted to see whirling red light ignite the houses and trees. He wished Doug would step on it. He wanted to feel speed press against his back. Anything, any spoor of ostentation that might compel a witness's attention.

But there was nothing. Doug moved it along at the same careful, defensive driver's pace Druff had noted earlier.

Fearfully, the City Commissioner of Streets raised his head and dared to look out the window.

They were not in the woods. They were in Druff's neighborhood. Relieved, astonished, he said so.

"I knew this shortcut," Doug said.

They were on Druff's block. They were at his house. Doug pulled the big machine to a stop.

"Thank you," Druff said. "Thank you for the lift."

"My pleasure," said Mr. Mayor.

"Hey," Druff said, "if I said anything out of line—"

"Forget it," the mayor said airily, "you were shitfaced."

"That's right," Druff admitted. "I'm not much of a drinker. Well, the pressure of the situation. I don't want to sound like I'm making excuses. Well, I *am* making excuses, I know that, but I get nervous around people's grief. I don't know what to say. I'm at a loss, so I drink too much and get so comfortable I don't behave well.

"Say," Druff said, "I heard you mention you might see Paula tomorrow? Would you do me a favor? If you see her, would you offer my apologies? If I embarrassed her and her guests in any way—— it's just I felt so bad about Marv, about missing his funeral. I wouldn't want her to get the wrong impression."

And on and on like that. Getting in deep. Deep, deeper, deepest. Until Doug actually got out of the car and, just as if it were the City Commissioner of Streets' own limo, walking behind the car (this being the protocol, never to pass in front of the windshield where the mahatmas in the back might see them), came around to the passenger's side and opened Druff's door for him, the poor man still talking, clipping along in a cloud of verbiage, like a magician. Just so, like a magician trying to distract his audience, bullying it with broad misdirection. And Doug, posed in a position of attention at the door he holds for him as if, had Druff any decency or at least conscientiousness left in him at all, he'd shut his mouth at once and scurry out of the car. Druff knows this but can't stop jabbering, hoping that the words he's so far spoken will cover over and perhaps bury the ones he can't bring himself even to take back. The brief, passing reference to his innocence and that by-now-for-sure-he-thinks little murdered girl.

Outside the limousine now and still filibustering even as Hizzoner rolls his window up.

"Oh, hey," says the City Commissioner of Streets, "I see you never went electric. With your car windows, I mean. That was a smart move. Well, hell, just another thing to go wrong. I've got them on mine and, knock wood, so far so good, but you never know. They get pretty temperamental I'm told, particularly in cold weather. As I say, *I* haven't had much trouble but my neighbor up the street drives, I don't know, one of those upscale Japanese luxury sedans, I forget which one, and his electric windows went out on him. It was only a fuse. Well maybe not a fuse exactly, but something relatively insignificant. Anyway, by the time it was working again it was like six or seven hundred dollars for parts and labor. They see you coming, those guys. Of course it's an altogether different story with the kind of machinery this is. Yours is more like a 'classic' car. I guess a limousine like this one, they probably charge the city extra for manual handles.

"Well," Druff says, holding his tongue, actually almost biting down on it for fear, perfectly capable of it as he is, of again blurting out the hideous non sequitur perched on its tip like irresistible candy. "Well," he says. "Well."

The mayor stares impassively out the window at him, then abruptly raises his jaw with an abrupt, quick little snap of his head, indicating to Druff to step closer. As if he has some confidence to impart to his streets commissioner that no one else may hear. More often than not it's a political thing, this gesture. Druff's used it himself on the customers, hundreds of times, inviting them into the squeezed, tight quarters of his confidence. Sharing his opinions (as if they were state secrets) about a particular dessert on the rubber-chicken circuit anyone in public office was obliged to travel. Or telling them in strictest, ears-only hush-hush that it seemed to him that this one or that one had put on or lost too much weight, and how—no, don't look now—does it strike you, could something be wrong, do you think? What goes around comes around. Is that all this will amount to? Druff wonders. He certainly hopes so.

He still hasn't moved. The mayor purses his lips, shrugs his eyebrows. It's not just an invitation, it's a direct command. Druff is drawn in.

"Yes?"

The mayor cracks the window about an inch and a half.

"You like my limousine?"

"Yes. Of course."

"It *is* nice."

"It is."

He turned on a soft interior light. "All the comforts of home."

"Yes, I see that."

"All the comforts."

"Yes."

"Nice appointments."

"Very nice."

"Not too flashy?"

"No."

"Well," said the mayor, "you must be tired. I know I am."

"Thank you for the lift."

"You're welcome. No problem."

"To the Mansion, Your Honor?"

"Whenever you're ready, Doug."

And they were off, the limousine very quiet, almost silent, in fact, for a car so large. Perhaps, Druff thought, some of the sound was muffled by the small Oriental rug at Hizzoner's feet.

Yeah, the MacGuffin goes. How about that?

Jesus, Druff goes, why didn't you stop me?

Me? Stop you? You're a force, you are. Once you get going. A force. Some force.

Right down there with gravity.

Hold it. Where do you think you're going?

You live here, don't you? Ain't this the place?

You stay outside.

Don't be like that.

A man's home is his castle. You stay outside.

Suppose it rains?

Mr. Mayor, Druff goes to himself, why haven't we been better friends? Is it because I had nothing to do with that girl's death? Christ, he must think I'm some jerk. He shoots a look at the MacGuffin. The MacGuffin made me do it, he goes.

The City Commissioner of Streets enters his castle. Leaving MacGuffin to fend for itself on his streets.

"Rose Helen, I'm back," Druff calls out in the Mikey mode. He waits a moment. "I'm back," he calls again. The lights were on but the house was quiet. "It's me," he repeats. "I'm back."

He has a hideous premonition of disaster, of, well, retribution, revenge; and pictures Rose Helen in intimate, compromised positions of slaughter, of savage, indiscriminate massacre. Her pubic hair singed, her nipples cut off, switched and reversed and pushed back into her breasts like plugs, the distinctions blurred between crime and ostentation. He punishes himself with images of depravity so far beyond depravity it's no longer depravity but business, nothing personal, her execution only someone seeking to send him a message.

Then he grinned. "It's her batteries," he said. "Poor kid, they must be as dead as a doornail."

"Where have you been?"

"Rose Helen! Oh, Jesus, you scared hell out of me."

"Do you know what time it is?"

"Look," Druff said. He fished around in his pockets. "Look, I went out and got you these. They're zinc oxides."

"It's almost eleven o'clock."

"Not everyone carries them."

"Michael had no trouble."

"Mikey got you batteries? All right, Mikey!"

"I didn't wait supper for you. The rest of the turkey is already back in the freezer."

"Gee, Rose, I'm hungry as hell. I could eat a horse. Well, never mind. I'll poke around in the refrigerator. I'll find something."

"Do you want me to defrost a drumstick? Do you want me to make you a sandwich? I could slice up some white meat and make you some toast."

And then Druff, quite gently, was sobbing. Just like that. One minute he's talking about dining on horse, the next he's dissolved in tears of gratitude and thinking how genuinely splendid his wife is, how easily women can shift gears from put-upon and pissed-off back to nurture and duty.

"What's wrong, have you been to the doctor? Is that where you've been all day? Have you been having angina again? What did he tell you?"

"Curse me, why don't you, Rose Helen? *No* I haven't been having angina. Angina, my God, that's *all* I need! You think I'd let them have another go at me? After what I've been through? Their fucking tests.

Their so-called options. 'Let's take this one step at a time, Bob. You could be managed medically. Or you might be a candidate for an angioplasty.' An angioplasty! That's a laugh. Do you personally know anyone who's ever been a candidate for an angioplasty? *I* don't. Hell no. They talk medical management and angioplasty at you, and all the time they're sharpening up the long knives and prepping their chain saws so they can open you up to the air and oxidize your heart like an apple. No, thank God. There hasn't been any angina to speak of."

"To speak of."

"That was only a little tightness in my chest. It wasn't heart attack pain, and it never developed into angina. I lay down too soon after eating. I gobbled my food too fast."

"And chewing all that coca has nothing to do with it."

"No."

"You think that junk is Juicy Fruit? Does it come with pictures of baseball players? Promise you'll quit. It's not good for your circulation."

"Is that your scientific opinion?"

"It cuts off your circulation. That's why you get that tightness."

"It relaxes me. It's my one pleasure."

"Reality isn't pleasant enough for you?"

"You think it gives me visions? You think it makes my colors brighter or brings out the music? It *relaxes* me. It makes it easier for me to deal with Mikey."

"Don't put it off on Mikey. Mikey has nothing to do with it."

Druff was touched. He was many things at once. He was moved and hungry and exhausted and cranky. He might be coming down with something. Not eating. All that running around. Lying buck naked—all right, half-a-buck naked—on what was practically Meg Glorio's floor. He could feel a little tickle in his chest, the beginnings of what might be a sore throat. He'd feel better once he'd eaten. He hoped there'd be fixings. Turkey wasn't turkey without fixings—— stuffing, cranberry sauce, a little candied sweet potato. He was supposed to be this big-deal cynical politician, the big daddy of the city streets, and got all choked up at the thought of turkey dinner. Well, that was the clincher, maybe. It put him right smack in the middle of the tradition. A direct descendant. The pilgrims were politicians first or they were nothing. What was

Thanksgiving, anyway, if not a sort of open-air version of the smoke-filled room, doing a deal with the Indians?

He followed his wife into their kitchen. He took off his suit coat. He loosened his tie. He rolled back his sleeves and opened his shirt at the collar. Pouring a little dishwashing detergent over them, he washed his hands under the faucet at the sink. Rose, dressed for bed, has been padding about, retrieving the turkey from the freezer, removing its remaining drumstick, carving a few stiff slices of meat from its breast, wrapping Druff's dinner in aluminum foil on which she's placed a spoonful of congealed gravy that she spreads like a sort of turkey butter over the meat with a knife. She places this package into their toaster oven to defrost.

"What did you set that at?"

"Three hundred fifty degrees. Why?"

"No. I mean the timer."

"Ten minutes."

Druff dried his hands on a dish towel. "You know," he said, "this is kind of cozy."

Rose Helen looked at him closely.

"No," Druff said. "It is."

"For you. For me it's overtime."

It *was* cozy. Druff, safe, snug in his kitchen, was thinking of blizzards, of cold, stormy evenings. He was thinking of MacGuffin locked out in the street like a wolf.

He couldn't remember when he'd felt closer to his wife. How intimate they've been. Not the screwing, not even the two or three times she'd gone down on him. Certainly not the squeamishness he felt about *her* body, foreplay, occasions he'd had to stick his finger inside her to make her wet. But how intimate! When she'd brought him back from the hospital. If it hadn't been for Rose Helen he might have died just from the humiliations of his body. She'd sat on the lip of the tub and stooped to retrieve the greasy suppositories he'd too timidly inserted into his behind to loosen the stalled, compacted bowels he'd been unable to move in the hospital. Feeling himself still too weak to walk into the bathroom when he first came home, he'd used a urinal at night. More than once, with his cock not properly inserted down its oddly angled plastic neck, he'd had sleepy, inattentive accidents. While he sat naked on a towel on a chair, Rose Helen had changed their sheets, gone for a washcloth and basin, warm, soapy water, washed down his thighs, his unstirred privates—all the more intimate, Druff felt, for his lack of response, his limp indifference to the contact, less aroused than if he'd been touching himself—and offered fresh pajamas. (Even his impotence, his open secret.) Intimate. As reconciled as the insensate organs of his own body—— his tripes and kidneys, his liver and glands.

There, in the kitchen, chewing his turkey sandwich, eating the flesh off his drumstick, gnawing its bone, sucking its marrow, he wished he could tell Rose Helen what was happening. How Mikey figured in. But he didn't see how he could do that without bringing Margaret Glorio into it. In a way, Druff thought, he and Rose Helen had been through far too much for that, had been far too intimate.

On the other hand, if anything happened . . . He was thinking of the mayor, of surprises waiting for them in the morning papers, of impaneled grand juries, of the fallback fall guy Druff suspected he was all too rapidly becoming. He was guilty of nothing, nothing. But these days it wasn't enough to be innocent. They cared nothing for innocence. Besides, if you were innocent of one charge chances are you couldn't be innocent of two. In politics as in life there was no statute of limitations. All they had to do to bring you into the conspiracy was to have you show up somewhere on some arbitrary table of organization, demonstrate how you made a blip on the screen even as a statistical or demographical cohort. Show the most tenuous linkage, the long, complicitous, breathtaking genealogy of sin. Guilt by association was still guilt. All one could do was demand how it could still be counted as a conspiracy if so many were in on it. Is it a cult? Was it a covenant? A convention, another political party altogether? Perhaps it was a movement. Maybe it was history.

He could hear the MacGuffin howling at the door.

Not now, not now, Druff pleaded.

I'll huff and I'll puff, goes MacGuffin.

Not now. Not now.

"You know," Druff said experimentally to his wife, "that girl, Mikey's friend, Su'ad, I think she may have been a smuggler."

"A smuggler? Su'ad? Do you think so? Oh, but that's terrible. You think Michael's on dope?"

"Mikey on dope? Mikey's body is a holy temple. Oh, you mean am I saying was she Mikey's *connection?* No, I don't think so. Of course not. Su'ad's body was a holy temple, too. The kid was a devout, respectable Muslim lady. Dyed-in-the-wool Shiite. She wouldn't even take cocoa with us."

"That's right," said Rose Helen, "I remember. She turned down a candy bar."

"Sure, that's the one."

"Then I don't see how you can call her a smuggler."

"Rugs. She smuggled rugs. Oriental carpets."

"Oriental rugs," Rose Helen said. "Well, but how do you know?"

"Someone accused her."

She said, "What an interesting piece of gossip."

"Well, but that's just it, Rose, this isn't gossip."

"Did Michael tell you this? He's a dear man but he has an overactive imagination. I wouldn't set much store by . . ."

"He never said a word."

"What do you mean by that?"

"I'm sorry?"

"You said it isn't gossip. What do you mean?"

She was a smart cookie, Rose Helen. She made the fine distinctions. He'd probably failed her. Who could have been a contender. Who *should* have been a contender. Who'd settled for City Commissioner of Streets in a relatively out-of-the-way, not much more than middle-sized city with no major league baseball franchise. A kind of Indianapolis. A sort of Memphis, Tennessee. City Commissioner of Streets a thousand years in a sort of Memphis. Not fair to a First Lady manqué. Not fair to a girl with her eye on the statehouse or even just a mayor's little mansion. She could have done better. She could have done better even with old Edward R. Markey, the waiter at Rose Helen's sorority and Druff's former roommate, the one with a name like the clerk of the court or the fellow who signs the driver's licenses, and of whom, now a congressman from the state of Ohio, they'd been hearing such good things lately. She could have done better. He'd stood in her way with his bland ambition. He'd stood in both their ways—— his fearful big-fish, little-pond heart (and which even at that had gone soft on him, had brought him to death's door in the emergency room, had left him damned-near-for-dead on the operating table, as-good-as- in the recovery room, and practically so in intensive care, and not-much-better-than- in the at-last private room to which he'd been sent like some prisoner granted special, experimental privileges during the first stages of a long convalescence). And which, a non-starter, had somehow failed to kick in for him—even when he'd been successful—out on the hustings. Hizzoner was right. There was something rotten about his campaigns. "VOTE FOR BOB DRUFF! VOTE FOR BOB DRUFF ON APRIL EIGHTEENTH!" had been, from the first, almost all there was to it—— the centerpiece of his positions, his platform. He'd had no record, and made none. He had no overarching vision. He had grounded himself in no particular principle. Give him that lever that could have moved the world and he would not have known where to set the fulcrum. He'd never been moved by party. One seemed as good to him as another. The broadest divisions—all the fors, all the againsts—were all the same to him. Six of one, half a dozen of the other. He was not unfeeling, this most civil of civil servants, but he felt, and thought he understood, that almost anything in more or less the right hands could be made to work. If he believed in anything it was a bureaucracy. His Fourteen Points had been a joke, merely his Inderal kicking in at the time of a confluence of his energy and an opponent's boorish failure to recognize a joke.

So he'd failed her. Anyone with even half his cynicism could have gone further. So hitting—and recognizing—his stride somewhere between the zones of comfort and opportunity, he'd failed her. Rose Helen, that smart, sharp, unsuspecting Muse of his complacency. Waiting for her answer.

"Well," Druff began, not at all willing for all of it to come out just yet but quite willing for some to, "I'm kind of an eyewitness."

"Yes?"

"The mayor has a small Oriental rug on the floor of his limousine. He made a point of my seeing it. Well."

"That's why?"

"Hamilton Edgar's rabbi has them in his study. Even in his crapper."

"His crapper. I see."

"There's this buyer of men's sportswear for some of the city's leading department stores. The *buyer* has them."

"Well then," Rose Helen said.

"I know what I'm talking about," Druff told her, imploring her, falling helplessly back on some trust-me idiomatics.

Rose Helen cleared away the remains of Druff's supper. She rinsed his dish in the sink, the knife for the mayonnaise jar, his coffee cup, his spoon.

He knows he doesn't have it in him. He hasn't put it all together yet. He has no overview, as he has no guiding political principles. He's really quite tired. In his condition, the way he's feeling, he should probably just drop it. He probably would have if the mayor had not deliberately made everything seem so menacing. It wasn't the first time today he'd had a sense of hazard and jeopardy. He remembered going down Doug's stairs in a darkened atmosphere of danger like the threat of imminent rain. The handwriting was on the wall. The conditions were cooking. Took my Chevy to the levee but the levee was dry. Singin' this'll be the day that I die, this'll be the day that I die. Plus the dirty pictures he'd had in his head when he came home of what they might already have done to Rose Helen. So he wasn't only thinking of himself. So he couldn't just drop it. He owed her his best thinking on this one. All he could muster. For her own good.

"And when I asked Dick over the phone if he knew of any international rug rings working this town, the connection was broken."

"You spoke like this to your driver?"

"Ha!" Druff exclaimed. "*Not* to my driver! To some bimbo whose voice I didn't recognize except to know that it wasn't Dick's wife's voice. When I asked *her* to ask him!"

"I'm confused," Rose Helen said.

"It's very confusing," Druff admitted.

It was like her seeing his clumsily placed suppositories, his pissed sheets and open impotence, his incoherence another, further—maybe furthest—intimacy.

"Listen," Rose Helen said, "does Mikey have anything to do with whatever it is you're talking about?"

"Is he home, Mikey?"

"He's out."

"I don't know," Druff said, beats behind their conversation. "I can't honestly say," he told her, yawning. (Because the tryptophan from all that turkey was starting to work, the Thanksgiving enzyme loading him

down, clear and present danger or no clear and present danger, heavy-
ing, hypnotizing him.) "The kid may be an accessory," he said. "He
might even be an accomplice. Look," he said, "I'm falling asleep on my
feet. I've got to lie down or die."

"Go on up," she said. "I still have a few things to do yet. I'll be up
as soon as I can."

"No," said Druff. "I have to see Mikey. I'll just put my feet up on
the couch in the living room."

"Take your shoes off first, they're filthy. My God, you really must
have gone all over town to find those batteries."

But Druff had already made it to the couch. He was already sleeping.
Already deep into his rapid-mouth-motion version of REM sleep.

"I can place Su'ad with our Mikey. I can place Dick with our Mikey.
I think I can place Mikey and Dick with the buyer," he said aloud from
the hustings of his dreamed oratory. "I think, from something Doug
said, I can place Doug with all three of them. I can place Dan with the
concierge, I can place him with the buyer," he said, pleased how even
in sleep he'd subsumed Margaret Glorio's gender twice now under the
neutral, asexual term. He smiled, proud of his presence of mind. "It's
all pretty much circumstantial, I guess, but the world's pretty circumstantial, too."

"Bob," Rose Helen said.

"No," he said, "I'm on a roll."

"*Bob,*" she said, and shook him.

"*No,*" he said, "stop it! Do you know how frustrating it is when you
do that, Rose Helen? Let me have my say, will you? It's still America.
We still have something called the First Amendment, if you want to
know. Give a guy a break here a minute. *If* you'd be so kind. There,
that's better. Thank you. Now," he said, "where was I? Dick with
Mikey. Mikey with Dick with the buyer. The buyer with the concierge.
The concierge with Dan. Dan with Ham 'n' Eggs and Jerry Rector. (I'm
eyewitness to that part.) Ergo, by extension, all three of that lot with
the buyer as well as with—— as well as with—— did I say Doug with
Mrs. Macklin? Right then, Doug with Mrs. Macklin. Mrs. Mack with
the mayor. And Doug with the mayor, too, of course. And obviously
Doug with Dick. So Dick with the mayor. So Dick with Mrs. Macklin.
Mrs. Mack with Mr. Mack. So why not Mr. Macklin with our Su'ad?

Or our Mikey with Mr. Macklin? Or our Mr. Macklin with the little boy who lives down the lane? The cheese stands alone.

"Hey, is someone getting any of this down? Is anyone getting *some* of this down?

"No? Not? No? Maybe I'm talking in my sleep to the wrong party here. Maybe I ought to be sleeping with the buyer. With someone who takes me just a little more seriously, if you please."

"Come on," Rose Helen said, "wake up. Unless you're already awake. You *are* awake, aren't you? You do this on purpose. This is your way of making conversation. It's your way of making conversation, isn't it? Sure, you're gone all day. Then, instead of explaining yourself, you do this song and dance. Well, I don't have to listen to it. I *won't* listen to it! I'm going upstairs. If you get tired of talking to yourself and want to come to bed and behave, you come up too. Don't put the chain on the door; Michael isn't home yet."

"Rose Helen," Druff said.

"What is it?"

"The chain isn't on?"

"Mike hasn't come back."

"Please," Druff pleaded, "put the chain on."

"He isn't home."

"MacGuffin's outside."

"Does he have a key?"

"No, I don't think so."

"Well, there you are then."

"Yes, but you don't know my MacGuffin. He's pretty slippery."

"Good night," Rose Helen told her sleeping husband.

"Sure," he said, "run off just when I need you."

"What do you need me for? I gave you your dinner."

"I need you because."

"I'm going up. Good night."

"God damn it, Rose Helen, I'm not crazy. You think I talk to myself? I don't talk to myself. I don't talk to myself when I'm dreaming. I'm not sure I could do this if no one was there."

"Good night," she said, and Druff, in his sleep, could hear her going upstairs.

He was quiet. He felt as if the cat had his tongue. Well, he dreamed to himself, that's that. That's that, then. A politician to the last. He needed his audience, he supposed. With Rose Helen gone, there was no one to hear him. Now he'd never be able to work it out, all the linkages. All that complicated family tree of corruption and caper, the linchpin hidden in its leaves. Because I'm *not* crazy, he dreamed, thought, subconsciodused—— whatever. Because I'm *not* crazy. On the contrary, I'm a very decorumed, decorous guy. I have my flaws, I'd be the first to admit it. Oh, sure, he sleep-mulled, I'm no more perfect than the next fallen fellow. Well those surgeries. Well those collapsed lungs. Well that zippery leg where they took out my vein. Well that impotence. Well my itty-bitty paranoia, well my dreamspeak. But I have my principles. No talking aloud if no one's in the forest to hear me. Mum's the word, but you won't catch *me* saying it!

In his sleep he heard a noise.

"MacMikey?" he mumbled.

MacGuffin.

You don't have a key.

I have the key to your heart.

The chain's up.

I'm pretty slippery. I'm slippery dickory dock.

Amscray, will you?

Otway orfay?

Who needs you?

Well, unless I'm much mistaken, you do.

Do not.

Do too.

This is ridiculous.

This is ridiculous? *This* is? *You* invoked me.

When did I do that?

Oh, please, Druff. You can fool some of the people some of the time and part of the people all of the time.

Druff waited for it to go on, but evidently it had finished.

Well, Druff went, as long as you're here. This is my thinking on the thing. I can place Su'ad with our Mikey. I can place Dick with our Mikey. I think I can place MacMikey and Dick with MacMeg. I think, from something MacDoug said, I can place him with all three. I've got MacDan with the concierge, I've got him with MacGlorio. It's all pretty circumstantial, but the world's pretty circumstantial, too.

Now, MacDruff went, where was I? MacDick with MacMikey. Mac-Mikey with Dick and the buyer. The buyer with the MacConcierge. The concierge with Dan. MacDan with Ham 'n' Eggs and MacRector. Did I say Doug with MacMacklin? Right then, Doug with MacMacklin. Mrs. MacMack with Mr. MacMayor. And Doug with the mayor, too, of course. And obviously MacDoug with MacDick. So MacDick with Mac-Mayor. So Dick with Mrs. Macklin. So Mrs. MacMacklin with Mr. MacMacklin. *So why not Mr. MacMacklin with Su'ad? So why not Mac-Mikey with Mr. Macklin?* Am I pulling it all together, or am I pulling it all together? Am I way ahead you? Are you eating my dust?

Hey, goes MacGuffin, I've been there and gone. Are you psycho, or what? You fair give me vertigo. Until you've walked thirty-nine steps in my macmoccasins, kiddo, don't you go be comin' up in my face like you be some man who know too much.

Why?

Cause it give me the frenzy.

It do, do it, Mr. Bones?

Without a shadow of a doubt, Rebecca.

Well, I'll be spellbound, Druff went on.

You will, will you? goes MacGuffin.

Didn't I say so?

Yeah, you said so all right, but between you, me and the lamppost *I* say you're for the birds!

Oh yeah? Oh yeah? A bunch of rugs mysteriously shows up on a bunch of floors and the lady just vanishes?

I'd say so.

Su'ad and my son. That's where they met, in that night-school art class.

Mnh hmn.

She was a Shiite Muslim. Do you know all the trouble they get into?

So?

So she used Mikey's paints.

So?

Don't you get it? She drew Oriental rugs. Iranian carpets, yes? The Iran-Lebanon nexus? The Iranian-Lebanese-Syrian one?

Mnh hmn.

Su'ad was a *smuggler!* She not only brought carpets out of her country but got commissions for designs she worked out in night school in to her weavers. She used the place as her studio. She used their light. *She used paints and swatches of canvases I paid for!*

Ho hum.

What's that, ho hum?

Come on, MacGuffin goes, you ain't telling me nothing. Nothing. Zippo. Not a thing.

Wait up. Hold on. There were certain conversations in the synagogue. I'd made a reference to rugs. Dan, somebody, said I was warm. Other stuff was said. Double entendres, very cryptic shit about bankers. Macklin was a hardened banker. I asked MacMayor. He said it was none of my business.

Bankers.

And one of them said something about psychiatrists writing prescriptions for pianos, dinette sets. I don't know, whatever the traffic will bear.

I put it to you again. So?

Don't you see? Don't you get it? *Whatever the traffic will bear!* I'm City Commissioner of Streets. *I'm* in traffic! Who more than? Traffic's the key!

Again with the traffic, again with the key. Metaphors. Puns.

Have you got a better explanation?

What, are you kidding me?

There's already a question on the floor.

All right then, yes. Sure. The little red dot in the middle of the Hindu woman's forehead.

Little red dot? Hindu woman's forehead? I don't . . .

It's a microchip, silly. With the plans.

The plans.

No? All right. Say it's wartime. Say there's this Lord Haw-Haw type with a slight but very distinct stammer who broadcasts this very seductive, very seditious, very traitorous garbage on the shortwave back to our boys in the foxholes. We're losing the war. This is just insult to injury.

Fucks morale on all fronts. A major puts a commando team together to take the son of a bitch out. Very do-or-die mission. We're looking for a few good men. Montage of serious training. Cut to guy who splits his nuts open on the confidence course. To guy whose character ain't in it and he loses it. Okay, commandos finally get through. Countercommandos go after them. Armageddon. Heavy losses all around . . .

Commandos? Countercommandos? What are you . . .

Jerk, the stammer was a *code!*

A code.

Da dit dit dot. He was sending inside hush-hush on the enemy's secret plans and high doings. The major was just out of the loop.

You. *You're* out of the loop.

I'm out of the loop. What about you and your magic-carpet conspiracies? Connecting the dots—— A goes with B goes with C goes with . . . Trying to get it all to spell mother. Trust me, these are MacGuffin sorts of things. It won't wash, Druffish.

Why not?

Well, the coincidences for one thing, the things that don't track.

What doesn't track?

All right. Case in point. How could Hamilton Edgar know you were going to stroll past B'nai Beth Emeth? That you'd wake up this morning and, not realizing it's Saturday, get all dressed up prepared to go to work? Yet he seemed to be right there waiting for you, didn't he?

All right, that was accidental. I presented him with an opportunity and he took advantage of it. What's wrong with that?

Pretty farfetched, if you ask me.

I *am* asking you. Ain't that just what it says on your shingle? The MacGuffin: MacGimmicks Are Us. What else doesn't track?

Well, you make an awful lot of Margaret's seeming to know about your son and that Shiite character.

She did know about them.

Well, sure she did. In your sleep, in your sleep, didn't you put him behind the wheel? Didn't you keep her up half the night with your run-her-over discussions?

I don't *know* I kept her up.

Ri-i-ght.

And I never mentioned rugs.

You made a *point* of mentioning rugs!

When?

When? When? When you called her from the rabbi's crapper, that's when. That's one when.

Suddenly, he remembered. Just yesterday, Druff went, just yesterday my driver placed Margaret and my kid together! In the limo, after we dropped her off, *Dick* mentioned it!

But Dick's nuts. Dick's around the bend. He's across the river and through the woods. He's somewhere over the rainbow. Don't you even know that much?

Doug, then. Doug said some stuff, too.

Doug? Doug's nuttier than Dick is.

Gee, Druff went, no longer certain where he stood. Gosh.

I think my work here is finished.

You're leaving? But why? Wait. You can't. You mustn't.

Listen, life is either mostly adventure or it's mostly psychology. If you have enough of the one then you don't need a lot of the other.

"Mom, Dad, I'm back," Mikey called.

That's it, goes MacGuffin. I'm gone.

"Mom? Dad? I'm back."

"What? Who's—Oh, Mikey. It's you. You scared me."

"You're still dressed. What are you doing down here, Daddy? Is anything wrong?"

"What? No. I fell asleep on the couch."

"Is Mom all right?"

"Of course she's all right."

"Are you sure?"

"She's fine."

"Are you all right?"

"I'm fine and dandy."

"Because you were gone all day. I was pretty worried."

"No need."

"Well, when you didn't come back. And you're fully dressed. You didn't have chest pain, did you? You didn't have to lie down on the couch till your pain went away?"

"I didn't have pain. I'm fine. I was tired. As a matter of fact, I was waiting for you."

"For me?"

"As a matter of fact."

"Did you want to tell me something? Is it about you and Mom? Because just because you had that little quarrel this morning, that doesn't mean it's the end of the world. Your parents don't get divorced because they had a little quarrel."

"Nobody's getting divorced."

Mikey actually said "Whew." "Whew," he said, "that's a relief."

"It's about you," Druff said.

His son closed his eyes, he did his disappearing act. Then, having found somewhere in his intimate, immediate dark the courage to face him again, he opened them. "Am I in trouble?" he asked his father.

"I don't know," Druff said. "You might be in trouble."

"What did *I* do?"

"Do you remember all those times you used to ask if we were well off? What our financial condition would be if something happened to me?"

"Dad, I was a *kid.*"

"You were a teenager."

"A preteen. *Maybe* a preteen."

"Mikey, you were working out at the gym. You could have bench-pressed the dining room."

"I was nervous."

"I know you were nervous. You were scared I was going to die. You were terrified you wouldn't be ready."

"I had some stuff to work out."

"Well, do you remember the time we got this annual report from a company I had some stock in and we went over it together?"

"Vaguely. I think I remember."

"It was this *Fortune* 500 company, some utility, I think. I forget which one. They listed their assets down one column, their liabilities down another."

"I *think* I remember."

"The profits they made each quarter from the natural gas they sold to their residential customers? What they took in from their industrial customers? How the two were charged at different rates because their industrial clientele consumed the stuff in much greater quantities?"

"Yes?"

"The profits from fields they owned but had leased to other gas companies?"

"Oh yes," Mikey said.

"Then there were the debits. Well," Druff said, "you can imagine. Their terrific operating expenses."

"Sure."

"A big fire. Equipment that had to be replaced. Disappointing yields from new wells."

"I remember."

"Then there were the acts of God."

"I don't recall the acts of God, Dad."

"The acts of God, the acts of God. You remember."

"No I don't. I don't think so."

"The exceptionally mild winter they had that year. The unusually cool summer."

"Oh," Mikey said. "Sure."

"Sure," Druff said, "what finally accounted for their slight net loss."

"I remember."

"This was when you were still working stuff out."

"Yes."

"So I sat down with you and drafted my *own* annual report. I listed *my* assets and liabilities. I put down our savings and investments. My insurance. What my pension could be expected to bring in. The couple hundred bucks Social Security gives to help bury you. I listed the probable resale value of our house. I even put down the approximate worth of our possessions. The furniture, our car, the TVs and appliances, the appraised valuation on your mother's jewelry, everything I could think of. What I took in over and above my salary that didn't get saved or invested but was lying around the house in cash. (This part wasn't in the annual report. This part was off the record. I just mentioned it to you on the qt.) Then I put down my debits."

"What were those, Dad?"

"The twelve hundred or so dollars we owed on our charge cards. Whatever it was I'd pledged that year but hadn't yet paid to a couple of charities. Some bills, our monthly expenses. I don't know, maybe four thousand, forty-five hundred bucks tops."

"That wasn't too bad."

"Well," Druff said, "the mild winter and cool summer worked in our favor."

"That's right."

"But of course those weren't my only debits."

"No? What were the rest, Dad?"

"My heart attack, my bad circulation. Whatever it was going to cost you guys to bury me."

"Oh Dad," his son said.

"No no," Druff said. "You don't remember. I showed you. We went over it very carefully. It was actually a net gain overall. You just don't remember. A slight net gain, but a net gain's a net gain. I was helping you to work out your stuff. I showed you that even though I was only one small, sick human being, in certain respects I was better off than a great big *Fortune* 500 company, and that if you and your mom were careful you could be in the black for another fifteen years."

Though Druff waited him out, Mikey didn't say anything for a long while. Then Druff broke their silence. "It's all right," he told his son. "You can ask me."

"That's okay."

"No," Druff said, "go ahead. Ask me."

"That's okay."

"I'll tell you anyway," said the City Commissioner of Streets. "If I dropped dead tonight, you'd still be in the black. But, really, it depends."

"What does it depend on, Dad?"

"Whether or not you actually ran over that girl."

"Su'ad was my *girlfriend*, Dad. Why would I run over my girlfriend?"

"Su'ad," Druff said.

"I'm no dummy, Dad. Who else could you be talking about? How many accident-prone Shiite Muslims do I know?"

"Did Dick do it, did Doug?"

"Maybe. I'm not sure, Dad."

"You were a witness?"

"Yes. No. I don't know. I was a *sort* of a witness."

"What sort?"

"Gee, is this fair? I mean, I loved her, Daddy. What do you want from me? I planned to go back to Lebanon with her even if it meant they would probably have taken me hostage one of these days. So how do you think it made me feel when they ran her down?"

"Not over?"

"What?"

"Down, not over?"

"It was pretty confusing. All right," his son said, "I'll tell you what I *think* happened."

And then, quite suddenly, Druff began to feel bored. Physically. Bored physically. As if boredom were a symptom like a tickle in your throat, a fever, or a runny nose. Perhaps he'd been exposed to too much MacGuffin. Maybe it was in his bloodstream by now. Gunking up the works. Causing rashes, eruptions, potholing his flesh. Like some disease, say, serious enough in childhood but devastating if you came down with it as an adult. What was it the old schemer had advised? Something-or-other something, or something-something, something-or-other, and that if you had enough of the one you didn't need very much of the other. The fact was, thought the City Commissioner of Streets, solutions were boring, never as interesting as the trouble they were brought in to put an end to. Motion and sound effects. Like chase scenes. Shoot-outs. Guys scrambling over architecture or sprawled out in fields. Wrestling in water. Or caught, humbled on monuments. Dangled on ropes like clappers on bells. *This* far from vats, the various acid baths and boiled oils. Above great heights, precariously dancing. Fighting against time—— the two-minute warning of armed nuclear devices, a few last inches of sizzling fuse. Character forgotten, left behind, left out, and only the juices of simple, driving survival left over, remaining, separated out, like whey, reduced, clarified like butter.

But Druff was in it deep now. Mikey would have his say. Bored or not, Druff would have to hear him out. It was, he supposed, almost his official duty as City Commissioner of Streets.

So the kid spoke his piece. In his old dad's living room had, as it were, his day in court. Druff imagined Mikey rather enjoyed it, glad to get it off his chest finally, and probably feeling grateful that it was his father to whom he was telling the story, as if the story he was telling, no matter the light in which it put him, discharged, at least a little, some filial obligation he may have felt toward the old man, made up for never having brought home good enough grades, say, or given him grandkids.

It was full of detail.

He admitted that on the night Su'ad was run down he had been with her. They had attended the lecture together, an overview of the Arab-Israeli question delivered by an Arab congressman from the state of Delaware with whose conciliatory views Su'ad was in strong disagreement. Afterward, during the Q and A, Su'ad had quarreled with him. How, she asked, could he betray his own people? How, she wondered, could he even bring himself to lick up under the Israelis by referring to them at least three times in his talk as "our Israeli cousins"? The gentleman from Delaware said he felt both sides must rededicate themselves to finding a reasonable solution—he had suggested one, but Mikey had forgotten the details—to what, given the region's long, complicated history and the antagonists' apparently intractable positions, were problems that were only apparently insoluble.

"Solutions to apparently insoluble problems?" Su'ad had said. "But, sir," she'd said, "I believe in the fell-swoop theory of history."

"The fell-swoop theory of history?"

"Yes," Su'ad had said, "when problems are apparently insoluble, *final* solutions must apparently be found."

There were Jews in the audience. They made angry hoots and catcalls. Two or three started to come forward.

And Mikey, for love, rising in her defense, speaking out, backing her up, for love having his say in public, even if it was only "Stand back. Don't touch her!" In the dark, Druff imagined, his eyes shut, mediating between Su'ad and the two or three furious Jews with his big body.

It was only afterward, he told his father, as they walked together to the parking lot to pick up the car in which he intended to drive her back to her dorm, that he thought to remind her, well out of hearing of the last stragglers leaving the auditorium, that his own father was a politician, a man who'd devoted his life to serving the public, and that it was the duty of such people to find solutions to problems that seemed insoluble and that, really, she had gone just a little too far, really, didn't she think?

"Your father," Su'ad had said, "doesn't serve the public, he serves the infrastructure. He sends men to fix the streets. In winter he dispatches trucks to salt them, just as if they were soups or meats or vegetables."

"Me?" Druff said. "You stood up for me? I'm touched."

"Thanks, Dad, but that wasn't really exactly the way. She was in a bad mood. PMS. You don't normally think of women in *chadors* as even having periods, but, I don't know, something was eating at her. If I said 'black' she'd say 'white,' if I said 'up' she'd say 'down.' If I said 'rugs' she said . . . Well, you know what I mean."

"Rugs?"

"Sir?"

"You said 'rugs.' What did she say?"

"It's an example," his son said uncomfortably. "I don't think I ever actually said 'rugs.' "

"Did Su'ad smuggle rugs, Mikey?" Druff asked, closing in, getting on, he supposed, toward the bottom of things, though still not excited (despite the fact that several times now he'd interrupted his son's relation of the account of the proceedings on the night of—never mind, he'd actually forgotten—to stop them—Mikey, Su'ad—somewhere between the auditorium—those last, probably Jewish, stragglers—and the parking lot where he would admit her into the car she couldn't possibly be both riding in and run down by at the same time), really not even off boredom's dime, puzzles, as he'd just so recently noted, being always more interesting than their solutions, though how he, the most nouveau of gumshoes, could possibly know this he did not possibly know.

"Su'ad? Su'ad was a rug *merchant*, Daddy."

"Ahh," Druff said, "a rug *merchant*. She had a *license* to sell rugs?"

"I don't know, I don't know if she had a license."

"You never saw it."

"I never asked about any license."

"But Mikey," Druff said, "there are all sorts of city ordinances. Restaurants have to be licensed to dispense food and drink. People are licensed to drive taxis, to sell newspapers from kiosks. Elevators are licensed. Souvenir vendors pay license fees before they're permitted to hawk their wares outside stadiums—— jerseys with the team logo emblazoned on the front, pennants for the home team, pennants for the visitors. My God, son, the man who sells you your hot dog from his little cart has to have a license. His ketchup is licensed, his mustard and napkins and piccalilli. These were rugs from the Middle East, Iran, from all those problematic, difficult trouble spots the gentleman from Delaware was telling you about that night. Why would the licensing requirement on a high-ticket item like a Persian carpet from a region of hot, intractable positions and insoluble problems be waived when a man selling pencils out of his cap or an organ grinder with a monkey dressed up like a bellboy has to go through City Hall before he's allowed to hit the streets? Can you think of a reason?"

"No."

"I mean, think about it, if you were in Su'ad's position I should think you'd go around absolutely *flaunting* your license, waving it in front of you like someone surrendering on a battlefield with a white handkerchief."

"I guess."

"Well, of course," said Druff. "So if you never asked to see it, and she never offered to show it to you, don't you suppose it's stretching things to say she was a rug *merchant?*"

"I guess."

"Sure."

"Su'ad smuggled rugs," Mike said flatly, his face pale, his spirit without heft. His eyes were closed now. Squeezed tight. He seemed diminished in size to Druff, his very bulk deflated. Druff was as still as his son. He waited him out. When Mikey finally opened his eyes to look at his father, Druff simply stared at him. He offered no reassurances, and something new seemed gradually to creep across his son's face like a shadow—— bafflement, curiosity.

Because Druff was this hope pumper. It was his nature. He pumped hope for Mikey, for Rose Helen, even, as a politician, for his constituents, telling them their lives could be better, simpler, fixed like tickets, bargained for and traded up. It was not only his nature, it was his job. Maybe it had been his job even before it had become his nature. I have to be a hope pumper, Druff thought, it's what I do. Nevertheless, the hope pumper wasn't pumping no hope now. The well was dry. And he was waiting.

Then Mikey resumed explaining himself. Though he managed to follow him, Druff, distracted, was barely able to take it all in. He had to concentrate. Other things were on his mind, too.

"I don't know what she wanted from me. When we got to the parking lot she was still bitching. It was that lecturer she was angry at, not me, the audience that hissed her and booed her when she made that remark. A few of them were trailing us, some of them were actually lined up along the path waiting for her as we went by. Their quarrel was with Su'ad, not with me. They made fun of the way she dressed. They passed remarks. I don't think she even heard them, that she paid any attention. She was too busy complaining to me, arguing with me. As if *I'd* said those things. You've heard her. You know how she gets. She's pretty hipped on this Palestine thing. They followed us to the parking lot. They milled around. I'm saying, 'Look Su'ad, just get in the car. This isn't any time to be standing out here.' And she's still lecturing me. About U.S. policy, the Israel lobby . . . Bitching at me as if I were responsible for what was happening over there. Finally I just had to shove her into the car. I mean, they were *steamed.*"

"Jews killed her? Jews ran her down?"

"No. I don't even think they followed us. I could see them shaking their fists after us, though, as I drove off that lot."

And Druff, stabbed by a sudden, astonished envy of the dead Lebanese woman, mildly contemplated the notion of enemies, entertained the thought of them, wondered, even momentarily wished that he'd had more in his life, people who would have pushed him in directions not of his choosing. If nothing happened to you you had to fall back on your character, spinning your life out of whole cloth, disaffiliate from the world. What he had had for an enemy had been merely his own body, his diseases, how they'd made him look in his suits. He wished now he had gone further in politics, drawn opponents from out of the woodwork, campaigners who might have gotten the goods on him, or even just slung a little mud. He'd been lazy with his life. Some stinginess of energy had stalled his heart, disengaged him and woken MacGuffins.

"What?" Druff asked. "I'm sorry, what did you say?"

"I asked what she wanted me to do with that rug in the trunk."

"You had a rug in your trunk?"

"In *your* trunk, Daddy. I was driving your car."

"My car?"

"Don't you remember? Mine was in the shop."

"Well, what were you doing with a rug in the trunk?"

"Come on, Dad, I told you. I drove for her, Daddy. I was the wheelman."

"The wheelman."

"When she made her deliveries."

"Of the smuggled rugs."

"Yes," he said.

"Jesus Christ, Mikey. Do you know what you've done?"

"Gone and gotten you in trouble?"

"Goddamn right."

"Are we well off?"

"Oh, Jesus."

"I'm sorry."

"All right. What happened then?"

"Well," Mikey said, "like I told you, she was bitching at me so bad it was hard for me to concentrate on my driving. It was your car, Dad. I didn't want to smash it up in an accident. That's why I told her that if she didn't stop shouting and screaming at me I'd have to let her out at the light."

In dread, the City Commissioner of Streets asked, "Which light?"

"Well, that push-button one on Kersh Boulevard," his son said, his eyes shut, his own lights out. "Where they're going to put that crosswalk."

"Scene of the crime," Druff said.

"Well, I pulled *over*. Well, I let her out at the *curb.*"

"Scene of the fucking crime."

"Well, no," his son said, "not exactly."

"Near enough. Scene of the fucking crime."

"No," his son said. "Because after she got out of your car I drove another fifty or sixty feet before I remembered about the rug. That's when I stopped and called out what did she want me to do with the rug in your trunk. She was still standing by that light."

"Well, of course."

"No," Mikey said, "that's just the thing. It was green. It had turned green in her favor."

"Did anyone see you?" Druff said. "Did they hear you call her?"

"No. Absolutely not. Well, maybe whoever ran her down."

"Someone was at the light?"

"In a car. Stopped in a car there, yes."

"Sure," Druff said. "Because the light was against him." His heart was pounding furiously. He began to feel not angina but the conditions for angina, his heart tightening, circling his wagons. Sure, Druff thought, this happens too. Your mouth dries up, your tongue gets thick. You get nervous. You need your pills.

"Yes, but that's just the thing, Daddy. Su'ad didn't even answer when I called to her. She was staring so hard at the driver in that car stopped at that red light, it was as if she hadn't even heard me."

"Why didn't she cross?" he asked slowly, as carefully as he could. So as not to spook the horses. To keep them from rearing, to keep their hooves from trampling his chest. (And *this* happens. You get too excited, too caught up in shit for your own good.)

"Well, I don't know. I mean it was like she was hypnotized, fascinated. You know?"

"Why didn't she cross the street, the light was in her favor?"

"Well I don't know," Mikey said again. "I mean then the light turned against her, and it was the driver who didn't move. Then it was in her favor again and finally she just stepped out into the street."

Druff's eyes were squeezed shut.

"Next thing I knew there was this dull thump. I mean, that's what it was. A thump. Su'ad was dead in the road but it made less noise to kill her than a fender bender, a little chip when a stone jumps up and breaks your headlight."

Druff was drawing short, shallow breaths.

"And it wasn't the Jews," he said.

"Someone I recognized from the lecture, lined up along that path we took or in the parking lot, you mean?"

Druff was slow to answer. "That's right," he said finally.

"That's right," his son said. "But it isn't as if I got a really good look. I was maybe seventy-five feet in front of him when he was stopped at that light. Then after he ran Su'ad down, she got like caught on his car somehow and he was doing these really wild maneuvers, throwing it into reverse, making wide swings, coming forward hard and braking. To shake her loose. You know? I was watching Su'ad," Mikey said. "I

2 7 3

couldn't keep my eyes off Su'ad. Her wild ride," he said, his voice breaking. "When he passed it was like a blur. I mean I couldn't even tell what make he was driving. I was all blinded by my tears."

"Hey," Druff said, "Mikey, take it easy. It's all right."

"It isn't all right," Mikey said. "I loved her. I was going to go back to goddamn Lebanon with her. I was going to let them make me a hostage."

Then, in the event, dread or no dread, thick tongue or no thick tongue, heart pressure or no heart pressure, angina or no angina, pills or no pills, *this* happens: You forget yourself, you forget you even have these things or that you need your medicine, and you make a MacGuffin-like leap.

"How," he asked his son, "did she get money for the rugs?"

"She told me she borrowed it, Dad."

Druff had no proof. He *could* have done it. She'd been screaming at him, bitching at him for some incompetence or other. She might still have been shouting when he threw her out of the car. She could have gotten his goat, screamed some devastating thing at him that just might have torn it. Maybe he was on steroids. Christ, he was big enough. Maybe he was on steroids and they had brainwashed his heart. So he *could* have done it. He'd never know, would he, not *really* know. He was a mysterious kid, had been a mysterious kid, was now a mysterious man. Mikey. Jesus Christ Jesus. Mikey! So it was conceivable. So he *could* have done it, the mysterious man-kid, thrown some sudden, thunderous tantrum, some killer snit. But he thought not. For love he'd been willing to go for a hostage in Lebanon, he'd said—— some foolish fate. Only an innocent was capable of inventing something like that. He hadn't run anyone down. He was innocent. As innocent as he'd been in not coming forward in the first place, everything mitigated by fear. His son hadn't done it. The very terms of his telling it had cleared him. So that should have been a relief. A load off Druff's mind. But his body was still doing its things. He was short of breath now, too.

It's the excitement, he thought. I'm sound as a dollar.

"What's wrong, Daddy? Is something wrong?"

"No," Druff said, "nothing. Not a thing."

"Are you feeling all right?"

"I'm feeling fine."

Stanley Elkin

"Shall I go get my mom?"

"Hey," Druff said, "I'm fine. I'm fit as a fiddle."

Because she would probably have had an inventory. Not many people would put out a few hundred bucks, let alone several thousand, for an expensive rug without having something to compare it to, seeing a selection. So she needed money up front. Forget the people working customs, here, overseas—— guys guarding the borders, working the stony, sandy, various desert checkpoints where they inspected the crates or boxes or whatever the hell they came packed in—— bribes, according to Druff's hierarchical imagination, for the still-more-official officials at the ports and air terminals, some compounding, snowballing sum of cash to get them to look the other way. So forget whatever considerable consideration it took to do just the stiff, burdensome logistics of the thing. She needed it for the terrorists. Who would get it to the weavers, who would get it to their wool suppliers and dye manufacturers, and all the hidden, unseen, unknown rest of the backstage, baksheeshed personalities who contributed to the production of a smuggled rug. Where would she get such sums, a poor student who didn't even have a green card and had had to enroll in a night-school art class in order to use its facilities and find and take on an accomplice or accessory just to have the use of his father's paints and canvases? Well *of course* she borrowed it. From those bankers he'd been hearing so much about. Probably from the hardened Macklin himself until he was retired by his long illness and, then, the even harder Hamilton Edgar, the steely Dan, the adamantine Jerry Rector. Su'ad was killed when she couldn't pay off her loans to the bankers of B'nai Beth Emeth. Well, it was only a theory. He didn't know for sure, but dollars to doughnuts.

"It works for me."

"What?"

"Oh boy," Druff said. "A new symptom. Now I talk out loud even when I'm awake."

"What?"

Cautious, tentative, like someone testing exactly how much weight he can put down on a bad ankle, Druff took short, experimental breaths.

Mikey hovered. "Are you feeling all right?"

"Terrific."

Because MegGluffio had taken a few rugs off Su'ad's hands. Almost

certainly on some no-strings consignment. No different, surely, from her other arrangements with the trade—— the nifty, voguish lamps and spiffy, à la mode furniture. The folding Japanese screens and futons. In keeping with all the other provisional terms of her life—— her plastic cutlery, Styrofoam cups and paper plates—— all that fast food paraphernalia of her get-out-of-town, one-night-stand ways.

"You're sure?"

"Your ma is rich and your daddy's good-lookin'," Druff said. He looked at his son, the wheelman, full on.

"I don't like this much," Mikey said nervously.

Because he'd said Su'ad hadn't answered when he'd called to her. Because it was as if she hadn't even heard him, he'd said.

"The rug's still in my trunk, isn't it," Druff said. It wasn't a question.

Mikey shrugged.

Sure, he thought, because he thinks Dick's been watching him, that Doug has. No, Druff thought, I'm wrong. Because they're watching me, Mr. Mayor's deputized observers. No, because he simply doesn't know who it is who's supposed to take delivery. Because she never said. Because he knew she didn't have enough confidence in him and wouldn't have told him until they were already on the way. Because he figures there'll be time enough to switch it if he ever finds out.

Oh, Mikey, he thought. Oh, oh, Mikey.

"Dad?"

"What?"

"Is something wrong?"

"Sure," Druff said.

"Oh," said his son. "Do you need a doctor? Should I wake my mom?"

"I heard from Scouffas and McIlvoy," Druff said. "They're not going to let us have the marathon."

And watched as Michael closed his eyes, a voyeur to his son's humiliation. Because as much as Druff had hurt and disappointed Mikey, he was up to here with the kid's character, its rigorous, repetitious, lock-step ways. His son's impervious shell of stunted, undaunted, familiar behavior. His peace-at-any-price conditions. Because he knew what Mike was thinking now—— that there'd never been a Scouffas, that McIlvoy was an invention. That his father had lied to him.

And waited till the long, extended blink was finished. And then, very deliberately, threw one of his own like a willed fit. Thinking, *I read yours, now you read mine.*

Thinking, she was financed by bankers, by bankers, not usurers, not loan sharks who required exorbitant interest, bankers, these merely hardened *bankers* who, when she couldn't pay back her loans (because Druff's middle-sized, rather backwater city, with its good-enough symphony orchestra of the second rank, its undersubscribed newspaper and losing football and basketball franchises, and narrow, four-story, dressed-limestone City Hall—once a department store—old-fashioned and less imposing, finally, than a county courthouse—for where were its cannons, its respectful, generic, de rigueur statues of Civil War rebs or Yankees or doughboys or G.I.'s?—in a town square; the building still, despite its conversion, faintly mercantile, vaguely pro tem, giving off trace elements of officious red-tape vibes, as if it were the headquarters of some army of occupation, was a fairly conventional, fairly conservative middle-sized city, whose relatively timid consumers wouldn't much care for, so didn't much buy, the risky frills and back-of-the-truck furbelows of contraband rugs, and whose conventional, conservative loan officers in its great gray banks and S&Ls would have pretty much written off the Third World and have had nothing to do altogether with the out-and-out nutso fringe doings of a subterranean Fourth One, let alone any shady arrangements of a black market venture capitalism, who wouldn't so much as consider, even out of politeness, handing over a loan application to be filled out by one of its representatives, never mind that they wouldn't have bothered to read it if they had, and so Su'ad had miscalculated, had been taken in by what she perceived— poor, dusky, benighted, cause-ridden, wacko Shiite Muslim maiden lady that she was—to be the advertised, universally obtaining Satanic condition, although—fortunately for her short-range goals, however disastrous it turned out to have been for her longer ones—this particular middle-sized city had fringe arrangements of its own, even its own quiet, stylish, hardened-banker terrorists not so squeamish or choosy as their éminence grise banker cousins with their stuffy, institutional FDICs or as their snooty enough second cousins with their FSLIC ones, and who would extend her cash, Druff imagined, not for her signature on a contract, or even, he imagined, for her marker, but just—they must have insisted on this, worked it into the deal like the devastating fine print in some apparently innocuous clause—on the basis of her given word alone) then, though I can't prove this either, struck her down in what wasn't quite yet even her prime, because, well, just because, because downtown had become too tame, and what was a fellow to do, where was he supposed to go to if he wanted to go wilding?

Yeah, Mikey, Druff thought, go ahead. Read *that!*

Which, of course, Mikey didn't, couldn't. They had different agendas. Mikey and Dad were on two separate, totally different, entirely arrested beams. Mikey into his preoccupations with Health and a sort of immutability on command of anything that might once have pleased him. (He would have gone back to Lebanon with her, even if it meant they might have taken him hostage! The trouble with his son, Druff thought, was that he didn't think things all the way through. He was going to go back to Lebanon with the woman he loved, willing to accept the risks, to take his chances on becoming a hostage. All right. So far so good. But had it once crossed his mind that they might not carry Blues hockey in the Middle East?) And Druff, Druff thought, never one to let himself off lightly if he could shoot himself in the foot with both barrels— with his own opposing preoccupations, with finding the action and recklessly throwing himself into harm's way, not only forbidding the immutable but absolutely encouraging it, not only inviting a MacGuffin into his life but positively becoming one!

Well.

Druff's eyes open again, he saw his son shake his head, mournful, woeful.

"Hey," he said apologetically, "I'm sorry, Mike. I really am."

"Did they give you a reason?"

"A reason?"

"For not letting us have the marathon?"

It was Druff's last straw. He practically exploded. He could have awakened Rose Helen, upstairs sleeping, but he was past caring. "God damn it, Mikey, do you even know what I do for a living?" he demanded. "Do you? Well, *do* you?"

"You're City Commissioner of Streets."

"That's right," Druff said. "Now what do you suppose that entails?"

"You're in charge of the streets."

"Good," Druff said. "Now where are the marathons run? Look at me. Don't shut your eyes. *Look* at me! Where are they run?"

"In the streets."

"Excellent. They're run in the streets. Excellent. They're run in the streets and I'm their commissioner. Why would I need a Scouffas, why would I need a McIlvoy? I'm City Commissioner of Streets, the streets are my jurisdiction. I could cross without looking both ways if I wanted. So if I wanted to put on a marathon why would I need the permission of people who don't even live or pay taxes here?"

"You wouldn't."

"I wouldn't. Wonderful!"

"Then you'll do it?"

Druff stared at him.

"You'll do it? You'll put one on?"

And stared at him.

"You promise?"

"Sure," said Druff, "honor bright. Cross my heart. Hope to kiss a pig."

Then Mikey said something in a manner so completely neutral and uninflected that, at first, Druff, though he'd heard the words, had no notion, none at all, what they meant. "Oh Dad" was what he said. But for the separation of the two discrete syllables, it could almost have been some sound of the body— some incoherent, vaguely natural (though not nature proper: not the wind, not the water; not fire, not earth) noise of the emotions, of displacement, like the tuneless, interstitial creak of bones. He said it again. "Oh Dad." Was it nerves? It was grief.

Then—to give himself time, Druff would have said "gradually," but there was nothing gradual about it, nothing calibrated, nothing stepping-stoned, nothing scalar, nothing runged; there were no easy stages—he recalled its terms, and understood that whatever their agendas, they were on the same beam, all right. Even before Mikey asked him if he remembered Diosodidio Macospodagal. Why, the kid *was* a hostage. He was Druff's hostage.

"The doctor?"

"Yes," Michael said.

"You were a kid," Druff said. "How do you remember his name?"

"I remember," Michael said.

"Well," Druff said, "it's a funny name. The kind of name you never forget. Hey," Druff said, "what's this? What's the matter with you? Do you want to wake your mother? Hey, Michael, come on. Stop it, Mikey. You're a grown man. Stop it now."

"I'm sorry. I can't help it."

"Of course you can help it. Take a deep breath. Go on, take a deep breath."

"Fuck a deep breath."

"Do you know how silly you sound?"

"Fuck a deep breath. *Fuck* a deep breath."

"All right now. Cut it out. Will you cut it out, please?"

"Fuck cut it out. Piss on cut it out up the ass."

"You're making a scene."

"Suck my scene's dick."

"I'm tired, Mikey. Why are you carrying on like this?"

"And I suppose you didn't? You made a scene! You made a son of a whore's bitch of a scene. God damn it to pus shit. *You* made a scene!"

"Come on, now. Jesus. Get hold of yourself please. Here, take my handkerchief. Your nose is running."

"Stick my nose. Stick your handkerchief."

"Right."

"*You* made a scene. I'll say you did. I'll say so. 'Your pop's dying, Mikey. I'll miss you, Mikey. You're the one. I love you, kid. *You're* the one I love. I'm sorry I crapped out on you, son. You're man of the house now; take care of your mother, Mikey. Study hard. Behave yourself. Don't get into trouble. Promise, promise me now. Your dad's dying, kiddo. He's had a massive cardiac infarction and he's slipping fast. Put your hand over my heart like you'd pledge allegiance to the flag.' Jesus, Daddy, I wasn't even ten years old."

"He was crazy," Druff said. "He had the bedside manner of an elephant. No idea how to talk to people."

"And you did."

"Did I say those things? I must have scared hell out of you. I'm sorry. I said all those things?"

"Oh Dad. Every word."

"Well, how do you think *I* felt, he told me the shape I was in, that the first ten or so hours were critical and I might not last the night? How do you think *I* felt, he said it might do me good I set my house in order and told my loved ones good-bye?"

"And I did it. *I pledged allegiance to your heart!*"

"He was irresponsible. No, really. That was irresponsible. A bull-in-a-china-shop doctor. I was so *scared*, Mikey. More frightened than when I found out I had to go in for the open-heart surgery. Jeez, I can't get over that guy. How can people talk that way? Doctors hold people's lives in their hands. Don't they realize the part the mind plays in healing the body? The brute force of attitude? He should have been brought up on charges, a guy like that."

"And what about you? What about the way *you* talk to people?"

"I *did* love you, Mikey. I swear it. I meant every word."

"Sure you did. I was cute. I was this cute fat kid."

"I was barely thirty. He told me to set my house in order. I wasn't that much older than you are now. I was too young to die."

"You were saying these things and crying. *Your* nose was running. Under the oxygen mask. I didn't know what to do. Why wouldn't you let me ring for the nurse?"

"How many times do I have to tell you? I was setting my house in order!"

"Tit piss fart wind on your house!"

"What is that? What's going on down there?" Rose Helen called. "Do you know what time it is? You woke me up."

Druff and Mikey looked guiltily at each other.

"I bought new batteries for her today," his son said.

"Yes," Druff said, "I know. So did I."

"She sleeps with them in?"

"She's afraid the smoke alarms will go off and she won't hear them if she doesn't wear them."

"Are you two fighting?"

"We were having a little argument. Sorry we woke you. It's all over."

"It isn't," Mikey said softly.

"It is for now," Druff said as quietly. "I'm exhausted."

"You *look* worn out," his son said.

"I am. I'm beat," said the City Commissioner of Streets. "I might be coming down with something. I didn't eat. All the running around I've been doing."

"What running around?"

"Well, Scouffas. McIlvoy. A lot of little shit."

"Are you having any chest pains?"

"No no."

"Because even if you're not having any right now but only just feel they might be coming on, you should take your pills. There's no need for you to wait. That's what the doctor said."

"No," Druff said. "It's not chest pain."

"You were taking these short, shallow breaths."

"Fuck my short, shallow breaths."

Mikey smiled. "I was worried," he said.

"You worry about the wrong things."

"What is it?" Rose Helen said. "Aren't you ever coming up?" She'd put on her robe and slippers and come downstairs.

"Dad's exhausted. It's an effort for him to move. He practically can't put one foot in front of the other."

"It's *not* an effort for me to move. I can move. I can put one foot in front of the other." He tried to push himself upright. He struggled to stand.

Rose Helen and Mikey stood at faltered Druff's side.

It *was* an effort for him to move, but suddenly all three of them were in motion in the living room at the same time, in each other's way. Rose Helen pushed in front of the City Commissioner of Streets while Mikey still stood at the coffee table in front of the couch where he'd offered Druff a hand up, and which Druff had refused. He was waiting until his father passed but Druff hesitated, uncertain of his son. It was one of those fits-and-starts things, some stalled comedy of errors in a doorway, on a sidewalk, in a street. Druff, wiped out, finally making the move, almost ran into his son.

He was so tired.

"I don't know about you two," Rose Helen said, "but I'm going to bed."

Pulling on the staircase's wooden handrail and leaning against the wall, he dragged himself up the steps, following her, leading Michael in the slow procession and watching for any depressions in the carpet as though they were tiny potholes that could trip him up. "Go ahead," he told his son, waving him on, "pass me."

He went into their bedroom where Rose Helen was already under the covers. Exhausted, wasted, he shuffled out of his clothes, let them fall to the floor. Awful, he thought, dreadful, awful what they had done out of boredom. Then he remembered. It was Druff, not Dan, who'd said there ought to be something malevolent, something personal. So he posed a question. If MacGuffin was the principle of structure to Druff, of pattern and shading, and all the latent architecture of the old man's life, what was Druff to MacGuffin? Why, raw material. Like pitch, like tar, like clay or sand or silica, like gravel and the trace elements of all the asphalts.

Then, hoping not to sleep, not daring to dream, he got into their bed.

ABOUT
THE
AUTHOR

STANLEY ELKIN, winner of the 1982 National Book Critics Circle Award for fiction (for *George Mills*), is the author of fourteen other works, including *The Living End, The Dick Gibson Show,* and *The Franchiser.* Mr. Elkin is Merle Kling Professor of Modern Letters at Washington University, St. Louis; has received fellowships and awards from the Guggenheim and Rockefeller foundations; was nominated twice for the National Book Awards, and is a member of the American Academy and Institute of Arts and Letters.